PRAISE FOR THE LEGAL THRILLERS OF R. A. FORSTER

CHARACTER WITNESS

"The author of *Keeping Counsel* and *Beyond Malice* does what one expects of a good writer of legal thrillers—drives the plot through unexpected twists without overstretching the bounds of credible law. Forster adds a bonus by transcending the flat stereotypes of the genre and creating diverse and realistically drawn characters."

—*Publishers Weekly*

"A challenge to figure out until the very end. Full of great twists and turns. Definitely a must read!"

—*The Snooper*

"*Character Witness* is another riveting legal whodunit from R. A. Forster."

—*USA Today*

KEEPING COUNSEL

"*Keeping Counsel* reinvents the legal thriller, with a whalloping premise. Read this one with a friend, during the day, with all the lights on—and do not answer the doorbell on any account."

—Polly Whitney, author of *Until Death* and *Until the End of Time*

"*Keeping Counsel* is the perfect legal mystery. I found it impossible to put down, even when I was supposed to be watching the 'Trial of the Century.' "

—Laurie L. Levenson, legal correspondent, CBS Television Network

"*Keeping Counsel* is creepy and compelling. It's the best read I've had in a long time."

—Herb Nero, American International Network

Books by R. A. Forster

Keeping Counsel

Character Witness

The Mentor

Published by Kensington Publishing Corporation

THE MENTOR

R. A. Forster

Pinnacle Books
Kensington Publishing Corp.

http://www.pinnaclebooks.com

PINNACLE BOOKS are published by

Kensington Publishing Corp.
850 Third Avenue
New York, NY 10022

Pinnacle and the P logo Reg. U.S. Pat. & TM Off.

First Printing: March, 1998
10 9 8 7 6 5 4 3 2 1

Printed in the United States of America

For JSC

My Mentor

and his mentor

DWW

ACKNOWLEDGMENTS

I cannot thank Jenny Jensen enough for her wisdom, insight and friendship. I would like to thank Dr. A. F. Forster for his good-humored assistance with a crucial scene, Barbara Benedict for all the time she spent listening and looking, Jack Trimarco, Jack Trimarco & Associates Polygraph and Consulting for taking the time to talk, Damaris Rowland, my agent, for her great support and belief in the future and, as always, my husband and children, for enduring with such verve.

Prologue

"Girlfriend, it is time to go!"

She talked to herself, gripped the edge of her chair and looked around the empty office. Deserted desks, silent phones, blinds closed in front and something going on behind the emergency exit to the alley were making her jumpy. Outside wasn't going to be much better than in, but outside, in front, she'd see that boyfriend of hers coming. She'd jump in that car and they'd hightail it out of downtown before he had time to stop. If, of course, he ever came.

She looked at her watch, the sixth time since she'd heard the last skittery noises in that alley, twice since she first heard voices. Barely ten minutes had passed and now the urgent whispers were starting again. That's when she decided, outside was where she wanted to go.

Quietly she eased her desk drawer out and got her purse. Keeping her eye on the closed, locked and bolted back door she hunkered down and checked the wall clock. Eight-thirteen. Slowly she raised her wrist. Eight-fifteen by her watch. On alert under the overhead lights that made everyone feel sickly, she froze and listened hard. Suddenly there was silence. *Oh, Lord above.*

Holding her purse close, she sidestepped across the floor and pushed through the little gate that separated the IRS workers from a generally crazed public. How a little swinging gate was going to protect any of them was beyond her. But now that gate was her ticket to freedom. She backed through it, bumped up against the door, groped with her free hand and pushed the lever. It opened only to slam shut and lock behind her as she stumbled out into the surprisingly cool night.

"Hey. Hey."

She shrieked, spun around and dropped her purse. Oh, God! A drunken bum had touched her. She shivered and snatched up her purse. Shaking, she clutched it to her breast, never taking her eyes off his milky right eye and the left that looked everywhere except at her. When he shuffled on, her shoulders slumped. Her looks-like-silk rayon dress was damp under the arms. It had been a bum, back there behind the building. A stupid bum scaring the living daylights out of her. How goddamn stupid could she be? Now she was stuck out here in the dark, alone on an all-but-deserted street. A sitting duck. She was beginning to hate her boyfriend, her job and Los Angeles in that order. She was starting to cry as she prayed in her head. *Sweet Jesus, please let it be eight-thirty.* She cocked her wrist to check the time once more but, to her amazement, her watch was gone.

In that split second of surprise, she heard the deafening explosion behind her and felt the hot-cold sear of flame at her back. Her looks-like-silk-rayon dress melted against skin that was already curling away from the bone. In a blink she was caught in a maelstrom of wood and glass; suddenly she was starring in a heavy-metal music video, a big-budget disaster movie without benefit of lights and cameras. And, in that seemingly endless second before a shard of glass pierced her throat and another took off half her scalp, there was time to consider something else. Her watch wasn't the only thing that was missing—so was her hand.

* * *

Someone pushed him, kind of slapped him on the back. He turned all the way around when that happened. He heard the roar of the explosion at the same time and half lost his balance because the earth bucked beneath him. He held his hands up against the wave of junk that rolled his way and squinted at the blaze of fire leaping out of the building a block behind. When he could, he looked to see who had tried to get his attention—like anyone needed to tell him that all hell had broken loose—but no one was there.

At his feet there was a hand with nobody attached. Lord above, this was it. Fire, brimstone and body parts. The dead were rising, the world was ending. Falling to his knees, clasping his hands over his chest, the drunken bum raised his face and waited for the ground to open and spew forth wrathful spirits from its evil molten bowels. Lord in heaven. When none of that happened he focused his milky white eye on a Chevy Camaro blowing down the street, the driver at the wheel looking damned surprised. That's when he heard the squeal of tires behind him and looked to see a pickup cutting through the night like a bat out of hell.

Damn right.

Hell.

Officer Readmore belched and reached inside his car for the radio. Half the restaurant had followed him to check out what was happening.

He looked cool, so no one could tell, but Jimmy Readmore was thrilled at the sight of the fire a mile away. He was sick of this beat. L.A. downtown from two to midnight was shit work. Readmore wished he knew what he'd done, or who he'd ticked off, to pull this kind of duty. Whoever it was still wanted him punished because the dispatcher was telling him to stay put even though half the city's fire units were on the scene.

Frustrated, he chased everyone back to their cold meals,

got in his car and convinced himself that he really had better things to do anyway. Still, as he patrolled the streets, he thought about the fire. Could be a gas explosion or a bum's fire crackling out of control. Messy stuff that. There'd be bodies. Nothing worse than a burned bum. So, a bored Jimmy Readmore was chuckling about his alliteration when he noticed a blue pickup heading for the 405. Jimmy wouldn't normally have given the truck a second look, but something had run afoul of his antennae. Nothing major. Just enough to make him do a double take on the truck that was so conscientiously following the speed limit even though there wasn't another car in sight and half a city block was on fire not more than a mile away.

He turned on the lights and gave the siren a once-over. The truck picked up speed for an instant, then pulled over before Readmore could get too excited. He took inventory as he rolled up politely behind it.

Blue Chevy pickup.

California plates. Riverside dealership.

A bumper sticker: *Take Back America.* The guy was a Republican. Otherwise the truck was real, real clean. His eyes flickered to the back window. This big boy had been to the Grand Canyon. There was a gun rack in the cab but no gun. The bed was covered.

Holding his flashlight high as he approached, Officer Jimmy Readmore's boredom blew away with the cool breeze. He shined his mighty light on the driver and smiled at the handsome blond boy behind the wheel. The kid couldn't meet his eye. Jimmy bent down and scoped the passenger sitting on the other side. Same hair and eyes only this guy was fleshier. Had to be the kid's dad. He didn't have any problem focusing. Dad looked Jimmy Readmore right in the eye.

"Evening, sir. Son. Think I could get you to step out here?"

Jimmy smiled his best public-servant smile. He stepped away as the older man opened the passenger door and got out of the truck.

Officer Readmore moved back toward the truck bed,

letting his eyes flicker away long enough to check it out. He lifted a corner of the bed cover.

That was his second mistake.

His first was stopping them at all.

"Turn it off."

"No." She breathed the word out along with a cloud of smoke.

"You're a pain in the ass."

"Even if I am, you need me." She never took her eyes off the television set.

"Yeah? What do I need you for?" His voice was clear as a young boy's still thrilled by the possibility of seduction rather than the inevitability of sex.

Edie was glad her back was to him so he wouldn't see how much she adored the sound of his laugh. She swiveled her head when he stopped, her jaw slicing dark hair swinging over one eye. The other one was black as coal; the look she gave him cold as ice. She'd practiced it because he liked it. Allan grinned at her, proving her point. Edie, he believed, was an equal-opportunity woman. Equal satisfaction, equal cravings, equally decisive and independent. That was his Edie. Edie, on the other hand, knew the truth.

While Allan Lassiter would never love her, he often wanted her and that meant something to Edie Williams. She pushed the left side of her hair behind her ear, holding her cigarette away so that it wouldn't singe, but close enough so that her squint looked almost nasty. He unwound one arm from behind his head and touched her breast: small for a tall woman, naked, excellent.

"Oh, you need me to fill in when the darling of the day bores you." She took another drag and shook back her hair. She exhaled leisurely, thinking of all the nubile young things that had probably been in this bed before her. None had lasted as long as she. "You need me to convince you it isn't your fault when you can't get the one you want."

"Never happens." He laughed again and this time she was looking right at him.

Generous to a fault with his money and time, Allan

Lassiter reserved his affection for himself—and maybe the old man. There had never been another man made like him: one who physically lacked for nothing yet needed so much. It was a need she understood.

"Lauren hasn't got the time of day for you," Edie reminded him flatly. He colored. Edie lowered her eyes. She hadn't meant to hit so hard, but sometimes hitting below the belt was the only way she knew how to get his attention. She covered her discomfort with something typical, a comment he would expect from her. "Lassiter, your lust is as transparent as your ambition."

"And your ambition is as unfulfilled as your libido," he shot back. That was the kind of relationship they had. That wasn't the kind Edie wanted, but there was the rub.

"I'd rather you help me take care of the ambition, Allan." She took another drag of her cigarette. This time her eyes teared. It was probably from the smoke. "I can always handle the libido on my own. Most women can, you know."

The bantering was tiring, so Edie turned away. The flickering images on television held more allure for her at the moment than even Allan. Channel Two had their cameras trained on an IRS annex that was burning downtown. It was a wonderful fire that threatened the entire shabby block. But there was even something more intriguing. Edie recognized Mark Jackson and two of his FBI cohorts, before the cameras closed in on a beautiful Asian newsreader obliterating the rest of the scene.

"... Just eight-thirty when the explosion occurred. One woman is confirmed dead, a man is severely injured and in critical condition at USC Medical Center. Fire units were on the scene within minutes and it appears that they have the fire under control. A fire department spokesperson refused to comment on how long it will take to determine the cause of the explosion, but speculation is running high that this might, indeed, be linked to the rash of bombings that have plagued government offices across the country in the last eighteen months. Witnesses say ..."

The set went black. Edie's prayers had been answered. Here was the key to her quite modest ambition. She tried not to think that this opportunity would lead to any spectacular change in her position, for to do so would be to tempt fate. She'd learned a long time ago you only fooled with Fate when it was a sure thing she would take the bait.

Edie tossed the remote on the bedside table and leaned after it. Her cigarette was stubbed in a crystal ashtray she liked to think Allan kept there for her. The brass lamp was switched off. She climbed atop Allan Lassiter. The room was warm and her imagination on fire. He was ready and she lowered herself carefully before angling her body over his.

In the dark of Allan Lassiter's immense condominium high above Century City, Edie Williams, Chief of Special Prosecutions for the U.S. Attorney's Office of Los Angeles, whispered.

"You know what I want?" She lowered her head toward his chest, lips parted. Allan sighed beneath her, his hands roaming over her back. He didn't bother to ask what it was she wanted. Edie answered anyway.

"I want just a little more than I've got."

Lauren Kingsley was foaming at the mouth. She brushed her teeth the same way she talked: with vitality, style and a great sense that she knew exactly what she was doing. Tonight she walked and talked while she brushed her teeth so that the words were garbled and the toothpaste foamed into big, blue gel bubbles. She went back and forth between her bedroom and bathroom practicing her closing arguments.

"Forgery is the altering . . ." a quick up-and-down on those two front teeth, ". . . legally significant instrument . . ." to the back teeth, ". . . intent to defraud . . . no one disputes . . . the defendant must . . ." a final flourish along the gums, ". . . Your Honor!"

She paused in the bathroom doorway, her toothbrush resting on a molar as she considered the intent, content, and inflection of the argument. All of it was passable, but passable wasn't good enough. Her argument needed to be perfect. Perfect. Up and down that brush went as she envisioned the word perfection in her mind. And while

Lauren was considering just how to reach such a goal she couldn't help but notice the news on the television. In the dark bedroom it flickered like a nickelodeon. Fire, cops and more fire. The sound was down but she knew there weren't many script choices. The anchor was either lamenting the fact that they didn't have any details, was trying to make up details or was speculating that a downtown fire was just a prelude to a riot that would tear the city apart. Of course, everyone would find out in the morning that the fire was nothing more than a faulty electrical connection. A drop of blue foamy gel falling at her feet reminded Lauren that she had bigger things to worry about.

She rushed to the bathroom and turned on the water. Bending over the sink, she rinsed her mouth. Lauren had a cup but couldn't quite remember where she'd put it—probably in the dishwasher waiting until there were enough dishes to actually run a load. She was too busy to find it, too busy to cook, too busy doing what she'd been called to do. It didn't matter that she hadn't named this wondrous goal. It was personal, it was out there, it was waiting for her and she'd know what to do when the time came.

Raising her head, Lauren looked at herself just long enough to see that everything that needed to be done was done. She turned off the bathroom light, cleaned the toothpaste off the carpet, slipped off her watch and put it on the bedside table as she climbed under the down comforter and turned on her side. The television still flickered, so one of Lauren's arms snaked out, grabbed the remote and shut it off. She missed the shot that Edie had seen. Lauren didn't know that the FBI was on the scene nor that the destroyed building was an IRS annex. That would have given her pause. But now it was dark, and the apartment was silent save for the sound of Lauren Kingsley's voice. She practiced her closing arguments over again not knowing that what she was really doing was talking herself to sleep, finding elusive comfort in the sound of her own voice.

Chapter One

They had descended like locusts on the places George and Henry Stewart were taken after their arrest. They went to the police station where the duo were booked and to the Federal Detention Center where they were held by the authorities. During the long months of investigation, the tedious weeks of jury selection, they had disappeared, losing interest in equal proportion to the attention of the press. Now the Stewarts' trial was about to begin in the courtroom of Judge Jonathan Lee, and they were back at the foot of the steps of the Federal Courthouse.

They were guys the likes of which Los Angeles had never seen. Guys with guts. Guys with beards. Gaunt guys made up of sinewy muscle. Guys in jeans and T-shirts with slogans about guns and liquor screen-printed back and front. They were guys who looked as if they came from a gene pool nobody should swim in. They wanted meat on their women and had disgusting pet names for the female anatomy. They condemned the government, blacks, Hispanics, and everything and everyone that wasn't white, male and spoke in one-syllable words. They championed gun ownership and animal rights for pit bulls. These were the kind of guys who didn't play by the rules because they couldn't read them.

But these were definitely not members of the militia, Independent or otherwise. They were pretenders with nothing better to do than cause a ruckus and they were having the time of their life.

"Are the mountain men still out there?" Abram Schuster talked to Edie from the doorway. She glanced at him. Abram was top dog, Edie second in command. He had rewarded her with position for her service, she responded in kind with her loyalty. It was a fine line they had been walking for years. They weren't friends, they were excellent colleagues.

"Yes, they're out there. I just love the media, they'll buy into anything. Those guys are no more militia than I am." Edie cocked her head. "It's sort of the difference between reading a Stephen King novel and finding the Night Stalker in your bedroom. Half those reporters would pee in their pants if they spent ten minutes alone with George Stewart. He's the real thing. He's worth writing about, not those people down there."

"And what about you, Edie? I'd venture to guess George Stewart doesn't scare you at all." Abram chuckled as he came into her office. She made room by the window.

"No, he doesn't scare me. He's my brass ring. Besides, men are predictable, Abram. It's women who aren't." She tapped her finger against the windowpane, focusing on the woman who walked past the cameras without notice. "She's the one who's frightening. Have you seen her up close?" Edie raised her chin, indicating the woman in yellow.

Abram was by her side now, having stepped over boxes of files that comprised the investigation which would build Edie's case against George and Henry Stewart, the men accused of killing two people in the course of a domestic act of terrorism. They were charged with blowing up an IRS outpost with 500 pounds of high explosives. Conspiracy charges made the whole package heavy with possibilities, and so damn politically correct. Abram focused on the woman below.

"Yes, I have. I assumed you'd already seen her, too. Perhaps even talked to her. Falling down a bit aren't we?"

"I've been busy. Or maybe you haven't noticed?" She leaned against the sill, arms crossed.

"Oh, I have noticed. I've noticed many things. Lauren Kingsley, for example. Your second seat has been putting in long and tedious hours while you've been showing up more regularly on the news, Edie. I thought, given the task of prosecuting two members of the elusive Independent Militia, you would have been burying yourself in strategy rather than tying yourself up with television cable."

Edie's smile was now small and tight. He was testing her. She was up to it.

"Lauren's been with this office for three years. She needs to burn the midnight oil. When I'm the U.S. Attorney, and she's been here fifteen like I have, then you can worry about her."

"I do hope you won't have to wait that long to take my place, Edie," Abram laughed outright.

"So do I." She gave him a lazy, honest look that hid her sudden attentiveness. "Any chance the job will be opening up soon?"

"I'm ready, Edie." Interrupted suddenly, they looked toward the doorway before Abram could answer.

Lauren was there, wound tight and ready to spring into action the minute Jonathan Lee gave the go ahead. Edie eyed Lauren's charcoal pant suit, the ascoted blouse, the flawlessness of the younger woman's personal presentation, then she disregarded it. Style was not a level playing field. You either had it, or you didn't.

"Fine, I'll meet you downstairs," Edie answered.

"Abram, it's going to be a great trial." Lauren reassured him with a nod and then she was gone. Edie half expected to find the space filled with flashbulb pops of light, residuals of Lauren's momentary, and blazing, appearance.

"I would say she looks none the worse for wear, Edie," Abram chuckled.

"I would say you're right." Edie reached for her briefcase and whipped it up atop the desk. Obviously he hadn't come in to announce that his position was about to be vacated. She fiddled with the latches and asked woodenly, "Has Lauren complained about the way I'm handling things? Is that why you're worried about her hours?"

"Our Lauren? She doesn't complain. She states facts and spouts her opinion, which she somehow manages to make sound like fact." Abram dismissed Edie's concerns with a cursory wave. "Just don't make her a lackey because she threatens you. Use her because she knows what she's doing. Remember, Lauren clerked with Wilson Caufeld. That's about as good as the federal bench gets."

"That's probably where she learned that every call is black and white," Edie smirked as the gold locks clicked on her briefcase. She turned back to look out the window and then at him. "But, Abram, let's be honest. Threatening is the last thing I find Lauren. I'm just practical. She's won six cases to my fifty. If you're worried about the hours she's putting in, take her off the case, otherwise we'll do what needs to be done."

Abram smiled and peered at the crowd of cretins below. He was pleased with Edie's sovereignty. Lauren Kingsley should count herself lucky to work under such a woman. Still, there was a danger in not recognizing the more human aspect of the work they did. Emotions and desires, rather than the simple intellect, needed to be considered, if outcomes were to be more easily predicted and objectives achieved. Edie, he feared, would never learn that.

"It was only an observation, Edie. I'm a voyeur at heart. I never like to get involved in the fray if I don't have to." They were face to face now.

"Why don't you observe how I work instead of how often you see Lauren hunched over her desk," Edie said, companionably cool.

Abram's nod was the only sign that he'd heard her. She raised her hand self-consciously to her head. Her dark hair was parted on one side as always and it lay against her head like a helmet. When she spoke, the slight curl of the cut moved as her wide lips did, like a punctuation mark calling attention to the fact that she meant every word she said. "I'll make you proud, Abram. I promised you that when you hired me and when you promoted me. I'm not going to let you down now."

Abram reacted charmingly with that sort of Ronald Reagan "there you go again" chuckle the broadcast media loved. He looked good in print, too. Abram was an Alistair Cooke clone of sorts, a gentleman's gentleman unless you looked too closely. Then you saw his skull was a bit too large for his body, his silver hair was slicked down too tightly against his almost-patrician head. His suits, of superb quality, weren't quite tailored properly. That twinkle in his eyes was not one of delight but a trick of his chemistry. But no one every looked that closely because Abram moved on before they could find his flaws. Edie saw them and understood them. She didn't have to like Abram to appreciate what he had, and probably would, do for her.

"Quite right, Edie. You run this case as you see fit." He ended the administrative talk and pointed casually out the window. "So what do you think about the mother?"

"I think she's as scary as her husband. She won't walk ten paces behind bringing up the rear with a rifle, I'll tell you."

"Do you think she's calling the shots?"

"Who knows?" Edie shrugged, more comfortable now that they were back to the business at hand. "This is supposedly an offshoot of the Guardians, but none of the big groups are acknowledging the Stewart boys. They haven't denounced them either, so I guess it's a wash. The case agents interviewed the mother and said she's a tough nut." Edie smiled. Abram did, too, knowing Edie felt a certain kinship with that kind of woman. "Mrs. Stewart is proud of her men, Abram. She didn't even try to alibi them. She'd probably hand over George without blinking. They'd both love to be martyrs. She may think twice about the boy, though. I'm not sure he's really with the program anyway."

"That's nice to know, but I'm not handing over either of them." Abram moved away from the window and slid onto her desk, letting one leg hang over the side.

"Don't you mean 'we,' Abram?" Edie said, emphasizing the partnership.

He raised only his eyes toward her and smiled. "Of course, Edie. In for a penny, in for a pound. But the sad fact remains that I am where the buck stops. You're simply not the boss—yet."

He laughed and Edie colored. One day she probably would be, but the job was his until the Federal administration changed. Even with that, though, Abram Schuster felt rather secure having survived two presidents. There was no reason to think he wouldn't outlast a third. Black robes and a lifetime appointment to the federal bench, or a presidential housecleaning, were the only two things that would send him packing. Edie could have her dream when he had his. He had thought that moment was close at hand until he took a good look at the Stewart case. This terrorist act wasn't quite a national disaster with only two dead but it had its merits. It also had its problems.

"Officer Readmore's stop wasn't good, you know. It was a bad mistake that could ruin you before you get started, Edie."

"We've got it covered. There are precedents," Edie shot back, annoyed that he should think she hadn't covered such basic ground. If the stop was flawed then the defendants could walk. Luckily, judges were human. They weighed the law against public perception, then seasoned the whole stew with their own prejudices and beliefs to come up with their unique recipe for justice. "Judge Lee is a good man. He's ruled favorably for the police every time there's been a fine line of admissibility. We couldn't have drawn a better judge on this one."

"I hope you're right. It isn't just your lovely ass, Edie. It's this office's reputation that's on the line. The national eye has turned upon us once again." He sighed. Menedez and O.J. were both disasters so they had to make this one good. Few people understood the distinction between the D.A. and the U.S. Attorney. To them, lawyers were lawyers and when they worked for the government incompetence was assumed. "People want someone to be punished. You better be definitive on the issue of Officer Readmore's stop or the defense will be all over you and the judge. Unless, of course, you can make a case without the physical evidence from that truck."

"I don't intend to try." Edie felt worn out, and the day hadn't started. Abram, half politician, half attorney, had that effect on her. He might not be able to pontificate so easily if he were to step back into the courtroom for a minute. Sometimes she simply didn't have the energy to be the hard-driving, hard-working, hard-edged professional everyone expected her to be. Sometimes Edie wondered when the rug would be pulled out from under her.

She looked for a way around Abram, found none and moved past him to put on her jacket. Edie was transformed. She stood taller, her eyes were sharper, she became an even more powerful-looking woman. Sometimes juries and judges didn't like that.

"They're waiting. I've got to go. You want to come watch?"

Abram looked at the clock on the wall and slid off her desk. "Thank you for the invitation, but I'm sending my best. Go defend the People against the evil men who would dismantle our government, rape and pillage." Abram chuckled, thoroughly amused with himself for just a moment. "I think I'll let you ride off to battle on your own."

Edie was skeptical. "You're turning down a chance to see and be seen?"

"It's your party, Edie. I assume you'll tell me when you think my presence might be beneficial. I'll show up after we hear how Judge Lee rules on the arrest of our anarchists, but only if he rules in our favor."

Edie swung her briefcase off the desk. When she looked back at him her eyes were filled with amusement.

"Thanks for the lesson in deportment, or was that a vote of confidence?" She stepped past him. Before she had cleared his path Edie hesitated. Though she would hate to admit it, she did need Abram's approval. Without it she felt too alone despite Lauren Kingsley by her side or, perhaps, because of it. "I've got Lauren handling the motions this morning. There isn't a man on earth who can resist a strawberry blonde standing at their feet pleading for them to do right by her. What do you think?"

"A wise decision, Edie. I admire a woman who knows how to work effectively with those of her own sex." *Or use them to the best advantage.* He sent her on her way with another smidgen of self-assurance. Edie thought a pinch was all she craved. Abram had a feeling bushels wouldn't be enough.

In her wake Abram sniffed, but Edie hadn't left a trail of burning doubt behind her. That was good. Prosecution was nothing more than guts and the desire for glory. Outgunned, out-financed, a prosecutor needed to be focused by a desire for right to triumph in the face of evil, or an equally strong need to triumph for the sake of proving oneself superior in the face of such odds. Edie, he thought, was the latter.

She was a funny, personally secretive woman. He would like to be around when that incredible passion of hers couldn't be contained one more minute. No matter how she tried to hide it, Abram was sure the passion was there. But that was for another day. Edie and Lauren had worked their tails off for this day. All in all, they had each done what they could to insure the success. Now the battle had begun and the troops had been sent forth.

Looking about, his practiced eye saw nothing intriguing in Edie William's office. At the very least he didn't have that sense of despair that often precedes disaster so Abram Schuster went to attend to his own important business. Mark Jackson was waiting in his office.

"Your Honor," Lauren said firmly. Judge Lee gave her just a bit more of his attention for her effort. "There is no question but that the restraint of Henry Stewart was lawful. As the driver in the car in which his father, George Stewart, was riding, Henry's presence was inclusive in the officer's detention. Now, I admit that the driver can challenge detention, but, Your Honor, I can point to numerous cases which override the challenge. For example, United States v. United States District Court, both of which uphold the notion that if the vehicle in which the passenger was riding is lawfully stopped the driver himself is lawfully stopped and can be detained."

Lauren raised a hand and pointed to the judge as if she had just called the eight ball and popped it in. Joe Knapp, young Henry's counsel, rolled his eyes. It must be nice to still get revved by your own arguments. The kid talked like she knew everything. He chanced a glance toward the end of the defense table. Eric Weitman, George's attorney was honed in on Lauren like a laser. The man was a barracuda. When this thing got going in earnest, and Edie hopped into bed with them, Joe knew he was going to have to fight for poor old Henry's share of the covers. If, of course, they ever got into bed. With a sigh he noted the time. If Lauren Kingsley was as smart as everyone said she was, she'd wrap it up. Not that it looked like she was in any danger of losing Judge Lee's attention. The man was giving her more than her due.

"If the courts did not recognize such lawful detention of the driver of a vehicle, Your Honor, we would have criminals—" she cast a stony look toward the defendants, "—murderers—hiring lawful citizens to sit in the passenger seat while the bad guys drove. Criminals would all be set free based on the theory that a driver cannot be detained because of a reasonable expectation of privacy."

Edie, sitting at the prosecution table, rose slightly and handed Lauren a note. The younger woman didn't miss a beat, nor did she read the note. Edie sat back and picked up a pencil to cover her annoyance. It wasn't that she didn't like Lauren, sometimes Lauren simply annoyed her. She never seemed to stay still long enough to learn what Edie had to teach. She would remind Lauren who ran this case and whose experience would guide them through the trial, if Lauren ever stopped talking.

"You, Your Honor, would be providing the criminals with the means to their end. That would result in anarchy, Your Honor, something I'm sure these two gentlemen would relish."

"Behind the lectern, Ms. Kingsley. And, may I remind you we are hearing motions, not closing arguments."

Jonathan Lee looked over his bifocals and motioned her back. His smile was so slight she almost missed it. Her impassioned contention still ringing in her own ears, Lauren sidestepped back to the lectern lamenting the lack of drama in Federal Court. She must remember to ask Wilson if her mother had been as cool in the courtroom as Judge Lee. She took a deep breath and centered herself. Her mother always said that an attorney who was centered was the one who moved the quickest. Her mother . . .

"Ms. Kingsley? Is there anything more?"

"No, Judge." Startled and ashamed to find she had stood silently before the bench, Lauren walked back to her table.

"Counsel?" Jonathan Lee looked toward the defense. Joe came to attention and took his place, ready to go through the motions. There wasn't much that would influence the judge at this stage since Jonathan Lee wanted to go to trial. The best bet would be to get every possible argument on the record for an appeal.

Lauren watched Henry's attorney. She paid attention the way her mother had taught her, and forgot her mother simultaneously. It was getting easier all the time. Joe Knapp was standing in the proper place.

"Ms. Kingsley makes up for her youth with her enthusiasm, Judge. United States v. Gonzales disagrees with anything she can throw out to this court. The point of this whole exercise is moot. I will let Mr. Weitman speak for his client, of course, but in regard to mine, Henry Stewart should never have been detained. There was no reason to stop the vehicle he was driving in the first place . . ."

"That's not true, Your Honor," Lauren muttered. She stuck her pen in the weave of her braided chignon before raising her voice. "A half a city block had just exploded. That's reason enough to stop anything moving within a five-mile radius."

Lee was hiding a grin when his clerk, moving more quickly than was appropriate, came into view. She reached toward Judge Lee. He wiggled his fingers, signaling her to put whatever it was on the desk in front of him. The clerk persisted, shoving the piece of paper at him while she leaned down and whispered loud enough for Lauren to know it was urgent. Judge Lee screwed his face into a look of displeasure, and it was in that moment Lauren became aware of everything: George Stewart jotted a note, a reporter cursed her inkless pen, Edie was reaching into her briefcase, Joe Knapp kept right on talking and Jonathan Lee was suddenly engrossed in what his clerk had to say.

"The officer should have been on that block then, offering assistance to those who were injured instead of stopping an innocent citizen, a young man . . ." Joe was still talking.

The clerk had her hand on Jonathan Lee's shoulder.

He was reading the note and then he stood straight up. An anguished "oh, my God," was heard over Joe Knapp's arguments.

Everyone was stunned. Even Joe, who found it impossible to stop his discourse, and rolled on like a car with bad brakes, ". . . A citizen who, by Officer Readmore's own admission, had not violated any law, whose vehicle was in good working order. Officer Readmore was bored . . ."

"Shut up, Mr. Knapp."

Joe faltered and with a last sputter fell silent.

Judge Lee towered above them all, white with fury. The muscles in his neck and jaw constricted. His eyes were red with the sudden madness that gripped him. There was a rustle. People squirmed. Comments passed from stranger to stranger. Henry moved in his seat. George remained still. Confused, Lauren tried to nudge the proceedings back on track.

"Officer Readmore," she said quickly, "was explicitly told he wasn't needed at the site of the explosion . . ."

"Did you not hear me, Counsel?" Judge Lee swung his head Lauren's way as he growled. "Shut your mouth. Don't say another word."

"Your Honor," Edie cried, on her feet, "I object . . ."

"And I object to all of this, Ms. Williams. I object to the drivel that you and your associate have presented here when you should be pointing the finger at these monsters, all monsters, who roam our streets taking innocent lives."

"My Lord!" Eric Weitman exclaimed.

"Don't even think about saying anything, Mr. Weitman. You're no better. Look at you. Look at all of you." Lee glared at the prosecutors. "You're arguing about the minutiae of stops and standing." He threw his head to the other side and pegged the defense. "This side is defending sociopaths, idiots who believe they have enough brain cells to think their way through the ills of the world when all they're doing is creating them. People like that should be . . ."

"Your Honor! We're still in session. We're on the record!" This time it was the court reporter who found her courage.

"She's right, Your Honor. Call a recess," Joe Knapp urged. Instead of listening, Jonathan Lee ended his career.

"You're right, Mr. Knapp, I should call a recess, but I won't. In fact, I'd like to speak to Henry and George Stewart—for the record. They are slime. They are the worst our world has to offer. I sit here and listen to these ridiculous motions and arguments using conflicting case law when what we should be doing is sitting the jury and showing them pictures of the maimed bodies of the two people these men . . ."

Everyone looked toward the Stewarts as Lee pointed a finger. Lauren caught Joe's eye then flicked her gaze over to Edie who stayed still. Lauren moved forward without a clear idea of what it was she could do to stop this. Edie turned toward the marshals to assist when all hell broke loose.

"This is unacceptable!"

Hearts stopped, barks of surprise peppered the air and George Stewart rose phoenix-like from his chair. He pushed Joe Knapp's neatly stacked papers, his briefcase and a cup of coffee off the defense table and onto the floor. In the next blink he slammed his fist atop his own attorney's portfolio. So calm, so disciplined for the last hour, the elder defendant was suddenly active and angry.

"The man who claims to be a judge in this court is nothing more than a vigilante able to abuse my son and myself publicly. He can use his words, and the power this so-called government gives him, and he can make us disappear. Until he does, we are guaranteed a speedy trial under the constitution and a trial by our peers. You are a crazy man and you are not my peer ..." George bellowed at Jonathan Lee. His eyes blazed as he threw himself across the table. Both his hands came down with an awesome sound that made the courtroom itself shiver. It was an explosion of outrage. Instantly they all remembered what this man was accused of doing.

A hysterical scream pierced the air.

Other observers scrambled to their feet only to realize there was nowhere to go.

Eric Weitman lunged at his client, but George was quick and evaded him.

There was a cacophony of exclamations and half-formed questions. A camera flashed. The photographer scurried out the door. There was money in that exposed frame. Later, someone would try to figure out how a camera had been smuggled past security. Now they wondered what else might have been smuggled in. A bomb, perhaps? George would have sacrificed all of them, even ...

"Dad!" Henry Stewart called to his father like a child terrified to be left behind. The back door of the court flew open. The woman in yellow made it three steps into the room before raising her voice.

"Henry!"

Henry reacted instantly. A look of disappointment passed between them. He wasn't beside his father in this fight. Then there was a softening, a hope, perhaps, that Henry would be smart and stay where he was. Henry looked back at his father. Mrs. Stewart advanced and Jonathan Lee did the same. He leaned over the bench, screaming at George Stewart who hollered back. George Stewart was ready for a fight but he hesitated. The face he turned to those behind him was twisted with hatred and cold with disgust. The woman in yellow looked directly at him with beautiful blue eyes and that gave him purpose. George offered her a ghost of a smile before whipping 'round to the bench. He vaulted around the table that stood between him, his son and the judge.

"What the fu- ..." Edie yelled but before she could

finish, Lauren threw herself in the path of the angry defendant. Edie called for her, pandemonium reigned, and the marshals finally got legs.

Two of them tackled George, hitting him hard, pushing him to the floor. His political protests turned to grunts of pain as they whipped his arms behind and cuffed him. They pulled at him like a wishbone. Lauren dashed back to the table just as Henry made a move to help his father, but fear kept him tap dancing where he stood until another marshal got him in a headlock. He looked like he was going to cry.

One marshal hollered, another moved past the bar to the rear of the court. Carolyn Stewart was on the inside of the closed doors. Everyone chattered, a few moaned and George Stewart was held tight against the broad khaki-clothed chest of a marshal who would break his neck if he wasn't wearing a badge. In the front of the courtroom, another deputy had his hands on Jonathan Lee, restraining him, too. The judge didn't struggle. One look forced the big man to release him. When Jonathan Lee spoke again it was quietly, with a coldness and conviction that sent shivers up Lauren's spine.

"You people are wrong." He glared at the Stewarts. "This government is valid but it sure as hell is weak. If it were strong, my hands wouldn't be tied by technicalities. There are times I long for the days when the only voice in a courtroom would be mine and the hanging tree was just outside of town. You would have been swinging from it . . ."

"Your Honor, I demand a mistrial. Your Honor!" Joe Knapp had sufficiently recovered his wits to realize he had an opportunity here.

"Your Honor. A recess is in order . . ." Lauren cut him off fast.

"You're right. You're both right." Jonathan Lee threw up his hands. "Talk yourself blue in the face. I can't tell who's honest. Everybody does what they want anyway, and we're killing each other. Go ahead, kill each other! I've been so dumb to think that I could do anything about any of this. I'm the fool. I'm the biggest fool of all."

The judge crumpled the note that started the mayhem. There would be no explanation. He looked at the ball of paper then at the uniformed men in the room. Finally he took a look over his shoulder at the great seal of the land that hung above him. He tossed the paper onto the floor. He took off his robes. Snaps popped. Spectators jumped. He threw the robes on the floor behind the bench, Jonathen Lee looked around the courtroom then talked to everyone.

"Do whatever you want with these two. It won't make a difference. One way or another we're all dead."

Chapter Two

Edie stood in the ante-chamber of Abram's office and looked at him. She was stiff as a board, her eyes darted from one side of the room to the other. She looked at Abram. When she spotted Mark Jackson, Edie turned on her heel and disappeared as quickly as she had materialized. Abram stood up and walked across the great expanse of his government-chic office and through the outer office where the secretary sat. He looked down the small hall, unable to see the reception room from where he stopped. Curious, Abram followed. He didn't bother glancing at the artistically challenged photos of his predecessors lining the walls. Instead, he looked into the reception area to see if his number two was, perhaps, waiting for him. She wasn't. The oasis of green carpeting that supposedly designated this a rarefied space, separate and apart from the concrete gray motif of the rest of the U.S. Attorney's Office, was empty save for the wing chairs, couch and table that were of the same mold as those gracing a thousand motor inns across the country.

Much as Abram would have liked to find out what had brought Edie back so suddenly and fiercely from the hearing, that's where he stopped. There was other business, so

Abram retraced his steps, noting that his secretary, Monique, didn't look up for fear Edie had come back with him. Gently he closed the door to his office and briefly wondered where Edie had left Lauren Kingsley. If anyone was bloodied, it would be her.

"I'm sorry, Mark." Abram took his seat behind the desk. Mark Jackson, FBI Special Agent in Charge, sat in the chair opposite him resting his elbows on his knees. He was quite a man, carrying satisfaction and disappointment alike with a macho flair that was anything but off putting. Honest, trustworthy and dedicated, he was the kind of man Boy Scouts and Marines dreamed of being. Add to those exceptional qualities a right to carry a gun, listen in on conversations and raid the bad guy's lairs and you had quite a combination. Abram smiled.

"Now, where were we?"

Mark shifted and referred to the third manila folder on his side of Abram's desk. It was weekly update time for the two. This week the update was fairly pleasant. The mental scale of screw ups each man kept in his head was tipped slightly in favor of the U.S. Attorney's office. All in all, though, Abram and Mark Jackson were on fairly even footing.

"The Mexican Mafia." Mark cleared his throat to give Abram time to find the folder. "We've got a slight problem with Little Joey."

"He doesn't want to testify?" Abram jotted a note on his file while he spoke.

"No, nothing like that," Mark answered. "He'll still talk, but he wants to take his girlfriend along into the Witness Protection Program. Normally that wouldn't be a problem, except he wants us to pay for the wife and kids, too. The cocky little bastard wants us to support a harem."

"Shall we?" Abram asked.

"Naw. I talked to Jamison—good guy by the way—and he says as far as the prosecution is concerned, Little Joey's got some interesting stuff but nothing we can't piece together on our own if we have to. I say we offer one or the other but not both."

"Done. Anything else?"

"The good news is, we don't have to worry about the press getting hold of the videotape of our surveillance. Judge Ferguson doesn't admit exhibits into evidence until the end of the trial to save his clerk a little trouble. It's a fine line, but public domain access doesn't kick in until the evidence is actually booked. This way the media can't get their hands on any of it. We can still keep this out of the limelight for a while." Mark chuckled thinking of the reporter's frustration with the black out. "They call every day looking for something. They've even hit up the mail clerk, can you believe it? The media can't move without a visual."

Abram pulled himself out of the reverie he had fallen into.

"Yes, yes, of course I can believe it. The ladies and gentleman of the press are nothing, if not tenacious. I'm quite proud of how this has all been handled. It's nice to be in control of the information for once."

"So, what's bothering you?"

Mark sat back, not terribly worried about Abram personally, but if his counterpart was preoccupied, the FBI should be, too. And, if it affected the FBI then it affected him, his reputation and his pride as an agent of the United States Government. In this jurisdiction Mark Jackson was the man and he didn't want to just cover his bases, he wanted to know what was growing underneath them.

Privately Mark thought Abram prissy. The U.S. Attorney was a man with a mediocre mind who lacked a certain character. That made Abram politically correct rather than public-spirited. The difference between them really boiled down to the fact that Mark felt privileged to work for the U.S. government. Abram, he suspected, just felt privileged.

"Edie's bothering me. She and Lauren were arguing motions this morning in front of Jonathan Lee. They should still be there, yet here she is, back already." Abram looked out the window toward the California mountains that, on this gloriously sunny day, were snow topped. He wasn't impressed by the beauty, so he swung his head back toward Mark. "I can't imagine why, can you?"

Mark became wide-eyed, a "duh" gesture. "They got it

done. Lee probably ruled, the Stewarts are back under lock and key, and everyone's ready for lunch. I wouldn't sweat it, Abram. Everything is set on that one. It's been top priority with my office since the blast. We're not only taking down the Independent Militia, we're taking down GOAL, Abram. The Guardians of American Liberties.''

"That would be so very nice, Mark. Quite an ambition.'' Abram sighed. "But, I'd feel better if you were focused on getting this conviction.''

"No problem. We'll do both. I'm going to turn the boy. He's scared and I'm betting he's going to roll over. Don't forget, Nick's still undercover. With his information we'll be able to indict a bunch of folks who will wish they never even heard of George and Henry Stewart. Put these guys away, make a public spectacle, really work the press and we will have renewed the public's faith in the Bureau. Your office, too, of course.''

Abram stiffened at the slight. There had, naturally, been setbacks in the last months. Abram could point to juries, judges and poor evidentiary work on the investigator's part to explain the few problems his office experienced. But they were hardly at a critical turning point.

"A conviction isn't as easy to get as it seems, Mark. Readmore's a hero now but he walked a fine line with that stop. If the stop was bad, then we won't be able to use the hardware in the back of the truck. Without it there's no comparison to what you picked up on post blast. Without it, your confidential informant better be good as gold.''

"Judge Lee won't toss the evidence. I'd bet you even the Supreme Court wouldn't screw up this one.'' Mark stood up and put his folders in a pile before wandering to the window. He ignored the view of the mountains and focused on the street below.

"What's happened to Los Angeles, Abram? What's happened to this country? We're overrun by foreigners who don't want to jump into the melting pot anymore. All those damned leaders—minority, community, whatever— they're loudmouths trying to make a buck or get their faces on TV. Human megaphones, that's all they are, and they're tearing this country apart. The more they scream about their rights, the more the good old boys holler back about theirs."

Mark took a step left to the low table on which Abram had lovingly laid an intricate battle scene full of little metal soldiers. They must have cost a fortune. Mark picked up an infantryman. It was an apt choice. That's the way he thought of himself even though he was a general in his own, very real world.

"I'm not saying I agree with the militia, you understand, I'm simply saying I understand how they've been pushed. Their kids have been pushed out of schools, they've been pushed out of jobs and its government mandates that are pushing them. Heck, half the television stations are foreign language and they need translators at McDonalds." He was smiling when he looked over his shoulder.

"I'll tell you Abram, we wouldn't be having these problems if there was more assimilation. I know it's not politically correct, but it's common sense. We've got a lot of organized groups from the Mexican Mafia to the Independent Militia, and it's the militia that scares everybody because they're our own. They're the ones pushing back big time now, Abram, and we've gotta do the same before we lose control completely. Judge Lee knows that."

"You're right, in theory." Abram was polite but not convinced. "But things happen, Mark. We can't speak this plainly to the judge. At the very last, the decision is beyond our control."

"I've controlled this one from my end, Abram. I'll leave my confidential informant in place until the last minute. He's the best and with the physical evidence in that truck, the eyewitnesses . . ."

"How many witnesses again?"

"Three. Homeless guys, but they all saw the truck and one swears he got a real good look at the Stewarts." Mark waved the little tin solder and shot down Abram's concerns. "We can't miss on this one. We're heroes. We acted so fast getting them indicted the afterglow alone is enough to see us through. The *L.A. Times* has had Readmore on the cover of their Sunday Magazine for Christ's sake. It's just like the movies." Mark warmed to his favorite subject.

"Ever see *The Man Who Shot Liberty Valence?* The guy who got the credit didn't really shoot Liberty Valence but he never tells. So Readmore made the stop because he was bored, because he'd been dissed by his captain, but he's not going to tell anyone that. He's going to be the dragon slayer."

"And if Lee won't allow the evidence?"

"Have a little faith in the man." Mark's fist tightened. The little soldier's bayonet plugged him in the palm. He looked at it, as if surprised to find it there. Carefully he put it exactly where he found it. "We got them. All that matters now is that we keep them, and the judge knows that."

Mark walked around the office, feeling invigorated by his sense of righteousness. He checked out the framed citations. Abram was lauded more than any man Mark knew but the reasons eluded him. The U.S. Attorney was full of affectations; well versed in the law, but hardly well practiced. He had few friends, yet a great many people were willing to go to bat for him. Funny thing, he never seemed to reciprocate. Mark never saw Abram Schuster reach down to give a leg up. He was a curiosity, this small man with the great view of himself as the general of the battle. Abram was no more a leader than half the men and women who had sat in that chair. They were political appointees. It was his office, the Federal Bureau of Investigation, that brought the cases and initiated the action. His agents put their lives on the line, Abram's assistants only put their reputations there.

"My CI is good, Abram. The best. I trained him and he'd do anything for me." He almost added that he loved Nick Cheshire like a son but decided Abram would never understand what that really meant. "We'll put the Stewarts away for a couple of lifetimes and the country will applaud. This case will be the banner that will show how effective we government men can be in Los Angeles. You, me and Judge Lee. We're on trial, too. I'm sure it's dawned on you that this is important to us individually."

"How long has your informant been in place?" Abram

asked, not willing to comment on the last. One never knew who was really listening, after all.

"Three years. He lives just like any other guy in the neighborhood. He goes to a job, comes home, dates. His story is that he's divorced and the system screwed him out of a fortune, by the way." Mark sat again, excited about the quality of his work and willing to share it. "See, that's what makes this particular cell so frightening. They're patient. They look like any other middle-class guys, living in middle class neighborhoods. They have wives and kids and pets. It took a solid year for Nick just to get himself into a meeting. There hasn't been a traffic ticket since our man went in, but there's been lots of talk. When we found out what kind of talk was going down, we decided we didn't want them for conspiracy to commit, we wanted them for something a little more dramatic. Nick's committed to that."

"So you let them blow up half a city block? Mark, that's going a bit far even for you." Abram looked absolutely shocked and that was a first.

"They were supposed to blow an IRS storage facility in Ventura. There's no guard on the weekends which meant no one would get hurt. These people really believe they can generate some sympathy with the general public by attacking the process, not the people who work it. Anyway, Nick steered them to that target because the building was scheduled for demolition next year. We had them move up the schedule and empty the place. Nick confirmed that target twenty-four hours before the downtown blast. Same crime, different location. We've got enough, Abram, as long as we don't lose Nick's information, eyewitness testimony and the post blast evidence."

"Somehow, Mark, all this isn't that comforting considering the fact that this is a government building. Even you spend your day in one. I'd hate for anyone from the Independent Militia to decide to blow up this building, for instance, and not have an informed heads up." Abram chuckled. It was a droll sound.

"I'll put you on speed dial." Mark laughed, but he was amused. It would be fun to see Abram in a real emergency.

The test of a man's mettle was what he did when he was cornered. Looks, words, big talk, it could all be deceiving. Abram would probably crawl over a woman who was down to get out of harm's way, but Mark knew he could be wrong. "Look, Abram, Edie's been on top of this since day one. She's got her act together."

"And Lauren, too," Abram muttered, only to find his casual comment ringing like a bell in his ears when Mark fell silent. "You have a problem with Lauren Kingsley?"

"Not really." Mark fingered another soldier as he confessed, "She has an attitude."

"Don't we all have a bit of that," Abram commented as his sense of dread lifted. "Don't forget to deal with her fairly, though. The young lady has some rather high-profile gentlemen championing her," Abram reminded him.

"Actually, I figured her history would have kept her out of the running for a position like this. Ms. Kingsley's professional cloth is full of holes and that means one of these days, when it counts, her work won't hold water. Right now, every move counts."

"She's aware of that, Mark. Lauren has such a need to wipe her mother's slate clean that her own work is always above board. She is ethical, meticulous, and righteous to a fault. The fact that the FBI isn't her favorite agency has never inhibited her performance. Her only vice seems to be that she loves the sound of her own voice, but who didn't at her age?"

"I guess you're right. Still, I wish you'd assigned Remillard or Jensen. Those two have some real time behind them. Then there's the thing about women prosecuting."

"Sexist are we, Mark?" Abram laughed. The gloom was gone.

"No. No, of course not." He colored just above his collar. Abram took note, looking for a weak link in the man's rather strong chain. Just for his own edification, naturally. "I'm thinking about a jury. I think a man would have helped the situation, subliminally."

"The first one dead in the blast was a woman. Women should prosecute when home and hearth are threatened."

Mark threw back his head. The gray at his temples

glinted under the overhead lights, his eyes actually twin-
kled. He laughed long and hard. Winding down, he
smoothed his well-trimmed mustache as if that would put
him back in the proper frame of mind. "You think female
jurors will relate to Edie or Lauren? The men might, but
I'm telling you it won't be because they think those two
can whip up an apple pie and stitch a flag at the same
time." He stood up, shaking his head. "You've got to get
out more, Abram."

Abram stood up while Mark was talking. Mark did the
same, shaking his head, chuckles still bubbling up. They
walked to the door but didn't shake hands and that was
odd for both of them. Abram usually offered his as a matter
of course, Mark to those he considered his equal. Perhaps
Mark Jackson made Abram think just a little deeper about
his political ways, and Abram made Mark wonder just
where it was he stood in the pecking order. Surprisingly,
though, Mark put his hand on Abram's shoulder and
smiled a white, bright, agent smile beneath his more-silver-
than-gold mustache.

"I'm pulling your chain, Abram. Edie will be great.
Lauren's good at what she does. A little too much baggage
for my taste, but good. We've got this knocked. If anything
gets in the way I promise, I will personally make it go away
no matter what it takes. You've got my word on that."

Mark gave Abram a thumbs up as he left the office, case
folders under his arm. Abram didn't see that optimistic
gesture. There was a tickling in the back of his mind as
he closed his office door and mentally spread the hand
he'd been dealt. It looked good. A full house: evidence,
attorney power, witnesses, a sympathetic judge, a jaded
public who would heap accolades on those who saved them
from home-grown terrorists. Still, something wasn't quite
right. Two cards were stuck together and hard as he tried
to separate them in his imaginary game, he couldn't.

Feeling ridiculous, Abram left his office and went to see
Edie. But Edie was gone, out for a late lunch—or an early
drink. He found Lauren in her office tossing paper balls
at her trash can. She colored when he found her like that
but didn't stop her last toss, or apologize for taking it.

She never apologized. The kind of surety wasn't good in someone so young.

"You're done early, Lauren." He pulled out a chair, noting she missed the trash can more often than she'd hit it.

"We're done for the day. Maybe the year. Maybe for life," Lauren muttered.

"Really?" Abram said.

That's all the encouragement Lauren needed. She started talking and kept it up until she'd told him everything, exhausting every possible ramification and permutation of what had gone on in Jonathan Lee's courtroom. By the time Abram left her office he had it all in perspective. Mark Jackson might have to work a little harder than he anticipated when it came to making the Independent Militia go away, and Abram was glad he hadn't assigned himself front line duty.

"I can't believe it. Poor Judge Lee. What a way to tell him. They left a message with his clerk. That is so tacky."

Lauren Kingsley's feet were propped on Judge Wilson Caufeld's coffee table. Her shoes were off, her hands laced behind the back of her head and her head was tilted up to stare at his ceiling. She looked as if she lived there, and in a way she did. A judge's chambers had been her second home since she was ten and nothing about the trappings of that office surprised, scared or intimidated her. The world at large sometimes did, but when that happened, Lauren Kingsley just talked louder and moved quicker until the boogie-men went away. What happened today didn't scare her, though, it made her feel terribly sad. She swiveled her head, watching Judge Caufeld go about his business.

"It's a horrible thing. Horrible. I don't think there would have been any other way of doing it," Caufeld intoned. "Frieda Lee was hurt so badly they couldn't have waited for a recess. I still can't believe it. That poor woman, carjacked right in Santa Monica. What is this world coming to? Someone had to tell Jonathan that he was needed at the hospital and his clerk wanted to be the one to do it. Better her than having the LAPD disrupt the courtroom, or a reporter.'' He shook his head like an old bull elephant. "What I feel so badly about is that Jonathan reacted so poorly. Given his outburst, I'm not sure he'll be able to return to the bench. I understand his distress, but public opinion, the system, neither will be forgiving of something like this. Despair is not allowed for a judge of his caliber. His emotions should be private. The law demands that we look with a knowledgeable eye, not an emotional one, at the business at hand.''

Wilson Caufeld shook his head again as he thought of Jonathan Lee's situation, but a glance at Lauren made him sorry he had voiced his thoughts. He hoped Lauren hadn't connected his comments with her memories, but one look was enough to know she had.

Lauren's eyes were closed, her body just a tad more rigid than it had been a moment earlier. She looked beautiful though she would have preferred a more generic adjective like polished or handsome. Her mother, Lauren was quick to point out, had been beautiful. To Wilson, the two women were identical. Fair of hair and coloring, chiseled face except for that nose. A Kingsley nose, just a tad pug, charming enough to soften that jaw of hers that was now clenched so tightly. The fair hair that nature curled was still caught in braids wound in a figure eight at the back of her neck the way she had worn it for more years than Wilson could count. Her color was heightened, not through make-up, but by hurtful memories of another judge who had kept silent during a time of despair. That silence led to disastrous results.

"No long face, Lauren." He scolded himself for his insensitivity rather than her reaction. "This is a special lunch, and I won't have anyone ruining it. Not Jonathan Lee or the sad circumstances in which his wife has found herself. Not you. Not me. Not even Allan. I told him to be here exactly at noon and now it's twelve-thirty. Sit down and eat. We won't wait. That young man can never be counted on. I shouldn't put even the smallest bit of faith in him.'' Wilson Caufeld motioned Lauren to the far end of chambers. She swung her legs off the table, put her shoes back on and stood up. Her trousers were beautifully cut, pleated, full and breaking just so on top of her Italian loafers. Wilson hadn't seen her legs since she was sixteen. Pity. He waved her to lunch again and she laughed. All was well.

"You better not let anyone hear you say that about Allan. Last I heard he had a client list that looked like the *Who's Who* of corporate America. If you slander him, he'll have your head on a plate."

Lauren shrugged out of her double breasted, dusk colored blazer and put it carefully over the back of her chair. Beneath it was a blouse made of ivory silk that fell beautifully over small breasts and covered her thin, strong arms. Another inch shorter, a less-refined profile, fewer absolutes and ultimatums falling from her lips and she would have seemed almost childlike.

"I was the one who recommended Allan as counsel to half those corporations. I've seen his press, Lauren. The greatest defense attorney of the century, indeed. Silliness. Greatest con artist. Most glib lawyer to hold a bar ticket," Wilson protested affectionately as always. "He's forgotten where he came from. I gave him his first job. I'll tell anyone who will listen that Allan Lassiter can't be trusted if he can't even honor his luncheon dates. Allan is no gentleman, Lauren."

"Oh stop grumbling. You adore him, and you know it. Besides, he adores you back."

Lauren swiped an olive from a platter as the judge turned it to a more pleasing angle. He gave her a paternal slap on the wrist and she smiled. She kissed him on the cheek, pulled out her chair and waited while Wilson bustled about complaining about a man for whom they both forgave everything. She watched Wilson Caufeld with her chin on her upturned hand.

A black man so light he could have passed for white, but would never think of it, Wilson Caufeld was Lauren's friend, her substitute father and mother, her mentor. Her mother had told Lauren about Wilson Caufeld instead of reading her to sleep with fairy tales.

Wilson Caufeld began the practice of law when it was almost impossible for an attorney of color to make his mark in the mainstream. He was proud to call himself a Negro rather than hide behind his light complexion to forward his career. Decades later, to the horror of the politically correct, he still referred to himself that way. A private man who longed for a family, he had suffered the loss of a beloved wife before being blessed with children. He never found someone special enough to replace Victoria in all the years of being a widower. Wilson Caufeld was a funny man, but shy of his own wit. In public, his intelligence and single-mindedness overshadowed his kindness. Few knew exactly how endearing he was. In his entire career he had taken only two people under his wing and into his heart. Allan Lassiter and Lauren Kingsley. They had grown up with Wilson, while Wilson had grown older and wiser.

Wilson had taught Allan Lassiter to be an excellent attorney, but he'd taught Lauren so much more. She learned how to function through hurt, keep her chin up, win by throwing small punches, protect herself though there were chinks in her armor. Sometimes he told her she was beautiful, but she knew that couldn't be true because an essential part of her was missing. All Lauren saw was the masculine cut of her jaw, the broadness of brow. Her mirror didn't register the fullness of her lips, the softening curl of her hair, only the pain-filled eyes that looked back when she wasn't on her guard. He said she was smart, but Lauren knew that, when it was critical, she had been too stupid to see tragedy looming ahead in her life. No matter that she was hardly more than a child at the time. She had still been blind to her mother's despair.

Wilson Caufeld clapped his hands, "We're ready. If Allan hasn't the decency to join us at the proper time on such an important day then—"

On that cue the door opened and Allan, in all his glory, stood on the threshold ready to be admired. Though the act was old, and they knew the scene well, they admired him anyway. Allan Lassiter was a breath of fresh air, a crystalline wave breaking over a snow white beach, an expanse of sky so blue it brought tears to the eyes. In short, Allan ranked right up there with every breathtakingly beautiful thing God had ever made. If Lauren Kingsley was the daughter Wilson Caufeld never had, then Allan was the son and just that much more adored. It was a narrow margin and one Lauren didn't begrudge him. Allan kissed the top of her head while he took the spotlight and adjusted it on himself.

"I know you were talking about me. I hope you were saying good things." He placed his hands on Lauren's shoulders. "Judge, when are you going to convince this woman she'll do better in the courtroom if she doesn't dress like Dick Tracy. Show a little leg, Lauren."

"No jurist in his right mind would be swayed by such a blatant bid for attention," Wilson sniffed, trying to hide his pleasure that Allan had finally arrived to fill out his family. "And we were only talking about you to lament your shortcomings."

"I have none, and you know it," Allan laughed. He put his arm around Wilson Caufeld and squeezed, grinning the whole while. Lauren swore the old man blushed. "Must be big news if you've got the table cloth on." He slipped out of his jacket and tossed it onto the couch without thought for its fine quality. Sliding onto a chair he gave Lauren a smile as his voice dropped, the way it did when seduction was on his mind. "You look good, Lauren." This part of the act she'd stopped taking seriously years ago. He cleared his throat and broadened that grin. There were more interesting things to talk about. "Considering the morning you had, I'd say you look stunning. Drove old Jonathan Lee right off the bench, did you? Better work on your oral skills, Laurie. You can't win if you let the judge lose control before he hears what you have to say."

"Boy, good news travels fast. And don't call me that."

Lauren rolled her eyes until they landed on him. Allan folded his hands and propped his elbows on the table. His cuffs were monogrammed white-on-white, the initials repeated on the pocket of his shirt to catch the eye no matter where it roamed over him. Sometimes she hated him because he was cold and that core in him would never warm to the world. Sometimes there was a warmth that scared her because it seemed to envelope her completely. But that frigidity kept her from him and him from being lovable. Sometimes it kept Allan from being likable. That coolness, though, was always interesting to other women who couldn't resist trying to melt his icy charm. What a waste of time.

"It's just gossip, Lauren." He pronounced each syllable of her name, chastened but unrepentant. "A nervous breakdown on the bench is kind of exciting. I heard Judge Lee actually took one of the marshal's guns and tried to use it on George Stewart."

"That's stupid rotten gossip, Allan, and it wasn't a breakdown. Lee was in shock. He was outraged. He just reacted." Lauren looked away. Allan's hand rested on the back of her chair. Lauren reached for the water. He touched her neck and she brushed his fingers away. "Don't tease. And stop looking at me like that," she said. "It was awful. Why is it you think everything is just a lark? What happened to Judge Lee isn't funny. His wife's in critical condition at St. John's Hospital. Shot in the head and for what? Her car. That's disgusting. And it wasn't exciting when George Stewart started in either. He's scary and, Allan, if you don't start acknowledging that there are real people involved in everything that happens around here, then I think you are one very sick puppy."

"Wilson, Wilson, what have you done to our little Lauren? She's beginning to sound like you. Right, wrong; black, white. You'll never survive in this business." He nudged her and dipped his head. She turned hers away. He lowered his head further until she almost smiled. "Lighten up, Lauren. I was just kidding. I feel for Lee, but admit it, hysteria doesn't do much for the resume."

"People don't think about their resume when someone they love is endangered or hurt. You don't know what it feels like to lose control or to have something horrible happen because you couldn't do anything, or didn't do anything, or did the wrong thing. Your problem is there's no one more important to you, than you."

Lauren's voice caught. Surprised at herself for becoming

so emotional, a wide-eyed Lauren pulled her head back. In the silence that followed she bore Wilson Caufeld's wordless empathy, Allan Lassiter's pitying look. Finally, Wilson ran interference.

"Stop baiting her, Allan. No more bickering, Lauren. We all feel for Judge Lee. If we don't, then we are not fit for our work. Knowing the history between us, I suggest we are ever careful of what we say, especially to one another. Today I want you both to be wonderful and attentive. I want to look at you and be proud." From the credenza he took a bottle of champagne that had been chilling in a bucket. "We have more festive things to discuss."

With that the cork went flying. Allan reached up and tried to catch it, but missed. Lauren squealed and pounded the table, face bright, her expression animated.

"Judge, are you getting married?"

"Absurd. I'll have no romantic talk in my chambers."

"He's retiring," Allan hooted, raising the glass Wilson had just filled and taking a drink as soon as his guess was made. "You're retiring, aren't you Wilson? Come work for me. My talent, your name, we'll make a triple fortune. It will be like old times."

"Put that glass down," Wilson admonished, hiding his delight. "I have something to say. There's a toast. Show some manners."

"Okay. If I can't have you, I want your secretary when you retire." Allan laughed. Wilson cracked a smile, his eyes sparkled.

"A fate worse than death for any woman. I wouldn't wish that on anyone. Besides, Barbara's coming with me, hopefully."

"Oh, my lord," Lauren howled again. "He's marrying Barbara!"

"Enough. You're both children, teasing about things like that. I'm just happy Barbara's gone to lunch, so she can't hear what you're saying." He pulled back his chair then changed his mind. He cleared his throat. "I suppose something like this is better said standing. If I thought it would help, I'd put my robes on and hold you both in contempt, that would put you in the proper mood. Now, glasses at the ready.''

Dutifully, Lauren and Allan did as he instructed, giggling until the portly man in the light gray suit lowered his eyes. Wilson Caufeld was choosing just the right words to match the moment. His every utterance changed a future. In his career he had sentenced men to death and men to life, he exonerated and condemned. Seldom were his thoughts directed inward nor did he speak of loneliness, or confusion or how heavily his judgments weighed on his heart. Allan and Lauren remained still. When Wilson spoke, it was with regard for them before a word about himself.

"I don't often tell you how proud I am of the both of you. I assume you know that I hold you dear.'' He looked at each of them in turn then let his gaze rest on Allan. "Allan, for many years I wasn't sure if I would find you on the right, or the wrong, side of the law. You are a talented young man who can make anyone believe anything. Your charm could have been your undoing, instead it was the key to your fortune. Thankfully, you have a good mind to go along with the rest of your nonsense. Your clients pay you handsomely for it. When I first saw you during that moot court session in your law school years, I thought you were a boy who would be disbarred soon after you passed it—if, indeed, you passed it. But then, when it was all over, you thanked me for teaching you a bit of humility. It took a man of character to do that. You have done well, you have turned tides that I know were often overwhelming. I am proud to know you, Allan, prouder still to have had a hand in growing you to such an excellent attorney.''

Allan raised his glass in gratitude. Lauren looked to see if that lovely speech had brought tears to his eyes. Before she could decide if it had, Wilson was talking to her.

"Lauren, I have known you even longer than Allan. You are as dear to me as if you were my own daughter. I watched you grow up. After your mother's death, I was honored to be the one you turned to, not just for professional advice, but for solace and friendship. I was terrified when a young girl looked to me for guidance. Thankfully, I seemed to have found a few meager words that helped you become the lady—or should I say, woman—you are today. In all honesty, though, I believe you have become what you are through your own will and fortitude and intelligence. Your future is as bright as Allan's. You will never get rich representing the People as I have, but you will always make a difference. That dedication to seek out what is right is in your blood. You have the determination to overcome all obstacles. I only wish that there will be no more in your life that must be faced with the courage you've already shown."

Wilson Caufeld ran a hand over his gray hair, tightly waved and slicked down with pomade against his head. The color of his eyes had faded over the years, yet the passion he felt for his young friends shined bright through, of all things, tears. Lauren steeled herself. In her heart of hearts there was no sense of foreboding. But perhaps this wasn't good news at all. He was speaking of their singular futures. He was speaking as if he was saying goodbye and Lauren wasn't sure she could bear that. Not again. Especially not him.

"And so, because you are the children of my heart, the apple of my professional eye, my family, I want to share with you the news I received this morning before you read it in the paper. Allan," he raised his glass, "Lauren," he tipped it her way. "I have been nominated to the Supreme Court. With God's help I will be confirmed, in due course, to sit on the highest court of this great land."

Chapter Three

The law, like any business, is sensitive to the winds of fortune. The degree of its sensitivity depends on whose fortune is blowing in that wind and whether the gale forces predicted will actually materialize. In the case of Wilson Caufeld, Federal District Judge, and newly nominated to the Supreme Court, those winds blew hard and fast throughout Los Angeles.

Those who did not know the judge barely swayed with the effect of the news, but acknowledged his nomination seemed well deserved.

Those who knew him, even marginally, reeled with the report. Stories were told of personal bondings in which Caufeld's affection for the storyteller grew in proportion to the number of times the tale was told. Dreams of grandeur blossomed in the minds of all who hoped to sit on the coattails Wilson was barely aware he was trailing. The judge, reserved though he had been all his career, would remember them all they were sure, even if they had been third seat on a trial that lasted less than a week in Caufeld's Los Angeles courtroom.

There were the gossips, too, who speculated regarding the nature of Wilson's nomination. Many a brow was raised when considering that Wilson Caufeld was no longer young. He may not sit the court through two presidential terms, so why appoint him? No arguments were pending that might require the weight of a conservative vote thus creating a political victory for the president who appointed him. No African-American groups pushed an agenda. If anything, a woman would have held the president in better stead. The gossips contemplated many a scenario over an equal number of beers and scotches. Finally, only one conclusion could be reached: Wilson Caufeld was a merit appointee, an anomaly in this day of calculated moves and minimized risks.

But there was an exclusive and knowledgeable group who understood his nomination thoroughly. They knew Wilson Caufeld was long overdue for such a singular honor. These were the ones who looked to the judge's future with an understanding that theirs would be inexorably linked. Though sincerely exuberant at Wilson's good fortune, they couldn't help but consider the personal ramifications of what was happening to Wilson Caufeld.

Allan knew that his considerable influence would grow in exponential proportion to the judge's good fortune if he used their relationship right. With each step Wilson took, Allan would be there beside him. He imagined himself holding the Bible upon which Wilson would pledge himself to his lifelong task. When that fabled first Monday in October came around, Allan would have free access to the most powerful chamber in the country and, with that, would come unbridled influence. Prominent on the West coast, Allan couldn't help but see himself distinguished throughout the country thanks to Wilson Caufeld and his fate.

Lauren Kingsley looked at Wilson Caufeld and saw her mother's friend, and, on some level, the father she had never known. Overjoyed at Wilson's success, she indulged herself in those selfish moments and felt the pride of knowing that, while others would fear, revere and possible revile Wilson Caufeld, she would always share his devotion, his counsel and his joy. She, Lauren Kingsley, would be privy to history and she was awestruck and humbled that he had chosen to care about her. She looked forward with excitement to the days to come as she hadn't looked forward to anything in a long time. Even more amazing, Lauren Kingsley found herself speechless as she considered what the future held for all of them.

Those who practiced before Wilson Caufeld walked on eggshells, waiting for any sign that his judicial nature had changed. When it did not, they wished him the best of luck and it was business as usual. Nominations, after all, were fraught with peril and Caufeld, while nominated, might never be confirmed. So they treated the judge as always but added a little more weight to the deferential spin of their argument.

For Abram Schuster, the ramifications of Wilson Caufeld's nomination were a bit more personal than even Allan or Lauren's. Wilson Caufeld's move would leave an opening on the Federal District bench and Abram wanted to fill it. Calls had been made putting people on notice. His good friend, the Democratic Senator from California, had already written a letter of nomination to be presented to the President of the United States as soon as Caufeld was confirmed. The lieutenant governor, two state senators and a gentleman in private practice who had, at one time, served as assistant attorney general of the United States had letters of recommendations for Abram in their files. A president of the right party was in the White House for a second term and Abram's checkbook reflected that proper donations had been made at the proper time. His long tenure as U.S. Attorney had been spotty with victories but, thankfully, the victories were showy and pressworthy. He could point to his curriculum vitae with pride.

Bottom line, Abram Schuster wanted Wilson Caufeld to be confirmed in the worst way. It would take awhile for Wilson's confirmation and, in the meantime, Abram was determined to add one more star to his resume. He wanted the Stewarts convicted.

So Abram Schuster walked the gray-carpeted halls of the U.S. Attorney's Office to a meeting that would be the first move in accomplishing that objective. His step was light but brisk and he couldn't seem to rid himself of the small

smile of delight he'd worn since planning his strategy.
When he opened the door to his office, Edie Williams and
Lauren Kingsley knew that they were dealing with a happy
man who would let nothing mar that happiness.

"Ladies, I'm delighted you could join me."

Edie murmured a hello. Lauren smiled back and Abram
admired the expression. She looked like a woman on the
edge of another time, running around in suits and silk ties
like men before it was acceptable, her face still cameo
perfect. Her hair was almost red gold in the morning light.
Very nice. He headed to his desk, stopping only long
enough to rearrange some of his soldiers. When he was
done, the little iron men stood aggressively facing the
enemy instead of eyeing one another across the field.

"English wool, Lauren?" he asked when he was finished.
"There's nothing like it for the fall of a jacket. You have
a fine tailor."

She laughed, amused by Abram Schuster's pretensions
but never fooled into thinking that's all there was to him.
Smart cookie, her mother had called her. Her mother was
right. She was smart enough to know when it was time to
lift her feet.

"Off the rack. Domestic. Glad you like it. I know it's
three-button these days, but I still like a double-breasted
cut." Always one observation too many. She bit her tongue
when she saw him bored.

"I agree wholeheartedly. Well, I admire the buyer's taste
then. And yours, naturally." He sat in his chair, throwing
off the last. It was a compliment on her clothing and
nothing more. Abram's sexual etiquette had never been
questioned by anyone in the office. Men and women were
treated alike by the U.S. Attorney. All were admired, or
subtly derided, for style or talent. It was as simple as that.
Lauren's suit forgotten, Abram looked at the lay of the
land. The troops were wary, but not divided, on the real
field of battle.

"Edie, why don't you join us here?"

She unfolded her long body from the low couch. He
didn't comment on her dress. She was not the kind of
woman who wore a dress well and he would not be the

one to tell her so. As she settled herself beside Lauren, Abram put his hands together and looked pleased.

"Better. Now that I've got you both in front of me, we'll get to it. This is a good news/bad news situation, ladies. The bad news is that Judge Lee will not be returning to the bench for an unspecified amount of time."

"Damn," Edie breathed. "The momentum is now. We can't have the Stewart trial continued indefinitely while he takes care of family problems."

There was a silence as they all considered whether or not a woman, shot in the face for her car, qualified as a "family problem." Abram decided when they were finished with that. It hadn't been given more than a minute.

"Oh Edie," Abram noted, "you were optimistic to think he could ever come back after what he said in that courtroom. No, I think when Mrs. Lee recovers, she will find her husband has quietly retired." Enough said about Lee. He was history. "However, the wheel, as the federal government is so fond of calling our simplistic, yet effective, way of assigning cases, has already been turned. The computer kicked out the next name on the list and the Stewarts have been reassigned." Abram lifted his chin slightly, looking at the women from beneath his silver lashes. The right corner of his mouth tipped up slightly and Lauren leaned forward to hear. He looked at Edie when he gave the news. "Wilson Caufeld will be seeing this through."

"Oh my God," Edie breathed. "We don't stand a chance on the stop."

"It will only be tougher to convince him because he understands the law so well," Lauren muttered, defending what they considered Caufeld's intractability. She would have taken Edie to task for her comment, but Abram was talking. She made a wise choice and listened.

"Wilson Caufeld is a special friend of yours who is at a very special time of his life, is he not, Lauren?"

"You know I clerked for Judge Caufeld," Lauren answered cautiously. Abram looked at her as if waiting to see if he would have to explain chapter and verse.

Lauren cocked her head, raised her hands and popped the arms of her chair lightly until she realized how juvenile

she must look. She grimaced at Abram and took a deep
breath before pushing herself to the edge of the chair.

"Well, I guess that's that. I think I can get the motion
files together within twenty-four hours, the case files by
Friday. I'm sorry about this, I was looking forward to the
trial. I certainly do understand the conflict, though."

Abram motioned her down and waved away her resignation. He looked disappointed in her, but not for long.
"Lauren, Lauren, of course you'll be in court. Tomorrow
Judge Caufeld wants to continue the motions in the morning. He's on the fast track with this."

"But, I clerked . . ."

Abram batted his eyes at her ignorance. "If every former
clerk had to recuse themselves from practicing in front of
their judge, then I'm afraid the courts would be busy playing musical chairs. Unless, of course, you're worried that
Judge Caufeld will be prejudiced by your involvement?"

Lauren lowered herself slowly, concentrating on the
glimmer in Abram's eye, and that telltale pacing of his
words. Beside her, Edie was tense and silent. Now there
was more to Edie's concern than Wilson Caufeld's reputation as a stickler for the letter of the law. Something was
up.

"No, he won't be prejudiced," Lauren answered carefully. "Judge Caufeld is the most ethical man I know."

"Yes, we're well aware of that in this office," Abram
muttered, then looked her in the eye. "Do you foresee a
problem with your performance, then?"

"Not at all." She shook her head with certainty.

"Perhaps you might even be able to give a hundred and
ten percent for the man who taught you so much?"

"I give a hundred and ten percent no matter what and
I work for you, Abram, not Judge Caufeld," Lauren said
flatly. Edie made a noise at such self-aggrandizement.
Lauren shot her a look, undaunted by the editorial.

Abram breathed deeply, "Yes, you always give your best,
Lauren. Knowing that, I've made an administrative decision. Publicly, I'd like Lauren to handle this case, as lead
attorney." Immediately he swung his head toward Edie
and looked her straight in the eye. "You will, of course,

be there to assist in your usual capacity, but you will not be designated first seat.''

There was a beat when nothing happened. Lauren stared at Abram. If she cast an eye on Edie Williams she would certainly turn her into a pillar of salt, and Lauren wouldn't blame her for it one bit.

"Like hell I will," Edie breathed and the office turned cold.

"I don't know that I'm ready for that." Lauren made an appropriate gesture to appease Edie or from shock, she had no idea. "Our strategy is set and, now that Judge Caufeld will be handling the case, I'll have to work harder than ever to argue on the Readmore stop. We'll both have our hands full. Edie understands the underpinnings . . ."

"I don't need your qualification." Edie was on the edge of her seat.

"I don't need your resentment," Lauren snapped back without thinking. The two women looked at one another. Sudden adversaries, they were surprised to find the line between them when moments ago they had stood on the same side of it.

"And I won't change my mind," Abram said sharply. Now he had their attention and it pleased him. "Is that the way it is then, ladies? What a pity. I thought you were both above this kind of female thing."

"Don't patronize either of us, Abram." Edie stuck an elbow on the arm of her chair and raised her hand as if ready to catch whatever he threw her way. Slowly she eased back in her seat and half turned her head toward Lauren. "And you don't need to speak for me."

"You're right. I'll speak for myself." She'd been to hell and back in her personal life. A miffed Edie Williams didn't come close to the devils Lauren had lived with. "I'll be happy to try this case. I was doing my best to be politic, but I am ready and I'll win. Thank you, Abram, for the chance to prove myself. I'm sure, I'll be able to handle . . ."

"Yes," he cut her off, not a real fan of Lauren's glibness. "I'm sure you will."

He shifted in his chair, though he was far from uncomfortable with this exchange. Getting hackles up only made

lawyers that much more effective. Lauren would have something to prove not only to Wilson Caufeld but to Edie
Williams, too. Whose admiration, he wondered, would the
young prosecutor consider the greater prize?

"Will you forgive us, Lauren," Abram said quietly, sorry
to see that neither of them were onto his thinking. "Edie,
if you'll stay please."

Lauren hesitated. Whatever was going to happen would
affect her. She should insist on staying, but Abram spoke
to her profile and changed her mind for her. "Remember,
Lauren, you were already quite effective with Judge Lee.
Let's see the same energy in front of Judge Caufeld. Edie
will be down soon to start working with you on the rest. I
assume you'll be open to her counsel?"

"Don't worry. I'll be fine."

"I know you will. How long do you think we'll be, Edie?"
Lauren had been dismissed.

"Not long, Abram."

The dynamic had changed. Lauren was neither needed
nor wanted. This was personal and the silence she left
behind lasted only long enough for her to close the door.

"What in the hell do you think you're doing?" Edie
asked quietly. Abram didn't have to hear. Her fury was
written all over her face and etched in every muscle of her
body. Abram tented his fingers and tapped them against
his lips.

"There are times, Edie, when you still surprise me."

"Why? Because I want what's mine? I don't know why
that should surprise you. You're the one who invented the
concept."

"There's a difference. You only think this case was yours.
As the U.S. Attorney, it's mine, Edie, and I have a larger
picture to consider than how you feel."

She stood up, so taut a good wind could snap her in
two. Abram gave her her head. She paced, her words keeping time with her gait.

"I don't want to hear that nonsense. What I don't understand, Abram, is how you can do this to me?" She twirled.
"No, how dare you do this to me? How dare you?"

Edie took a deep breath through her nose and shook

her hair back. She couldn't look at him. He would see the hurt and, damn, there was a lot to see. She stopped by the window wondering why she put up with this. Any firm in the city would have her at three times her salary, but any firm wouldn't do. This was where she was meant to be. This case was hers and, with that thought, control was back.

"First," she said evenly, "explain why you took me off this case and second why you felt the need to do it in front of Lauren."

"You've been around long enough. Take a wild guess."

"You think Caufeld will give her special treatment on this?" Edie was incredulous.

"Wilson Caufeld would never do that." Abram countered, disappointed at such a pedestrian answer. "He's too above board. There's too much to lose, now that he's nominated."

"Then he should never have accepted the case in the first place," Edie snapped.

Abram sighed at such absurdity, "Don't be ridiculous. He couldn't possibly turn it down. The ramifications would be overt and covert. People would see him as weak, unable to handle the rigors of the Supreme Court if he couldn't take on what he was assigned at home. Caufeld has always held himself apart from the politics, so he wouldn't refuse the trial for fear of suddenly seeming political himself. No, no, Edie, don't even think he might decline on that basis."

"Then you think he'll recuse himself because of Lauren? Is that your strategy?"

"Please, Edie," Abram responded. "We simply have an opportunity here that we can't ignore because it is a certainty Wilson Caufeld will judge the Stewarts." Abram was excited by his own thought process. "Did you know, for instance, that Wilson Caufeld is Lauren Kingsley's surrogate parent? He probated her mother's will, saw to her schooling, he practically raised the woman. There is a bond there that goes beyond any oath Caufeld could ever take. I doubt even he is aware how strong it is. I'm counting on that subliminal desire to see his protégé—his daughter by proxy, if you will—succeed."

Edie grasped the back of a chair. She needed support if she was going to listen to such nonsense.

"Abram, this is so rich. You, of all people, counting on an emotional tie between an old man and a neophyte attorney in braids. We're facing one of the most media-sensitive trials we've had in a long time and this is how you handle it? Please tell me this isn't true. I want you to call her back."

His smile was gone. Abram was pulling rank.

"I'm sorry, Edie, but it's not just Caufeld. Lauren under-stands him, and she'll use that knowledge to play to his weaknesses and her strengths."

"She could do that as second seat," Edie scoffed. "What about when push comes to shove? Will Lauren make him look like a fool if she needs to? Will she fight with him?"

"Who knows, Edie? But I'd bet with Lauren out front, Wilson Caufeld will see this thing through expeditiously. He won't want to give her anymore time than necessary to do what she has to for fear she'll fail. He wants this case off the books as soon as possible with an outcome that will make him look good. Favoring the prosecution is what he should do. He can then sit in front of the Senate Judiciary Committee crowned with laurels."

"And what about me?" Edie rubbed her bare arms.

"What about you?" Abram asked, eyes widening.

"What about what I want and need?" she insisted, sure he would understand—but all she got was a blank look.

"Well, Edie, I would suggest that's up to you." Abram opened his hands as if to show her there were no tricks up his sleeve. Then it dawned on him. He saw it in the twitch of her jaw, the faint shading of disappointment in her eyes, the shaking of her fingers still wrapped over the back of the chair. "Oh, Edie, what is it you thought? That I was going to take care of you? Edie, what on earth gave you such an idea?"

"You did," she whispered. "You hired me. You gave me the big cases. You promoted me. You've always made the way for me, Abram." Her fingers kept tune with her lament. Edie felt sick to her stomach knowing, somehow, that once again she was about to find out she had never really been a factor in life's big equation.

"I did all those things, Edie, because you were the best person for the job, nothing more. Edie, Edie," he laughed with honest amazement. "I'm sorry if you thought there was something more. No, no. Not at all. I don't believe in mentoring. The process is never quite fair. Either I would give too much or you would take too much; I wouldn't give enough, you would flounder because of it and make me look bad. And, if a protégé surpasses a mentor? My, but there's a pickle."

Abram licked his lips. Perhaps he should have sensed this dependency in her, but he hadn't. That Edie had such professionally intimate expectations was a revelation, indeed. Edie, of all people.

"There always comes a day, Edie, when the teacher is taken advantage of by the student. Worse, there comes a time when the teacher fears the student. I fear no one because I am beholden to no one. I trust you because I've assumed you felt the same way. Your talent and determination allowed you to excel. That is the highest praise I can give you. That and assigning you to high-profile work within my power or my pleasure."

Abram sighed. He hadn't thought Edie would have been so full of anger. But now that he looked back he could see so many little things that should have given him a clue. Her tension probably took root the minute Lauren Kingsley was hired. A pretty little thing with a big mind and the recklessness to say what was on it. A young woman with connections. A young woman whom Allan Lassiter held in great esteem. All the things Edie didn't have, Lauren did. But Abram would have been wrong in that assumption. Lauren wasn't the thorn in Edie's side. It was damnable Fate.

"I have my objectives," Abram went on, "and I assume you have yours. Do what you must to meet them, and I'll stand behind you. I would suggest it would be to your benefit to stand behind me, but that's your decision. Mine is to make sure that Lauren Kingsley tries this case. Put whatever spin you want on your participation. You may call yourself anything you like, but you will second-seat this. If Lauren says she believes something is the right way, you will find out the bearing it has on Caufeld. Believe me, Edie, Lauren has an agenda, too, whether she knows it or not. If she doesn't, then I've sorely misjudged her. Now, my decision is made. Take it, leave it, or get out of the way. That's what I want. That's what will be done.''

Abram picked up the phone. So much could happen between now and the time the Stewart case was finished that to carry on this conversation was a waste of time. Caufeld could be confirmed, Abram appointed to a district judgeship and Edie appointed the U.S. Attorney. He doubted any of it would happen in such a short span of time, but stranger things had happened. If and when Edie sat in his chair she could make her own assignments. For now, the discussion was simply over.

Edie dipped her head as a sign of acceptance, not agreement. It was her only option. She had thought him more loyal. She had thought Abram was her undeclared champion. To find out differently meant a change in strategy.

Edie left Abram to his calls, his networking, his schemes, whatever it was that Abram did when he was alone. There was nothing more to learn from him, now she had to put that knowledge to work. First step, make sure she looked good no matter what Lauren did. Second step, find the only one who could still help her get what she wanted.

Edie was so lost in thought as she stormed down the long, undistinguished halls of the office that she barely noticed the man coming toward her until they turned toward Lauren's office simultaneously.

Edie glared.

The man smiled politely. "Lauren Kingsley?"

"No," Edie said flatly.

"I mean, is this her office?" he said.

Edie pointed to the nameplate as if he'd put her out royally.

"I'll leave her a note then she's all yours."

"Thanks." He stood easily in the doorway until Edie was finished at the desk.

He stepped aside to let her pass then brushed at the sleeve of his jacket where she had rubbed up against him before he could move. He half expected to find fabric singed, which would have been a pity. It was one of two jackets in his closet that came close to bureau dress standards. Leaning back, he checked the hallway, stepped into Lauren Kingsley's office and took a seat. He was a patient man and innately curious, so his mind worked while he sat.

The picture on her desk was familiar. Though he'd never met Marta Kingsley, he'd seen her photo a number of times way back when. Her face had been splashed all over the papers for a solid week until the story fizzled out. Then it was as if she'd never existed. There were other things to write about in those days, other peoples lives to look into.

He looked up. Nothing on the ceiling. Government types in the old days were fun. They decorated the ceilings, since wall space was covered with trial strategy charts, calendars and notes. On the ceiling he'd seen mug shots of the bad guys, happy faces, moon shots—and he wasn't talking the celestial kind—bar scores and bullseyes up there. Luckily he'd never looked up to find the dart hanging above his head. Kingsley's ceiling was clean, as were the walls except for a chart outlining opening arguments on the Stewart trial.

He leaned forward to look, interested but hardly seduced by the intricate planning. He knew where his talent lay and it wasn't in crime investigation. His was a more delicate calling. He reached down to tie his suede bucks, black and brown for this occasion. He gave them a little buff.

"Can I help you?"

Hips came into view and then passed out of sight again. He had an image of inky black worsted cut with a gray pin stripe, of a fine body under designer trousers. He sat back and focused. Those clothes fit well. The body was definitely worth imagining underneath them. Tight and tiny. His eyes went up. The face was interesting and pretty. Very pretty. It carried an expression of fatigue, perhaps worry. It hadn't been a good day for the lady and he was so very, very sorry.

Chapter Four

"Lauren Kingsley?"

"Yep." Lauren pushed a box of files out the way with her foot and dropped her books with a thud on the only free space on her desk. She put her hands on them. No rings. Short nails. Small hands. The books were the bibles: Title 18, the criminal code and The Federal Rules of Evidence.

"Eli Warner," he said.

Eli stood up and put out his hand. She took it briefly. Eli sat back down without a clear idea of whether or not it was enjoyable to shake hers. He had a card ready and put it on top of the books, sliding it just under her fingers. She frowned. This, he decided, was not a playful person. He flipped out his credential. That seemed to make things worse.

"What'd you bring me? I hope it's the wire tap transcripts. You guys have been dragging your feet and we've been reassigned to Caufeld. Knowing him, he's going to cut this thing down to weeks instead of months so I need whatever you've got like yesterday."

Lauren plopped herself in her chair. It rocked precariously. Eli guessed there was a wad of paper stuck under a leg somewhere. She rode it out well.

"Sorry to disappoint you, but I don't have what you're looking for." He raised a finger heavenward then cocked it toward her. "Want me to look at that chair?"

"No." Lauren screwed up her face. "If you don't have my transcripts then you better have something else I can use. I'll call the engineers for the chair. You bureau guys should learn to stay on topic."

"Yeah. Thanks for the tip," Eli said amiably and that seemed to peeve his hostess.

"Well, what've you got?"

Lauren leaned forward. When she found she couldn't really see him past the stack of reference books and files she pushed them aside. It would make her happier is she didn't have to see him at all. FBI agents were all alike. In a suit, or cords or a paper bag they couldn't hide their spots. They were arrogant. They could do anything better than anyone else and when they were wrong, they never admitted it. Lauren shook her head. It was getting hot in the office, or at least under her collar.

"Actually, I haven't got anything," Eli said. "I came hoping to get something. Information on Wilson Caufeld."

"Then look somewhere else." Lauren took the top book off the stack and slammed it onto her desk. "You guys don't have to strategize about this. I'll call you to the stand, you tell the truth. Period. Don't try to second-guess the judge, for God's sake," she said then mumbled to herself, "I think that's supposed to be my job." Finding her center again, she instructed him. "I just want you to work up the case. There's no need for you to know, or do, anything else."

She dismissed him but he didn't budge. In fact, he was still smiling.

"Stress can kill, did you know that?" Eli dug in his pocket. "M&M's? They'll give you something good to think about."

Flabbergasted, Lauren was speechless for a moment.

"What are you? An FBI agent or a kiddie-show host? No, I don't want some M&M's, and, no, I don't want to talk about Caufeld. This case is going to be tried on its merits. This isn't a football game, we're not interested in Caufeld's weakness. He isn't the enemy, much as you people would like to think judges are."

"I don't think he's the enemy. As a matter of fact, I think Wilson Caufeld is probably one of the all-time good guys. I just came to find out if you thought he was."

"Of course. Yes, of course. I think he's sterling." Lauren drummed her fingers. He imagined she was taking a deep breath through her nose to disguise her confusion. She wasn't quite so snippy when she spoke again. "You're not here about the Stewart case?"

Eli shook his head. He pocketed the candy.

"Sorry." Lauren's bottom lip dissappeared under her top one. He imagined her biting her tongue. "It's kind of been a tough morning."

"Hey, Kingsley!" Lauren looked up, Eli looked over his shoulder. A gangly middle-aged man was grinning at her, giving Eli only a slight nod. He stage-whispered, "You kicked butt this morning. I want lessons. Edie Williams second seat to you is stunning!"

She waved him away, embarrased that he would think she had engineered the assignment. "Give me a break, Carl."

"I think you've already got it. Kick butt, Kingsley," he said again gleefully.

"Yours if you don't cut it out," Lauren called as the man disappeared. Eli looked back at her and she at him and she saw it in his eyes. He knew who she was. He knew her relationship to Caufeld. He knew what was going down. By quitting time, every agent in the FBI's Westwood office would know about the shake-up if this man was true to locker-room form. They'd think she pulled strings, or Wilson had. That's not the way he'd want it, nor did she. "Look, Mr. . . . ." she referred to his card. "Warner. What is it I can do for you? I'm really busy today."

"I can see that." He smiled with his lips and no teeth. He seemed kind of pleased with himself but he said to her, "Congratulations."

"You know, that would be nice if I thought you meant it."

"What makes you think I don't?" He seemed genuinely taken aback. Lauren hadn't expected that, nor did she quite know how to answer it.

"Forget it. Just forget it."

"Okay."

Eli took a note book from the pocket of his jacket and flipped it open and that threw her off completely. There wasn't an agent or assistant or defense attorney in the whole of Los Angeles County that didn't care what was going on with the Stewarts. When he looked back, pen poised, Lauren realized she'd been staring, waiting for him to admit he was curious like everyone else. But when he smiled at her and those hazel eyes of his narrowed almost to a half moon there was nothing to see in them at all. They were beautiful and clear and happy. They were the eyes of a content man. Lauren relaxed and clasped her hands in her lap. She didn't believe it for a minute.

"As I said, I'm Eli Warner." He sounded like a doctor introducing himself to a skittish patient. "I'm with the FBI, and I'm here to ask you some questions about Wilson Caufeld to complete his background check. This investigation is being conducted in anticipation of his hearings in Washington for confirmation to the Supreme Court of the United States. I'd like you to answer some questions as best you can, feel free to tell me if you'd rather not answer. It will not reflect badly on you or on Judge Caufeld. I'm simply interested in your personal impressions and knowledge of his activities as they might affect his performance should he be confirmed."

Eli finished in the same manner he'd begun, pleasantly businesslike. But no smile, no kind manner, could fool Lauren. His job was to dig for dirt and she imagined he did it rather well. Most background agents seemed worn, on their last professional legs. This one actually seemed delighted with the business at hand and that would definitely be an advantage with most people.

"I see. I'm sorry. Fine. I just assumed you were here on the other business. I'm sorry to have wasted your time."

"I would have let you know if you were."

"I'm sure you would have."

"So, can you do this now or shall we do it another time? I can fit my schedule to yours. Morning, noon or night. Coffee, tea or anything else." Eli grinned.

Lauren almost smiled back. He was very good—and excellence deserved credit.

"Now is fine. What can I tell you?" She pulled at her books and straightened the spines meticulously before looking at him again. His head was down and the pen was on the paper.

"How long have you known Wilson Caufeld?"

"Does it count if I was a kid?"

"Yeah, I think it counts." He crossed his legs and jotted a note.

"Okay, seventeen years."

Eli raised a brow but not his eyes until he'd written those two numbers. He wrote quickly. She would have liked to peek at his book to see if he wrote neatly.

"In what capacity have you known him?"

"Friend. Family. He's my family now. Wilson Caufeld was my guardian after my mother died twelve years ago." She paused, waiting for him to comment. As she waited, Lauren saw that his hair didn't have that razor-sharp cut most agents favored. She had the impression that he'd combed it back just for the occasion, and that it would normally part naturally in the middle. When he made no mention of her mother's death Lauren relaxed. "When I came of age we continued our relationship."

Eli wrote in his notebook. "Did he support you?"

"Not if you mean financially. My mother's estate was sufficient to see me through law school and more. If you mean emotionally, professionally, yes. If you mean has he ever done anything that could be construed as improper, or favoritism, in any of those areas the answer is no."

Eli was writing but his pen hovered when he raised his eyes. This time there was amusement in them. "No, I didn't mean anything like that. I just asked a question. Believe me, if I want to know something more than what I'm asking I'll rephrase."

"Fine." Lauren colored. She could feel that blush climb right out of her cleavage, minimal though that cleavage was. The last time she'd blushed like that was when Wilson introduced her to Allan. She was fifteen. He was twenty-six, an attorney and gorgeous. Luckily by the time Lauren was sixteen she'd gotten over it.

"Are you always this defensive?" Eli asked.

"Is this part of the interview?" Lauren inquired archly.

"No."

She sighed. Something was wrong with a man who conducted such serious business as if they were at a tea party.

"Then let's move on."

"I'll bet the Stewarts keep you hopping." Before she could comment he was on the next question and the next and the next. *To your knowledge has Wilson Caufeld ever been a member of the Communist party? Demonstrated against the United Stated of America? Burned the flag? Spoken out against mother and apple pie? Do his socks match?*

Three other people stuck their heads through her door during the interview. Two managed a comment about Edie, the third decided to let it go since she didn't know if Eli was friend or foe. The secretary she shared with two other assistants brought her the subpoena list. It didn't escape Lauren's notice that Cheryl lingered a bit longer than necessary, her eyes trained on Lauren's visitor. Eli Warner was oblivious. Allan would have managed to proposition the girl with a wink and wrap up the interview at the same time. But Eli seemed content to stay where he was. Content, in fact, to stay longer than was strictly necessary.

"Well, I can't think of anything else, off the top of my head, but then that doesn't mean I won't think of something else. It works like that sometimes. I'll hear something one day, but it doesn't raise a question until a week later. It's fascinating how that works."

Lauren found herself staring. He was handsome as could be, but he was such a choirboy.

"You can come back, but I can't promise I'll be accessible. Leave a message with Cheryl, and I'll get back to you if you need me."

"Cheryl?"

"The woman who was just in here." Lauren twirled a finger, her brow furrowed. The man must be brain dead if he missed Cheryl. "My secretary who was just in here? Redhead."

"Sure, but I'll probably try to catch you first. I'll be here a lot. I have over two hundred assistants to talk to not to mention the department heads."

"You've got to talk to all of them?"

"Everyone who's practiced in front of Judge Caufeld. Not to mention his neighbors. If he had a dog I'd talk to the vet."

"You'd probably talk to the dog."

"Probably." Eli got up. This time when he put out his hand Lauren took it firmly. "If you don't mind me saying so, you seem older than twenty-seven."

"That's a switch. Usually I hear that I look like a kid."

"You do. But you seem older. You gave me a lot on Judge Caufeld I didn't expect. He's pretty special to you, isn't he?"

"You could say that. But so is this trial. So, if you don't mind?" Lauren held her hand toward the door. "I've got a lot of work to do."

"Me too. I'm on my way. Nice to meet you, Ms. Kingsley."

When he was gone Lauren pulled up her chair with the broken wheel. She looked at him as he was passing through the doorway and called.

"Mr. Warner, you seem young, too. I mean, to be doing background checks. Why did you ever decide to give up case work?"

"I didn't decide not to do case work," he said with a devastating smile. "I decided to do background work."

With that and a wave he was gone, off to ask his questions of people who knew Wilson Caufeld less well than she, of people who held the FBI in higher esteem than she, of people who would probably find him more charming than she.

Perhaps not more charming. For certainly Lauren did find him nice and memorable and it wouldn't truly disappoint her to see him somewhere else again. Then again, she was too busy to think about men. Then again, he was FBI and that, above all else was what really counted.

Edie's body was anuglar, honed by a lifetime of nerves standing at attention waiting for the next thing to happen that would call for her to make a decision. She was always having to decide whether an event was a good thing or a bad thing for her. In all her years, the answer was never obvious. Edie walked a tightrope, knowing that if she tried to sprint ahead of the pack she'd probably be stopped just before the finish line; if she stayed behind, she'd be lost and probably forgotten. This cycle had begun when her father one-upped her by dying in the audience as the principal was handing her a middle school diploma, forcing Edie to decide whether she should take the diploma or run to his side. Before she could make her decision, the principal dropped the diploma and he ran to the stricken man.

She'd become pregnant the first time she had sex, and the father-to-be had vanished into thin air, leaving Edie alone to decide what to do about the situation.

Her law school scholarship dried up when one of the trustees invested the school funds in a pyramid scheme. Her scholarship was buried in the rubble and the question was whether to continue and starve, or drop out and get a job.

She wasn't the prettiest nor the wittiest, never the last to be chosen but certainly not the first, not the smartest but no dummy either. Edie Williams had rebounded from each disappointment and every setback because she figured it didn't mean the end of anything. For every bad thing there was a good one. Not quite as good as the bad had been bad, but Edie truly believed that somewhere the brass ring was waiting for her. Someday she would get what she wanted because she deserved it. No one worked harder, or was more patient, than Edie Williams. So when she was turned down at the private firm she applied to after law school, and the door opened at the U.S. Attorney's Office, she decided this was the good thing she'd been waiting for.

From the moment she stepped into the courtroom and took her seat alone at the prosecution table Edie felt powerful. She was David to the Goliath of drug dealers' multiple counsels, murderers' arrogance and kidnappers' slyness. They had things they didn't deserve—money, freedom, the power to terrorize—but Edie had determination. Fate had brought them together and, in this place, she could win. She fought tooth and nail. She was every criminal's bit of bad luck. Edie never lost a case in fifteen years.

Today, though, she lost to one of her own and that galled her. She'd been willing to share her knowledge with Lauren. She'd accepted her, treated her professionally, if not kindly, despite the fact that Lauren was everything she was not. Thinking about Abram's betrayal, Edie left the office and walked. Still thinking about Lauren's willingness to take what had been hers, Edie stepped off the curb. She'd been seeing red since she left Abram so she didn't notice that the light was against her.

A horn blasted. The fender of a car grazed her leg. Edie reacted angrily though she had been in the wrong. She was angrier still when she saw the horrified look of the woman behind the wheel of the car. A terrified woman. A woman who could never have lived with herself if she hurt Edie. A stupid woman. She didn't have a clue what real hurt was.

"There are better ways to stop traffic." A man had her arm and, with one strong sweep, she was back on the sidewalk. She shook herself free as she watched the frightened woman drive on before turning to her Gallahad.

"I don't need any . . ." Edie, feeling idiotic, never finished her sentence. Of all people to be there to see her looking so foolish and out of control. Allan. Cool, calm, gorgeous and perfect Allan. He took her arm again and worked his magic. She almost let herself fall into his arms. Edie almost let herself cry. Instead she took a step. A second later they were headed back the way she had come.

"You okay?" Allan asked after a bit. Edie lowered her lashes. It was nice to hear him ask so she slowed her manic pace just a little and walked beside him instead of racing with him.

"Yeah. I'm fine. I mean I didn't get hurt. Not by the car."

"Really? You look like death warmed over. I'd say you need a little TLC."

Allan put his arm around her and gave her a squeeze, his beautiful face was close to hers. Edie closed her eyes, knowing a thousand more eyes could see them. Gossip could run like wild fire if she wasn't careful. Not that it would hurt Allan. He reveled in the attention. Conquest was a badge for any man, for Allan another jewel in the crown. But Edie was private. She was sure there were many who knew about her relationship with him, but public acknowledgment of the good things in her life had always led to disaster, so she was cautious with Allan. He was the best thing in her life, especially now that Abram had turned on her. She pulled away and gave him her most grateful smile and a hand on his arm.

"You have some to spare?"

"I don't know. Depends on what the problem is. Lose your first case or is it PMS?"

Edie pulled her lips tight. She should say something. She should stand up for herself, perhaps point out the wound he had just inflicted. Instead she walked. "Everyone in the world knows that you don't say stuff like that any more. You leave yourself open for lawsuits."

"That's my Edie. It can't be that bad if you're still politically correct. Besides, that might be kind of fun. Who better to defend the bad me than the good me?" Allan laughed and caught up with her in a stride or two. How easy things were for him. Stuffing her hands in the pockets of her dress Edie wished she knew how to slow down, to just feel sorry for herself instead of banging her head against the wall. She wished she knew how to ask for his help.

"I was coming to find you," she said, and that was a start. "I thought you were over at the *L.A. Times* building."

"I was. That business is over, and I've got to pick up

some stuff at the courthouse, but I'm a little early. I'll walk with you if you can slow down."

The minute they were side by side again she blurted it out. "Lauren's going to handle the Stewart thing. Lead prosecutor."

"No kidding?" Edie cast him a sidelong glance. He was grinning from ear to ear "You really know how to play it, Edie. Smart move. Not that Wilson's going to really be swayed by anything Lauren does, but why not throw the kitchen sink at the old boy. I didn't think you had it in you. That was a brilliant decision."

Edie didn't break stride, only her mind stumbled over his unfounded admiration. If she could get away with it she would have taken credit. But Lauren was the apple of his eye, the object of his close-to-incestuous desire. The two of them talked often and Lauren talked constantly. Allan would know the truth soon enough, so Edie was truthful before Lauren could tell him.

"It wasn't my decision. Abram did it."

They'd reached the courthouse steps and tapped up them quickly. When they hit the top, Edie was half a step behind Allan. He threw open the door—brass, glass, heavier than hell—as if it were light as a feather. She went through first.

"Ouch." Allan finally commiserated. It wasn't much but she'd take what she could get.

"I don't think it's going to buy us that much."

"Probably not," Allan agreed.

"I think it's a transparent play."

"You're right." He was getting bored.

"When you thought I made the decision, you said the assignment was a stroke of genius," Edie drawled.

Allan grinned charmingly as they passed through the metal detectors and were pronounced unthreatening. They covered the hall in seconds.

"Busted," Allan quipped, unruffled that he'd been caught making appropriate noises. The elevators opened for him without touching a button. "Sometimes I lie."

"Tell me something I don't know," Edie muttered as the doors closed on them. When they opened on the fifth floor she was talking. "I could have wrapped that case the way it was laid out. Lauren would have been high-profile enough even for Caufeld. If there's any benefit to her it would have been used up in the motions. Abram's wrong if he thinks the old man isn't even going to be aware that he's favoring the prosecution because of Kingsley. Christ, Allan, why didn't you tell me this was where you were headed? I don't want to see Caufeld."

She looked at the small brass plate on the wall. They had come to Judge Wilson Caufeld's courtroom and Allan tugged on her arm.

"You won't. He's being interviewed by some FBI agent who's doing his background. I'm supposed to meet him here for a late lunch. Come on." Allan shifted his briefcase, dug in his pocket and dangled something in front of her. "The key to the inner sanctum."

"I'm impressed," Edie deadpanned. So little of what Allan did impressed her anymore, but she cared for him so much that she put up with him. Even he would find himself on the wrong side of luck one day. When all his tricks failed, then she'd be there to impress him.

"I know where the bar is," Allan sing-songed. He unlocked the second door. Edie followed him in.

The courtroom was cool and dark and Edie shivered but only because she always did when she stepped into one. The seal, the bench, the grandeur of it all was the stuff of which great dreams were made. No matter that half the population of the country didn't know what went on here. Edie knew and this was where she shined. That's why Allan liked her and others respected her. She *was* good. Edie stopped. It took Allan a minute to realize she didn't dog his tracks.

"Edie?" Allan was still grinning, but he was annoyed that he had to come back for her. Edie can't care. This was about her now.

"I deserve to prosecute the Stewarts, Allan. That case was mine and I want it more than I've ever wanted anything in my life."

"More than anything?"

He was giving her that seductive look and that wasn't

fair. In fact, it was insulting. This was her life and to him it was game. Allan had the money and prestige, both earned in the defense of corporations that spent more on their letterhead than she made in a year. He couldn't understand a need as all-encompassing as hers because each compartment of his life was full to bursting with good things.

"Yes, yes. More than anything." When she had his attention she pressed her advantage. "Help me get it back, Allan. You have Caufeld's ear. Make him deny Lauren. I'll find someone else to replace her."

"He makes his own decisions."

"You could try." Edie took his briefcase from him and put it on the long bench beside them. She took both of his hands in hers. "He does things for you. Look, he's nominated to the Supreme Court, Allan, so asking us to reassign could be good for him, too. He doesn't want any question of impropriety. If he doesn't object to Lauren handling this assignment, then point out why he should. Please, Allan."

He was silent a minute. Then he asked the consummate Allan question.

"So, what's in it for me, Edie?"

Edie didn't miss her cue.

"You'd be saving Lauren grief. She's not ready for something like this. The decision should be made before he actually starts the trial and has to face her. Caufeld wouldn't want her to look like an idiot. Tell him that when you're with him."

Allan moved closer. He was fooling around as he took her in his arms and Edie felt suddenly uncomfortable. She put her hands flat on his chest as if she could press into his heart the need for him to take up her cause. She tipped her face up to him, he was just tall enough that she could do that. Her hair had fallen over one eye and she didn't bother to push it back. Beneath her fingers, Allan's body warmed. For the first time since they'd known one another Edie wanted to step away. She didn't. Instead, she closed her eyes when he put his lips against her hair.

"No, I mean what's in it for me?" Edie shook her head.

Nothing, she wanted to scream, *do it just for me. Do it because you care.* He held her tighter, pressing against her. "Come on, Edie. Here we are. The courtroom. Judge won't be back for at least half an hour. Come on, Edie. Let's have some fun. Sometimes I think we're the only ones who know how to have fun."

Edie bit her lip so that she wouldn't talk while she tried to decide what she wanted more. Perhaps she was just trying to decide where her luck lay. Allan and a relationship, one-sided though it might be, or the trial. Just once she'd like not to have to chose. Just once she'd like to have everything she wanted and deserved. She tried one more time to get through to Allan.

"You could just talk to him because I asked you to," she murmured, but Allan wasn't listening and his hands were busy. Edie shut her eyes tight, so tight a tear couldn't escape even if she had some to shed. She put her own hands on his belt buckle and she felt his lips part into a smile.

"I could talk to Wilson," he whispered, "if that's what I felt like. If there was a good reason."

"For me?" Edie whispered, coaxing him down the right path. "Because I'm you're best friend, Allan, and you're mine."

His silence told her what she needed to know. It wasn't enough just to be her. Someday it might be, but not today. He lifted her skirts and she didn't stop him. That's when Edie Williams knew what she wanted most in the world. She wanted to have made a different choice.

Chapter Five

"That's enough, counsel."

Wilson Caufeld took a deep breath. His barrel chest filled out his robes, the knot of his tie was impeccably neat and his expression exceedingly controlled. From the moment Wilson Caufeld read into the record that he and Ms. Kingsley were close friends, from the minute defense offered no challenge, the courtroom was alive, crackling with fast words and quick thinking. Wilson was alert, the attorneys on guard and the two marshals who watched over a now shackled, but unrepentant and silent, George Stewart were ready for anything. Henry Stewart's nervous fidgeting seemed to be in response to the intense and amorous interest of a row of young women who had come to watch that day. Everyone was primed for something to happen. So far, it was business as usual.

The motions had been argued again for Judge Caufeld's benefit. Joe Knapp, Eric Weitman, Lauren—especially Lauren who had taken possession of this case as if she was fighting her young—had put their heart and soul into the job at hand. From one side of the courtroom Knapp and Weitman raised their voices for their respective clients. The arguments were the same:

There was standing . . . a reasonable expectation of privacy, Your Honor . . . Yes, yes, for both Henry and George Stewart. A guard against unreasonable search and seizure is what the Fourth Amendment promised . . . they are protected by it . . . the Constitution is sacred . . . under that protection any evidence within the truck must be suppressed. It is the law. It is just. Suppress. You can do nothing less.

Lauren, fiercely outraged from her side of the courtroom, feeling Edie beside her watching like a hawk, shot back:

There can be no question of standing in special circumstances. Impossible for the protection of the Fourth Amendment to be applied here. I have cases, Your Honor. I have proof of the government's righteousness. Deny the montion. Deny it. I urge you, Your Honor.

Wilson Caufeld called a halt just after he'd heard enough and just before emotions ran too high. Both Weitman and Kingsley tried for one more word but Caufeld stopped their anticipated impertinence with a slice of his hand. Lauren took a deep breath and watched Caufeld intensely, knowing he would rule from the bench. It was his style. No slack. Not a wasted minute, no scurring to chambers to think in private when he knew he was right.

"There was no probable cause to stop the vehicle," he began quietly and leaned forward as if to discuss the sad state of affairs more personally. "Therefore it is my opinion that Henry Stewart was unlawfully detained on the night in question. As both the driver and owner of the vehicle, he is entitled to a reasonable expectation of privacy. The motion to suppress the evidence found in the back of his truck is, therefore, granted in regards to the charges against Henry Stewart."

As Wilson Caufeld ended his thought, Joe Knapp stood. He didn't bother to approach the lectern since this would take only a moment.

"Then, Your Honor, I would request that all charges against my client, Henry Stewart, be dropped immediately."

"I can't believe you would even consider that, Your Honor. Such action would be beyond ridiculous." Lauren was up, too. Today her slacks were beige, her blazer blue and now her color high. "The man is a murderer and a conspirator."

"With no case against him." Knapp had moved to the lectern and claimed it. He spoke into the microphone and made only a passing nod Lauren's way. It wasn't she, after all, who had to be convinced, it was the judge. "Given this ruling on his standing and the suppression of evidence, circumstantial evidence is all the prosecution has at best in this matter, Ms. Kingsley."

"He is a young boy caught up in circumstances beyond his control. He was at the wrong place at the wrong time. A kid . . ."

"He is a terrorist," Lauren shot back and moved toward the center as if she might knock Knapp out of the box. "Why don't you say what he is? I don't care if you dress him in knee socks and a sailor suit. Henry Stewart is a man, not a boy. He and his father conspired to plant a bomb, planted the bomb and killed two people, one of whom died a horrible, lingering death."

"That is for the jury, Ms. Kingsley," Caufeld said flatly. "Move away." She stepped back to her table, but he wasn't done with her. "I would have to speculate that your case against Henry Stewart is not as strong as it once was, considering this ruling. Am I correct in that assumption?" Lauren was silent, but she didn't look away. Wilson Caufeld gave no sign of empathy and she raised her chin a bit higher. "I thought so. Perhaps it would bode well to spend more time with the elder Mr. Stewart and discuss the matter of his son. That might afford you a new outlook on this matter." Wilson threw her a bone. It didn't do much to appease her growing peevishness. She'd thought of turning to George Stewart. Who hadn't? But the man was tough, and Caufeld could have done more to help her. Instead he said for the record, "The motion for suppression of evidence is granted. There will be no more argument or discussion on this point."

"Then, Your Honor, in light of your ruling, I once again request that all charges against my client be dropped." Joe Knapp tried once more.

"Over my dead body," Lauren said despite being

stunned by Caufeld's ruling. She could feel forty sets of
eyes on her. She felt like a kid having a tantrum in the
grocery store. No matter how valid the tantrum, no one
wanted to see it once she had been swatted. She was the
government's representative and her voice shook with
righteous anger as she made her position clear. "The U.S.
Attorney's office has charged this man and the charges
stand. I doubt Mr. Knapp has an idea what our evidence
is, and I would caution him not to count his chickens,
Your Honor."

"Fine. Let Ms. Kingsley bring her case. My client is an
upstanding citizen. He will submit to the due process of
law. But, Your Honor, I must insist—no request—a reduc-
tion in bail at least. Henry Stewart is no threat to our
society. In fact, since Ms. Kingsley and her cohorts at the
FBI will be looking for any sign that he is, I can assure you
that Henry Stewart's behavior will be exemplary given this
scrutiny."

"Fine, Mr. Knapp." The court reporter typed like the
wind into her tiny machine. A computer would later trans-
late at an enormous cost to the People. Lauren would
need it later to make sure she had heard Wilson Caufeld
correctly. "I'll hear the motion to reduce bail now."

"We request that the defendant be released on his own
recognizance."

"Your Honor!" Lauren raised her hand in frustration
but sat back down without waiting for the judge to point
out the obvious—he didn't want to hear from her.

"I can't go that far, Mr. Knapp." Wilson put on his
glasses and looked over his paperwork. "Bail is now set at
$500,000. I'll reduce that to $100,000 with the provision
that Mr. Stewart surrender his passport. I will also make
it a condition of his release that he check in with this court
twice weekly to report on his whereabouts and activities.
Should I have any concerns, Mr. Knapp, I will have your
client brought back and the bail revoked. There will be
no second chances. Is that clear?"

Eyes were on Henry Stewart. He colored. The smile that
came to his face was electric. He could do this. Sure, a
piece of cake. He was, after all, after everything was said

and done, just a kid. He looked at his father in the hope that there would be some sign of paternal relief. His hopes were dashed. George Stewart sat with his eyes forward, his jaw tightened and trembling, not in relief but with outrage. Henry Stewart paled.

"Of course, Your Honor ..." Joe Knapp droned, unaware of his client's disappointment despite their victory. "We are grateful that Your Honor ..." Knapp's brown-nosing played on a background track as Edie whispered and Lauren focused on her.

"Looks like dad's not too happy. Maybe we can use that," she said quietly over Lauren's shoulder. Lauren nodded slowly. Indeed, what should have been a celebratory moment on the part of father and son was not. Was George Stewart angry that he wasn't on the verge of freedom? Angry that his son wouldn't share the burden of incarceration with him? Angry that his son did not insist on martyring himself in this court neither of them supposedly acknowledged? Or was he just an angry man? Lauren turned her head slightly. Her lips hardly moved when she spoke.

"Think there's a chance to roll George?"

Edie smiled and nodded as if to say there's always a chance. Lauren smiled back. That was good. At this moment, they liked one another. They were doing their jobs and proud of it.

"Your Honor." Lauren was ready to put Wilson on notice. Now that he was giving her a lesson in hard ball, she would show him how well she could bat. "The prosecution will have no choice but to take this matter up with the Ninth Circuit if you set such an outrageous bond and do not insist upon electronic monitoring. Henry Stewart can make this bond four times over and it is well within the militia's powers to disappear him anytime."

Caufeld was unimpressed with her threat and Lauren sat down heavily beside a vindicated Edie. Abram had made a bad call. Caufeld was no more inclined to give Lauren a break than he would her. In fact, he seemed to be bending over backwards to do just the opposite. What a pity. "Do what you must, Ms. Kingsley, but until you manage to complain to a higher authority, this is where all discussion ends. Now, in the matter of George Stewart," Caufeld intoned. Lauren tried again, her tact more courteous, her only request was time. If he gave her that, Lauren was sure she could insinuate herself long enough to convince him she was right.

"Your Honor, I apologize. I realize the place to appeal this decision is here, in this courtroom. I respect your autonomy in this matter. If Your Honor will give us the leeway to file additional points and authorities, I'm sure you'll see that lowering Henry Stewart's bond to such a manageable sum is, perhaps, not a wise course given the mood of the people of this city, not to mention the country. The government want to prosecute the younger Mr. Stewart, and I fear he won't survive to stand trial as he should."

"Ms. Kingsley, you are trying my patience and exhibiting the limit of your reach. If you are trying to intimidate this court by painting such a grievous scenario, you have failed miserably. I doubt there are vigilantes waiting at the door. If you'd like to suggest a lynching, I imagine the better place to do that would be outside on the steps of this courthouse. The media will assist you with great delight. Regarding your request to submit points and authorities, the time to do that was before the ruling was made."

"I know, your Honor. I know that I try your patience—" *I have since I was a child but I want you to give me a break here* "—but now I have a clear idea of what you're focusing on—" *and I know you're not going to give me a break*—"and I believe that I can find additional case law that will more fully support our position regarding Officer Readmore's stop."

"Fine," he said, raising her spirits only to dash them a second later. "However, Mr. Stewart may still post his bond. Should you convince me otherwise, bond will be revoked. I believe you know that whatever you bring me had better be good, Ms. Kingsley."

"Yes, Your Honor." She left off the thank you. Caufeld didn't seem to take note. Lauren knew he did.

"Now, to the matter of George Stewart." Caufeld watched her through the first few beats of his talk with

Eric Weitman. Finally, he dismissed her and Lauren knew that all were aware of the visual wrist slap. "There is some question in my mind whether the defendant, George Stewart, has standing in this particular situation. The question of whether or not, by search and seizure via a stop that was not sanctioned, George Stewart's Fourth Amendment rights were violated is a bothersome one which I would like to have more time to consider. If it is found that the defendant, like his son, is protected under the Fourth Amendment, then it stands to reason that the physical evidence against him must be suppressed and the burden will be on the prosecution to prove their case without introducing evidence found in a search deemed illegal."

Lauren found it impossible to hold her tongue. Beside her, Edie scribbled notes.

"Your Honor, the government vehemently object to any consideration of possible standing for George Stewart."

"Your objection is noted, counsel."

"No, it cannot simply be noted." Protocol was abandoned. Lauren was behind the lectern arguing with Judge Caufeld, not pleading with her friend, Wilson. "George Steward was in the truck as a passenger. It was not his vehicle. He did not object to Officer Readmore's search of the truck bed. This was a good stop, one based on experience and caution by the officer in the face of an unknown disaster. Anyone can see that." Caufeld's eyes narrowed. Lauren didn't back down as she drew the line. "Anyone, Your Honor."

His response was glacial. "I am not anyone, Ms. Kingsley. If your case cannot survive suppression, then you have no case, and I would suggest you think about that deeply before you waste this court's time and the people's money. Perhaps a discussion with your superiors is in order before you come to any conclusion. You are charged to convince me with your knowledge of the law and not try to sway me with your rather impressive, and insistent, outbursts. That is what your survival depends upon."

"And you cannot survive a ruling in favor of this defendant. The People will not stand for it."

"You overstep your bounds, Counsel," Caufeld thundered. "This is not a matter of what is good for me or the defendant or you. This is a matter of what is just under our law, I think you'd be wise to remember that." He was on his feet, towering above her, furious and godlike. Despite all she knew about him, and all he meant to her, Wilson Caufeld intimidated her and that made Lauren mad. She clamped her jaw tight while she listened to his final pronouncement. "I will take two weeks to explore the question of George Stewart's standing and reacquaint myself with papers and positions already filed. Prepare your cases, counsel. If you wish to file additional points and authorities, do so within the week. Make it worth my while to consider them. As soon as I have rendered my opinion, I will expect all of you to roll on this. There will be no excuses."

He was looking at Lauren and taking his leave when, surprisingly, he let his eyes meet George Stewart's. The two men looked at one another, both powerful in their own right, each striking fear in other people's hearts in their own way. Something passed between them and Caufeld could not continue. He seemed to be waiting. George Stewart didn't make him wait long.

The defendant gave a little snort as the right side of his mouth curled up. He seemed to have forgotten Henry and the marshals and the rest of the world, but Wilson Caufeld intrigued him. "You can't deliver, mister. There can't be justice because this isn't a fair trial. I can only be judged by a citizen of this country."

"Your Honor, I apologize for my client." Eric Weitman moved elegantly from behind the table, shooting a glance at George Stewart as he tried to control the situation with tone. Caufeld ignored him.

"Sir, I am a citizen of this country, who serves a system of justice that has stood us all in good stead for over two hundred years. It is not . . ."

"I don't recognize your citizenship under the provisions of the Fourteenth Amendment." Stewart smirked. "I am a citizen under the original constitution, you are a recipient of a second-class citizenship based upon that amendment to which I just referred. I do not recognize that citizenship.

If I am to be tried for any crime, I demand to be tried in a court of common law and judged by my true peers. The people's court is already convening to bring charges against you, Mr. Caufeld, for daring to pretend to a position that your kind cannot hold."

Wilson Caufeld stood still. George Stewart's bravado didn't fool him and the Fourteenth Amendment was one he knew well.

"That Amendment that you cite so blithely, extended constitutional protection to the newly freed slaves after the Civil War, sir. I am no slave. I am your judge. I put it to you that you cannot hide your bigotry behind rhetoric. I have heard it all before and you cannot shock me." After all these years Wilson was tired of such discussions. It showed behind his eyes but not in his stance. "You will be judged by your peers, Mr. Stewart, have no fear. You will be judged with all the fairness the law allows. In fact, Mr. Stewart, this court will make sure that your hearing is fair and equitable under our laws and the constitution you interpret so loosely. This court will do so, Mr. Stewart, so that neither you, nor your associates, can point a finger and frighten someone weaker, hurt another human being, incite a riot, or in any manner harm this country that is so dear to so many and only coveted by you. I would judge you the same way if you appeared before me for a traffic ticket . . ."

"Or if you sat on the Supreme Court?" George Stewart taunted. "How will you judge me then when it isn't a matter of evidence but of constitutional content? No matter where you sit, I don't recognize you and there are more of us than you can ever imagine. You've shown your weakness toward a man you consider a child. My son is no child, Caufeld, and he is not afraid of you. I'm not afraid of you."

"You should be, Mr. Stewart," Judge Caufeld said with certainty.

"No." He half stood then regained his seat. Better not to struggle with his shackles. He would wear martyr's trappings and use the words of a prophet. "*You* should be afraid. You and your kind took everything I had. There was no one to talk to, no one who would listen to me when it was only me fighting to save what I had earned. Where were you when the IRS took my home and my savings? Nobody was there for me. Now I have my armies, I have a son and I have a reason to fight. You've forgotten what my ancestors fought for and that was freedom from tyranny. You won't be able to hold me. Vengeance is mine, sayeth the Lord and He avenges his own who are mistreated."

"Justice is mine, and I'm the one saying it," Wilson answered back and all heads turned to George Stewart. He was a study in mediocrity gussied up with an ego, a mouth and a modicum of intelligence. That was nothing unusual in California, but when firepower and a sense of fatality were added, mediocrity was frightening.

"Watch your back, Mr. Wilson Caufeld. You and everyone who has anything to do with this farce. Watch those you care about. Watch them all." George Stewart looked away from Wilson and directly at Lauren. Or did Edie have his attention? Perhaps George Stewart thought them all of one mind, one body, all equally despicable. Lauren, mesmerized as she was, looked to Wilson for reassurance that this was only a crazy man talking and no one to truly fear. She was too late. He was leaving the courtroom with shoulders back and head held high. The threat was left behind and it chilled everyone who had heard it. All except George Stewart who seemed pleased.

In the time it took for Lauren to remember to breathe, people in the courtroom became reanimated. George and Henry, oddly subdued, were led away. Indignant, Lauren packed to go. A threat hung over her head too, but Wilson Caufeld had caused the real damage. He had betrayed her even though she had remained true on all counts: to herself, to his counsel and to the law.

Eric Weitman walked with Joe Knapp through the swinging gate. This was all in a day's work for them. Spectators left like the faithful filing out of the church after the bride had been left at the altar. No one knew if they should smile and make the best of it, or wail that life was unfair. Lauren followed, silent and concerned, stung by Wilson's ruling and decision to deliberate.

"What do you want to do now?"

Lost in thought, she didn't notice Edie come up behind her, she only heard her ask the one question she didn't want to answer. Lauren's guilt at having replaced Edie was just below the surface, the same way disappointment must lay beneath Edie's skin.

"We have points and authorities to submit. I suppose I'd like to get to work on them. We'll just have to broaden our interpretation of standing."

Lauren hefted her briefcase, walking fast as if she could dodge the self-recrimination that went with her. They'd all been stupid: Abram for changing the line up and Lauren for stepping up to the plate. Edie could only be blamed for being professional and not putting up more of a stink. Lauren raised her chin at defense counsel who were huddled in the hall. Weitman and Knapp smiled back out of habit. Everyone was lost in their own thoughts and Lauren's was a simple one: Wilson Caufeld had twisted the axis of the world as Lauren knew it. Her balance was off.

For the first time in her life, she didn't admire Wilson's concern for the letter of the law. His rulings that morning were absurd and he should have taken into account the spirit of the law. Her arguments were solid, her research impeccable, her credentials and history should have given her a leg up. He should have considered her spirit, too. Lauren punched the call botton for the elevator, missed and hurt her finger.

"Which way do you think Caufeld's going to swing on George?" Lauren used both hands to hold her briefcase, pretending like her finger didn't feel hot and throb. Edie talked on. "If he suppresses everything in the truck we're looking at fifty/fifty on the conviction, even with Mark's information and the post-blast work and everything."

Lauren was tight-lipped with her reply.

"You're putting too much emphasis on this. It's a minor setback. We can beat it. The confidential informant's testimony and the blast fragments are our real case. Besides George is the one we want and he's still in custody. I'm not worried. Not worried at all." Lauren looked up. The elevator seemed to be stuck on the third floor. She pushed the button again and this time she was right on target, pretending it was Wilson's chest she punched. Maybe she was putting that finger in Edie's face. "And I don't know what Wilson will do. I'm not a mind reader or his confidante."

"Okay," Edie said. She joined Lauren in her observation of the painfully slow progress of the elevator.

They stood in silence. Lauren's shoulders pulled back, her briefcase held close down by her knees, clutched in both hands; Edie resting her weight on her back leg as if completely relaxed, even though that was far from the truth. Abram's little plan had backfired and Lauren was caught in the middle. That was the bitch of it. At least it was a position Edie could sympathize with. "I think Abram put you in a bad place, for what it's worth. Small-town politics don't even fly in small towns anymore." Lauren didn't smile, but Edie could tell she was listening. "I should have handled this."

"I can handle it," Lauren snapped. Gratitude that Edie hadn't crowed was taking second place to the affront of the other woman's magnanimous commiseration.

Edie scrutinized Lauren. "All I'm suggesting is that it was unfair to assume that your relationship with Judge Caufeld would give you any greater insight than I had. Abram thinks that this office is just a bigger board than the one he keeps those toys on." She chuckled. "Doesn't it ever amaze you that a guy who plays with tin soldiers is the one calling the shots here?" Even Lauren had to smile. Edie had a point. She went ahead and made a few more. "Confidence is one thing, dreaming another. I won't undermine you because in the end all this reflects on me. But since I have a few more years under my belt than you, I'm not going to sit here and let you charge ahead without saying something. So here goes. The CI and the lab stuff isn't going to mean much without the truck. It's a minefield we're walking into and I think you better face that reality right now."

"I'm not afraid if that's what you're worried about. I always knew there was a chance Wilson could do something like this. We all did." Lauren punched the button again.

"You approved the motions and the arguments. They were exactly the same as the ones we presented to Judge Lee. I even think the presentation was stronger this time."

"Hey, no need to get defensive. I didn't expect you to have any special magic. You did good, now we'll work a little harder."

Lauren waited just long enough so her "thanks" seemed reluctant.

The doors of the elevator opened. Lauren preceded Edie. By the time they reached the twelfth floor Lauren had faced the facts: her Merlin had deserted her and she needed help with the sword in the stone. "Why don't you take the issue of standing and I'll take the stop? We only have a week to pull it together so he can have a week to consider the new material. What do you want to do about Abram?"

"I'll fill him in. He doesn't want details, just wants the Stewart's convicted."

"The press?" Lauren asked. They were almost at the twelfth floor.

"No interviews until Caufeld rules, then a short statement."

Lauren looked askance, glad she asked. She wanted to present their side to the public immediately and it was a surprise to find out that Edie didn't. "Why?"

"Mystery. Never look worried. Don't get defensive. Pick one. Besides, no one matters but Caufeld. The general public doesn't really understand the preliminaries."

"Sounds like you think everything's settled."

"You're just figuring out I'm a fatalist?" Edie half smiled. "Just keep your ears open. Caufeld's going to tip his hand at some point, and you'll be the only one who can see over the top."

"I'm not going to do anything unethical. I'm not even going to see him socially until the trial is over. I won't compromise him, myself or this office," Lauren warned.

The elevator stopped. The women stepped out. Lauren was headed to the office but Edie reached out and guided her toward the far wall for a little talk.

"Here's a clue Lauren, no one expects you to. We're

expecting you to take advantage of opportunities and that's a whole different thing. I know you're thinking about your mother's situation, but this is yours. Play it straight but play it smart."

The look in Lauren's eyes was flint and Edie met it head on. A spade was a spade after all.

"That was uncalled for," Lauren said.

"Okay, so let's assume you're right up there with Mother Teresa. But even Mother Teresa wanted to win, so I'm betting you'll ram this thing through because you believe we're right. We need to be just this side of dirty to make sure the bad guys go away. If we don't, we might as well quit because we're not doing anyone any good."

They were at the window now. It was noon. A jury had gathered by the elevators looking like overgrown kids on a field trip with their big white juror tags strung around their necks. The marshal, a handsome young man the color of chocolate, sported a uniform over a body to die for. Two assistant U.S. attorneys were trying to skirt the crowd without much success. Edie ignored them all as her head dropped left, her eyes locking on the scene below.

"Look out there. See all those people? They'll hate us if we lose. When it's over, they won't even remember our names, or the Stewarts for that matter, they'll just remember that there was danger and we failed to protect them. They'll hate a generic us."

"You don't give the man on the street much credit, do you?" Lauren murmured.

"How can I? They're not part of the system so they get in the way. Funny thing is, they don't want to know what goes on here. The system is scary, they can't manipulate it and they're terrified they'll get caught in it. If they can read the bad stuff in a paper and their names aren't attached, it means they're safe for a while longer. Fear and confusion are both collective and the most personal emotions in the world."

Edie stood back, embarrassed to see she was still holding Lauren's arm. When she spoke again, Edie sounded almost affectionate as she talked about Los Angeles, as if she and this faltering city had a lot in common.

"This really isn't a sophisticated place. People here believe the whole country has to have their cappuccino by 7:00 A.M. They think everybody in the world worries about their abs. They can't fathom living anywhere that shopping malls don't come three to a mile, Seven-Elevens don't carry tofu and cars aren't traded every two years." Lauren laughed as Edie swept her hand toward a horizon that was packed with buildings, threaded with freeways and smothered under a heavy layer of yellow smog. "Los Angeles is the exception to every common sense rule for living. We're not normal. The Stewarts are. Normal is sitting right here in Caufeld's court, and we better figure out how to deal with it."

"They're criminals," Lauren interrupted, thinking Edie had lost a little of her mind. Edie pushed one brow up, reacting to Lauren's incredible ignorance.

"Not to some they aren't. There are millions of people who want to feel important again by controlling their lives. Politicians talk about fixing things, but don't. Judges and lawyers talk about protecting people and don't. Normal folks don't want their kids to access the Internet, they'd rather have the family veg out in front of Roseanne reruns. They don't want fads and pop psychology. They want their boys to have jobs and their girls to get married and have babies. People like George Stewart used to decide what happened in their towns. Now someone they don't even know, and probably didn't vote for, does."

"So what's your point?" Lauren moved away and turned her back to the window. She leaned against it, thinking Edie looked softer in the midday sun then decided it was a trick of the light.

"The point is, Lauren, your idea of justice isn't the same as everyone else's. In your deepest heart you expected Caufeld to cut you some slack today. You thought that would be justice and now you're mad because you didn't get it. George Stewart and his wife and his kid are exactly the same. They think it would have been just if Caufeld called a halt to the proceedings, apologized and called the IRS on the carpet. So who is going to give the world the ultimate definition of justice? You? Them? Me?"

"Someone's got to."

"Then it will be Judge Caufeld's definition, unless you can rewrite it for him. I'll admit George Stewart is the exception. He was pushed over the edge when the government took away his house and business for back taxes. Every person in the militia has a story like that. When they snap and cry out for justice, they terrify us because they disturb the equilibrium. We've got to do everything in our power to regain the status quo. We've got to convince everyone that our definition of justice is the right one. The Stewarts and their kind play dirty, Lauren, and if we have to get in the mud, too, then let's do it."

"I'll play hardball." Lauren wanted this conversation to end. Edie was not accommodating.

"We'll see when push comes to shove." Edie shrugged and sighed. "This isn't a contest to see how much you learned from the old man, it's a test of how fast you can think on your feet. Most people just react. Think about that. Understand it. Then do whatever you can to work around it. If you don't, there will be anarchy—of one sort or another."

Lauren's eyes narrowed. Edie was laughing at her.

"Isn't it just a little arrogant to think that World War III depends on the outcome of this trial?"

"Nope." Edie shook back her black hair. "Oklahoma City, Atlanta, Ruby Ridge and a zillion other isolated incidents have made this an aggregate trial. If we don't keep stopping them here then they'll get bolder and more people will die."

"I understand that. We're doing what we can, but it's not a personal fight, Edie," Lauren objected.

"Oh, it definitely is personal. Whatever happens here is going to affect your career a lot more than it does mine. You'll be blamed for letting the Stewarts get away with murder, and you'll never be anything more than what you are now. Caufeld will be seen as making the tough calls, which is perfect for someone who might sit on the Supreme Court. Abram will be blamed for making a personnel mistake and I'll come out smelling like a rose because, ultimately, the matter was out of my hands. On the other hand, if we win, we'll all be fine."

"This isn't a publicity campaign. The issues are bigger, Edie. The issues are constitutional, legal, moral."

Edie shook her head and laughed. It wasn't a rude sound, just incredulous. "You are such a Girl Scout, Lauren. The issues and the laws change every day because men change and manipulate them. Don't count on any of it. If you want to be a player, take those calculated risks and anticipate what the next revision will be." Edie picked up her briefcase. The hall was empty now. "But hey, Abram put you out front, not me. Do what you can live with. Just remember, the only way to get what you want is to go after it."

She and Lauren looked at one another. Women in the U.S. Attorney's office had no need to band together for respect or power. It was conferred when you filled out your W-2. In an office overrun with cases, few women had time for such posturing. For a moment, though, there had been something more there than mere professional concern. Edie had offered Lauren hard earned wisdom. This might be the only time she would do so.

"Okay, I'll think about it."

Edie nodded and walked away, giving a curt wave to the receptionist behind the bulletproof glass as she buzzed in. Two assistants came out, managing some deferential murmurings as they passed Edie.

"Lauren." Brendan flashed his Irish grin. She'd found that grin more than charming when she was new to the office. Unfortunately, he seemed to be committed to pick-up basketball at the beach on off hours. Lauren was too short for one and too fair for the other so it never went any further than drinks after work. Still, he was always good to talk to. Until now.

"Tough break on the Stewarts," Brendan called as he ambled toward her. "Are they really going to bail the kid?"

Lauren pushed herself off the wall, meeting him and Michael Vane halfway. She drawled, "Good news travels fast."

"It could have been worse." Michael's long face was

serious, as he put in his two cents. Lauren looked at him
hoping for words of wisdom. He smiled wickedly. "Caufeld
could have let cameras in. Then you'd have to worry about
your hair, too."

"Shut up, Michael." Lauren glared. The two men's
chuckles trailed off. Brendan put his arm around her shoulders. It felt nice. She needed someone's arm there.

"Come on, it was a tough break. But you know Caufeld,
he doesn't shoot from the hip unless he's sure of the shot.
Maybe a couple of weeks and he'll come to his senses."
Brendan chucked her under the chin and she pulled back.
He dropped his arm and stuffed his hand in the pockets
of his pants. Okay, a shoulder to cry on wasn't what she
needed. "Listen, Reno was arguing the constitutionality
of removing a passenger from a lawfully stopped vehicle.
Well, the justices came back with a decision and they gave
it the green light."

"That's great," Lauren muttered, not quite pouting but
not in the mood to fool herself with false hopes.

"It could be. Hey, it's worth throwing Caufeld's way."
Michael stuffed his hands in his pocket, too. Brendan tried
to perk her up, "I've got some time. How's about I check
it out and get you the low down. I'll read the whole thing—
even dissenting opinions."

Lauren smiled wanly. "Who dissented?"

"I don't know, but someone had to. God, Lauren, don't
be so grateful."

"I'm sorry. Thanks. I appreciate it. Really, I do."

"Good. Now, how about lunch? We're going to Colima
for burritos. They just recovered the booths. They're purple vinyl. That ought to cheer you up."

The two men stepped forward as the elevator arrived.
Brendan was on one side, Michael, tall as a tree on the
other, their arms outstretched to keep back the doors that
insisted on trying to close. Lauren walked through taking
the dark cloud over her head with her. By the time they
hit the lobby, she'd changed her mind. A burrito at Colima
held no allure, purple vinyl booths or not. Brendan's ban-
ter would be tiring today. Michael, as usual, would spend
the hour justifying his government employment with a

litany of private firms that were in bankruptcy. All Lauren wanted was to sort out her feelings about Wilson and get on with the business at hand, so the men went their way forgetting Lauren's problems the moment hey hit the street.

Lauren reached into her purse, found her sunglasses and slipped them on. Cell phone in hand, she dialed and waited to be put through. When she finally was, Lauren hardly noticed, because there, on the steps of the Federal Courthouse was that FBI agent. Warner. Eli Warner. He stood with one leg bent as he leaned back against the concrete banister that led visitors up and into the building. Their eyes locked. He pocketed his notebook. It seemed to take him a minute to place her. When he did he grinned, lifted his hand and waved. She took a step toward him but he was already on his way, heading inside.

Lauren was sorry he had to go. It would have been good to talk to him. Then again, she hardly knew him and this was a private thing, needing to be discussed with someone who knew Judge Caufeld intimately. The impatient man hollering on the phone was a better choice. She held the phone to her ear. She'd nearly forgotten him.

"Hi. You busy for lunch?" she asked and was surprised to find her lips dry, her eye still on the door of the Federal Courthouse as if she was expecting Eli Warner to come right back out the door. Lauren shook her head and got him out of it while she flipped the phone closed and put it back in her purse.

Eli Warner didn't come out the door. He was busy for lunch.

Allan was busy for lunch, too.

Tough for Allan.

Chapter Six

The Sports Club of L.A. West Los Angeles. Valet Parking. Movie stars, kids in tow. Indoor rock climbing. Have your nails, laundry and car done before, during or after your workout. It was a cool place, if cool places were your thing. It was a place of business, if that's how you did business. Allan Lassiter was both cool and one to do business wherever he happened to be. The club initiation fee would have eaten up half of Lauren's salary; for Allan it was pocket change. She found him on the fake mountain, rock climbing in a climate-controlled, man-made environment that he had come to think of as natural. He was harnessed, shirtless and an all-around gorgeous spectacle as he moved from toehold to toehold.

"I told you I was busy, Lauren," he grunted, making her name sound like a rude noise. "Come on. Give me a break. Cameron's due back any minute and he and I have got some serious talking to do. We're going to do it in the steam room, so unless you're planning on . . ." He heaved and lifted his muscular body up another inch. He wasn't as young as he thought he was. She could hear the sounds of extra effort from where she stood on the floor, head tilted back, brow furrowed, chignon firmly in place at the nape of her neck. He looked down at her, passing along a compliment to hide the fact that he was pausing for a breath. ". . . God, you look gorgeous today." When she didn't say anything he grinned and started climbing again. Lauren was tired of watching him. She paced and let her voice climb up after him.

"This is important Allan. It's really important. I wouldn't have driven across town just to watch you climb up that thing."

"What can be that important?"

Lauren looked up then back again just in time to keep from running into a stunning blonde whose attention was focused on Allan's rear end.

"Excuse me?" Lauren cocked her elbows, raised her palms towards the ceiling to give this Barbie Doll a clue. Business was going on here and it wasn't the kind this woman would understand.

"Lucky," the blonde clucked, obviously deciding she was eyeing Lauren's territory.

Just as obvious was the thought flitting through her platinum-haired head that, given time, the hunk above would tire of the little lady so firmly planted on the ground. The blonde smiled. The light caught her lips and bounced off shell pink gloss. If she'd had one more collagen injection, Lauren was sure they'd have to call in hazardous waste and designate those lips an oil spill.

With a sigh and a snap of her thong, she gave Allan one last, lustful look and left. Lauren watched her go. What kind of idiot put on makeup when the objective was to sweat? The same kind that thought a small piece of fabric emphasizing where-the-cheeks-meet was attractive. Lauren sniffed. Liposuction. She'd bet the blonde never lifted a weight and that she was a good five years older than she seemed. She'd also wasted too much time on her. Lauren looked up again.

"Hey, Allan, come on. I haven't got all day."

From above a laugh, a whirring sound and Allan rappelled off the mountain to land at her feet. He looked so happy, so pleased with himself. She couldn't help but smile. Free from his harness, he grabbed a towel.

"Look, I don't even have ten minutes, Lauren. I really did mean it when I said I was busy. As partners go, Cameron is on the more neurotic side. He and I are due for a meeting and if we don't have it on time he'll have to spend an extra hour with his therapist tomorrow to figure out why I've suddenly taken a dislike to him."

"Tell him you love him and you'll talk to him at the office. I know that's a novel concept, but you're always up for something different."

"Sarcasm will get you nowhere, Laurie." Allan took his towel and wrapped it around her neck, trying to pull her closer.

"Will you cut it out. I swear, if you were my brother you couldn't be more bothersome. What's so important anyway that you got Cameron down here?"

"We've got to figure out how we're going to position the firm when Wilson is confirmed. I know, I know." He stopped teasing when he saw the look on her face. The towel went around his own neck. "You think I'm less than dirt for capitalizing on our relationship, but believe me Wilson won't object. He knows the score. Anyway, Cameron has to take off for Boston tonight and this is the only time we have to talk."

"Geez, Allan, I never say things like that," Lauren said as she walked beside him. "I only think it. You may be a lot premature, though. Wilson may never leave L.A." That got his attention. Ten minutes later, they were in the health bar, two untouched Smoothies melting in front of them while Lauren filled him in.

"I can't believe he's doing this. He's crazy. He should have ruled for you immediately."

Allan didn't move while he groused. Though he had cooled, his color was still high, his face still glowing with the last of the sweat-sheen. An outsider would have seen a man coming down from a physical high, focused on his companion. Lauren knew better. Allan was furious.

"That's an astute assessment of the situation," Lauren said quietly.

"Okay, then he's selfish not crazy and he's not thinking straight. This isn't just about a goddamn issue of standing, and he better get it through his head fast before he blows his nomination. Christ, that old man is going to be the death of me."

"Don't you mean the ruin of you?" Lauren reached for the strawberry smoothie. "Come on, be honest. Weren't you selling tickets to his swearing in?"

Allan slid a look her way then turned sideways in his chair. He watched his fellow club members ambling out, their long self-indulgent lunch hours at an end. It was time to go back and do what they did best: make money. He was seeing dollar signs flying out the door with them. If Wilson didn't make it to the Supreme Court it wouldn't exactly ruin him, but it sure wouldn't do him any good either.

"Lauren, look, you and I go way back. I know that we've never had the same professional interests, but the one thing we've always had in common is concern for Wilson. Neither of us has made any bones about what we owe him. Both of us have used his influence, so don't take that sarcastic, righteous tone with me."

"Whoa, wait a minute. I'm not your daughter, your wife, or your latest lay," Lauren shot back. "I'll take whatever tone I want, because I'm not just concerned about Wilson undermining his chances for confirmation because I'll make more money if I know a Supreme Court Justice. I think he's wrong, and I'm worried that this is going to impact a whole lot of people. Yes, me included."

Allan's hand had been raised to his cheek, his legs spread out in front of him, his back up against the wall. At first he only moved his eyes. They slid toward her and she saw the shrewdness in them, layers of it like the intricate pattern inside a cat's-eye marble. Closer to the surface was the affection he felt for her. He dropped his hand on her folded ones, squeezed and patted.

"You're right," he sighed. "I'm sorry I jumped the gun."

"Fine. Thank you." She pulled her hands back. "I apologize, too. You told me you were busy. Now that I'm here I realize it was a knee-jerk reaction to just show up. But I felt like I'd done something wrong, you know? Like I had forced him to be so cautious that he was incautious. Do you think I did that?"

"You're thinking too hard about something that's Wilson's problem. People don't know standing from sitting. All they know is that the Caufelds of the world seem like arrogant, overpaid, intellectual snobs. They don't care if he hatched you . . ."

"Okay, I get the message. So you think the U.S. Attorney's going to come out looking okay. If we win, we're saviors. If we lose then it's because of Wilson so we get some sympathy factor. God, I hate that. I don't want him in that position." Lauren considered this, an opinion diametrically opposed to Edie's.

"Neither do I," Allan muttered. "Washington is going to be watching this real close. Given what he's doing, I'd advise Wilson not to quit his day job." Allan brought his fist down lightly on the table. "Stupid man. Really, really stupid call for him to make." He looked at her and his expression was closed, his eyes dark. He was saying all the right words but Lauren knew there was a lot going on behind the eyes. Allan was looking at this from angles she never thought of. "Sometimes Wilson can be maddeningly meticulous but he comes through in a pinch. He's not going to hang you out to dry." Allan smiled. Lauren wasn't reassured.

"But will that be the right thing to do? I mean if he puts me into the equation will that be the right thing to do?"

"Yeah, Lauren, it's the right thing to do. When push comes to shove, it all boils down to who you care about. We care about him, he'll bend over backwards for both of us. If that weren't the case, I'd walk away from him right now."

"You are so selfish," Lauren said lazily. "That's really all you care about isn't it? What he can do for you."

Allan shook his head and spoke with surprising sincerity.

"No, I care about what we do for each other. Who is it you go to when you're scared or nervous or want to bounce ideas around? You come to me or him. I go to him or you and Wilson has us. I don't expect him to always help us. What I really expect is that he won't hurt us, and right now Wilson is the only one in a position to do that."

"He would never do that, Allan." Lauren pulled her bottom lip up, considering this new thought. Any hurt he'd inflicted that morning had not been intentional, only necessary.

"Yeah, well, maybe," Allan said and grabbed his drink.

"He wouldn't," she insisted. "He would expect us to give him reason to favor us and that's what I have to do. God, Allan, I made this really personal and it's not."

"Yes, it is. Wilson, for all his talk, can't separate us from himself and our jobs from his. I promise. The greater good he's always talking about is a big part of this but when it all shakes out, he'll choose us. I speak from experience on that."

Allan put both hands to his face, groaned and pulled those hands down so that he looked hang-dogged. He stopped before his fingers cleared his nose and opened his eyes wide at her. She laughed.

"I can't even imagine what Wilson went through with you, Allan."

"Someday, I'll tell you," he said, only to be distracted. "There's Cameron. I've got to go and sweat through some of this stuff." He stood up. His workout shorts, what there was of them, fit so very well. When she looked up, he was looking down, fully aware of what she was thinking. She buttoned her jacket, ready to go.

"Thanks, Allan. I'm sorry I barged in. If I can't get myself on track, I'll talk to Abram. He's probably trying to figure out why he put me on this in the first place. I did think it would be a piece of cake, you know."

Allan chuckled and took her in his arms. He pulled her close, loving the delicate feel of her body. All the women he'd had and it was still her he wanted and for no other reason then he couldn't have her. "We are so alike." He pushed her back and held her by the shoulders and kissed the top of her head. "Go on back to work, listen to Edie. Believe it or not, she can be your best friend. Just do what you have to do."

"And Wilson will do what he has to," she said, closing her eyes as his lips met her forehead.

"Yeah. Sure he will." Allan murmured against her warm skin. His voice was low and detached. But when she looked at him it was the same old Allan who smiled. "I've got to run."

And he did, trotting right past the blonde who gave him a second, then a third look before focusing on Lauren as she tried to figure out what the attraction was. Lauren passed her on her way out, leaned over and said, "The mind is a muscle, too."

Lauren didn't need to look back to know the blonde would never get it.

"Here, I'll take it."

Her persimmon-colored dress had shoulder pads that were just a tad too big, out of date by a season or two. She wore that dress as if it was a cloak of gold. Against her persimmon dress she hugged a brown jacket, a yellow tie and a short-sleeved white shirt with a stripe in an unidentifiable color running through it. She was handed a watch. She turned it backward and forward, looking at its face as if to determine it hadn't been damaged. But damage wasn't what she was looking for. Telltale signs of tampering, that was what she had on her mind. She'd have one of the men check it out later. Last thing she wanted to do was bring a bug into her house even though she knew there was probably one or two about anyway.

"Right here." The officer pointed at the papers.

She signed the forms that were pushed in front of her and finally, finally, offered her son a tight smile that seemed more for the benefit of the custodial officer watching them take their leave.

"Henry? Are you ready to go?"

He nodded and followed his mother out the door, leaving the officer shaking his head. If he'd been that judge, he would have kept the kid under lock and key. Damn shame he was going home with his mother. Henry Stewart, of course, thought differently.

He looked neither left nor right as they stepped outside. Acne had flared during his weeks in jail and now cut a fiery, swollen path down the right side of his once handsome young face. Dark circles hung under his eyes and he'd lost weight. At least now he wore his own clothes: jeans, a T-shirt with a bulldog holding a beer silk-screened on the back, and big sneakers that looked like the soles were made of lead. He walked with a slight bounce that betrayed his anxiety. It was as if he was afraid to break into a joyful run for fear someone might change their mind and make him stay in jail.

Yet, as excited as Henry was to be leaving, he was also cautious, not knowing what his mother thought about him. She'd think the same as his father and his father hadn't said a word to him in the van that returned them to the detention center. Henry was disappointed that his dad wasn't happy with him but he, Henry, had a lot to learn. That was George's pronouncement, that was Henry's charge and that was probably why George wasn't happy.

Outside felt like summer but it was only spring. Inside his head was a flash, a thought that the man and woman who died in the bomb blast would have given anything to be walking down the street like he was. Henry stopped thinking after that. His dad always said he shouldn't think too hard because he confused issues with opinions, right from wrong, honor from cowardice. His dad was always right about that. He felt confused almost all the time and never more than now when his mother was walking kind of ahead of him, kind of trailing her displeasure like other women might trail perfume. Still, she carried his clothes, had paid his bail, even put her hand on his shoulder like she had some comfort to give him. She might even have been happy to see him.

"Over there. We've got to go quick. Reporters are going to figure it out soon, and I want to get home before they do."

Henry veered left and folded himself into the hatchback that was the family's other car. The truck was impounded. They'd never see it again. Carolyn Stewart swung expertly out of the parking lot and drove silently toward Riverside, half smiling because traffic was light and they were moving fast. She wore sunglasses. When Henry looked at her he could see her long lashes touching the lenses. One day he'd tell her how pretty her eyes were, but now they were home. They were just inside the door, when he felt she was ready for him to speak to her.

"Thanks, Mom."

Carolyn was half bent over a chair, putting his court clothes down, when he spoke. She straightened and seemed to think hard about what to do next. When she faced her son Carolyn made the move that she wasn't sure she should. She put her arms around him and pulled him close. Henry closed his eyes, feeling tears of relief well up inside him. Thankfully she didn't hug him, just held him against her. If she had hugged him he would have lost it.

"Carolyn, think George is getting any hugs where he is?"

Mother and son turned toward the man in the doorway of the living room. He was bigger than George Stewart but not as impressive. He looked like the kind of guy whose car dealership was the biggest in town because his father-in-law kept the books. He certainly didn't look like a revolutionary leader.

"Paul, think you could let me do what I want in my own house?" Carolyn said stiffly.

"It's not your house," the big man reminded her. "That's what this is about, isn't it? You lost your house same as I lost my business. This is just a roof you rent."

Carolyn gave Henry's arm a short pat but distanced herself from him. "I don't need to be reminded of that. I don't need to be reminded that my husband isn't here because he's fighting for all of us. So, if you don't mind let's just get on with it. Is everyone here?"

"Yep. The feds took pictures, though. We all got snapped, but we didn't try to stop them."

"Thank God for small favors," Carolyn muttered. Henry was heading for the stairs that would take him up to his room just as she took the first step down to the basement. She paused on that first step. "Henry. You'll be wanted."

"Mom, I . . ."

One look was enough to know that there was no choice. He closed his eyes. He was so tired. He wanted to put on headphones and listen to music. He wanted his mom to bring him a sandwich and ask if he was okay after such a horrible experience. She would do neither, so he would go with her downstairs and listen to the men who were already there and talking about him. He hated them all. Well, almost all of them. He didn't hate Nick Cheshire, but he didn't know him very well either. The others, well, they weren't the ones who had been in jail and still they were the ones who talked like they knew all about it. Reluctantly he followed his mother and Paul into the paneled room. It was worse than he thought. They stopped talking when they saw him.

Carolyn sat between Paul and Nick. Henry would have liked to have sat there. He had a feeling that Nicholas, so gentle when he talked, would have understood that sometimes all this just didn't seem worth the effort. But tonight shy, quiet Nicholas was looking at him curiously, same way as everyone else. Well, almost the same way. Nicholas seemed to actually be trying to communicate. His smile of encouragement was so small Henry wasn't even sure he saw it, so he just told himself he did whether it was the truth or not. Henry sat down on a chair without arms.

"So, here we are." Paul had taken over now that George was gone. Henry admired his father in a lot of ways, but he didn't admire Paul, who was full of hot air. Like a big balloon set down in the middle of the basement, he had everyone's attention. He tried to look wise. He looked stupid. "Why don't you tell us about it, Henry."

Henry moved, kind of rocked from one side of his rear to the other. "It was okay. Food was good." He yucked once, still a kid laugh at eighteen. One look at the men and women in the room told him no one was laughing with him. He lowered his eyes and muttered. "It was okay."

"That all you did in there? Eat? You been in there a good long time, Henry. We want to hear who you talked to."

Henry chanced a glance at his mom but she didn't give him any help. He took a shot in the dark. "I talked to other guys sometimes. I didn't see much of anybody. They let me and Dad hang out sometimes. That was nice."

"Oh, Lord," someone swore in disgust. It was James Harker. James had taught Henry to shoot when he was ten. It was one of the few things his own dad hadn't taught him.

"It was, James. It was nice," Henry insisted, proud he had been courageous enough to say that.

"Where, Henry? Where did they let you see your dad?"

"In his cell. Sometimes mine." Henry smiled wanly. Those gathered around did not. Carolyn didn't give him one of those "listen-and-learn" looks. She didn't give him one of those softer ones that said "I know this is hard to understand now." All his mom did was look at him like the rest of them. He would have preferred his father's lectures to this. He tried again. "They let us sit together for meals."

"Who else did you talk to, Henry? The FBI must have come around at least." This was Nicholas asking softly.

Henry's skinny shoulders raised. "Yeah. I mean sometimes. I talked to the guards sometimes, too. I don't know. I read a lot. Oh, there was one really nice guy . . ."

Suddenly, Henry was still. He was so still he believed those around him could actually see his heart beating in his chest. Under lowered lashes he looked about, catching his mother's guarded eye. He had seen that look before, on his twelfth birthday. There had been a meeting that day instead of a party for kids. The gathering was sober, as it was now. Those who spoke did so one at a time. There had been no lively discussion about the ills of the country, the failings of the so-called leaders, the sad plight of the true citizens of this land. That night they discussed the need for action against one of their own who seemed to be questioning the militia's objectives. Henry had listened from behind the closed door of the bathroom, catching only bits and pieces of what was said. It was enough to scare him silly when he was twelve. Now eighteen, he was frightened again because it was him they were talking about.

"I didn't tell them anything. I did just what my dad said to do. I talked to them, but I didn't tell them anything about us, not even when they tried to trick me."

Henry's voice faded away, leaving his defense hanging in the air. His heart beat faster. He grabbed the side of his chair, just now realizing it had been the only one left for him to sit in. It had no arms and was straight-backed, like the chairs in jail. He tried to swallow but his throat was dry. He wanted to go to his room and sleep in his own bed. He'd been scared since the minute he got in the truck with his father and saw that they were pulling the trailer behind them. It wasn't until he saw the explosion, though, that Henry knew he shouldn't have been scared—he should have been terrified.

"You know, Henry, we've been talking about just that. We've been having a discussion on what it is you talked to all those people about inside that prison." Paul sat back and heaved a big sigh. He carried a spare tire at waist level and it made Henry sick to look at all that flesh in one place. Paul looked like he was melting. "We know your dad's not talking. That's why we all look up to him. We can trust him with our lives, Henry. And believe you me, Henry, this is about our very lives."

"I know that, Paul. I can be trusted, too. Mom? Mom? Tell them. Tell them I didn't say anything that would hurt any of us."

Henry turned toward his mother. Carolyn smoothed her persimmon skirt, it covered legs that half the militia men would love to have wrapped around them. But Carolyn was George's wife and George was a natural-born leader. Right now, though, George was a martyr commanding them from the stake while Caufeld tried to decide whether or not to light the tinder. They would take care of business at home while they waited.

"He didn't say anything," Carolyn answered, but she evaded her son's eyes and her tone was resigned. As

George's wife, she was the final say in how far they would go with Henry. As Henry's mother, she wished things could be different.

"We appreciate that, Carolyn." Al Johnson cleared his throat after every word even as he lit another cigarette. "But you have to admit, it's pretty odd. That judge did everything but pat Henry on the head and tell him to go home. I find that awful strange, Carolyn. We put up his bail, and Henry didn't put up a fuss. He ran right out of there."

"Why shouldn't I?" Henry wailed. "He said it was the law that I should be able to go home."

"We don't recognize that law, son," another man piped up. Henry heard it but couldn't identify who spoke.

Yet another. "Now I'm worried. If Henry doesn't know that, then we've made a big mistake."

Grunts and murmurs of approval. No one wanted to hear what Henry had to say. Carolyn stood up while the only other woman in the room put in her two cents.

"We put up his bond. I think we ought to get something for that. I think we ought to be sure about your son, Carolyn."

Carolyn raised an eyebrow but that was as far as she came to defending Henry.

"If you have any concerns, you put him to the test." She looked around the room so everyone knew she wasn't afraid. Finally Carolyn looked at Henry. "Go ahead. You know what George wants, and I suppose you figured out how you want to handle it before we ever got here. Henry will do what needs to be done."

Carolyn left Henry behind. He wished he was back in his jail cell. He wished he was back in that truck with his dad. But this time they'd head anywhere except toward that little building, in the middle of a block, on the wrong side of downtown LA.

Lauren left the Sports Club, headed up Sepulveda, made a right on Wilshire Boulevard and drove through West-wood thinking it had been a long time since she'd seen a

movie on the big screen. Fresh from her talk with Allan,
feeling better about the morning and confident about what
lay ahead, she thought about doing something fun. She
could take surface streets all the way downtown just to have
some time to herself. She'd cut up to Sunset and wind
through Hollywood. She'd take any road that would get
her slowly back to the office. Then Lauren wondered why
she'd want to do something like that. To be completely
quiet, at peace, at rest and actually enjoy driving the city
streets was frightening. It meant that you were sliding down
the chute instead of climbing up the ladder. She was fighting the urge to zip down to Westwood Boulevard and head
for the freeway when a multicolored Toyota ran the light
at Veteran and Wilshire and crashed into the side of her
racing-green, rag-top MG.

As she was thrown against the driver's side door,
Lauren's eyes rattled in her head. Her first thought was
that her car was totaled. Her second was that she might
be, too. Then her eyes closed and Lauren sat stupefied
while the rest of the world came to a screeching halt.
Behind her, people cursed, screaming the battle cry of Los
Angeles to those ahead: go around! Slowly Lauren lowered
her head onto her outstretched arms, fully aware that it
would be a few minutes before she could unwrap her fingers from the leather-bound wheel. She was also fully aware
that the man in the Toyota that hit her had taken everyone's advice. He hadn't just "gone around," he had gone.

Sliding her head to the right she saw that the little bucket
seat on the passenger side was mangled, the beautiful walnut paneling on the console was buckled. It was that walnut,
polished for years by her mother, and by her own hand
after her mother's death, that made this all seem so tragic.
As the West-bound lanes of traffic slowed to a crawl and
horns began to honk, as the driver of the car directly
behind her got out and began to yell at her in Spanish,
Lauren Kingsley started to cry. She was still crying big tears
when the door opened and she heard:

"Are you hurt? Can you talk?"

That voice was so nice; it was a savior's voice. Rational
and calm. He reached around her. From the corner of

her eye she could see him and there was the sense that he was a big man. Then he was gone. The next voice she heard was one that made her feel as if everything might be all right after all.

"It's okay. I'll take care of it. I know her."

Chapter Seven

"How's she lookin'?"

Eli Warner stood in the doorway of Casey Mallon's office and watched Casey put a final flourish on a Band-Aid gracing the small cut on Lauren's hand.

"I think she'll live."

"I don't know if that's good news or not." She looked up at Casey then over to the doorway. Eli stood exactly the same way he had on the courthouse steps, but this time she was the only thing on his mind. Lauren smiled to show him that his efforts hadn't been wasted on someone without, at the very least, manners. "I'm tired, but I'm okay. I have a headache."

"I'm surprised that's all you have. That MG is about as safe as a sardine can." Eli walked into the office and stopped to lean against the wall. Casey said, "You'll probably be really sore in the morning. It'll take a few days for that to go away. I saw it all the time in Nam. Guys would yell medic and I'd get there only to find out it was the noise of an explosion that made them lay on the ground like they were hit. Their muscles would be so tight you'd think they were atrophied. The way I see it, you have a couple of choices. Go see your own doctor, take a handful

of aspirin and head back to the office if you're the worka-
holic type. Or you could go see your doctor, take a bunch
of aspirin and hop in bed. Course there's always option
number three.''

"What's that?'' Lauren mumbled, testing her shoulder
to make sure it still moved.

"Have this guy take you down for a bowl of soup while
you decide if you even want to see your doctor.'' Casey
smiled at Eli Warner as he walked past him. "I've got about
twenty hours of surveillance tapes to watch so I'll let you
guys figure it out. Nice to meet you.'' He nodded at Lauren,
tapped Eli's shoulder and was gone with a, "See ya.''

Eli stayed on.

"So, do you really want soup or does a stiff drink sound
better?''

"Thanks. No.'' She looked around for her purse but
couldn't seem to focus. He was there, her bag dangling
from one hand, her briefcase in the other. She reached
for both. He gave her the purse.

"Get your sea legs before you take on the heavy lug-
gage.''

"Look, Mr. Warner . . .''

"Eli,'' he corrected with an easy grin showing teeth so
darn straight Lauren almost laughed thinking about the
mother somewhere who was proud to death of that smile.
She reached for the case again and kept her hand on it
when he didn't let go. "I really appreciate it, but I've got
to see about my car . . .''

"Been towed. I have the number. Bill's a friend of mine,
and he'll do all the insurance paperwork.''

". . . and call the office. I've got to get to get back to
work.''

Eli tugged on the briefcase, "I took the liberty of talking
to Edie.''

"She a personal friend, too?''

Eli shook his head. "Naw, but it's not exactly a secret
that you two are working together. She said she'd see you
in the morning.'' He smiled. When she didn't he kept
smiling. "You know, there are worse places to be stuck
than an FBI office. Especially with an agent who's ready

to do your bidding. You know, I can get anywhere with my
nifty official badge."

"Right." Lauren winced as she finally pulled the briefcase out of his hand.

"Okay. So there are better people to help you out than
me."

This time Lauren did smile. "Look, it's not that I don't
appreciate what you did. I couldn't have picked a better
place to get nailed than in front of the Federal Building."

"Or a better time. If I hadn't needed my daily candy fix
I wouldn't have been crossing that street."

Lauren looked askance. It was hard to argue with that.
A friendly face and a strong voice to deal with the cops, a
stronger arm to take her away were all better than standing
dazed in the middle of Wilshire while angry motorists
craned their necks for the pleasure of giving her dirty
looks. He was right. Seeing him, was like seeing a hero.

"M&Ms, huh?"

She was walking slowly to the door now. Beyond it,
agents, secretaries, probably an informant or two, went
about their business. They had given her a passing glance
when Eli first brought her up and through the secured
doors but that was it. The FBI, as Lauren well knew, didn't
pay any attention to anyone until they decided you were
interesting. Then you couldn't shake them if your life
depended on it. Sometimes it did.

"Look, I appreciate the help, but I'm really better . . ."
Her knees shook and one crumpled. Eli was smooth. He
didn't hurry. He just steadied her by the elbow, his other
hand taking the briefcase back like she'd passed him the
ball on a crowded playing field.

"I know. You're tough. There are dragons to slay. But
I'll let you in on a little secret." He leaned close and she
smelled only man. No sweet aftershave like Allan was partial
to, no pomade that Wilson liked, nothing except the scent
of skin. "You can't slay a dragon if you can't hold the
lance. Did you eat before the accident?"

She shook her head and couldn't help leaning into him.
"I had part of a smoothie."

"Doesn't count and don't think you can shake me. I'm

just protecting my butt. I don't want to be dragged into court for negligence. What happens if your head falls off? They'd probably tell me I'm liable because I didn't listen when you said you had a headache.'' Lauren laughed. "Now, do you want me to take you to the hospital, your doctor, or a place you can just sit down and have a bite?''

Ten minutes later they were seated in a dark corner of La Grange Restaurant, a little French place with a *prix fixe* menu and no other patrons at three in the afternoon.

"Boy, he wasn't kidding was he? I mean about being sore.''

"Wait until tomorrow,'' Eli laughed and moved around his brandy snifter. Three in the afternoon wasn't exactly the time he felt like a drink but Lauren refused to have one unless he joined her. She took a sip and let her head fall back on the padded bench.

"I don't even want to think about tomorrow. I've got so much to do, and I need to be sharp. I don't know if I can even think straight if it gets any worse than this.''

"Do you want to call someone? Allan Lassiter? Judge Caufeld? Lassiter's closest in Century City.''

Lauren's eyes were brandy bright, cut with a world-weariness he didn't think odd given what he knew about her.

"You've done your homework. Kind of sad when you only have two people in this world who you can call in an emergency.''

"Better than not having anyone.'' There was something in his voice that made Lauren realize, of the two of them, she was probably the luckier.

"Sorry.''

"Don't be.'' There was no self-pity in him. "Time gets away, so do people.''

"It sure seems to.''

"So, who will it be? I've got a dime.'' He grinned; Lauren liked it.

"It's twenty cents for a phone call these days.'' She lifted her head and her glass. The brandy burned. Water came next. She wanted a bath. She wanted to know if her car was all right. She wanted to call Wilson but decided against it, knowing that was too ridiculous. If there was trouble, Wilson would be the first at her side. Still, she would let her snit go on a while longer. Righteousness could be satisfying even if right had nothing to do with anything. She'd already disrupted Allan's day so she crossed him off the list. Besides, Eli seemed to like being with her. She'd rather look at him looking at her, than look at Allan, who would have a hard time hiding the fact that he was always anxious to be somewhere else.

"Okay, I'll spot you the twenty cents for the phone call. You just tell me when you need it." When she didn't move, he curled one leg up on the booth and put a hand under his head. "So, aren't you a little out of your territory? I mean you live downtown, you work downtown, the Stewarts come from Riverside. Don't tell me you're a closet West-sider?"

Lauren snorted, almost laughing, "Don't be ridiculous. I wouldn't be caught dead being that chic. I was out here seeing someone. It was personal."

"Oh." Eli nodded. Part of his lower lip disappeared between his teeth. How delicate and quaint. She knew what he was thinking.

"Okay. You've got me. I was down here having a quickie at lunch with a married man who also happens to be an informant on the case I'm working on." Lauren looked at Eli. Eli looked back and took his lumps well. He raised his glass to her without a word. "You deserved that. You may have been investigating the judge, but you don't have me all figured out. You probably haven't even got him all figured out."

"Darn, you mean I still have work to do?"

"Probably more than a bit," Lauren laughed.

"You forget, I've been doing some deep background investigating . . ."

"On Wilson Caufeld," she reminded him.

"On everything about Wilson Caufeld and you're pretty much joined right at his hip," Eli reminded her.

"Yeah? So that means you had to look into my life, too?"

"Let's just say I know some things."

"Like what?" Lauren was flirting. It was actually fun, until she moved, and a knifelike pain shot up between her shoulder blades. He raised his arm, mindful not to touch her unless it was absolutely necessary.

"Careful. You got whacked pretty good out there. Maybe I better take you home even though I wish you'd see a doctor."

She shook her head, not ready for the rat race quite yet. "No, why don't you tell me what you know first. Then I'll figure out if I want you to know where I live?"

Amused, Eli hailed the waitress. "I already know where you live," he said then ordered two bowls of French onion soup.

"You are twenty-seven years old, your mother died when you were fifteen. She named Wilson Caufeld as your guardian—"

"Do you know how my mother died? Do you know why my mother died?" Lauren interrupted. She hadn't meant to ask that. She especially didn't mean to challenge him.

"Yes. I do." There was no sympathy in his answer; there was no apology either. He recited her history like a well-prepared student trying to impress the teacher. "She killed herself. You found the body, and her suicide was a direct result of an FBI investigation into allegations of wrong-doing on her part that would have removed her from the bench. Criminal action would have been brought if the allegations proved true."

"And no one ever proved a thing, did they?" Lauren was cool but the pain was no longer limited to her body.

Eli nodded once. His eyes never left hers. If asked, she couldn't tell you what color they were because her own were glazed with the anger she'd never quite been able to control. Eli, on the other hand, was extraordinarily controlled.

"And if you want to talk about that right now, I'll be happy to oblige." He leaned close so that she could hear him but no one else could even if there was anyone else about. "But that's the sort of thing people talk about when they know each other very well. You've got to get past the

first layer. Even then, that's something you may not want
to talk about until we are old and fast friends. So, since I had
nothing to do with that investigation, since it happened a
while back and since I'd like to get to know you a whole
lot better, why don't we skip it for now? Given all this, I'd
suggest we kind of go back a few steps. If you don't want
to do that, I'll just leave you as that old footnote on
Caufeld's file and take off.''

The waitress was back with crocks of soup. Eli leaned
away, thanked her as she served and never took his eyes
off Lauren. He wasn't exactly smiling, he wasn't exactly
trying machismo on for size. Eli knocked the wind out of
her sails by suggesting she put away her arsenal of affronts.
No one had ever told her she could really talk about her
mother, not even Wilson. This was new and weird. It had
never occurred to Lauren that she actually had a choice
in the way she dealt with her history until Eli allowed her
to do just that. When he lifted his spoon, Lauren did the
same. The soup was delicious and her puzzlement taxing.
Lauren put her spoon down.

"I don't know that I want to know you that well."

"Okay, that's fair." He reached for a basket and held
it up to her. "Bread?"

Lauren shook her head. "But, then again, maybe I do."

"Then that would be better than fair."

He grinned without any of Allan's overcompensation.
There was no wariness that often accompanied a man's
smile, nor was there any suggestion that time was being
calculated until he could move forward to whatever his
objective: professional, personal or sexual advancement.

So Eli Warner was a good guy. That's why he was doing
background checks at his age instead of handling more
notable field work. That's probably why she liked him. He
was an agent, he just didn't seem to be of the FBI.

"Your soup's getting cold." Lauren pointed to his bowl.
At that moment there was no doubt Eli Warner was a happy
man. He picked up where he left off, finishing his story
and his soup at the same time.

"Allan Lassiter is one of your best friends. You've never
dated him, according to my sources, and Caufeld treats you

both like you're his own. Lassiter was Caufeld's protégé. Worked for him for four years before going out on his own. Caufeld is a class act, a guy with brains, a conscience and courage. He has everything except a blood-line family because his wife, Victoria, died young and he never remarried. I'm proud to be working on this. I think Caufeld is an all-right guy. I'd like to call him my friend. I'll be happy to see him sit on the high court."

"He'd probably like that, too," Lauren said encompassing both the ambition and the desire for friendship in her answer.

She pushed aside her empty bowl and left the brandy half finished. It had been a long time since she'd sat in the dark with a man and enjoyed it as much as she enjoyed being with Eli Warner. There was something about the way he talked that made her feel as if she didn't need to say anything. The way he imparted information, the way he waited for her input, made her feel safe. He could keep that bogey man at bay. He listened so well. He should have been a priest to whom people could bare their souls without regret. She was glad he wasn't.

"So," she sighed and plucked her napkin off her lap and put it on the table. "How much longer before you wrap everything up?"

"I like to be thorough, so probably another couple of weeks for my end. The hearings aren't scheduled and those senators want a couple of months to look for dirt using their own investigators."

"They won't find any on Wilson," Lauren assured him.

"Don't I know it. Life's been pretty boring since I started in on him. I have a funny feeling, though, that since you're part of the package things might heat up. How long do you think the Stewart trial will last?"

"Knowing Wilson? We'll have it wrapped up in three weeks."

"Perfect. We'll both need a break. Dinner? A movie? I'll even drive."

"Very funny." Lauren started to move out of the booth but her muscles were locked. She muffled a groan and squeezed the tears back behind closed eyes.

"Hold on." Eli got out first. He held out his hand. She took it and he half lifted her away from the table.

"Lean on me." She did and they stopped only long enough for him to pay the bill. She was walking stiffly, but on her own by the time he finished. The sun was almost down, rush hour was in full swing. "Come on, I'll take you home."

"I should go back to the office."

"You should see a doctor."

"I won't feel like inviting you in."

"It's good to know where I stand." He put his hand under her arm and took her briefcase. This time she didn't object. She was tired in body and soul, suddenly aware she had been lonesome. She didn't mind that other people rushed past them. Their slow pace gave her time to look at the Federal Building.

"I used to think this building was the most beautiful thing. It looks like a ghost building because the light shines at an angle through all those windows."

"I used to love it when anyone could come sit on the grass—before they put in those concrete barriers. Oklahoma City changed a lot of things," he said back. "Sometimes I just hate how we all have to be so careful. Maybe you'll put the Stewarts away."

"There are a million others waiting to take their place if I do."

"You're right. Even if there weren't, they'd never take the barriers down. Once something like that goes up, it doesn't come down unless it's torn down. Somehow, I don't think there's anyone passionate enough in this city to do that. We like our walls. Yes, indeed we do."

Lauren looked askance. He wasn't looking at her. He seemed to be talking to himself as much as her. The streetlight was red now and still he didn't hurry though they were only three-quarters of the way across. Eli seemed to know nothing would happen to them as long as he was alert and his head was up. He seemed to be mindful of all her injuries, even the ones deep inside. Lauren didn't ask how he knew to do these things.

She simply said, "You're right."

* * *

"Wilson, you know that I admire you more than anyone in this world, and I know that I owe you everything. I haven't forgotten that, Wilson. But things have changed and the stakes have changed. Remember when you told me not to take risks that weren't absolutely necessary? Well, now I'm telling you the same thing."

Allan talked fast as he followed the old man through the house. It was a rambling place full of memorabilia of Wilson's travels, his speeches, his education, his years as a judge. The house was too big for a man alone, Allan always told him that, but Wilson didn't listen. Neither did he stop to consider the framed pictures or plaques or citations often, but Allan knew they were comforting to him. These things were proof of a life well lived and that's what counted to Wilson Caufeld.

Allan ignored the trappings completely, well aware that there was a hole in this shrine of Wilson's, a year that wasn't remembered, and that he was partially responsible for it. But all that was long ago and far away and Allan hardly even thought of it anymore. He was different now. Wilson was the same.

"I cautioned you against greed, Allan, and pride and all the seven deadly sins you seem so fond of. That was my warning."

Wilson reached up and gave the hanging plant above the piano a little drink. It was the kind with the tufts of leaves on long tendrils. College girls called the tufts "babies" because they trailed from the mother plant.

"I hate this thing." Allan swiped at it, sending a baby flying as he followed after Wilson Caufeld. Wilson didn't blink, but kept on with his chore. Allan was ready to beg. "Wilson, please, listen to me."

"Allan, I have been listening for the last forty-five minutes. I'm tired. I had a long day as you well know and, to tell you the truth, I've only allowed you to stay this long because I hoped you'd run out of steam. I thought we could sit and have a cup of coffee together and relax. But if you're going to go on with this argument then I want you to go home."

Wilson carted his copper watering can into the kitchen. His leather slippers made a swooshing sound and the whole scene gave Allan the creeps. On his home turf Wilson Caufeld looked like an old man, he sounded like an old man, and Allan didn't admire old men. He admired the professional and powerful Caufeld. There were times Allan worried that he might be looking at his future when he looked at Wilson. Tonight, though, he was angry because he couldn't make Wilson Caufeld see that the future was exactly what was at stake.

Taking a deep breath, Allan stuck his thumbs in the pocket of his jeans, threw back his head and counted to ten. Wilson was making the coffee. Allan took his fingers out of his pocket and leaned his elbows on the counter.

"Wilson, think of what you're doing to Lauren if nothing else. Ever since I've known you, all you've talked about is how much she needed a break after her mom died. Now you're in a position to give it to her and you're not."

Wilson raised his eyes. In that moment he was the all-knowing, all-but-wrathful, near omnipotent Wilson Caufeld whom Allan used to fear. He had looked at Allan like that before. This time Allan didn't look away. Wilson picked up the coffeepot.

"Remember where you are and who you are with, Allan. This is my home. This is my decision and my business. What I do about George Stewart has nothing to do with you."

"It has everything to do with me, Wilson!" In his fervor, Allan jostled Caufeld's hand as if that childish gesture could change his mind. But Wilson had the pot in his hand when he pulled back, the hot coffee splashed out, burning the judge. The pot crashed to the floor, shattered irreparably. The two men looked at the mess and then at one another through the dim light. It was Allan who looked away first. His anger vanished in the face of Wilson Caufeld's wounded expression. That look still made him feel like a young boy, unworthy of the affection the old man lavished on him.

Allan moved around the island. He took a sponge from the sink, crouched down and picked up the pieces, opening the cabinet to throw them away while Wilson ran his hand under cold water. Allan nudged Wilson's leg. He moved and went to get the first-aid kit.

"Where's the sponge mop?" Allan muttered.

"Same place it's always been," Wilson said on his way out the door.

He was in his study reading when Allan came and stood in the doorway. He had finished with his chore but not his mission.

"The kitchen's clean." Wilson remained silent. "I'm sorry . . . about the coffee." He stepped in and put a cup on the table next to Wilson. "I've brought you some more. Extra cream." Wilson didn't respond. Allan put the cup on the coffee table. "I guess I better be going."

Allan turned around then back again.

"Wilson, I only wanted to point out that this could hurt you. You are nominated for the Supreme Court, for God's sake. Your confirmation would have been a snap if you didn't take this hot potato case. But you did. No trial like this is about the law. It's about drama and you're making it more dramatic by the minute. You've got a lot to worry about, Wilson: the press, the senators, the president. I talked to the assistant attorney general, Gil Stern. People back there are taking notice of your ruling and the fact that you're taking two weeks to think about George Stewart. They can't believe it. The best thing you can do now is make George Stewart stand trial inclusive of that evidence. To do anything less is political suicide." Allan sighed as if he had just come a great distance and found he had reached the wrong destination. "It's wonderful to think that politics isn't tied up in this, but it is. I would have passed on the whole thing if I were you."

"I know you would, Allan, and that is the difference between you and me. You can make use of your contacts, you can tell me about the politics, you can advise me that I have options that are legal in this matter and you can convince yourself that you do all these things because you care. But it's not right to act out of fear of not gaining something. I'd rather forego the nomination and make sure that the Stewart problem is handled correctly. I thought you understood that. I thought you understood me."

Wilson sighed and took off his glasses. He looked at his protégé, grown now into the most handsome and successful of men but still holding onto the desires of a spoiled boy. Allan's decisions were rooted in what was best for Allan. Who could blame him when he had come from so little, fought so hard for the few things he had when Wilson met him? All one could do was encourage and teach, and that was a job Wilson had dedicated himself to years ago. The fact that it had been a harder, and longer, job than expected didn't mean he could give up.

"Allan, what do you think my charge will be if I am confirmed? Do you think that I'll test the waters of public opinion before I render my own? Do you think I'll consult with the politicians from whom, by virtue of the constitution, I stand apart? When I sit on the Supreme Court, do you imagine I will be concerned about the individual who brings the action, or the constitutionality of the cause itself? If we all worried about the individual's desires where would the world be? What kind of judge would I be?" He scoffed. "I wouldn't be fit to sit this bench much less the Supreme Court."

"Oh please, Wilson. What kind of man are you if you can't bend on this so you can go on and accomplish bigger things? I'm not asking you to do anything illegal." He hit the doorjamb lightly with his open palm then turned his back to it, hiding his hands as if he was afraid of what he might do. "We'd be better off, Wilson, if you worried about the public good when it came to the Stewarts. People wouldn't say you were worried about your nomination, they'd say you made a decision based on the need for safety. You know Henry Stewart was bailed . . ."

"As was his right," Wilson reminded him curtly. Allan ignored him.

"And George Stewart is acting like some kind of vengeful spirit putting a price on your head and Lauren's. Maybe he even included Edie in that threat. Who knows what he's going to do. He'll do it though, Wilson, because he's mad enough and crazy enough and you're not going to stop them.''

"It's not my place. Let Lauren convict him in a court of law, using the law, in front of me, a judge who understands that law." He pushed aside his coffee, frustrated that Allan refused to understand, or at least accept, his position.

"Help her, Wilson," Allan wailed. "Just help her do it. It's in your power. Even the ACLU isn't going to pipe up on this one, believe me." Allan pushed himself away and stood tall. He was tired of talking. They weren't getting anywhere. Tomorrow or the next day, he might calm down, but right now he was angry and that wasn't good for either of them. "Just think about it, Wilson. Just make the right decision."

"I always try to make the best decision, Allan."

"I know that, Wilson. But this time it's fucking important that it is right for everyone."

Wilson raised his head and looked toward, not at, his protégé. There was nothing to say. He wasn't Allan's father. He couldn't wash out his mouth to rid him of a dirty word, but how he wished he could clean away the cobwebs in the younger man's mind so that he understood the difference between his welfare and what was moral.

"I'm sorry, Wilson," Allan finally muttered and bade Wilson a quick good-night.

Wilson put his glasses back on but closed his eyes when he heard the door close. He had heard Allan's argument for personal satisfaction years ago and had made a decision he'd regretted. He wouldn't do it again. Not this time. Not even for Lauren and definitely not for Allan.

Eli Warner closed the window. It was cold by the beach this time of year. The temperature had begun to drop off suddenly around eight-thirty and Eli spent each night shivering, even in his sleep. Funny how he still hated being cold at night. When Eli was young, he would go to his mother's room with the hopes of banishing the chill. But

there was always someone else there, someone he didn't
know, taking advantage of his mother's voluptuous warmth.
She would half wake, sensing him standing hopefully in
the middle of her room. His mother would smile sleepily
and, even through the dark, Eli could see she was beautiful.
She would murmur, reach for him without ever quite making contact, then send him on his way. He would still
be cold through the long night, but he appreciated her
honesty. When he was enveloped in her arms, and held
against her, it was because she wanted him there. Honesty
was the one thing Eli Warner had learned from his mother
and that made him so good at what he did. Few held his
seemingly mundane job in great esteem, but he did and
that's all that really counted.

His mother died when Eli was twenty-four and he loved
her still. Thinking of her now, he adjusted a picture of
her, him and a man whose name he couldn't recall. Every
once in a while it occurred to Eli that he should cut out
the nameless man but then, if he were to be honest, that
guy was as much a part of his history as his mother. He
represented all the guys who had been in his mother's life,
and one of them could have been his father.

Eli slipped on a sweatshirt and put his feet into his well-
worn moccasins as he grabbed a handful of M&Ms on his
way to the kitchen. The pizza was half eaten but he could
manage another slice. He promised to curb his wicked
nutritional ways as soon as he saw a roll at his middle. In
the meantime, another piece, a cold beer, a quick listen
for his neighbor who had recently taken up with a heavy
metal rocker and he was ready to work. The neighbor was
out, probably at a concert that wouldn't bring her home
until Eli was gone again.

He flipped on the stereo with the remote and flopped
in his favorite chair. His butt fit so nicely in the cracked
burgundy leather and the ottoman was just the right length
for his long legs, it was amazing he didn't fall asleep. Johnny
Mathis classics were playing. A stack of financial records
had been subpoenaed from various accounts that Wilson
Caufeld had opened and closed over the years sat on the
table. The records, that began with Caufeld's fledgling

defense firm and ended with the carefully invested funds of the present, were standard and clean. It was a pleasure working on this man's background. As far as Eli was concerned, Caufeld could pass GO and head for Washington whenever he felt like it.

As he pulled out the first manila folder, the song changed and the buttery croon of "Funny Valentine" oozed out of the speakers. Eli Warner closed his eyes, enjoying the music, imagining a young woman, small and delicate-looking, tenacious and talkative when he heard the lyrics. She was more than half his age, thank goodness, because Eli liked Lauren Kingsley. He'd like to have her here and find out if Johnny Mathis made her think of romance, true romance the way he thought of it and the way his mother never did. He'd like to know if she got her vitamins eating vegetarian pizza. He'd like to do a lot of things with Lauren Kingsley. He opened his eyes. That would all come later, hopefully. Right now Caufeld had a deadline. Lauren didn't.

Eli began to read, filling in the background on Wilson Caufeld. He didn't even question what he read until a few days later when it dawned on him something wasn't quite right.

Lauren had soaked in a hot bath for more than an hour. For the last two she'd been curled up on the couch looking at the paperwork spread out on the coffee table and glancing at CNN on the television. She'd propped her shoulders up with a pillow from her bed and wrapped her mother's afghan—crocheting was the one thing she'd seen her mother do that didn't have some connection with the law—and fixed herself some instant chicken noodle soup. The soup tasted good, the afghan was warm, the CNN commentator exceptionally mellow. The closest she'd come to work was making a list of things that had to be done: contact the car repair shop, send Wilson a note to let him know what happened and that she was fine, call Allan for a doctor's referral, and thank Eli Warner. Yes, thank Eli Warner. The next time she saw him. Whenever that would be. Perhaps, she would call him. Perhaps, she would go see him. She fell asleep planning how exactly to thank Eli Warner.

Mark Jackson was glued to the television screen. It was three in the morning. His wife was asleep. His three kids were asleep. Half of Los Angeles County was asleep. The other half was up to no good—with one exception. It was that exception that kept Mark awake and watching "Fargo" for the second time that night.

He was getting up to replenish his drink and make a pit stop when the phone only he answered sounded with two quick, quiet and distinctive rings. He was fast for a well-muscled man. It was all those hours on the tennis court that made him nimble. Mark picked up the phone on the second ring.

"Yep."

He listened, his expression betraying none of the emotion that was instantaneous and violent, given the news. There wasn't much to say, so he didn't say it. He replaced the receiver quietly then picked it up again to dial. Mark spoke to two men who would, in turn, call two others. When that was done he used the remote to turn off the television.

In the bedroom he was quiet as he slipped between the sheets. His wife murmured and rolled over. He kissed her cheek. The house creaked. The children dreamed. Mark closed his eyes, knowing the forty-five minutes of sleep he would allow himself were necessary. When he woke, he would kiss his still sleeping wife once more, take one look at each of his children and go to work—with a vengeance.

Henry Stewart sat alone in a shed. He was far from home, in a town that looked like a zillion towns along the freeway. Outside there was a car with stolen plates attached to the back but not the front. Inside there was a cot, a hot plate, a small refrigerator and a worktable. On the worktable there were wire cutters, ammonium nitrate, wire and other bomb stuff. That's what he used to call it when he was a kid, when his father first started showing him what to do. Bomb stuff. There was a shotgun, a revolver and some food. Not a lot of food because no one expected him to be there long but at least he had everything he might need. His mom told him they would move him at odd times to keep him safe. Then, one day, after he'd played his part, it would be over and he would go away for good.

Too bad.

He only wanted to go home.

There were four men in the car. Three were drinking. The fourth was bleeding. They were all only half conscious.

They didn't say a lot. Most of it had already been said. The guy at the wheel, a huge man, drove pretty well considering his inebriated state. He knew exactly which offramp he was looking for, found it, took it and parked under the overpass.

Three doors opened and then the fourth. The bleeding guy fell half out of the car so the man closest to him tossed his beer can and dragged him the rest of the way. The three guys gathered round.

"Think he's still alive?"

"Maybe. Won't be for long." Another beer can clattered on the rocks. "Let's go."

Two of them trudged back to the car, the third thought about it for a minute and gave the man on the ground another swift kick with his steel-toed boots. One more for good measure. The man on the ground didn't even groan. Wasn't fun if you didn't hear anything. He tried again. Third time was the charm.

Now he felt better. Now he could go home.

Chapter Eight

Abram drummed his fingers on the desk. Edie sat across from him. Both watched the small television screen. Had it not been so horridly ill-timed, so terribly important that nothing like this happen, the tape would have been fascinating entertainment. As it was, the scene was the stuff which felled governments, or at least those mid-level bureaucrats who were called on the politician's carpet and symbolically castrated for such faux pas. It was a most interesting tape, indeed, shot by an insomniac in Riverside who just happened to have his videocam sitting right there next to his easy chair when he saw some suspicious movement across the street.

To the poor sod's surprise, black-clad men descended upon the home of Nicholas Cheshire, the quiet man who lived in the green house across the street. The insomniac didn't know Nicholas well, but it struck him as odd that people should be letting themselves into that house, much less so many men dressed in black. Three doors down, two other men sat in a plain gray car outside the Stewarts' door. That, at least, he could understand. Cops, he assumed, still persecuting the poor Stewart family. But the silent men in black, breaking into the house across the street, were another matter altogether, so he whipped up that camera and pushed the record button.

It was like a movie: one guy giving hand signals and the rest of them snapping to. The insomniac got a real good shot of the leader when the man looked over his shoulder. It was a picture *People* would like. Being a good citizen he called the cops instead. Then he called the television station. By seven he had a check for a couple of hundred dollars. By ten he was sorry he hadn't held out for more. So was Edie, she would have paid handsomely for that tape just to keep it out of the media's hands.

"Mark Jackson looks good in black, doesn't he?" Edie drawled.

"I wish it was a shroud. My God, Edie, this is going to make everything so much more difficult," Abram sniped.

They watched it twice more and, as Abram worried, Mark came through the door. He'd changed from the black jacket and turtleneck he'd worn to bust into the home of Nick Cheshire, private citizen, into a suit and tie that made him look like a banker. No one said a word as he walked the length of the office. Lauren followed slowly behind. She was late and limping. She didn't explain and no one asked, because all eyes were on Mark Jackson.

"Do you want to see it again Mark or are you still in the throes of that wonderful adrenaline rush that replays every instant of your ridiculous behavior in your head."

"Jealous that we're actually doing something, Abram?" Mark nodded at Edie. He didn't bother with Lauren. She wasn't in his line of sight.

"We'd like to know what went on this morning, please," Abram's voice was tight as he ignored the dig. "Who ordered the search warrants, Mark? Neither Lauren nor Edie heard from you. I certainly didn't. Without us there could be no request for a warrant, without a judge there could be no warrant, ergo, Mark, I believe you acted illegally at worst and brutally at best. Our office is going to have to prosecute this action and answer questions as to why we, the government, are intimidating the families of men on trial. Do you know what the press is doing with this tape? Do you know . . ."

"Yes, I know. I know." He shifted and popped the button on his jacket, pushing it back. He was wearing a shoulder holster.

Mark clasped his hands. He wouldn't let any of them see that he felt like scum. Not because he didn't have a warrant, not because his clandestine operation was caught on tape, but because he hadn't found Nicholas Cheshire. His CI, his friend, hadn't been heard from in days. He leaned into the conversation, his light good looks taking on an icy cast, but life and fire burned deep in his eyes. "I'll tell you something else I know. Nicholas Cheshire, one of the best agents I have, is gone. Disappeared. That was his place we were going into."

"Our informant?" Lauren asked alive and alert. "Where is he?"

"If I knew that, Lauren, I wouldn't have gone looking for him in the middle of the night. To keep up appearances I should have had a warrant. But if I asked you three to rouse a judge in the middle of the night and get me a warrant I might have been wasting time that would mean the difference between life and death for Nick. He works for us, for Christ's sake."

"Nobody out there knows that," Edie snapped, "and we can't exactly get on TV and tell everyone this was just a misunderstanding. Excuse us, but we were really on a mission of mercy."

"Exactly my point. That's why I called a few of Nick's buddies and asked them to help. They didn't know what was going down, or that there was no warrant, okay? It was my call. I made it. I blew it. We'll settle everybody with cash and that will be it. But Nicholas is gone. There was nothing in the house, no sign of a struggle, no blood, nothing. Not even a message. He knew what to do if he was tagged. He didn't do it. The place was too clean."

"I thought you were going to pull Nick," Lauren insisted. "Why was he still there?"

"I couldn't pull him with Caufeld dancing around the way he is. I told Nick to turn the screws just in case Caufeld throws out the stop. Nick went after documentation, recordings, paperwork, anything to hedge against Caufeld doing something stupid. You should be thanking me for trying to get what you're going to need to win this case when Caufeld screws up." Mark relaxed. They had the picture. "You're not implicated, so don't worry. I took it on myself for Nick and for this case. You want to blame someone, then you blame Caufeld. Who knows what the militia started thinking when Henry got cut loose and George is making all that noise?" Mark leaned forward, his mustache twitched on the right, his hair shined gold and silver under the overheads. "I'll tell you another thing. The kid isn't in the Stewart house either. What do you think the press is going to make of that?"

"Lauren, get Joe Knapp on the phone and find out what he knows," Edie directed. To Mark, "He should have been wired."

"Caufeld didn't order it." Mark added to the judge's scoreboard. "After we couldn't find Nick, I sent one of my guys over to check. Carolyn Stewart says he went to visit a cousin and that Henry isn't under house arrest. She wouldn't give the address—like I believe there is a cousin—then she called us assassins. She gave me the same old crap, Abram, about not recognizing our authority and having the right to protect themselves from us." He turned to Lauren and pointed a finger. "I want you to tell your friend Caufeld that I hold him personally responsible for this."

"I wouldn't even if I could." Lauren was quick. "And don't point your finger at me. If you want to point it anywhere turn it around because you're the one that pushed Nick when you should have taken him out. Don't you people ever learn? God, you push and you push until people do stupid, ridiculous things. If he's dead it's because you made him that way. You've done it before. You blame other people and think there won't be consequences for your actions. Well there are always consequences, Mark, and it's time you started thinking about them in terms of a body count."

Lauren's face flushed. It was as if her mother was standing there in the room with them. Only Lauren could see her but they all knew the specter was there. But it was old news and therefore not relevant to anyone but her.

"Lauren." Abram steered her back with a word, but Mark Jackson pulled the other way, not ready to give her up yet.

"I think about my men all the time." Mark made sure there was no question but that Lauren's mother was excluded from his concern. "I trained Nick, and I wouldn't hang him out to dry the way Caufeld is doing to you. If it wasn't for that old man, I wouldn't have had to make that call. If you were doing your job right we'd have a ruling, we'd have viable defendants. I could kill Caufeld for what he's done. I could just kill him."

Mark half rose from his chair and realized how he must look. Instead of sitting back down, he took a breath and walked the length of the room while Edie filled the silence.

"Okay, now that we've got everything off our chest, let's look at the situation. Mark, I assume you'll go ahead with your investigation into Nick's disappearance, but quietly. Since it was Nick's house there won't be anyone to press charges." Mark nodded, his back to her even as she spoke. "We still need his testimony desperately. I heard through the grapevine that Caufeld is going to throw out the baby with the bath where George Stewart is concerned."

"Who'd you hear that from, the secretarial pool?" Lauren asked wryly.

Edie swiveled her head slowly. Her eyes were hooded by a sweep of deep, dark lashes. She looked like a raven-haired Garbo.

"I have it on good authority. I believe you're privy to the same source."

Lauren froze. Allan. The ultimate good authority. His pillow talk was more than likely nothing but speculation, yet there was a chance Wilson had said something to him. This was a fence Lauren could have peeked over without compromising her position yet Edie had done it first.

Mark Jackson took one, last intense look at them all then walked quietly across the room to stand behind Lauren. She shivered and moved a step away. He didn't say a word while he listened to Edie.

"What about the people who were affected last night, Abram?" Edie asked.

"We'll wait and see if we hear from their lawyers. Contact the cameraman and thank him for his public service, Lauren. I want him on our side. We are going to have to set ourselves apart from the Bureau operation until all this calms down."

"Fine," Lauren crossed her arms. The politics, the personalities, the intentions were polarizing and personalizing. The circus surrounding the Stewart case was now so melodramatic as to be ridiculous, but it was reality and that was electrifying.

"I think we better talk to the press," Edie offered. "If we don't say something now it will look like we condoned, maybe even planned, that whole thing to intimidate the militia. We've got to remind everyone we're the good guys."

"Agreed." Abram's patrician face screwed up into a look of exceptionally pedestrian concern. He had commandeered both generals from his exhibit of miniature war, and held them in his open palms as if weighing which would give him the best advice. Abram gave a little toss to the Union general. He spoke smoothly and with surety.

"I want you to find something that will make Caufeld revoke Henry Stewart's bail. We need something that will make the press jump. Henry Stewart is dangerous. His father has threatened Judge Caufeld and Lauren. Edie, I want the marshals with you when you hold the press conference."

"No problem. We'll make it look good."

"I know you will." Abram smiled at Edie and Lauren saw the look that passed. They were of one mind and she was right there with them but still on the outside. Lauren decided she would be a part of this team even if it meant pitting herself against Wilson Caufeld.

"Do you want me to be there, too?" Lauren asked. Edie looked her over.

"Considering you're still leading this prosecution I think you have to be," Edie answered.

"We'll underscore the fact that these people are dangerous, but that we're not intimidated," Abram reminded them all again. "We want everyone to forget Mark's little party last night."

"Right," Edie agreed. "I'll call a conference for ten."

"I'll write up a statement and be ready for questions," Lauren offered.

Edie looked over her shoulder. "Do you want us to handle your end, Mark?"

They had all but forgotten him. He had been standing so still and now all eyes turned his way. Mark took a minute then said: "No need for you to speak for me, Edie. I'll just wait until they come my way." He glanced around the room then focused on Edie again. "How reliable is your information on what Caufeld's going to do? Do you really think he'll suppress?"

"It's as solid as any for now," Edie answered absently. There was a lot to do and she didn't want to dwell on speculation. "He'd be a dead duck if he did."

"I agree, Edie. He's a dead man," Mark said quietly. Edie heard him and something in his voice made her look up. Mark looked right back then smiled slowly. "I mean as far as his nomination is concerned."

"That's what I meant, too. He'll never make it out of Los Angeles if he doesn't do the right thing, will he?"

Lauren opened her mouth to protest such incautious talk. Yet, when Mark looked at her, his expression so calm, his attention so focused, she hesitated and the moment was lost. Edie barely noticed when Mark left. Abram was leaning over his desk, little metal generals abandoned for a Mont Blanc pen.

"Lauren?" Edie called her back to the circle. "We don't have much time."

"Sorry. Yes, I'm ready."

"We need a statement."

Edie and Abram began to talk. With the spin they put on this renegade raid, Caufeld's indecisiveness and the U.S. Attorney's noble intentions, Lauren began to wonder who it was the real people—the ones Edie had argued felt powerless—should be afraid of. Maybe it was Mark Jackson. Maybe it was all of them.

* * *

Los Angeles was anxious now, more anxious than during the first few days of Wilson Caufeld's silence. During the first days anxiety stemmed from the fact that voices less reasonable than Caufeld's filled the airways. Channel 2, Channel 7, and Channel 5 offered ever more frenzied commentary. The television flashed stock footage of Klan rallies, explosions, the aftermath of Oklahoma City, funerals, Iranian terrorists and German skinheads. It didn't matter what pictures came across the local news, people got the message: danger lurked as close as next door. Through it all, there were pictures of Wilson Caufeld and some were not too flattering. The media was having a great deal of fun; some seemed to believe they were actually doing a public service. The first was forgivable, the last unconscionable.

With the advent of Mark Jackson's raid and the U.S. Attorney's press conference, the tone of the newscasts changed, and the level of apprehension on the part of the people rose ten degrees. The national news discussed Wilson's silence. His inaction was not just as a footnote to their important news of presidential affairs, the fiscal health of the nation or the most recent coup in a third-world country. Who, the news readers asked, were the bad guys? Perhaps Wilson Caufeld was not as crazy as he seemed. Perhaps he was protecting the rights of citizens who had been abused by legal vigilantes like Mark Jackson and his FBI thugs. Worse yet, the rhetoric of the prosecutors sounded hollow and defensive leaving people to wonder who, exactly, was in charge and who, exactly, had their best interests at heart. Through it all, Allan Lassiter remained silent. Listening. Watching. Conferring with his partner. Checking in with Lauren. Unfortunately, he didn't learn a thing from her.

When he coaxed her to lunch she had been as close to silent as Lauren could ever get. When she did talk, it was about Eli Warner, an FBI agent who seemed to have captured her imagination but left Allan's wanting. She chatted about Eli's love of books and music, his M&M habit. She tried to convince Allan that Eli Warner was not like other agents. This afternoon, Allan ordered a drink during the silence between stories of Eli Warner and reports on the status of her car.

"You know, Lauren, you're getting really boring. You're not telling me much I don't know."

"I heard you're the one who knows things. Edie swears that Wilson is going to rule against us. She says she has it on good authority. Intimate authority, no less. You know, it would be better if you would just shut up in situations like that."

"It was speculation. You're not giving Edie anything and she's worried. I gave her my best guess." The waitress brought his drink but he didn't really want it now.

"Well she's spouting your speculation like it's God's own truth, Allan, and Mark Jackson believed it. I swear, this could do more harm than good if Mark's bad-mouthing Wilson in Washington. I'd never second-guess the judge."

"Now there's a news flash. If you had, Henry Stewart might still be in custody." Contrite, he reached out and ran a hand down her arm. "I didn't mean it. Nobody could have done more." They were quiet for a few seconds before Allan tried to make up. "How's it going on the new research?"

"Fine. Everything's good. I've got the final P and A's to deliver to chambers."

"Great. I'll come with you."

"He won't see you."

"I just want to say hello," Allan insisted and finished his drink.

"If you know Wilson well enough to call his decision, then you know him well enough to know that he means what he says. You'll be lucky if he talks to you ever again. What did you say to him to make him banish you?"

"It doesn't matter. All that matters is that I make up. I've been talking out of both sides of my mouth to anyone in Washington who will listen."

"That must have been taxing," Lauren drawled. He reached for the check. She let him take it and finished her iced tea.

"How are you feeling?" Allan asked.

"What about?" Lauren asked, busying herself with her lipstick, sans mirror.

"Your accident? Or has the M&M treatment miraculously cured you?"

Lauren leaned over, crossing her arms on the table. "You should take a lesson. It would be cheaper than the way you treat your women."

"I don't need candy to make any woman melt, Lauren."

"You're disgusting, but I'll admit I feel pretty fine. The car's another matter. Probably won't be out of the shop for at least a month. It breaks my heart to look at it."

"It's a cherry vehicle." Allan slid out of the booth and reached for her. She took his hand and patted her chignoned braids with the other. "What are you driving now?"

"The insurance got me one of those little four-door things. Smoother ride than that old MG but it doesn't even compare when it comes to class."

"Just like you, compact, a tough drive, but wouldn't give her up for the world."

"I'll take that as a compliment. At least it doesn't look like every other car in the world. Your Lexus looks exactly the same as the government issue."

"Inside is where luxury counts when you're talking cars," Allan assured her. "Now, let's go see Wilson."

"Bet you a dollar he won't even come out of chambers." Lauren looked over her shoulder and grinned.

"I'll take that bet," Allan said and put a hand on the small of her back wondering why she hadn't figured out the obvious yet. He never lost.

Chapter Nine

"Barbara, come on. Pencil me in on Wilson's calendar. I just want to say hello. I promise, I won't upset him. I won't talk business. You know me, I can't go a week without sitting down and chewing the fat with my friend in there."

Barbara held up her hand. "Judge says he doesn't want to see you until the fourteenth, Allan. He's tired of you haranguing him about George Stewart." She turned with a smile to Lauren, "What have you got for me?"

"Final points and authorities." She handed Barbara her paperwork and the secretary turned toward chambers.

"I'll keep my fingers crossed that this convinces him." She cast a glance over her shoulder. "I imagine you two will be gone by the time I come out so I'll say good-bye now."

She disappeared behind the door and Allan grabbed for the appointment book and a pencil.

"You're being ridiculous now," Lauren laughed as she stopped him. "Barbara memorizes that calendar. She'd notice if you penciled yourself in."

"Just a joke, Lauren."

Lauren wasn't laughing, she was grinning from ear to ear at the man who walked through the door.

"Eli!" Lauren exclaimed, obviously surprised to see him and more obviously delighted. She started for him. "I thought you'd be finished with this."

"Not quite. But you're the last person I expected to see here. Thought you'd be worn to a frazzle by now." He met her halfway and put his hand out. She took it. He put his other hand on hers and neither seemed to notice Allan was there.

"My nose was knocked out of joint by the grindstone, but I think I've got the situation under control. How's it going on your end?"

"I'm plugging along." He let go of her hand and put it out to Allan. "Mr. Lassiter, you're on my list." They shook hands briefly.

"Eli's doing the background check on Wilson," Lauren said.

"I've heard. A number of times, Lauren." Allan looked back at Eli and smiled. "Kind of boring, considering your subject."

"I don't know. The subject matter is getting more interesting all the time. Think we could sit down sometime soon?"

"Nothing I like better than talking about Wilson. Call my office. My secretary's name is Shelia. She'll set you up."

"I have called. Sheila's great, and you're a busy man." Eli reached in his back pocket then handed Allan his card. Allan pocketed it without looking.

"Sorry about that. I'll carve out some time. Why don't you call again?"

Lauren nudged him. "You could call after you check your calendar Allan. It might make it easier."

"Nope. That's fine. I track everyone down eventually." Eli smiled but it was clear he wasn't amused. Neither was he curt. Agents had a wonderful way of remaining polite while getting their point across. "I've tracked down a whole lot of people who knew the judge but I've really been anxious to talk to you about a few things in particular, Mr. Lassiter."

Lauren's eyes flicked toward Allan and back to Eli. She was about to suggest they simply make a date and stick to it when the doors opened in front and behind. The two men looked one direction and saw Barbara close the door to chambers. Lauren glanced the other way as a messenger blew in.

"It's a party," Barbara said dryly, accepting and signing for the envelope the messenger handed her as she raised a brow at Allan. She nodded at Eli. "Goodbye, Allan. Hello, Mr. Warner."

"Barbara." Eli nodded deferentially. "Is he in?"

"Yes. Do you need to see him?"

"Christ, everyone is on Wilson's calendar but me." Allan's laugh was strained and Eli's answer was full of camaraderie that galled Allan.

"Guess some of us are just lucky." Eli nodded at Allan and took a step around him.

"Yeah. Some are luckier than others. But then I guess you knew that, since you've been poking around in Wilson's life." He leaned over and kissed Lauren's cheek. "I've got to go."

"Well, I'm not too great at interpreting innuendo, Mr. Lassiter, so I'll just wait until we can talk plainly to know whether I should be upset." Eli's grin didn't falter until Barbara's cry cut the exchange short.

"Oh, my goodness! Look!"

Eli was quick and the first to examine the paper she held in trembling hands. Allan and Lauren joined him, pushing close. Allan reached for it, but Eli caught his wrist hard, squeezing Allan's ego at the same time.

"It would be best if you didn't touch it. The lab doesn't like to work any harder than it has to when it lifts prints." His advice was friendly, the pressure on Allan's hand wasn't. Lauren stepped around and took Allan's other hand. Connected to her, he finally stepped away.

Taking a Kleenex from the box on Barbara's desk Eli protected any existing prints on the paper while he held it up. This time they all read the rambling treatise that pretended to political substance. There was no signature; none of them doubted what it would be if it were there.

"Henry Stewart." Allan looked at her, but Lauren shook her head.

"I don't think so. Cranks are a part of the business. I think this is a piggyback and I'm surprised it didn't happen earlier. Henry's been so docile through this whole thing. I just don't think it was him."

"That could have been an act," Allan suggested.

"It could be anyone in the cell, or it could be anyone else with a grudge or a fantasy," Eli said then asked all three, "Are the marshals on Judge Caufeld?"

"He keeps dismissing them," Barbara said. "He thinks the idea that anyone would hurt him for doing his job is ridiculous."

Eli barely looked at any of them. "We'll have to put our men on him then. I'll talk to Mark Jackson about it." Eli slipped the message back into the original envelope and held it gingerly. "Do you have a bigger envelope I can put this in?"

Barbara gave him one and Eli slipped it in, smiling his thanks. Allan started toward chambers.

"Mr. Lassiter," Eli called, "I'd appreciate it if you could hold off going in there until I've had a chance to talk to the judge." Eli hesitated. There seemed to be more he wanted to say but decided against it. He held up the envelope. "I want to talk to him about this for one thing."

The moment was tense and Allan did little to ease it.

"All right. I'd like you to tell him that we were here and that we're concerned." Allan walked to the door. "Call me, Lauren. Tell Wilson to call me, Barbara. Let's not play any games. If anything happens to him, I'll hold you personally responsible." That was said to Eli and it was Lauren who offered an explanation if not an apology after Allan was gone.

"They're close. You'll have to forgive him."

"No problem. I'd feel pretty bad if everything wasn't done to protect that man in there, too." Eli put his hand on her arm. "This is a tough spot for you to be in what with the trial and everything. If it makes you feel any better, I'm going to be here for a while. I'll give you a call just to make sure you know he's handling things okay."

"Thanks. If you can ID this back to Henry, I know Wilson will revoke bail. I won't let him say no." She lifted her chin toward chambers then smiled at Barbara. "Promise you'll call me if you need anything." With a nod to Eli, she said something she never thought she would say to an FBI agent. "I'm glad you're here, Eli. Thank you."

"Just doing my job the way I was taught to do. Same way you do yours."

"Yeah. Taught by the best, huh?" Lauren smiled gently. "He just really doesn't need any more trouble right now. Not now when so much is happening." She left with a small, sad wave.

Eli watched her go knowing Lauren Kingsley had no idea what trouble might be in store for Wilson Caufeld, or that he was the one who was bringing it. Without another word, Eli knocked on the door to Wilson's inner chambers and was admitted.

"Eli." Wilson took off his glasses and smiled a greeting. His pleasure was perceptible and Eli walked with measured step to shake the man's hand.

"Judge." He nodded, still smiling though not with his usual ease. "I've got something you should see."

Immediately sobered, Judge Caufeld waited patiently while Eli removed the threatening letter. It was half out of the envelope when the door opened and an anxious Barbara poked her head inside.

"Everything all right in here?"

Eli nodded and the woman backed out, closing the door quietly. Still Wilson said nothing. He put his glasses back on as Eli put the paper in front of him. Hands clasped under the desk, Wilson leaned over and read it. When he was finished, he sat back and sighed, rubbing his eyes as Eli refolded it and sealed the envelope.

"Trouble, Eli. Nothing but trouble. That's what this case has been. I'm too old for this much trouble."

"Yes, sir." Eli sat down. He too clasped his hands in his lap and sat silently for a moment with the judge. He looked at the floor briefly, considering the word trouble. They looked at one another.

"You have something on your mind other than this drivel." The judge nodded curtly at the letter in the envelope.

Eli nodded gravely. "Judge, I'm afraid I'm not going to be making matters any easier for you."

Caufeld steeled himself with an almost imperceptible tightening of the muscles in his shoulder. But the judge's distress, if indeed that's what it could be called, was most evident in his eyes. Caufeld waited. Eli took another envelope out of his jacket pocket and passed it over the desk. It seemed that Wilson Caufeld looked at it for an eternity. When it was clear he was not going to take this envelope, Eli laid it on his desk and said quietly but without apology:

"I'd like to ask you a few questions about 1985, sir."

The air in Wilson Caufeld's lungs escaped through his barely open lips. The room seemed to darken, though it was hours before nightfall. Eli never took his eyes off Wilson. There was much to be learned at a time like this. Experience dictated that this was when he would discover something that usually did no one any good.

"I see, Eli," Wilson finally said as he touched the envelope lightly.

"Yes, I thought you might," Eli answered sadly.

Wilson listened to what Eli Warner had to say. He even managed to thank Eli for coming to him first. A flaw in a subject's background was usually worked up and presented in writing and given to the powers that be. Eli's visit was a most welcome consideration. He spent no more time than was necessary imparting his information, outlining the course he'd be pursuing in his investigation and determining that Wilson would not be shedding any light on these curious findings until the time was right. Eli was respectful when informing Wilson Caufeld that he would continue with his investigation, then he was gone.

Two hours later, Wilson called Allan, who promised to come to chambers by seven. He was there at seven forty-five. Late, as usual, and unrepentant. Wilson heard Allan's hearty hello to the men in the hall who had appeared to guard him an hour before Barbara left. He watched as an agent held the outer door open for Allan and almost chuckled at the appropriateness of it as an analogy for

Allan's life. Doors were always held open for him by those who assumed he deserved the courtesy or had earned the honor. Wilson heard Allan's promise: sports tickets for the men who kept safe the life of his precious friend. Yes, Wilson would have laughed if it all hadn't been so sad. The price tag Allan put on Wilson's safety was equivalent to a box seat at Dodger Stadium. But then Allan came through the door of chambers, brightening the office with his grin and energy and confidence and Wilson couldn't fault anyone for falling under Allan's spell.

"Glad to see you finally got smart, Wilson. Those are good guys out there. You'll be fine. What's the word? Was it Henry? Did they pick up prints? Did they pick up Henry?" Allan stopped at the credenza, flipped open the cupboard and grabbed a bottle of water from the small refrigerator hidden inside. He frowned at the label. "Judge, we're going to have to upgrade this fridge a bit."

He tossed his bottle of water from one hand to the other, and slipped out of his jacket, like a juggler, taking no notice of Wilson's silence. The last flourish as he sat down was to loosen his tie and cross one long leg over his other knee. He had arrived and was anxious to get this meeting going.

"I knew you wouldn't banish me till this thing was over." He sobered, but only slightly, and opened his water. "It's scary when someone's taking potshots at you, even if they are on paper. You need people around who care about you, Wilson. I only want to say one other thing and then we don't have to talk business. I really hope you'll reconsider and revoke Henry Stewart's bail. I suppose there's no question as to what you'll be doing about George."

Wilson had meant to take control of the moment but his resolve had deserted him. He felt dry inside, as if the life had been sucked out of him. He would have given anything not to have to face Allan with this news. Eli would have been kinder to demand an answer to his questions rather than gifting Wilson with time to consider a course of action. Actually, Eli would have been kinder to put a gun to his head.

"So," Allan said, tiring of the one-sided conversation.

"Is this a celebration, or have you just decided to break the news to me gently that you're going to ruin your entire future and let George Stewart walk?"

Wilson was still. Allan took another drink. This time, when he was done, he let the little bottle swing by his side, held casually between two fingers. With his other hand he touched the knot of his tie. It was already loosened.

Wilson took a deep breath. He felt a hundred years old as he moved far enough so that he could lace his hands on the desk in front of him. Wilson's head was lowered. The desk lamp was on but not the overheads so the shadows cast were deep and long. In that light, Wilson's heritage was more evident than it had ever been. His dark eyes may have pointed upward but they looked back to a time in history when men like him had to swallow their pride, standing mute and strong to keep their neck out of a noose. That time was past. Wilson's survival was no longer that of the body, but of the soul and that was a much harder fight. Allan, Wilson knew, believed in survival but he doubted he believed in the soul.

"Allan, this isn't about the Stewarts. This afternoon the FBI agent who is conducting my background check came to see me." Wilson tipped his head up just enough so he looked like Wilson again.

"I met him," Allan acknowledged tentatively. "Lauren seems to think he's a great guy." Allan was watchful, attuned to the nuances of the judge's behavior.

"Lauren suffers no fools. Eli Warner is a man dedicated to finding the truth and he has stumbled upon something in my history that affects you. He has discovered our lie." The word caught in Wilson's throat. He held his head high so that the lump would pass away. "Mr. Warner is most concerned about the last year you were with the firm, the year before I took the bench."

Allan Lassiter froze, only to relax with extraordinary grace and alacrity. He was a talented chameleon, changing with the light, conforming to the lay of the land in anticipation of danger.

"Really? Well, that's interesting." He swung his water bottle up, took a drink and then put it on the desk. "I don't know why I thought I wanted this. How about a real drink? Still keep Jack Daniel's on hand for me?'' Allan walked to the credenza again and opened the cabinet. He bent down, one hand holding the cabinet door, the other on the top of the piece of furniture. When he spoke, his voice was even, his words well thought out. ''I can't believe you're even worried about it. It happened so long ago. I don't know what he could have found, since there was no paper trail.''

He poured himself two fingers then wandered toward the desk. Gone was the playful, irreverent man Wilson loved, replaced by the lawyer Wilson had taught and trained and been so proud of.

''There was obviously something that made Mr. Warner take notice Allan. He asked appropriate questions.''

''Did he lay it out for you? Everything?'' Allan put his glass down on the desk and it hit hard. When he took his seat, he was wiping a bourbon stain off his cuff. It was unusual for Allan to be so careless, or to betray his agitation. Wilson had lived longer, so he could control his disappointment.

''No, but he has astute questions to which he will find answers. He alerted me to his concerns as a courtesy, and asked me if I would prefer answering his questions immediately.''

''And?''

''I asked him for some time. I told him there was someone else who would be affected by this investigation. I told him I had to consider his situation.''

''How nice of you. Why didn't you just bring him over to my place for dinner so we could all talk about it?'' Allan waved, letting it stand as an apology for the sarcasm. ''It's all right. Damage control shouldn't be too tough.'' Allan planted himself on the edge of his chair. His body was taut, his jaw locked. Here was the intense Allan who could work until dawn and argue with the angels on the devil's behalf. Here was the man that Wilson always hoped Allan would not become. ''I can call Mark Jackson and see if we can have this guy reassigned. I'll tell him that I was disappointed with the way Warner handled the threat.''

Allan's mind churned with options. He discarded the first and tried the second on for size. "No, no, we'll tell him that we believe he's a competent investigator, but there's some sort of personality conflict that's alienating your colleagues. Jackson will read between the lines. If he decides not to, then I'll be here with you when you talk to Warner. We're not talking rocket scientist here if this guy's spent his career doing background. We can convince him that to go further would be detrimental not only to you, but to the president who nominated you."

Wilson raised a hand wearily. "Allan, stop. You don't demean Mr. Warner by saying things like that, you only prove how short-sighted you are. I might point out that you demean me when you assume I will agree to such action."

"That was never my intent," Allan objected. "My intent is to protect you, Wilson. It's the least I can do after all you've done for me." Wilson watched him spin his tale. It was a good one, with just the right inflection of humility. Pushing away from the desk, Wilson stood, turned his back and walked to the window. Gently Allan rapped his knuckles on the desk as if to call him back. "What's going on Wilson?"

Wilson didn't answer. He looked out at the city. Twinkling lights gave the whole damned deserted place the look of a fairyland. He wished day would never come. But the sun was coming, Eli was bringing it.

"Allan, while I waited for you to come I thought about what we did all those years ago. I thought about what I'd become and what you'd become." Wilson tired of the view and looked at Allan. "I concluded that we were never the same after the moment we made our pact. We were never quite as close, never quite as open with one another, and that's because you can't be totally honest in a relationship if there is a secret that's kept and consequences aren't faced. I've spent my life making sure the people who come before me face what they've done and accept the consequences of their actions. Sadly, I made an exception in your case and it ruined us both."

"No, Wilson, it did not. You're about to make sure that

it does, though, and that's what I can't fathom. I'm willing to accept that you don't give two cents about me, but your future, Wilson!" Allan raised his arms as if framing Wilson's glorious destiny.

"Oh, Allan, don't play-act with me." Wilson's shoulders fell in disappointment. "You know that I acted because I loved you, and now I must act for me and my conscience. In my courtroom I've been harsher than I should, to people I don't know, because I tried to make up for my failings when it came to judging you. It's time to set the record straight. It's time for me to accept my punishment if it comes to that."

Allan blew out a breath, his head tilted up. Wilson was reminded of a picture from a childhood storybook where an ominous cloud with cheeks full, and lips pursed, blew the cold north wind across a cowering earth. That picture had frightened him as a boy. He wasn't afraid now, but he was sad that they would have to face a storm which neither of them would survive.

"You're going to tell Warner about what happened, aren't you?"

"No, I'll let him find out on his own if he can."

"And if he does and if he reports it?"

"I'll answer any questions put to me by the Senate," Wilson said flatly, "and I will answer them truthfully."

"You'll ruin me, Wilson."

"I suppose it would be too much to ask that your first thought would be of me," he said sorrowfully. Wilson shook his head when it appeared Allan might backtrack toward feigned sympathy. "Yes, there will be problems for you. Obviously there can't be any prosecution, but there will probably be action by the bar, your clients will have to decide if they would like to continue their association if you retain your license."

Allan stood up quickly and reached across the desk, startling Wilson as he picked up the telephone and put it in front of the old man. He wrenched the receiver off its cradle and held it out to Wilson. His voice was calm, in contrast to his actions.

"One phone call, Wilson, and this goes away. Take your

pick: the president's appointment secretary, the chief of staff, the president himself if you like. You can spill your guts to them and get your absolution. You won't scandalize these men. They'll look into things and figure out what to do. If they can't do anything, they'll let you walk away quietly. No one will be the wiser."

Wilson eyed the phone then let his eyes meet Allan's. Both men knew exactly what his answer would be, but for Allan hope sprang eternal until he heard the words.

"I will not cover a crime with a lie again. God has seen fit to present me with the crowning glory of my life, my nomination. At the same time He has reminded me that I am truly not worthy of the honor bestowed on me. This is a test of my mettle, Allan. This is a test of what kind of judge I will be, because now I must judge myself and you."

"This isn't about God, it's about circumstances." Allan pushed away and spoke clearly. There would be no mistake about where he stood. "It is about men doing what men do. You protected me and gave me a second chance. I've paid you back a hundredfold by being the kind of attorney you could be proud of."

"I wanted you to show me that you became a man I could be proud of," Wilson thundered, his voice rising so that the men outside took note. Almost instantly he lowered it. "I'm sorry. I'm sorry. I don't mean to lose my temper, but it breaks my heart that you miss this point. The mere fact that you do, means I failed and it means what I did was wrong beyond any measure." Wilson's eyes were tearful, yet in the face of Allan's selfishness Wilson put aside his emotions. "This is about ethics, not power. It's about character, not success. If I had done the right thing all those years ago then we wouldn't be having this conversation."

"No, we wouldn't. Then again, nothing would have changed for you back then, would it?" Allan goaded.

"Everything changed for me the minute I did what you wanted me to do. I just didn't know that until Eli Warner pressed me for an explanation and I had to face myself." Wilson listened to the silence and watched as Allan seethed. They were almost done. There was only a little more to say. "In my arrogance, Allan, I denied you an honorable future. You aren't the man you should have been because of me, not despite me. I am so sorry for that."

"I am what I was meant to be, Wilson. I'm successful, I have money, I have clients who respect me. That's a hell of a lot to destroy just because you want to ease your conscience." Allan's voice was flinty with fear. Wilson was stoic.

"If your material success is compromised, then so be it. Eli presented us with a second chance and I am going to take advantage of it."

"Nobody asked me if I wanted to participate, Wilson. Has it occurred to you that Eli Warner is a little man who sees a chance to make a big name for himself by taking the both of us down?"

"He is an honorable man doing his job, Allan." Now Wilson chuckled wearily. "There's a certain poetic justice that someone like Eli should be the one to call us into question. We pretend to such heights and yet who do we demand respect from? From men just like him. So why shouldn't he question our claim to it?"

"That's a bunch of esoteric crap." Allan snapped. "I don't want respect from him. I don't care about respect."

"Not even from me, Allan?"

"No, not even from you," he said, and it was the lack of hesitation that wrenched Wilson Caufeld. Allan leaned forward to underscore his frankness. "If it comes down to this, Wilson, I don't want your respect. I will accept that you are willing to give up a seat on the Supreme Court. I will help you decide the best way to handle that situation. I will accept that this is the end of our personal relationship. But I won't accept what you propose. You taught me the game, and I'm not going to let you change the rules now." Allan swallowed hard. He was forcing his anger back down inside because he knew Wilson too well. There was no way to argue with a man who saw so clearly that there were only two choices. Bad and good. There was, however, one way to appeal to him. "Walk away, Wilson. Please, I'm begging you. For me. Resign the confirmation, and the problem goes away. We can go on like before."

Wilson shook his head and it appeared to be hard to do so. "No. I owe a full hearing to the president who nominated me, to the people who have believed in me, and to myself. I must prove I'm not above the law, and you must accept that you aren't either."

"I'll be branded as a criminal. What we did was nothing compared to what others have done and gotten away with. Do you want me ruined? Is that what you want?"

"You know it isn't," Wilson said quietly.

"Then don't let them ask the questions. Don't say a word if they do."

Allan hesitated only a moment when he saw that Wilson remained unconvinced. He had no more time to waste. In three long strides he was back at his chair and putting on his jacket. He snapped the collar down and pulled at the lapels. He shook his cuffs. Anger rolled off him in waves.

"I don't have to even worry about this, Wilson. I don't know why I'm buying into this whole confession thing. If Henry Stewart doesn't get you, then the president's handlers are going to. They'll cut you loose the minute Warner turns in your file." Allan held his lapels and looked at Wilson Caufeld with clear, unremorseful eyes. "If that nomination doesn't die, Wilson, I'll call in my markers with the politicos and kill it myself. If that doesn't stop this nonsense there are laws against slander, Wilson, and I'll use them. I'll fight back with everything I've got. You'll be lucky to hang onto this seat, much less get another."

"Allan, please. This type of behavior will only hurt you more."

"No, it won't. I couldn't be hurt more. You betrayed me. You've betrayed the public. You're not winning any friends hedging on George Stewart's standing. You dealt yourself a blow by reducing Henry Stewart's bail. Now you're dead all the way around. Salvage what you can." Allan rotated his head. He licked his lips. He faced Wilson Caufeld and spoke concisely. "I want to be very clear,

Wilson, because I don't want another misunderstanding between us."

"There never has been a misunderstanding, Allan. We both knew exactly what we were doing."

"Oh, yes there was a misunderstanding. I thought what happened to us was between us." His voice warbled with emotion, and all of it was being expended on himself.

"It didn't happen to us," Wilson reminded him "We acted and it is time to face that."

Allan ignored the subtlety. "I'm going to start protecting my ass as of now. Do you understand that?"

"Yes, Allan, I do."

"And I'm not going to think twice about how I do it, and do you know why?" Wilson sat stoically in his chair knowing he would have to hear. "I won't think twice, because no one cares about honesty anymore, Wilson. They only care about the perception of it, and I can make people believe anything."

"You're wrong. I care. Eli cares about honesty. Lauren cares."

"Lauren!" Now Allan laughed harshly. "Lauren cares about rewriting history for herself. That's not honest."

"And this isn't about Lauren except in regard to how we will fare in her eyes," Wilson said forcefully, but that was not a subject that interested Allan.

"No, it isn't. In fact, I wonder what you'd be doing if all this was about Lauren." Allan's smile was cruel. He wanted to hurt, and he pulled out his arsenal indiscriminately. "But I suppose that's a stupid question. You're screwing her in court, you're going to screw me the minute you get the chance. Whatever the future brings, Wilson, I want you to remember one thing. You were my mentor. You showed me how far to push right and wrong. You showed me when to cut the corners. No one was hurt then, but a whole lot of people are going to be hurt now if you open your mouth. So, think about it, Wilson. Think who was the teacher and who was the pupil."

He stared at the old man with eyes that shined with one last desperate hope, but Allan's hopes were tied up with his fears and arrogance. Wilson's mouth tightened. Allan had no love for him and, with that understanding, Wilson knew there was no need to discuss the matter further so he said nothing.

"Fine, Wilson. Fine," Allan said quietly. "You're forcing my hand. I'll do what I have to do."

"And so will I," Wilson Caufeld answered. "So will I," he murmured again but there was no one left to hear.

Allan Lassiter was gone.

Wilson Caufeld was alone save for the men in the hall charged to guard his body.

Pity they couldn't have somehow saved his heart.

Chapter Ten

"Mr. Jackson?"

Mark put aside his magazine and stood up, adjusting his jacket as he did so. He was resplendent today. Pale blue shirt, white collar and cuffs. His tie was a subtle print of blue and brown and beige. His suit was navy. Blue was his color. Blue was his mood because he had found Nicholas Cheshire here, in one of the two places he hoped he wouldn't. The morgue was the first place on the list, a hospital the second. He supposed he should be glad he hadn't been summoned to number one.

"This way."

The nurse held out her hand to lead the way but followed it herself before Mark cleared the door. He tracked her down the hall, silently lamenting the changes in the world. Take nurses. They used to look like angels. This one looked like she'd just gotten out of bed. Her hair was permed and dyed once too often to look soft and touchable. No starched, authoritative little hat perched atop that horrid hair. Her clothes were no more a uniform than the sweats his wife wore around the house on cold days. She wore sneakers instead of those substantial, wedge-heeled white nurse shoes of decades past. He missed the days when women looked like women. Call him old-fashioned. If he was in a place like this an angel is what he'd want to see when he woke up, not someone who looked like they were just making a pit stop between carpool and the gym.

But he wasn't Nick, so he paid little attention to the woman when she ushered him into an office and closed the door. A doctor who looked like a doctor approached.

"Mr. Jackson. Dr. Temple."

The man smiled, and it didn't seem part of the job. They shook hands. The doctor's were soft and small-fingered. Mark would have been surprised to know that the doctor thought the same of his. But that's where the similarities ended. Mark's inscrutable expression was in direct contrast to the doctor's concerned one.

"Nice to meet you," Mark said evenly. "How's Nick doing?"

"I suppose as well as can be expected." The doctor moved, so did Mark and they both landed in chairs. The doctor made an offer before he actually sat. "Coffee?"

"No, thanks. I'm anxious to see Nick."

"I can understand that. I'm sorry it took us so long to find you. Agent Cheshire didn't have any identification on him when they brought him in. We had to work pretty fast just to get him stabilized and that really didn't happen until he was with us for about forty-eight hours. There was a mix-up with the local police, too. I don't exactly know what happened but no system's perfect. We're certainly glad you're here now."

"I am too, doctor. What are we looking at with Nick? He's pretty important to an investigation we're conduct-ing." Mark Jackson hesitated then added, "I might as well tell you, he's also a personal friend."

"I see." The doctor nodded and Mark wondered if he did, indeed, understand how Mark Jackson felt about Nick Cheshire. Mark couldn't have cared for him more if he was his own son. Dr. Temple seemed to read Mark's mind and pulled out all the stops on his bedside manner. He spoke with sensitivity and gentility. "Well, I must tell you Mr. Jackson, Nick isn't in any shape to help anyone, and I honestly can't tell you when he will be. Coma is unpredictable. He could open his eyes the minute you enter the room. It would be hard for him to talk because we've had to wire his jaw shut, but if he was to suddenly come out of it he might be able to communicate to yes or no questions. On the other hand, Nick could remain as he is indefinitely." Dr. Temple's voice softened even more. "We'll do everything we can, but eventually we'll have to transfer him to a facility that can properly care for him if his situation doesn't change. For now we're trying to deal with all his injuries, not the least of which is massive cerebral edema."

Mark Jackson plucked at the button on his jacket. His eyes never left the doctor's. He saw nothing behind them except professionalism, and that he could appreciate. That's how people saw him, after all. Everyone except Nick, who understood that Mark was his own worst enemy. There was something in Nick's demeanor that always made Mark Jackson stop and think, staving off Mark's natural impulsiveness. He owed him a lot for that.

"Doesn't sound too good, Doctor. What exactly is that and how are you going to take care of it?"

"Massive cerebral edema is an excess amount of extracellular fluid in the brain. That's what's causing him to remain unconscious. We did an MRI to determine there was no bleeding, so surgery wasn't necessary. Intravenous medication is causing decompression by absorbing the fluid around Agent Cheshire's brain cells. As decompression occurs, his status will change. Hopefully for the better." Dr. Temple gave him a tight-lipped smile. "Are you sure you don't want coffee?"

Mark shook his head and watched the doctor pour himself a cup. The man was thinking hard and, when he turned back, some decision had been made.

"Look, Mr. Jackson, I know this is none of my business, but whatever your agent was working on has really given me pause. I mean, in the final analysis, I'm just a citizen and what I saw when Nick Cheshire was brought in gave me the willies. I'm surprised he survived that beating. He must be dealing with some extraordinarily frightening people."

"I don't quite follow you," Mark said, and touched his mustache. He wasn't ready to confide in Dr. Temple no matter how good he'd been to Nick. But the doctor wasn't prying, he was trying to figure out what the world had come to.

"Nick's injuries weren't just sustained around the head. Those were serious, of course, but whoever beat him was extremely personal about the whole thing. Every single one of Nick's ribs were broken. That creates a flail chest, there's nothing to hold it up so he couldn't breathe." He used one hand to circle his own chest. "We had him on life support until the fibroblast . . ." Dr. Temple hesitated, even chuckled a bit. "Sorry, fibroblast are the connective tissue cells that grow between the ends of the fracture. Takes about four or five days for that to happen, and then he's okay breathing on his own."

"Sounds pretty standard to me. If someone's going to get beat up they're usually moving around trying to protect themselves." Mark still couldn't understand Dr. Temple's concern. "I can see how his ribs might be broken. People don't just lie there and let someone beat them over the head with a bat. That bat lands a whole lot of other places."

"Oh, certainly, I understand that. It's just the extent of these injuries. Agent Cheshire was meant to die, but he was meant to get an important message before he did. Someone wanted him to die, literally, without his balls." Doctor Temple cleared his throat. "I'm going to hate to tell him that he's actually going to have to live without at least one. He was beaten with great verve in the genital area and ended up with a massive hematoma. We had to do an emergency orchiectomy to remove the damaged testicle and control the bleeding."

Unprofessional as it was Dr. Temple shivered. Mark Jackson was statue still.

"I see," was all he could think to say.

He closed his eyes briefly. The bastards. Damn militia. He'd show them who had balls and who didn't the minute he got his hands on Henry Stewart and his buddies. He'd take one or two back for Nick—from each and every one of those slime buckets.

"We'll keep him comfortable, of course," Dr. Temple went on, back on track with his clinical talk and feeling quite comfortable the more he chatted. Mark appeared to listen, standing as soon as the doctor's tone indicated it was appropriate.

"I want to thank you for taking good care of him, doctor. Now, if you don't mind?"

"Of course. I'll walk with you. I need to check on him anyway."

They walked side by side until they reached Intensive Care, where Mark zeroed in on Nick's place before Dr. Temple could lead him there. He glanced at his friend, a young guy so dedicated to his work that he had followed orders and stayed where exposure was always a possibility. Mark let his eyes glaze over to buffer the shock of seeing Nick, then focused once more as Dr. Temple checked Nick's chart, fiddled with the machines surrounding the bed and spoke quietly to a nurse. The doctor pulled open one of Nick's eyelids and shined a pen-light then did the same to the other. Finally, he put his hand out to Mark.

"Stay as long as you like. Talk to him. Call me if there's anything more I can do."

When he was alone, Mark whispered, "Nick?" He touched the other man's hand. It was dry like his lips. His eyelids didn't flutter.

"Damn it all, Nick," Mark muttered as he hung his head.

He was actually finding a few words to say to God right then, and he used them over and over until he was exhausted with praying. He looked up when the nurse came in and laid his hand on Nick's bed, close enough so that the sides of their fingers touched, when she left. When another woman came in after midnight, Mark stretched.

"I'm going to get some food. Is it okay if I come back?"

"Sure, of course," she smiled softly and spoke quietly. He was glad she'd be with Nick. Before he left, though, she couldn't resist one question.

"Do you know who's responsible for this?"

Mark looked from her to Nick and his eyes lingered on the man in the bed. It was hard to recognize his friend given all the tubes and monitors.

"I don't know who did it," he said, "but I know exactly who's responsible."

She looked at him curiously, but Mark left without explaining further. The only thing on his mind was the man Mark Jackson held responsible for the situation Nick Cheshire was in: Wilson Caufeld. His damn letter of the law had kept Nick Cheshire in the militia camp too long. That was all that Mark Jackson could think about while he had a sandwich in the cafeteria. The thought that Caufeld deserved no less than what Nick had gotten stayed with him during the long night as he sat by the younger man's bedside. And, by the time dawn would have been breaking, if he had a window to see out of, Mark Jackson knew he had to do something to ease the guilt he felt for not pulling Nick Cheshire right out of the Independent Militia cell, despite Wilson Caufeld's idiocy. So, though it wasn't much, Mark Jackson flipped open his phone and dialed a number that put him in touch with one of the two agents who had spent the night outside Wilson Caufeld's home.

"Jerry? Mark. Listen, you're relieved as of now." Mark listened for a minute or two. "No. You're right. Wait until the day watch arrives and tell them the same thing. They're relieved the minute they get there. The old man doesn't want us there anyway so we might as well save the taxpayers a few bucks. As of now, Wilson Caufeld's on his own. He can call the marshals if he starts feeling scared." Mark Jackson disconnected and leaned over the bed. "I wish I could do more, buddy. Sure do wish I could do more."

From the Federal Courthouse in downtown Los Angeles it's a short hop to the charming town of South Pasadena. To get there, you drive the oldest leg of a freeway system that criss-crosses Southern California. You drive by China-town and Dodger Stadium then past the sign pointing the way to the Los Angeles Police Academy. That's where the Pasadena Freeway becomes two in-need-of-repair lanes in either direction. The off-ramps demand a certain daring-do to negotiate. It's not a ride to take drunk. Just when you think the curves will never end, you see a hill with a sign scripted in flowers or stone. It comes up so fast you can't tell what the town council had in mind when it came to gracing the entry to South Pas, as it is affectionately called. Not that it matters. Once you take the Orange Grove off-ramp, make a left, a right, and then a quick left you will forget that little sign and slow the car to admire the charming neighborhoods ribboned with classic California bungalows. You'd probably pull over to admire the one that belongs to Edie Williams because it is a showplace.

The privileged few to visit Edie's house inevitably come away impressed at how impeccably it is kept, how astonishingly feminine the trappings. The postage-stamp lawn, front and back, is green year round, the flower beds are cut to precision and always blooming with the season's best. The crowning glory of her castle are the hydrangea bushes with their antique pink floral pompoms. Edie would tell you that the bushes were planted by the original owner in the early twenties. She looks at the flowers when she says this, so a visitor won't see how proud she is to be the caretaker of plants that survived so much. The calla lilies are a bit younger, but not by much, and equally treasured. Edie's house is pink stucco with white wood trim and a front door that is as close to black as burgundy lacquer can get. She loves her house, but she loves it most when Allan is there. He doesn't come often yet she keeps the special coffee he likes so much on hand for when he does.

She was thinking about that coffee when the soft morning light came through the old multi-paned windows and cast shadows on the wall over the top of the walnut highboy. A lone hydrangea blossom rested in the crystal vase on the dressing table. It was a Martha Stewartesque still life and, lying in her bed, Edie was impressed by the perfect moment. From the Camille-like wilting of dying petals to the tortoise shell brush still kissed with pale face powder that lay beside the vase, to the sound of the birds in the tree outside her window and the man sleeping beside her, every detail of that instant was as flawless as any Edie had ever had.

But perfection was a thing with a life span as lovely and fleeting as her treasured flowers. Perfection only lasted as long as no one else knew about it. The second someone did, they spoiled it all. Abram had proved her theory when he diluted her involvement in the perfect case. Allan diluted the impeccability of their lovemaking when he gave affection so minimally as to be almost imperceptible. Lauren disturbed the superiority of Edie's cross examinations because everyone believed Edie to be second seat.

So, in order to survive, Edie redefined the concept of perfection. She felt superior knowing that she was the power behind the strategy Lauren would present in court. Edie had mastery over her relationship with Allan because she understood he was needy when he, himself, did not. Abram? He would not be the U.S. Attorney forever. One day, she would take his job and do it better.

She lay quietly thinking of all this, watching the shadows move, knowing she should have been up and on her way to work already. But Caufeld was still silent, and rumor had it he was struggling with his decision, so Edie knew there would be no surprises waiting at the office that might need her attention. But there was a surprise right there beside her. He had appeared on her doorstep the night before drunk as a skunk. That was new. That was a curiosity. She took him in, took him to bed. He passed out before she could get him coffee so Edie undressed Allan, and slept with him and now left him as she threw her covers off and got out of bed. Standing naked in the golden light, she leaned over the bed and used one hand to touch Allan's hair.

"Do you want to wake up?" she whispered.

He shook his head. Edie smiled. He wasn't running out, and he hadn't snapped at her. It was almost perfect, but she wouldn't know that until she knew what had put him in such a horrid state the night before. Then, when she had that information, Edie would decide if she felt privileged or used. She touched his hair once more and left him to wake on his own.

Her dressing gown was aqua, a stunning find at a small store that sold old clothes. The proprietress didn't know the difference between used and vintage so Edie got it for a song. She swore she could feel the woman, as tall as she, who had first owned this satin gown with the lace-trimmed train. Edie wrapped the belt as she went wondering what kind of man that woman had left sleeping in her bed so many years ago. In the kitchen she put on the favored coffee and reached for her cigarettes. She was half-way through the first of each when Allan came in.

"I don't like it when you leave before I do," he grumbled.

"I don't have the leisure you do. People notice if I don't get to work until noon." Edie looked him over. Pity he'd slipped into the underwear she had lovingly removed the night before.

"I may not even have to bother getting up soon. I can just stay here all day doing nothing."

Edie cocked her head. She took a drag from her cigarette and looked closely at Allan as he poured himself a cup of coffee and leaned his rear against the cranberry tile of the kitchen counter. He held the coffee and looked into the cup. Edie watched, trying not to appear meddlesome. She'd seen people act like this before, people who had things to tell. Usually they were criminals ready to confess to a crime. But this was Allan, and confession was not a concept he grasped easily. More important, if he had something to tell, why tell her when Lauren Kingsley and Wilson Caufeld, ever excellent and pure, shone in Allan's universe?

"I'm all ears, Allan," Edie said carefully.

He put his free hand to his face and rubbed. He closed his eyes. He breathed deep.

"I feel miserable, Edie. I thought I could hold my liquor." He laughed and it was at himself. Edie could hardly believe her ears. "Ever trust anyone completely, Edie?"

"No, I never have," she said, then added, "I guess that's why I can be trusted. I guess," she pushed her luck and tried to minimize the sound of her excitement, "that's why you know you can trust me. I know how it should be done."

She stubbed out her cigarette in the apple-shaped ash-tray on the table and shook back her hair. It was just long enough to graze the edge of her neck. Finally she screwed up her courage and looked him straight in the eye. Allan was looking right back at her, staring at her as if seeing her for the first time.

"You know what, Edie? You're right. I do trust you more than anyone on this earth. I thought it was Wilson I trusted most, but it isn't."

"Lauren?" Edie asked quietly, not unaware that a bomb had just burst right there in her kitchen, but too shell-shocked to assess the damage—or opportunity—yet.

"Lauren," Allan scoffed, then shrugged. "How can you trust someone who doesn't have time to be anyone's best friend?"

"I have time, if the friend's worthwhile."

"I wouldn't blame you if you threw me out after last night. I wouldn't blame you at all, so you better rethink what you're saying because this ship is sinkin', babe. So you can just shove me overboard if you want. Everyone else has a sword at my back."

"Ships don't have to sink. There's always a way to plug a hole, or bail the thing, Allan." Edie rose. She shimmered in her aqua satin gown. The world she was moving through was changing as she got closer to Allan. Finally, she felt powerful and connected to him. Edie took Allan's cup and set it aside. Her fingertips touched him first before her palms brushed against his face.

"I never realized you were an optimist, Edie."

"I'm a realist, Allan, and I'm telling you there's nothing that can't be fixed. You just need the right person to help you when the problem's big. You came here because you know that I'm the right person."

Allan eyed her, up and down. He seemed to dissect her, trying to find out what made her tick. Edie didn't shrink from his scrutiny. This was what she'd been waiting for and she knew she'd pass muster. She smiled.

"God, Edie, I'm glad you're here." He took her in his arms and held her almost tenderly. "I'm in trouble. I'm in very, very big trouble."

Edie didn't move. She lay in his arms, afraid to break

the spell by putting her own around him. He put his chin on the top of her head and started to talk.

By the time he finished, Allan had run the gamut from rage to near-tears self-pity. Allan's story made him wander from her, arms flailing, hands reaching as if there was something important that was just out of his grasp. Finally he sat in solitary misery and that was when Edie Williams knew this was an opportunity that would not come again. She considered what he told her. The historical circumstance was fascinating, the current situation amazing and the problem one that seemed almost impossible to overcome.

But when Edie knelt at Allan Lassiter's feet, she knew only one thing for sure. She knew that, between the two of them, they would figure this out or kill themselves trying. Nothing mattered except Allan's survival and Edie knew, if she insured that, they would be bound forever no matter what happened.

"Hi."

Lauren smiled as she stuck her head through the door. Barbara returned the smile and waved Lauren in even though she was on the phone. Lauren closed the door behind her and sat while she waited for the conversation to end.

"Yes. I'll tell him. I apologize again. No, he's feeling fine. Yes, I'll definitely call if anything changes. Thank you for being so understanding. I'm sure the judge will appreciate it. Yes. Of course. Goodbye." Finally, the phone was hung up and Barbara collapsed in her chair, worn out. She pursed her lips and puffed and tried to smile. The result wasn't quite reassuring. "I don't think I can handle another one of those calls."

"It didn't sound pleasant," Lauren commented, happy to bear the small talk to find out why she'd been summoned.

Barbara gave her a sidelong glance and picked up a pencil. It was red. She opened her calendar and drew a large X through one of the little date blocks.

"I probably shouldn't have called you. The judge would have my head if he knew I was doing this, but I'm kind of at my wits' end."

"What's going on?"

"This has nothing to do with the Stewart trial, Lauren. You know I'd never compromise you, or him, in any way on that. But something's happened. Two days ago everything was fine. Now I've got instructions to cancel everything. I mean everything." She flipped the calendar. It was filled with big red X's. "The dinner at Loyola Law School. He adores that school and was so looking forward to getting the award from the Alumni Association. Now he doesn't want to go. He told me to make up any excuse. Lunch with Judge Weems. Canceled. The Women's Defense Lawyers Luncheon. Canceled." Barbara looked up, Lauren raised a brow. "Take your pick. Every single appointment has been canceled, personal and professional."

"Look, Barb, we're heading to the wire here on the Stewart thing. Maybe he just needed to be alone while he figured this one out." Lauren couldn't catch the fever. "You've got to admit it's not exactly your run of the mill decision. Have you seen the papers today? The Independent Militia has been flooding the clerk's office with paperwork. I'm beginning to think they've got five hundred members stashed away somewhere churning out liens and complaints. Eric Weitman and Joe Knapp are holding daily press conferences and they've got George Stewart all spit and polished like he's a Cub Scout leader. The judge is probably just feeling the pressure. I am, and all I have to do is wait." Lauren winked. "Besides, the P and A's I gave him are stunning. He's probably drafting his opinion to include kudos for the most brilliant attorney on the face of the earth." Barbara didn't laugh. Lauren took her cue. "You're worried."

"I'm worried," the secretary admitted. "I don't know if I really should be, but, Lauren, there is something in his voice that just doesn't sound right. It's like he's just given up. He sounds awful, kind of like he's lost his best friend. He hasn't called the president's appointment secretary back either. They're trying to schedule the hearings. I keep passing the message along and the judge never calls."

"That's not good." Lauren bit her lip.

She sat back and considered the situation with one foot crossed over her knee. She touched the slender heel of her pant boot. The thought that she should have bought into the chunky heel craze crossed her mind and made her smile. Nothing like finding the mundane, or the insane, interesting when you want to avoid thinking about something serious. It was the laundry when her mother died, shoe heels for Wilson. It seemed appropriately balanced. Shoe heels were not as dire as laundry, Wilson's sudden solitude was nothing compared to her mother's suicide.

"Well, did he go to the doctor? Could it be something like that?"

"No," Barbara answered. She touched the calendar. "I can account for every minute until I left him that night."

"So, that was the day he got that stupid letter. I suppose I'd want to kind of lay low, too, if I were him." Lauren tapped that shoe heel a couple of times. "You know, everybody's antsy. Abram can hardly contain himself. He wants me to read tea leaves to figure out which way Wilson's going to call this thing so he can ready an appropriate press release. Mark Jackson's dropped off the face of the earth. Edie, well, Edie's wound tighter than a spring. I know she's worried."

"She must be because she's not thinking straight. Edie's been in here a couple of times."

"Looking for the judge? She never told me. I'm surprised she'd do that without me."

"It wasn't official, if you can believe that."

"No kidding? Something personal?"

Barbara shrugged, "She never said more than she'd check back when I told her he wasn't available. Finally, I just told her he was home and I'd give him the message. She said fine and that's the last I heard from her."

"Whatever, I'm sure she'd fill me in if it was something to do with the Stewarts."

"Right," Barbara muttered and Lauren tipped her head. Barbara turned big, innocent eyes up toward Lauren. "I mean right. I'm sure she would. Edie's a professional all the way."

The two women paused, then laughed. Lauren said, "You think she's still stinging about the change of assignment."

"Oh, I would think so."

"Well, I give her a lot of credit then, because you'd never know it. She's been working her tail off. She's been holed up in her office with the door closed for a couple of days now." Lauren stood up, still grinning. "Look, Wilson's fine. We're still on calendar for Monday. He'll give us an answer and we'll scramble to do whatever we've got to do." Lauren's voice softened. "You know, I'm not pleased about the roadblock he put in my way, but I wouldn't want to be in his shoes for anything. It takes a lot of guts to do what you think is right when the FBI is poking around and dissecting your life, newspapers are printing half truths and pundits are taking potshots at you." Lauren shook her head. "Let Wilson have some quiet time. The man's surrounded by agents sworn to protect him. If they do half as good a job protecting as they do harassing people then we don't have a thing to worry about."

With a rap on Barbara's desk, she threw her a grin and headed out, pausing before she closed the door behind her. Something bothered Lauren but she couldn't put her finger on what it was. In the hall she tugged on her jacket, feeling suddenly hot. Then she realized it wasn't the hall, but Wilson's office that had caused her to feel so odd. It had been cold as a morgue in there. Funny, she never remembered feeling cold in chambers before.

Passing it off, Lauren closed the door and headed back upstairs. Monday would come soon enough, the motion would be ruled on, the trial would proceed. Three weeks, tops, and they'd be sending the thing to the jury. In a month this would all be over and—win or lose—she'd be back in Wilson's chambers having sandwiches brought in at the end of a long day while they waited for Allan to pop in with a kiss for her, a slap on the back for Wilson. All would be well. All was well now, really, and there was work to be done. Just in case, though, on the off chance that something was amiss, Lauren put in a call to Allan. She left a message for him while she went through her own.

As she hung up the phone, Edie popped in with questions on the direct they intended for the clerk at the gas station where the Stewarts filled up the truck an hour before the bomb detonated. Lauren answered her. She almost asked what had taken her to Wilson Caufeld's office, but Edie was gone fast. Knowing it was really none of her business, Lauren flipped through the little pink slips in her hand. Phil, one of her case agents, called to tell her to hightail it over to the Westwood offices because they had a woman who was positive she'd seen Henry Stewart in a house behind hers. Phil wanted her to bring a warrant. Lauren wanted to see the lady first. There was a report on George Stewart and the visits with his wife. She put that aside and sat down to sift through the rest.

Right in the middle was the one that made her raise a brow. Allan had called. He wanted her to come to his place at seven. What a great coincidence. She'd definitely be there and get his take on Barbara's concerns. Lauren set aside the pink slips and picked up a report that had been left in the middle of the desk. That's when she saw her last message. Attached to a bag of M&Ms with nuts was a note: "I was here, where were you?"

Chapter Eleven

Her car was getting better. The mechanic, considerate as any specialist could be, consoled her that the cost was nothing compared to the health of a racing-green, rag-top MG. When Lauren stopped at the first stoplight she thought she should call Eli to tell him about her car, thank him for the candy and maybe figure out how they might be able to get together again. At the second light she thought about Allan. Funny how she just realized she hadn't spoken to him in days. When Wilson first began his deliberations, Allan called incessantly with ideas on how to sway his thinking. Then, suddenly, nothing. Perhaps Allan did know something she didn't as Edie suggested so long ago. By the time she hit the freeway Lauren was free-associating with thoughts of Allan, Wilson, Eli, her car, her checkbook, Eli and Wilson and Allan and back again.

The background noise for these thoughts was all the talk by all the people who had an opinion on everything from Henry's whereabouts to Wilson's chances for confirmation. Secretaries and people on the street, reporters hounding her and Edie avoiding her. Abram not quite as patient, not quite as accommodating as he had been when he first appointed her, added his two cents. And, to make it all seem a royal mess, she was assaulted with the sights of the night.

Cars heading East on the Santa Monica Freeway zoomed past, their headlights creating a stream of liquid gold. Ahead of her, an equal number of taillights left a fiery trail to follow. Mesmerized, focused on lights ahead of her and behind, and suddenly tired, Lauren almost missed her exit.

The rental didn't have the handling of the MG but she managed the turn just in time to zoom off on Robertson, wind her way up to Olympic Boulevard, hang a left then a right on Avenue of the Stars and another right into the high-rise that housed Allan's condo. Pulling into the underground parking she had two thoughts: she was late and Allan's parking space was empty, which meant that he was later still.

Carolyn Stewart wiped her hands on her apron when she heard the car pull into the driveway. She went to the front window and saw that Paul had left the headlights on when he pulled in. Anyone who was watching could see everything that was happening. Three men got out of the car, taking their time closing the doors. They hitched their pants, they pulled grocery bags out of the back seat and they laughed. Finally, Paul turned off the headlights and they all walked up to the porch that blazed with light. They rang the front bell politely. If anyone was watching it would look like a visit to a woman in need of company. That was Carolyn's cue. She hurried to the back door and opened it, hoping any surveillance had been diverted by the men on the front porch. Henry flew into her arms, a moth to a dim flame.

"I've got to get the others. You go on downstairs," she whispered even though they knew the house was clean.

She held him close for a second more and then pushed him on. He felt thin. He smelled awful. She was glad she hadn't seen the house where he was staying. She pirouetted back to the door by the second ring.

There were hearty greetings all around. A grocery bag was put in Carolyn's hand and much show was made of looking inside. Then the door closed against prying eyes. Grocery bags abandoned, they all went downstairs to the room where Henry waited. This time a table was set up. The meeting was smaller than the last. Henry didn't bother to ask why.

"Hey, son," Paul slapped him on the back, "how's our fugitive doing? You're giving them all fits disappearing like that. Still haven't heard anything about death threats on the news. You sure you sent that letter?"

Henry gave him a sickly smile. Carolyn touched her son's hand under the table.

"Yeah," Henry answered.

"Good boy. Let's just get down to it. Carolyn's been to see George. Told him we've been taking care of our end, right Carolyn?" The men chuckled and Carolyn nodded. "She's got some instructions. Is he happy about the liens?" Paul looked around the table with a huge grin. It had been his idea to start that campaign after he read about another group doing the same thing. "We've been giving that court a time of it. Put liens on every piece of federal land in Southern California."

"Yes, he's happy with the paper flood, but it's not affecting the judge. George says it's time to send a message to Caufeld. He's getting too much attention. We need to control things." Carolyn spoke softly, keeping her eyes on the table. She didn't want to see the glee in the older men's eyes and she didn't want to guess what she might see in her son's when she gave them George's directive. "He says to tell you he wants a warning only this time, and it's up to you as to how you'll do it."

"I don't know why we're playing these games." James was talking. "I think we ought to just blow him to kingdom come. We should get it over and done with. That would send a message."

"No." Carolyn was adamant. "That would just make people mad. George wants everyone to be afraid. If it's something that kills Caufeld they'll tighten security on all the Feds and none of the regular people are going to listen to us anymore. No." Carolyn looked up, her eyes ablaze. Her husband had been specific and remembering his voice, his passion, the feel of his hands on hers as he gave instructions, gave her strength. She turned to Henry. "He wants you to do it, Henry. He wants you and Paul to start a campaign now. He says it's time you took your proper place."

Henry's cheek twitched.

"I don't want to, Mom," he said quietly.

Beside him Carolyn didn't react. She was aware that Paul wanted to lay into her son but wouldn't until she set the tone. She licked her lips and pretended she didn't hear the comments of derision.

"Your father wants you to do something to make Mr. Wilson Caufeld aware that neither your father, nor you, nor any of our group of concerned citizens, recognizes his authority. Mr. Wilson Caufeld has not responded to our pleadings or our needs. Force is the only avenue left to us."

"You're not going to get him to change his mind." Henry sat up and took his mother's arm, forcing her to look at him. "You're not going to change his mind about Dad, or what Dad wants, or what any of you want. If we hurt him for doing his job isn't that wrong?"

"I can't believe you're even saying this. After everything your father and I have taught you." Carolyn shifted for the first time, uncomfortable, now that George's name had been personally invoked.

"Does it mean I have to agree with everything, Mom? I know what happened to you and Dad, but are we supposed to keep hurting people? What if they tried to hurt us?"

"You don't think that's just what they're doing?" Frank took center stage, anxious to be part of the conversation. "If they convict you and your dad, you're going to fry. You will be dead in the electric chair, kid, and you don't think that's hurting you?"

"Naw, they do that injection now." Paul grabbed Henry's arm and poked at the vein. Henry tried to pull back but Paul wouldn't let him go.

"You think they're going to look at your pretty face and decide you're too nice a guy to kill? Listen Henry, if you don't get them, they'll get you, and that's exactly what we're fighting for." Horrified, Henry looked into Paul's angry eyes. He pulled away, afraid to tell him that the last bit made no sense. How could they be fighting so that everyone would have the privilege of trying to get at one another? Paul didn't have a clue, he was just thrilled with the chance to terrorize Henry. "You want to tell your dad that you're not with us? Is that what you want to do to a man who gave you life, put a roof over your head and stood up to a government so strong it could take that roof away, destroy his credit, make him want to die? Is that what you want to do?"

Henry shook his head and hung it low.

"Then show some guts, Henry. That's what your mom and dad expect. Show some guts, or get out." James pushed his chair back and the legs scraped on the linoleum floor. He went to the chest and came back, putting a gun in front of Henry. "Show some guts," Paul whispered, "or get out. But if you get out, then you're one of them, Henry."

The three men stood up and went upstairs leaving Carolyn alone with Henry.

"Haven't you learned anything?" she asked wearily before leaving without another word.

Henry hunched over the table, the gun only inches from his nose, wished there was someone to talk to who he trusted. He wished Nick Cheshire had been there. Just looking at Nick could make Henry feel at peace even if he didn't know what was right.

But Nick hadn't been there and the others were waiting to take him to find Wilson Caufeld. There really wasn't any choice. He picked up the gun, put it in his belt and walked slowly up the stairs.

Edie Williams sat in her car and looked at Wilson Caufeld's house. It was a big house for a man who lived alone. A car was parked half a block down and Edie assumed Mark's men were either inside or about. They would probably recognize her even in the dark, so if she wanted to just walk up and ring Wilson Caufeld's doorbell she could. They wouldn't stop her. Caufeld would come to the door. She would say she was there to talk about Allan. Simple. Professional. A straightforward approach.

She could do that.

But what would she say after that?

Edie picked up her heavy purse and flipped off the headlights.

She would appeal to his emotions.

She put her hand on the door latch and got out of the car. Before she could close the door a car came down the street. It rolled slowly forward so she hung onto the door, waiting for it to pass. Suddenly her attention was diverted. A car came out of Wilson Caufeld's driveway, the headlights so bright she had to put her arm across her eyes but not before she saw the judge at the wheel.

Oh Lord. Damn it all anyway. Wilson Caufeld was driving away. The car down the street pulled out and the one driving toward her stopped then pulled into a driveway. Edie didn't know if it turned around because she was busy getting back in the car, and starting the engine.

Lauren used the garage elevator key. She'd knocked to make sure Allan wasn't home then used the other key on the ring to get in. Pocketing them both, she slung her purse on the couch, walked to the picture window and took a minute to enjoy the view as she always did.

The view was a stunner and Allan's home was a showplace that it never occurred to Lauren to covet. Even the thing she most desired, closure over the circumstances of her mother's death, seemed to be losing it's grip on her. That left one big, burning question. What was it she wanted? To put the Stewarts away? To have a relationship? To feel wanted instead of competent? To beat Wilson? Impossible, that last one. All the others were feasible.

Lauren smiled. What she wanted was for Allan to get home so she could find out what it was he wanted. She put on water for tea then dialed his office. Allan barked his hello, apologized absently when she identified herself and told her he'd be there in twenty minutes when she asked how much later he would be. Lauren added ten minutes to the twenty he promised, took much of that time deciding what she wanted to order in and finally decided on Kung Pao chicken, egg rolls and steamed rice. She had just tucked her feet under and turned on the big screen when the doorbell rang. Once, twice and a quick two shots at the end. Too early for the delivery man but Lauren grabbed her money anyway and opened the door.

"Edie!"

No little white containers, no smell of Kung Pao chicken, only Edie Williams looking as surprised as Lauren. Edie managed to compose herself first.

"Lauren." They looked at one another. Edie was uncomfortable, a laughable situation if she thought Lauren didn't know about her relationship with Allan.

"Is Allan here?" She cleared a slight catch in her throat.

"No. I'm expecting him any minute." Lauren stood back, both hands on the door, hoping against hope Edie would say no when she asked, "Do you want to come in?"

Edie's eyes flicked left, then right. She pulled her purse across her front.

"He's not here, then?"

"No," Lauren said again, then it dawned on her. If Allan wasn't there, why was Lauren? Lauren took the keys out of her pocket and dangled them. "I check his mail when he's out of town."

"Oh." Edie stretched her neck; it was long and beautiful and flushed and the woman was embarrassed. Lauren made amends.

"Come on in. Come on," she urged. "Were you supposed to meet him here, too?"

"No." She stepped across the threshold. "He wasn't expecting me. I just thought he'd be here, you know." Edie walked to the middle of the living room, her hands still clutching her purse strap, her elbows sticking out behind her as she bent from the waist to search for Allan. She twirled back to Lauren. "You know this is really uncomfortable. I mean, I like to keep things separate. You know, work and . . . well . . . this. I should probably go."

"He's probably on his way," Lauren looked at her watch. "I suppose I expected him by now."

Edie minced toward the bedroom. Lauren took a step after her then backed off. It wasn't as if Edie had never been there before.

"Listen, just have him call me. I'll be home in about forty-five minutes. He's got the number." Edie spun around. She almost lost her footing and that embarrassed her more. Worse, her clumsiness made her angry. Lauren had seen that look many a time in the office and really didn't want to deal with it here.

"If you think you should." Lauren counted the seconds until Edie made good on the suggestion. She didn't. Lauren couldn't figure out what she wanted exactly. "Look, Edie, I don't know what you're thinking about Allan and me, we're just . . ."

Just then the door opened and there was no need to explain anything. Allan was home. He could decide who it was he wanted to see and if it wasn't her she would gladly leave.

"Hey Lauren," he said wearily as he tossed his keys on the counter. He stopped, on his guard, a minute later. Edie and Allan exchanged a look that that seemed neverending. Pale and cautious, Allan recovered first. "Edie. What brings you here?"

"I . . ." Another glance Lauren's way. A fidget. Edie's jaw twitched. "Nothing. Nothing. I just needed to . . . You know, this isn't a good time. I didn't know you had company, and I feel like an idiot barging in. Call me, Allan. I'll see you tomorrow, Lauren."

"I'll walk you to the door." Allan put his hand out and she smiled as she took the first few steps only to lose him when the phone rang. "Just a second, and I'll get you all the way downstairs."

Allan went for the phone. The doorbell rang. The food arrived. Edie stood in the middle off the commotion, not quite family, not quite a guest, and her equivocating presence annoyed Lauren, who was trying to figure out how to stretch the food when she heard the thing that had kept Edie transfixed.

"Shot? Shot?" Allan kept asking.

Lauren put the bag on the kitchen counter and walked

into the living room to stand beside Edie. Tall and dark, petite and light, the two women were a study in contrast but they were both of the same mind. Who had been shot? Unfortunately, there was an answer a second later.

"Wilson? Judge Caufeld? Where?"

Lauren's hands flew to her mouth. "Oh, God."

"How?" Allan's mouth hung open. Pained eyes looked toward the women, darting from one to the other. Lauren stepped back, afraid he might hand her the phone, but it was held firmly to his ear.

"Dead?" Allan whispered and closed those eyes of his. "Wilson's dead."

"No," Edie murmured.

A moment later, Allan's hand fell to his side and Edie Williams collapsed on his perfect white carpet while Lauren Kingsley watched.

"Oh, God, no."

To Lauren her own voice sounded odd. How could such a hollow and frail sound come from a person so competent in a crisis? Crouched down, Lauren touched Edie's face. It was warm and pale. Her eyelids fluttered. Lauren was with her when she came 'round but Allan was the one who helped Edie to the couch. Relieved of duty, Lauren began to shake.

"Allan." She followed him to the couch. "Did I hear you right? Did I?"

Allan went rigid. He didn't straighten nor did he look at Lauren. How could he look her in the eye?

"That was the LAPD. The sergeant identified himself properly." Finally he turned to face her, keeping a hand on Edie's shoulder. "They found Wilson about half an hour ago, Lauren. Someone shot him and he died." Edie groaned and put her head low toward her knees. He seemed torn between the two women and then chose Lauren. Taking her by the shoulders Allan tried to pull Lauren toward him. "I'm so very sorry, Laurie. So very, very sorry. I'm going to see him. I'll take care of everything."

"I'll go . . ." Lauren pulled back, but his grasp was tight.

She put her hands onto his chest and held him back. Suddenly her eyes widened. It dawned on her what she was about to offer. Lauren raised her hands as if burned and broke from his grasp. Putting rigid fingers to her lips she whispered.

"I'm sorry, I can't go again. I thought I could, but I can't go to the morgue. I can't . . ." She was sorry she couldn't accept his comfort and was sorry she had none to offer. Lauren was sorrier still that she was a coward and glad he wasn't. Three strides and Lauren had her purse on her shoulder, her hand on the door and nothing but determination to leave. But she couldn't open it. Not without an answer. "Twice, Allan. First my mother and now Wilson. Am I cursed? Where is God?"

Knowing there was no answer, Lauren stepped into the hall. Before she closed it, Lauren heard Edie's voice not quite as horrified and hollow as her own had been, asking Allan:

"Is he really? Is he dead?"

Lauren called the LAPD from home. Wilson's death was confirmed. She had called Eli's office, but it was late and he wasn't there. She asked that he be paged. There was no one else to call. The apartment was deathly quiet, so Lauren got back in her car, heading nowhere in particular. She never made it to nowhere. Lauren stopped at the Federal Courthouse thinking she would try to work until her mind could fully function again.

She pulled on the glass door, anxious to get to her office, now that a decision had been made. She pulled so hard the building seemed to shudder. A cry came out of nowhere and Lauren fought it back, falling against this formidable and immovable object. The guard who came to investigate peered at her through the double glass doors as if she was a nut.

"Let me in. Let me in." She pleaded even though he couldn't hear her. Lauren pantomimed. He could see, for God's sake. Finally, Lauren fumbled with her purse, found her credential and slapped it against the door. The metal edge of her gold badge scratched the glass. The man moved closer and Lauren stepped back as he unlocked the door.

Lauren thought she remembered to say thank you when she finally got in. She might even have said hello. The metal detectors were turned off for the night so she ignored them, and walked past the high desk where the guard sat reading every night. She was almost to the elevators when he put his hand on her shoulder. Lauren jerked away and spun toward him. There were angry words on her pale lips, but she didn't have to say them. The look in her eyes was enough to make him drop his hand.

"Lauren Kingsley. I'm going to the twelfth floor. I'm going to my office." He could fill in the night register if it was that important.

Lauren didn't go to the twelfth floor, though. She stopped on the fifth and walked down the hall, going faster as the echoing of her heels bounced off the walls. At the high and wide doors that opened to Wilson Caufeld's courtroom Lauren dropped her purse and used both hands to pull at the handle of the locked courtroom door. That's when Lauren fell apart.

She pulled harder. Her chignon came undone. Her hair billowed out around her shoulders, falling over her face, obscuring her view as she grunted with the effort of her work. If she could just open the door, Wilson would be there waiting for her, smiling at her and telling her that hard work always paid off. They would speak once more if she could just get that door open.

"Let me in," she muttered as she pulled. "Let me in, Wilson. Don't be gone . . ."

Lauren's hands slipped once then she attacked again. The racket she made could have roused the dead. How she wished it would. Wilson had died when she was disappointed in him, angry at his rulings, miffed that he hadn't put her first. He had died trying to do the right thing while she had complained endlessly. Wilson was dead and she hadn't said goodbye. Wilson had died alone just as she was alone now.

Lauren heard nothing except her own pleas careening

around in her head; she felt nothing except her power-lessness against the stronger metal locks. So intent was she on proving everyone wrong, Lauren didn't hear the footfall of a man coming toward her. It wasn't until he pressed himself against her, grasping the wrists of her hand and throwing them up against the door to stop her near hyste-ria, that she even knew he was there.

Lauren whimpered but she didn't fight. Instead, she rested her cheek against the wood, almost grateful that someone had stopped her. She was so very tired and now she could rest. They stayed locked together until Lauren began to mark time again by the sound of her brutal breathing. It was only when the man behind her laid his cheek against the one she left exposed that Lauren began to cry.

Pressed against her, Eli Warner had a tough time not doing the same.

Death was a funny thing. Some people bore it well. Wilson did, as far as Allan could tell, but this was his first go round with the grim reaper. His parents were still alive but separated for years—from him not one another. Wilson was his family and still he didn't feel anything he expected to feel as he looked at the judge.

Perhaps, if he'd been standing right next to Wilson's body, there would be some sort of emotional upheaval. Perhaps, if he wasn't behind a plate glass window he would feel less detached. But he wasn't inside, so Allan didn't shiver with disgust or cringe with discomfort or feel wretched with sorrow. Instead he rested his arm on the glass and placed his forehead against it as he looked. A police officer, who had stood quietly behind him for five minutes, now needed to take his leave. The cop cleared his throat.

"Mr. Lassiter? I'm going to be going now, sir." Allan didn't look at him so he tried again. "We weren't quite sure who to call. The bureau agents didn't want us to call anyone. They wanted to make sure all the political stuff was taken care of. The President had to be called. You know." Allan could feel the man fidgeting. "But that just didn't seem right. Does it seem right to you that they didn't want us to call his family? I mean not that you're official family, but I understand you're the closest the judge had."

Allan finally looked inquiringly at the officer. What a funny question. This wasn't a matter of right or wrong, and it was funny the man didn't see that. Still, Allan's perception could be a little off so he answered as he thought he should.

"No, of course not. That doesn't seem right," Allan mumbled. It was hard to talk. Allan felt drained but he knew that now was the time to get himself together and he needed to do it pronto. He squared his shoulders. "I can understand their reasoning. You have to be careful of politics. When you make things known," he looked back at Wilson's body, "and how you make things known, can change the outcome of important events. You do have to be so very, very careful."

"Yeah, I guess you'd know about that." The officer spoke as a matter of course, but Allan turned cold. He waited for the other shoe to drop. Fortunately the cop didn't have a clue he even had one in his hand. "Well, wish we could have prevented it. It's tough out there. I don't think there's anything we could have done. It happened fast. He was a good guy."

"Yes, he was," Allan said as the officer backed away and finally disappeared.

Allan put his head against the cool glass of the window, relieved to be left alone. The officer had been right about one thing. Wilson Caufeld was a good guy. He was a man whose excellent intentions had gone awry at the end. When the coroner's assistant stood by the gurney and looked at him, Allan looked back steadily. The woman took it as a sign that he was finished with the viewing and tucked Wilson away before she left too. Allan stayed there, head on his arm, and tears coming to his eyes. They went no further than that.

Ten minutes later he opened the door to the anteroom. Edie stood up, her purse clutched in both hands in front of her. Her wide lips were set in a line that threatened to dissect her face, her eyes were smudged black with mascara.

"Well?"

"They'll do an autopsy, but it's pretty clear what happened. He was shot through the chest. The coroner said an inch or so to the right and he would have made it."

"An inch." Edie murmured, dazed and disbelieving. "An inch could have cost you a lifetime of work. It's so amazing, Allan. So amazing."

Allan took her arm and stood beside her, so close they were almost embracing. She slid his eyes over and up to meet his. Without another word, they walked back to the car. Allan opened the door for her. Edie got in, catching his hand before he could shut her inside.

"I'm sorry, Allan," Edie said. "I'm so very, very sorry."

"I am, too," Allan agreed.

When he rounded the car Allan couldn't help but smile. Inside Williams was doing the same.

Chapter Twelve

Lauren wore a dress. Actually, it wasn't as much a dress as a column of mourning: black, sleek, unadorned save for a long gold chain on which hung a perfect pearl. The dress ended at her ankles where one could just glimpse the sheen of dark opaque stockings before they fused into half boots the color of coal.

Wilson Caufeld had clasped the necklace around her neck the day she graduated from law school. Petite as she was, Lauren looked ever more delicate in her costume, yet her handshake was even and strong. She greeted people who loved Wilson and consoled those whose grief, in reality, was not nearly as overpowering as hers.

She wandered among men and women jammed into the offices of Caufeld, Gordon & Willard, the firm where, as a hopeful young man, Wilson had launched his career. The firm still carried his name but all interest in it had long been sold. Yet much of Wilson remained. The comfortable chairs, the burgundy carpet, the well-stocked library were all traces of his influence. Yet Wilson's influence wasn't relegated only to things.

People from the "old neighborhood" appeared out of nowhere and Lauren couldn't quite grasp where the "old

neighborhood'' was. Everywhere Wilson had lived the
neighbors had believed him to be theirs alone. There were
old men and young women, black and white, Hispanic, all
with a story to tell about how Wilson Caufeld had helped
them, if only by listening to their tales. Lauren listened,
smiling at the conceit of her claim to Wilson. These people
stood aside, unsure of themselves while the mighty mingled
and murmured about the travesty of Wilson Caufeld's murder at the hands of anarchists. They were all afraid, these
mighty men. Those from the neighborhoods were simply
resigned to the fact that things happen.

"Lauren," Allan took her arm and the old black man
she had been talking to melted away though she gestured
for him to stay. But Allan was insistent that she pay attention
to him.

"Yes, hello." She shook hands with the woman by Allan's
side without thinking; she smiled without feeling any joy.

"This is Marge Everhill," Allan said. "She edits *The Daily
Journal*. I was just telling her how much we appreciated
the fine article she did on Wilson."

"Marge, it's nice of you to come," Lauren said.

"I wish we were here celebrating Judge Caufeld's confirmation."

"Don't we all," Lauren said softly.

"Aren't we all just terrified? Whoever heard of the bad
guys going after the judges? I mean this stuff happens in
Italy, not here."

"It's happening here now, Marge," Allan said, turning
to take two drinks off the tray a waiter was passing. He gave
one to each of the women. "The militia doesn't recognize
judicial boundaries. What's really odd is that Wilson was
giving them the breaks. Shows how stupid they are."

"Not stupid enough. Nobody has found Henry yet. The
FBI has pulled out all the stops to find him."

"I heard there was a death threat a day or two before
the judge was killed?"

"Marge," Lauren put her drink on a table behind her,
"I hope you won't think this rude, but I don't think we're
up for an interview." She glanced at Allan who was surveying the crowd near the front door. He looked like he was

at a cocktail party scoping new clients. Peeved, Lauren apologized for them both. "I'm sorry. There are just so many people here. Maybe in a few weeks."

"No, my fault," the woman patted Lauren's arm. "It's the reporter in me. I can't shake it. I really just wanted to let you know I'm sorry, I'm shocked, I'm appalled. He was an excellent man. You know, though, I am curious about one thing. What on earth do you think he was doing in Baldwin Hills? That's the one part of this that just doesn't add up."

Lauren shook her head. Allan knew the answer. "That's where he first lived with Victoria. They were really young. In fact, That was about the same time he started this firm."

Lauren blinked back a sudden resentment that, even after all these years, Allan knew so much more of Wilson's life than she.

Marge talked on. "Well, that makes sense. Wilson Caufeld never forgot anyone. I think it's admirable he still had friends there." She gave a sigh and her drink went by the wayside, too. "It was a lovely service. I've got to get back to the office. Hang in there, the both of you."

Allan walked her a few steps but was back with Lauren before anyone else could corner her.

"Come on." He took her hand and led her toward the library. "I want you to go in there and put your feet up for a minute. You look like death warmed over."

"Thanks for the compliment."

"Hey, I'm trying to help here."

"I know. I'm sorry." She patted his hand.

"Do you want me to bring you some food?"

Lauren shook her head. "Are you sure you don't mind if I bow out for a minute? I can't listen to one more person speculate whether it was Henry Stewart or the whole Independent Militia that pulled the trigger. It's sick. It's such a waste."

"It's natural, Lauren. These people are no less prominent than Wilson was. If he can be taken out, they could be next. I doubt a government salary is worth the risk."

"Do you really think that?"

Allan looked at her and his face changed, there was a

ripple in his expression, a curious blend of foreboding and relief. It was gone as quickly as it had come.

"That a government salary isn't worth it? Definitely." The joke fell flat. He walked on. "Sorry and no, I don't think this will happen again. I know for a fact this was a unique situation, Lauren. Now, go."

He gave her a little push and she gladly disappeared into the dimly lit library. Grieving was exhausting, and Lauren leaned against the library wall trying to find the reserves of strength she knew must be there so that she could continue with her task.

From the chair at the far end of the library, Eli Warner watched Lauren. He was reminded of pictures he'd seen of weeping women in third-world countries. This one didn't weep, but no photographer could have made grief seem more personal nor the griever more beautiful.

Knowing she would be embarrassed to find her private moment not so private, he tried to bury himself in the wings of the high-backed chair. But Lauren was a woman used to being alone and attuned to disturbances in the equilibrium of isolation. Her head came up, her square jaw set and those light eyes of hers became sharp as she peered through the dim light. Knowing he was found out, he got up.

"Hi." Eli said.

"Hello." She pushed her head back against the wall and eyed him warily.

"I tried to see you after the service."

"It's been pretty crazy."

Eli stuck his hands in his pocket. He approached with caution, sensing her wariness. "I can see that. Wilson had a lot of friends. I hope he thought of me as one."

"I'm sure he did. It was nice of you to come, Eli." Lauren glanced through the door. "I better get back."

He was quick with a hand on her arm. She looked at the hand, then at him and that hand went up in a universal sign of peace.

"Sorry." He stepped away and was about to put it down

to a funeral thing or a girl thing but he had a feeling this was a Lauren-hates-Eli thing and that he couldn't let go. "You know, Lauren, I have this funny feeling that something happened between the night Wilson died and this very minute. Not that I mind if there's a good reason, but hey, if there is a good reason I'd really like to know what it is. I apologize almost as well as I listen."

"Let's just say that I was mistaken about you. I knew about bureau agents, I broke a promise to myself to stay away from bureau agents. I should have known you'd do your job just like all the rest of them and I think that pretty much sums it up."

Lauren took her first step, Eli dropped his head and raised his arm across the doorway, blocking her exit before he looked up at her again.

"No, no. Not quite yet, lady. You don't say things like that and walk away. I don't care what day it is."

"I appreciate the time you spent with me the night Wilson died. I don't know what I would have done without you to talk to."

"But . . ."

"But I talked to a few other people since then, and I think you had a great deal to do with the fact that Wilson was despondent and that his frame of mind somehow led to his death. When I went back over the last few days of his life, you were right there, all over him, one of the last people to see him the night before he just dropped out of sight. Barbara said when you left you looked so grim. The judge didn't say more than good-night when she left. That night he left her a note to cancel all his appointments and that's it. No guards on Wilson the night he was killed. Didn't you promise me he would be guarded? I don't know what you talked about or what you did, but Eli, I know in my gut whatever you did, or said, started the dominoes falling."

Eli dropped his arm. She could walk away but from the looks of her she would explode before that happened. Eli had no sympathy.

"First, as you well know, I couldn't order anyone anywhere. I logged the letter, I spoke to Mark, I was assured there would be a detail on him. Maybe it would have made you happy if I worked a twenty-four-hour day; investigate in the on hours, guard Judge Caufeld in the off."

Lauren shook her head, her hands, she seemed to vibrate with the desire not to hear anything more.

"I don't want to have this conversation."

"Well, I want to talk about this. You're making some suggestions here that don't make me feel too nifty. I may not have a clue what you're talking about but I do have my pride."

"Damn don't you just," she said coldly. "You're so proud of what you do, aren't you?"

"Yes, I am," Eli said easily, but there was no caprice in his attitude. "I do it well."

"So well that you drove Wilson away from the one thing he loved. What did you say to him that night, Eli? What miserable little thing did you blow out of proportion so that he felt his life was over? Allan told me he wouldn't answer the phone even when he called. Wilson wouldn't even return the calls from the president's appointment secretary." Lauren seethed. Disappointment in Eli, sadness at her loss of Wilson, desire that this man say something to make it all right roiled inside her. "Oh, never mind. Don't bother saying anything. I'm so sick of the FBI and the lies they tell and the despair they cause."

Lauren blinked fast. Tears were coming and she wasn't going to cry in front of Eli ever again.

"Are you done?" he asked.

"Yes. Yes, I am."

"Then before you go, let me tell you a couple of things," Eli said quietly. "First, what Wilson and I talked about was not definitive and I'm not sure I can divulge the content. I'll check on that. Second, Wilson Caufeld knew I was just doing my job, and third, I wasn't the last one to talk to him that night, and I'd bet I wasn't the one who broke Wilson's spirit. I never had that kind of power."

"I didn't say you were the last. I said whatever you brought him put his last days in motion and that something wasn't good. Why don't you deny that?"

"Why don't you ask if what we talked about was the truth?"

"I already know the answer to that." She stepped forward defiantly but Eli wasn't intimidated.

"Well isn't that just interesting. I thought you were damn cute, Lauren, but I didn't know you were omnipotent. Maybe you should take your little Romper Room mirror that sees all and point it a little closer to home. I'd bet you'd find your friend Mr. Lassiter looking back. Why don't you ask him when the last time was he saw Judge Caufeld? Ask him what they talked about. He doesn't have any confidentiality problems. Go ahead, ask Lassiter and then come back to me and tell me what he says."

"How dare you, Eli," Lauren breathed. "You might as well attack me."

"I have no reason."

"If you have a reason to attack Allan, then tell me. Tell me now and I'll listen. But if you're playing a game, remember that I've played before. I was too young to figure it out when my mother's life was at stake, but I know how you work now. Don't expect me to roll over and see things your way. The FBI creates havoc and leaves misery and then they just walk away until they find another person to torture. It's part of the job description. What an idiot I've been. I thought it was just the field agents who were beneath contempt. I thought you'd broken the mold."

Eli laughed gently, "You know, one thing Judge Caufeld always said about you was that you were fair. I would have agreed with him at one time."

"I don't really care what you think about me, Eli, and don't pretend to an intimacy with Wilson. You didn't get to know him, you discovered him. You pried into his life, you gathered information and that doesn't make you a friend."

Lauren turned away. She held a handkerchief to her face and it covered her nose and mouth. It was a big white thing that a man like Wilson might carry. In the dim light Lauren's braided chignon gleamed like golden sand, too many shades to identify, and all of them blending to a color that was dazzling. That braid wasn't quite perfect today, it was just a little off, like her perception of what had gone down that fateful night. Yet Eli had no proof to give her, only suspicions and those suspicions kept him up at night.

"I was an admirer, Lauren, and I know that something is wrong here." He spoke softly. "I might have set the ball in motion, Lauren, but I think you better look in your backyard to see who ran with it."

Lauren glared at him but Eli wasn't cowed. His interest was elsewhere and so intense Lauren was drawn to him. She stood by his side. Lauren looked over his shoulder only to turn away in disgust the moment she saw who he was looking at. Allan was accused under Eli's scrutiny.

"You are detestable."

Eli took her arm gently, leaving no doubt she would not be let go until he had his say.

"Just watch, Lauren. Ask yourself if Lassiter looks like a grieving friend? Is that a smile of condolence or relief?" He pulled her closer still, his fingers now digging into the soft flesh of her upper arm. "Funny thing is, Mr. Lassiter was so much more than just a friend to Judge Caufeld. Like you, Lauren. Wilson Caufeld loved him." She refused to look at Eli when he cast his eyes her way. "You grieve. I feel sorrow. Most of those people are devastated by the loss and, yet, Lassiter's eulogy was like a closing argument," he whispered low into Lauren's ear, abridging what had been a horrid homage, "let's wrap up the loose ends of Wilson's life and get on with our own." Eli spoke normally. "Now there's a touching way to send off a man you owe everything to."

Lauren shook off his hand. "Allan wasn't even sentimental when Wilson was alive."

"There's a difference between sentiment and downright glee. Do you think he's forgotten why we're here, or is he celebrating the occasion?" He side-stepped once and cocked his head so that he could look at her even though her eyes were downcast and her face turned away. "Can you tell me what he was doing the last few days of Wilson's life?"

Her eyelids fluttered. Her lashes kissed her cheeks once,

twice, three times before finally opening so her eyes could meet his. Those beautiful eyes were red-rimmed from crying, exhaustion and now rage.

"You are beyond contempt. You pretend affection for Wilson, and then attack the man he loved more than anyone in the world." She shook her head sadly. "I can't fathom what you expect to gain. Do you think by pointing a finger of suspicion at Allan that you'll score some brownie points? Think maybe Mark Jackson will take another look at you and say 'hey, this is my kind of guy'? Or do you just want to prove what a rebel you are? Well, I'm not going to let you take away the last person in the world who means something to me, Eli. I'll tell everyone who'll listen that you're not fit to investigate Wilson's murder."

"That's not what I want, so don't waste your breath," Eli countered.

"I don't care what you want. The most docile assignment and you managed to end it with a tragedy. I don't know what you did, but you played a part. I feel it. I know it and if it's the last thing I do I will make you pay for making Wilson's last days so painful."

With that she tried to sweep past him but the doorway was narrower than it appeared and Eli larger than his good nature led one to believe. He towered over her, making no move to shrink away. Eli enveloped Lauren with the force of his personality, the scent of a man, the warmth of his breath and the touch of his fingers.

"I find what there is to find. There are people who had a lot to lose with Wilson walking around and I'm not talking about Henry Stewart."

"That's absurd," she scoffed.

"Is it? I think someone didn't want Wilson to make it to the confirmation hearings."

"This isn't a movie, Eli. That's no reason to kill him," Lauren countered.

Eli relaxed and thanked God for small favors. She was listening.

"I know some people who think a pair of shoes is enough to kill for. What do you think a reputation goes for? A business? A license to practice law, for instance?"

"If you have an accusation, Eli, make it."

"I accuse when I'm sure; I investigate when I'm not."

"Not this time, you won't. I can promise that."

"Maybe, maybe not. Just do me one favor. Ask Lassiter about what happened in '85. That was the last year he worked with Judge Caufeld in his law firm." Eli opened his arm. She was free to go. But when she tried, he pressed his card into her hand. She was two steps out the door when he remembered to add: "Just so you know, I talked to the agents who were in the hall that night after I left the judge. The last visitor Wilson Caufeld had the night I talked to him left in quite a huff. In fact, they said he looked like he could kill."

Lauren took another step praying he wouldn't continue, but he did.

"It was Allan Lassiter."

Chapter Thirteen

"Lauren?"

Monique, Abram's secretary, was standing in the door of Lauren's office, looking like she'd rather be anywhere else.

"Yes?"

"Abram wants to see you."

"Do me a favor? Tell him I'm waiting to hear back on some test results . . ."

"I don't think so. You better come this time."

Monique didn't wait, which was just as well. Chit-chat was a pain when there were important things to think about. In the few weeks since Wilson's death, Lauren had learned how different people react to challenge and fear. Judge Martinelli, into whose court the ill-fated Stewart trial had landed, decided the prosecution was golden. She ruled on the motions without hearing them argued again. She reversed Wilson's ruling on Henry Stewart, simultaneously revoking his bail, terrified if she didn't get him behind bars, she would be next on the militia's hit list. Lauren missed the challenge of Wilson's court, but she understood Martinelli's desire to make all of this go away before anything happened or anyone else was hurt. Judge Martinelli had a marshal living with her.

Edie declined a guard opting to handle things on her own, relying on the gun she always carried to help her out of trouble. Lauren had thought about carrying her own revolver since she had a permit like every assistant, but decided against it and settled for parking in the secured garage the judges used. Abram, low-profile on the actual case, insisted on an escort morning and night. The spectacle made for great press. They were the good guys once again and everyone was pulling for them.

Now Lauren was being summoned and couldn't imagine why. Abram had been cool since the funeral. Monique wasn't looking at her when she came in. Not a good sign.

"Close the door." Abram's back was to her. Lauren paused and cocked her head. "Sit down." This order came with a turn of his head. She could see his profile as he stood over his mounted battle scene.

Lauren sat, waiting patiently while Abram fiddled with his soldiers.

"Do you know why the military is so fascinating, Lauren?" Lauren figured out the question was rhetorical without too much effort. She settled in for a soliloquy. "The military is fascinating because it is the one institution where all people work in incredible harmony, disregarding concerns for personal safety and individual desire, because the objective is the common good. That is stunning selflessness."

Finally, he looked at her, but it seemed she was lacking an element essential to his needs. Hands clasped behind his back, Abram walked to his desk and stood behind it.

"You are breaking rank, Lauren, and it bothers me a great deal."

Lauren's mouth fell open. "That's news, Abram. I've done nothing but work on the Stewart case for the last year an a half, and never so intensely as these last weeks. If anything, I'm doing more than my share."

"So Edie has told me. Judge Martinelli is predisposed to the prosecution and willing to move the Stewart matter along even more quickly than Judge Caufeld would have. However, I understand there are certain things Edie has asked you not to pursue because they are both irrelevant and time consuming. Yet you relentlessly, and aggressively do so against her wishes." Lauren rolled her eyes. Abram's hand came down on the desk. Lauren jumped. Something new was added. Force. "Giving you such a high profile on the Stewart case did not elevate you to administrative status. Edie Williams heads special prosecutions. When she says something is wrong, it is."

"Nothing needs fixing, Abram." Lauren pushed herself out of her chair. "Everything's under control. If I haven't made my strategy clear to Edie, or explained my objectives properly, I will . . ."

"Sit," Abram ordered before controlling his anger. "Why don't you make things clear to me, first, Lauren. Explain to me why it is that you have requested the LAPD release all records, including autopsy reports, witness reports and investigative notes, on the matter of Wilson Caufeld's murder? What possible bearing could that have on anything you are doing at the moment?" Abram lay his hands flat on the top of the desk. "While you're at it, tell me why it is that you've requested weekly updates from the FBI agents who are assigned to investigating that murder? Which, by the way, Mark Jackson has told them not to supply. Why have you petitioned Judge Martinelli for Judge Caufeld's phone records—chambers and his home? A petition she wisely denied."

Lauren set her jaw. "I don't think the bureau is following through as they should. The investigation is either stalled, or there are people inside the office who don't think it's worth a whole lot of time." Lauren paused, waiting for him to respond. When Abram didn't, she went on albeit with a touch less confidence. "Okay, they're doing what they can. I know Mark's pulling out all the stops to find Henry, but I need those police reports to see if I can link Henry Stewart to the crime. It would definitely have bearing on the prosecution of Henry, if not George, if we can establish that Henry was involved in the murder of Wilson Caufeld. The threats alone were enough to classify them as committing a hate crime. We certainly will have no trouble asking for the death penalty if we can tie Henry to Caufeld's death. If he was the trigger man and we can link . . ."

"That's enough, Lauren. That's enough!" Abram tugged at his slacks and settled himself in his chair, fatigued by her misplaced zeal.

He tapped his fingers atop a letter he had just received from a friend who was wishing him well on his quest for Wilson's now vacant seat. Beneath that was a message from his senator's office politely replying that they were considering all fully qualified candidates before making their recommendation to the President. It was a tasteful word of caution. A conviction was needed on the Stewarts before a commitment could be made to Abram. A lot of good Caufeld's death had done Abram's ambition. Now here was Lauren trying to run off on a tangent that would lengthen this trial for no good reason. Too bad Henry Stewart couldn't have taken her out, too.

"Save your breath, Lauren. You may have convinced yourself there is a natural connection, but I don't recall that anyone has been indicted for Wilson Caufeld's murder. I don't recall that we have even been officially advised that there is a suspect."

"Abram, everyone knows . . ." Lauren demurred with a condescending smile.

"No, everyone doesn't know. We have a system, Lauren, have you forgotten? Without a suspect, without an indictment, Wilson Caufeld's murder has nothing to do with you or the Stewart prosecution. Even with an indictment this will be a separate matter and a separate trial. Now, if you can't keep your personal concerns out of your work, then I suggest you remove yourself from this case."

Lauren opened her mouth to object and, thankfully, thought before she spoke. Martinelli was making things easy. No doubt Edie was pushing to be reinstated and Abram was willing to bend with whatever expedient wind was blowing. Well, she wasn't about to let the seasons change quite yet. Lauren wanted to convict the Stewarts and that was that.

"No. No, I realize this is business." Lauren smiled. "I was only trying to make sure that we used whatever we had to lock in a guilty on the Stewarts. I suppose now that we've got the standing issue resolved, everything is settled."

"I'm glad you understand," Abram said quietly. "Do the job you were assigned and do it properly, Lauren, and everyone will get what they want. Lengthen this trial by even one minute because of a personal agenda, and you'll find yourself doing T-check cases. Edie, by the way, is in complete agreement on this."

"No doubt," Lauren muttered.

"If you have something to say, Lauren, be adult about it," Abram shot back.

"You know, Abram, as much as I admire you as U.S. Attorney, I can't help but notice that my worth seems to have diminished just a tad now that Caufeld's no longer hearing this case. I'd say that sounds strangely like you're thinking about rearranging the players again, and that sounds oddly like you're playing politics simply because you have the power."

"Lauren, someday you will say something to someone who is not quite as admiring of your youthful spirit as I." Abram's voice was dark, his eyes were narrowed. She gave him something to target.

"Just an observation, Abram. I've always appreciated learning from professionals. I suppose that's just one more lesson I should be grateful for."

"And I always said you were an intelligent young woman, Lauren, who learns quickly. Perhaps now is the time to prove my admiration hasn't been misplaced."

They played stare down for a second or two because there was nothing more to say. Abram was working when she left his office. Lauren blew off her chores while she got Allan on the phone. But he didn't want to hear her story, he didn't tell her she was right, he didn't even sound like he really wanted to talk about Wilson, or the investigation or anything.

She thanked him for nothing, slammed down the phone and sat back in her chair. She didn't care if she was the only one who really wanted to find out what happened to Wilson. She'd do it, then they'd all be sorry they hadn't helped. She didn't care one bit that she was alone. She'd been alone before, though never, of course, so alone as now.

Chapter Fourteen

Lauren collapsed in her chair and rubbed both eyes with both hands the way a child would. She'd never make the cover of *Vogue* at the rate she was going. Throwing her arms over her head she stretched but her chair tilted on that cracked wheel so she went forward, letting her shoulders slump as she lay her head on the reams of paper, reports and case books littering her desk. Closing her eyes, Lauren listened to the dead silence. The cleaning crew had come and gone a while back, but she'd waved them out of her office. Lauren was busy then and now she was tired.

The next day's preparation was done for Martinelli, but Lauren was determined to go over the police report on Wilson's death one more time before she called it a night. There was something about the angle of the bullet entry that bothered her. Henry wasn't a tall man and Wilson was fairly short. The bullet should have gone in . . . Her thoughts strayed. Her steam had run out. Even the memories of Wilson were fuzzy.

It had only been a few weeks, and long hours of work were nothing new, but Lauren had lost sight of him. She was drifting off, finding her paper pillow surprisingly com-

ortable when suddenly she heard a noise, sharp, and loud
enough to make her bolt upright. Her eyes were heavy
and dry. They hurt when she moved them, looking around
her brightly lit office to the shadowy hall beyond. Lauren
tilted her head left, then right. Nothing. No boom. No
clap of thunder or retort of a pistol. It was all so still and
silent. Slowly she eased herself from behind the desk and
stepped around the boxes in her office. She looked down
the hall—both ways—twice—then chuckled.

Sleep noises, phantom sounds exploding in an over-
loaded brain, that's what she'd heard and it had scared
her half to death. She heard those noises in the night for
months when she was first orphaned, now they came again
like the slamming of a coffin lid to remind her someone
else she loved was gone and that sleep was not an option.
It was time for her to go.

It took five minutes to gather her things and straighten
her desk. Another five in the ladies' room where she
splashed her face with cold water and considered the day
in a vain effort to perk herself up before the short drive
home. It hadn't started well with Abram and had ended
worse. Allan not only ignored her first two calls but was
angry with her third. He accused her of being obsessed
and spiteful toward the FBI. Neither of which was true.
Lauren knew the agency was doing its job, it just wasn't
doing its job fast enough. Then her contact at the LAPD
had asked what was going on with Allan because an FBI
agent was nosing around. Eli was still stirring up trouble,
damn him.

Another duck into the sink, and another splash of water
and she was just awake enough to walk down the hall and
take the elevator to the hot garage. Lauren's heels clicked
on the concrete but the tune lacked its usual verve. Her
thoughts were more a ball of mush than laser points of
light and she liked it that way. Exhaustion forced the mind
to rest but exhaustion also made her inattentive, and
Lauren was a beat late noticing that something wasn't right.
She was almost to her car when someone moved. That
someone was extraordinarily near. Close and silent. Invisi-
ble. Just a sense, a flash, a stirring of the air. A breath on

the back of her neck. Where? Where? There. Under her car? Crouching by it? Yes, he was by it. Rising, rising, rising until he stood. A man. A boy.

"Oh God." Lauren dropped her briefcase. Her knees buckled before she could move. Lauren reached for the car while Henry Stewart stepped back again and then again. Lauren's eyes went up, down, she saw more of him, then all of him. He was dirty, as if he'd been rolling on the ground. Perhaps under her car. Perhaps working under her car. Two more steps and he crashed into the piling behind him, never taking his eyes off her. Henry Stewart faced off with Lauren Kingsley and she was terrified. But, then, so was he.

In the tomb-like silence they breathed out hard and back in with equal exertion. Lauren's stricken face was mirrored in the boy's saucer eyes. Yes, boy. She forced herself to think of him that way because, if she was wrong, she was dead. Since she was still standing, since his hand hadn't been raised to her, she must be right about that. Except there was something happening here that could be her undoing if she didn't attend to the possibility; something that would be the death of her yet.

"What?" she whispered. He breathed back, unable to answer.

Lauren took a step, then two. He pushed back into the unforgiving concrete then froze again as Lauren scoped the length of her car. Lauren started to bend at the waist, her eyes flickering to the chassis and back to keep an eye on him.

"There's nothing there," he whispered. Lauren froze at the sound of his voice. Her stomach turned.

It would be a gun then. He wore no jacket and she could see there was no gun. There was no knife. Did it matter? He could have killed her with a word, her fear was so great. Thankfully, her mind was still working. Slowly Lauren got to one knee and took a chance. She looked under her car instead of at him.

"There's nothing there," he said again, taking a baby step forward as if to show her. His arms were wrapped

around himself. Henry seen___ed to s___
have a bomb. I don't want to ___

Carefully Lauren got up, h___ead ove___
of the car to steady herself. H___ ___
could see how he had change___ ___s c___
was haggard. There were deep ___
skin was red and swollen from t___

"What do you want?" Lauren ___
in each passing minute. She use___ ___ could.

"I wanted to see you." One arm ___rapped, he pointed
to her hesitantly as if to remind her who she was.

"How did you know I'd be here?"

"My dad knows all about you." They danced again.
Henry one step forward, Lauren mirroring him with one
step back. Henry seemed to understand so he stayed still.
"My dad taught me everything I know. He taught me
how to make a bomb. He taught me how to listen to
conversations when nobody thinks you're paying attention," Henry sighed. "Now he tells my mother things and
she tells everyone in our cell what to do. We have charts
and schedules about people. About you."

Lauren's eyes fluttered shut. It felt funny to hear him
say that. She and Edie had wondered if there were enough
of them to watch and plan. Now she knew. The other thing
Lauren knew was that it only took one to kill. Henry read
her mind.

"Just because there isn't a bomb, it doesn't mean I can't
hurt you. I could kill you now." His voice shook with the
threat but Lauren took him seriously. She'd die alone like
Wilson; like her mother. People would come to lament her
passing and forget her within weeks. Even Allan wouldn't
mourn the way Lauren would hope. She wouldn't be a
pest if she was dead.

"You don't want any more killing on your hands, Henry.
How many is it now? How many are you going to take the
fall for? Two people in the bombing, Judge Caufeld . . ."

"No. No. That's what I came to tell you. I didn't do
anything to that judge." Henry's eyes grew fat with tears,
his hands fell away and wiggled at his side as if he could

throw off the accus___
Either Henry w___
"You sent___
But you d___
quickl___

...ations that were somehow stuck to him.

...s panicked or an extremely good liar.

...a letter telling him that you would kill him.

...dn't have the guts to sign it,'' Lauren insisted

..., giving him no time to gain his footing.

...t could have been anyone who sent that letter.''

...auren would have laughed at his amateurishness if this hadn't been so frightening.

"But they have fingerprints, Henry, and that letter was never made public. How did you know about it?'' She bluffed and he bought it.

"They made me send the letter. Paul said I had to do it. I didn't even write it. They didn't like my ideas. But they said if we sent that letter then the judge would back off my dad. I didn't think it would do any good. My dad's the smartest person in the group and I told them he wouldn't.''

"That's got to be tough when no one listens. You were right.''

"So you believe I didn't do it? I swear, I didn't.''

"Even if you didn't, the fact of the matter is he's dead, Henry. Tell me who did it before they come after me or Ms. Williams or anyone else. Henry, you're in enough trouble, don't make it worse.''

"God, don't you think I know I'm in trouble? I just tried to do what my dad wanted, but look what happened. I didn't think anybody would be hurt.'' He wailed and he wrung his hands. That's when Lauren snapped.

"For God's sake, are you brain dead? You detonated 500 pounds of explosive material and you didn't think anyone would be hurt?'' Henry stiffened and made to bolt, this young man who no one listened to. He was going. She held out her hands and talked fast, damning her big mouth. "Okay. Sorry. I didn't mean it the way it sounded. I know you didn't set out to kill that man and woman, but Judge Caufeld was different. That was premeditated, cold-blooded murder and that can send you to the electric chair ten times over, Henry.''

"Go ahead and send me. Nobody'll care if I get exe-cuted. I figured out there isn't much I can do about any-

thing now except tell you h⸺
judge cared. I appreciated tha⸺
Ms. Kingsley, I didn't do it. I ⸺
did the people I know. I just ⸺
looking at me, Ms. Kingsley.''

Startled by his respectful ton⸺
bringing her hands in front of ⸺
still held her purse. Slowly, she s⸺
shoulder and let it drop. Henry ⸺ ⸺ both
knew what that soft thud meant. She had no weapon either.

"What do you mean I shouldn't be looking at you.''
Lauren spoke soothingly, trying to refocus him. "Henry?
Look at me.'' He shook his head and finally looked away
from her purse.

"I mean it's somebody else that killed the judge. I was
there, I won't lie about that. I was supposed to shoot him,
but just scare him. My dad wanted everyone to be scared
so that they would know we weren't kidding about anything, but he didn't want him dead. It was like a campaign.
The letter, then we were going to shoot at him and then
maybe wound him just to keep everyone scared.''

"So you did see him that night?'' Lauren asked.

"Yeah, I saw him. Paul and some other guy drove me
to his house. But when we were coming down the street
there were two other cars parked on the street. We figured
it was the FBI watching him. So Paul slowed down and
they were talking about what to do when all of a sudden
the judge comes driving out of his garage. We were all
scared but Paul was really scared so he hightailed it out of
there. He made some stupid excuse because he wants us
all to think he's just like my dad. If he was my dad, we
would have followed Mr. Caufeld. But we didn't, and I
didn't kill him.''

"How do I know you're telling me the truth?''

"I'm here, aren't I?'' he asked plaintively. "I didn't fire
that gun they gave me. It was a thirty-eight if that helps
you check. We stopped and had a burger. There are people
there who saw Paul. I brought a picture. Here.''

He held it out to her. The photo shook along with

hesitated only a moment then stepped
ok it.

like a used-car salesman," Lauren muttered.
Henry laughed shyly. Lauren couldn't help but

Okay, you drove away. Then what?" Lauren asked.

"We went and had a burger. A place on Santa Monica Boulevard heading to the freeway. Jack in the Box."

"What time?"

"About seven-forty. We ordered three burgers and three Cokes and three fries. You can check it, Ms. Kingsley. Please check it. We sat in a booth near the bathroom." His voice caught. Lauren looked closer as he swiped at his eyes. He was tired and he was crying. "I just don't want this to go on anymore. I don't believe all the stuff my dad says, but he's my dad so I try really hard to believe. I don't want my mom to do anything that could put her in jail, too. I just want things to be right. Do you see? Do you understand when it's your parents? You've got to at least try to believe because they're supposed to show you the way."

Lauren nodded. "Yes, I really do, Henry. But it doesn't change the fact that you were involved in the bombing."

He hung his head, "I know. I know, and don't you think it keeps me up at night. Those people are dead and I pray to God he'll forgive me for that."

"You've already made a start by talking to me, Henry. I could make sure that you're protected. You plead to a lesser charge and I promise the U.S. Attorney will accept it if the information you give us is good."

"I'll be talking against my dad," Henry said. He touched his face and winced, as if George had reached from behind his bars and slapped him for his insolence. The acne had flared to open sores. "I don't know. I don't know what to do." Henry sighed and looked around the garage. Lauren did the same. This place was more hospitable than any jail he would be going to and that was a pity. "All I really wanted was to make my dad proud. I don't know how to do that, and I don't know who'll tell me the truth about whether it's worth it to try."

"That must be lonely," Lauren said, caught in this young

man's dilemma, recognizing her own in it. Henry relaxed, talking to her like a friend now.

"It is. My mom believes in everything my dad does. I can't talk to her. I tried, but she's getting worse now that my dad's in jail."

"Aren't there other young people like you in your organization. Maybe there's someone who feels the same way you do and you just don't know it."

Henry shook his head, so despondent Lauren thought he might just slide down that piling onto the concrete and never get up.

"Naw. Nobody. Except one guy. Nick, maybe. He lives a couple of doors down. I think he figured out how I felt. He's quiet but he would look at me, or kind of pat my back, like he knew. But he couldn't say anything. None of us really can."

"I'm sure he did. Nick Cheshire's a good guy," Lauren agreed caught up in the flow of the conversation. Then Henry raised his head. She saw the look in his eye, and Lauren knew she'd made a terrible mistake.

"You know Nick? How do you know, Nick?" Henry asked quietly. His hands were open, palms backward on the concrete piling. His fingers twitched. She had stepped on the frozen lake of his desire to do what was right and her weight proved too much. The ice spiderwebbed with cracks and disillusionment was in the stagnant water below. Henry was goin' in for a dunk.

Lauren back pedaled, calling up all her reserves of confident persuasion. If he fell back into that state of despair she could move him in the direction she wanted.

"I only know what our investigators have told me. We have files on everyone, too, Henry. You know that. That's what we do in an investigation. Collect information. We have so many more investigators. We have so much more than you do."

"You said he was a nice guy. You said that." Henry pushed himself away from the wall, fighting her every step. He had begun to think for himself and the road that opened up was the wrong one. He charged down it. "How would you know? Why would you think any of us were nice unless you knew someone before they were one of us? You want to put us all in jail. You want to send my dad and me to the electric chair. Why would you think any of us are nice?"

"I don't know Nick Cheshire. It's just the information we have on him . . ."

Henry kicked the side of her car and the sound was deafening. Lauren's hands flew up and covered her ears. Through her not-quite-closed eyes she saw his foot kick again. Her purse took flight and Lauren went down. Henry was on her, pulling on her arms until he had her wrists down by her side and Lauren cocked at a defenseless angle.

"Nick's a plant! He's one of you, isn't he? He put my dad in jail. He'd put my mom there, too. He's one of you?" Henry's Adam's apple, mined his throat as if trying to run from the flood of emotion that washed up from his gut. "I thought you . . . I didn't want you to get hurt . . . thought I could talk to you. Damn it." He pulled her wrist to the side and down. Lauren grunted. "Nick is just like you! Just like you! And I was trying to help. I felt sorry because that judge died. I'm as dumb as my dad thinks."

"No, Henry." Lauren said though the words were hard to understand through her panting. "You're not. You're smart to be here and Nick's not a part of this. I swear," Lauren's words slipped through clenched teeth. He was strong and her wrists felt brittle in his grip. He could snap them without thinking. "Think, Henry. Think. Why would he be one of us? Has he ever done anything to make you believe that?"

Henry laughed, near hysteria now. "He's never done anything and that's just what I'm figuring out now. He's never built the bombs, he's never drawn the plans, he never asked to drive a truck. He just sits and listens. He looks at me and tells me it will all be okay. Okay." Henry almost spit the word. "That's what he always said. So what's okay? My mom and dad and me in prison? The government taking away our house because my dad didn't pay taxes so welfare people could get his money? Is that what Nick meant?" Henry pulled her tight against him and Lauren pulled back. It was no use. "I don't think that's okay, Ms.

Kingsley. I think maybe my dad was right and I just wasn't learning my lessons the right way," Henry's teeth were bared now. Lauren had no choice but to kneel as he twisted her wrists.

"Henry, listen to me. Remember why you came here. Judge Caufeld did the right thing. You felt bad when you heard he was dead . . . Aaah," Lauren clamped her mouth shut. Henry was down on one knee beside her.

"I came because I didn't want anyone else to get hurt. Not you and not my mom and not anyone." He seethed, he aged with anger. Lauren turned her head away.

"But someone's already been hurt." She talked fast. Tears were coming to her eyes but her life depended on what came out of her mouth now. "Nick's been hurt. Yes, really. Nick's in a hospital almost dead. People you know did that to him. They aren't sure he's going to live and he was just doing his job. Just like Judge Caufeld.

"Shut up. I don't care anymore."

"Yes you do. You wanted me to know the truth, Henry, and that's why you came here. Nick was working for the truth. Judge Caufeld was working . . ."

He twisted hard and Lauren was silent except for a squeal of pain. "So you find out the truth by lying? That's crazy. One thing my dad never did was lie. Is there anybody on your side that doesn't lie?"

"Hey! Hey! What's going on?"

Henry fell back, taking Lauren with him. Still holding one wrist, they scrambled behind her car. He pulled her close as he put his back against the right front tire.

"The security guard," Lauren whispered. "He's going to find us."

Henry stayed silent. He turned his head one way then the other. Lauren did the same. Neither could tell which direction the guard was coming from.

"I'll take you with me," Henry growled.

"Everyone's already looking for you. If you try to take me with you, there won't be anywhere to hide." Lauren sat up and twisted away from him. Henry was too preoccupied to fight. The guard was coming closer, looking under cars, making his way up the ramp, not down. The lot wasn't full at this time of night and he would be on top of them soon. There wasn't much time. Lauren knew she should call out. Instead, she whispered frantically. "Look, this was the right thing. I believe you about not killing Judge Caufeld. No one can tell you how you need to live your life. Don't think about what other people want, think about what you want. Think who's been hurting people. It's not us. We're not the ones beating people up or blowing them up."

Lauren threw herself on her stomach and peered under the car, sighting the guard not more than 100 feet away. There was only time for a calculated risk. Scrambling back, Lauren took Henry's arm.

"Listen to me. Grow up. Coming here will go a long way in court. You trusted us before, trust us again. Henry . . ." Lauren grappled with him but he was up in a sprinter's stance. "Henry, no!"

"I'm sorry about Nick," he said and looked over the top of the car. She stayed on all fours, exhausted and afraid for them both. He hesitated; she took advantage.

"They won't let you get away again. I'll go hard on you."

"Nothing could be harder than what I've got now," he said and without looking at her again, he bolted.

He was thin and he was quick, but not quite quick enough. The guard hollered. Lauren called out his name, whether to stop him or alert the guard to who it was, she didn't know. In the cavernous garage she heard other things. A gun drawn. Calls to halt. Shuffling feet. Still down, Lauren let her head fall forward as she waited for the next thing to happen. But the boom didn't sound, there was no retort of gunfire, no cry from Henry as he fell dead. There was just the sound of running, fading into the night as someone touched her. Lauren didn't move, so the guard took her arm and pulled her up.

"You okay?" he asked. Lauren looked at him. She nodded. "You sure. What was it? Robbery?" He looked her up and down, but her clothes were intact. He couldn't bring himself to say the word "rape." "Did he do anything, you know, to you?"

"No, it's okay. It's okay." Lauren shook her head and

brushed off her pants. She straightened her jacket. She had a hard time looking at him. She was so tired. "Thank you. I thought you were going to shoot him."

"I couldn't get a clear shot, but I got a pretty good look at him. I called it in. Guy was running like a bat out of hell, though. I don't know if they'll get him. Did you get a good look at him?"

"Yes, I did. I'll make a report."

"You want to do that now? I'll call the cops to come here."

Lauren shook her head, "I just want to rest for a second. I work upstairs. U.S. Attorney's office."

"Then I guess you know what to do. Okay. That sounds good," the guard said and stepped back. Carefully he put his revolver in his holster and looked around. There were steps near the elevator. He led her to them. Lauren sat while he picked up her things. Henry had kicked her purse like a football and her stuff was spread all over the place. Meticulously, the man gathered it all while Lauren gathered her wits. By the time he handed her her purse, she had come to a few conclusions.

Henry Stewart was one confused young man.

Henry Stewart did not kill Wilson Caufeld.

That meant someone else had.

When the guard handed over her purse, Lauren thanked him. She was in her car when he hurried up beside it.

"Is this yours?"

He held out a business card with something scribbled on it. Lauren took it.

"Thank you. Yes," she said and remembered exactly who had told her that Henry Stewart wasn't the only one with a reason to see Wilson Caufeld dead and buried.

Chapter Fifteen

"I saw Henry Stewart. He says he didn't kill Wilson. I didn't try to stop him from running away. You were probably sleeping. Sorry." She stuffed her hands in the pockets of her jacket and pulled out his card. She flipped it between her fingers then held it up. "I found this. It was wrong to talk to you the way I did at the funeral. I was working late."

Eli lifted his right shoulder and the left corner of his lips. He didn't point out that hello would have been a nice opening, or that she was rambling, or that the last time they saw each other she considered him less than dirt.

"I was working, too. Must be time for a break."

He held the door open and Lauren walked into his world. It wasn't what she expected. There were family pictures. Comfortable furniture. The apartment was clean and small. The door shut. She looked at Eli.

"It's warm in here," she said.

He plucked at the worn robe he wore over his shirt and jeans. It had seen better days. "Metabolism. I'm always cold unless I'm running around. I'll take your jacket so you don't boil."

"No. Thanks. I won't stay too long. I just wanted to get your take on this. Look, Eli, I know I'm in trouble on this one and I just can't think straight so I'm here with my hand out." Lauren tried to keep this businesslike. It was tough. He looked so darn good.

"Okay. I'll listen." Eli rearranged a few things on the table, restacked some papers he was looking at. "Sit down."

"You have a nice place."

Eli moved suddenly, reaching for her. Lauren shrunk back. He lifted his fingers, then slowly reached for her purse.

"I don't charge for consultations and I promise, I don't bite unless I've been invited to."

Lauren looked grim, her posture was rigid. She gave up her purse reluctantly and sat on the edge of the sofa. Eli put her purse on a chair by a desk and disappeared. She heard him in the kitchen, was about to tell him not to go to any trouble but by that time he was back.

"I've got Pepperoni pizza. Cold. My favorite candy," he pointed to a bowl of M&Ms, "pretzels. Beer, wine or soda. Take your pick. Last thing, I'm not going to listen to you rag on me or the bureau unless you've got a reason. Other than that, talk away."

Lauren's jaw moved, her eyes slid left then right.

"Water," she said. "I'll have water."

Eli opened a beer and set it in front of her. "I don't buy bottled and I doubt you'd like the tap stuff."

"Okay." Lauren picked it up, took a sip and held the cold bottle atop knees that were held so tightly together they had merged. There was nothing left to do but admit she'd screwed up and hope to God Eli Warner had some words of wisdom. "Here goes. I was working late. Henry Stewart was waiting for me in the garage. He told me he'd been at Caufeld's house the night he died. He gave me a picture of the man who was driving the car."

"Can I see it?"

Lauren dug in her pocket and handed it over. Eli glanced at it and set it aside.

"When Caufeld drove away, this guy got scared and took off. Supposedly they had burgers and then took Henry back to where they're hiding him."

"Do you know where that is?"

Lauren shook her head. "Nick Cheshire was one of the people he trusted in their cell. He didn't know that Nick was hurt."

"I assume he does now," Eli said quietly.

Lauren looked toward the floor. She nodded.

"Can I assume that Henry Stewart also knows that Nick was working for us."

Lauren looked up, cocked her head. She had screwed up so bad. "Yes."

"I see."

"I could have called the guard. I didn't. I let Henry get away, Eli."

"Then I'd say you're in big trouble, Lauren." Eli was not vindictive. He only stated what she already knew. She took no offense. "I don't see that there's any way to keep the powers that be in the dark."

"I know. I know." Lauren was up. She put her beer on the table and paced as far as she could, turning on a pinpoint to come back. "I'm not asking to be excused, but I've got to sort things out before I face Abram."

Eli sat without eating or drinking. He watched and noted the nuances in her voice and her body language. It wasn't hard to figure out that she was tortured by what she considered wrong doing.

"He was so confused. It was as if he finally realized the kind of destruction he had caused, the kind of pain he had brought to the people who survived. This was a turning point for Henry and he was taking a stand. I could have turned him with a plea bargain. He was ready to give up his father to save his mother and his own sanity." She stopped abruptly. "Oh, wow. That's Laura Nero on the stereo."

"Do you like her?"

"Yeah. I really do." Lauren's smile was small and personal.

"Johnny Mathis?"

She nodded, comforted by the small talk and leaving it reluctantly.

"I could have called the guard at any time. It wouldn't have been difficult to detain Henry if I'd gone on the offensive, but I didn't. I forgot all about the bombing, Eli, and all I could think of was Wilson." Lauren threw her hands down to her sides, they were balled into fists that flailed in tight circles. "If Henry didn't kill Wilson then I didn't mind him going. I don't know what I thought. I suppose I thought I could save him. When he ran he was so angry, so different than he had been. I felt I'd taken his last chance away from him. Maybe I thought I was going to give him another one when I let him go."

Eli leaned forward in his chair. The living room was so small he touched her by just reaching out. Gently he pushed up the sleeve of her jacket and looked at the welts that were beginning to show around her wrist.

"Stress makes us primal. We react. It may not be the right thing, but that's the way it is," Eli said, letting her sleeve fall into place.

"I thought I was better than that." Lauren said sadly but there was no sympathy coming her way.

"Why would you think that?"

Lauren snapped to attention. Eli's eyes glittered but she wasn't sure if it was with pleasure.

"Because," she answered coldly. "I've been through this before if you recall."

"No, you haven't." Eli sat back, crossing his legs on the ottoman. "Your mother wasn't murdered."

"She was put through the grinder the same way Henry would have been if I'd made sure he didn't leave. He wasn't responsible for Wilson's murder."

"And the Bureau isn't responsible for your mother's suicide but you keep trying to find a way to blame it, or me, or anyone but her. Now you haven't got any answers about Judge Caufeld. When Henry couldn't give you any answers you sent him away, you weren't giving him another chance." Eli shrugged, satisfied that his diagnosis was the right one.

"Well, gosh," Lauren drawled. "That is just such a supportive attitude Eli. Thanks very much."

"Lauren, what on earth is it you want from me?" Eli asked.

"I don't want anything from you. I just thought since

you were part of all this you might be a good one to bounce things off of."

"You don't even like the part of the system I'm in. You don't want to listen to what I know. You don't want Henry to be subjected to the thumbscrews now that you don't think he had anything to do with killing Wilson. Lauren, what exactly is it you want?"

"I wanted Wilson to have died for something. If he died because he stood up to the militia, that would be honorable and heroic, but now I don't think they had anything to do with it. The Independent Militia wouldn't have had a tag team. Henry sent off one way, another team waiting to follow Wilson."

"I agree," Eli said.

"Henry thinks it was a law enforcement conspiracy. He said that before he even knew Nick was a plant."

Eli scoffed, "You expect someone who hates the government to say anything else? Look, Lauren, what are you doing here? If you want to know what I know I'll be happy to tell you, but I can't tell you everything will be fine."

"That's not what I came for." She flopped on the sofa and pulled a pillow onto her lap. "There was nowhere else to go."

"I know." She looked hard at him and saw no pity. "But you made it that way and it's about time you took a look at that circumstance."

"And that's coming from someone whose friends line up at the door." Lauren regretted those words the minute they left her mouth. A tremor ran through her. She may be a lot of things, but she wasn't cruel. She threw the pillow back on the couch. "I'm sorry. That was uncalled for. I'm going home."

Eli was up before she was. "Hey. It's okay. Nothing wrong with the truth."

"There is when it hurts."

Eli shook his head and offered a wry smile, "The truth hurts more often than not, believe me."

"Where'd you hear that?"

"Nowhere. Just figured it out on my own. I learned from a master."

"Yeah?" Lauren pulled the pillow back onto her lap.

Eli settled on the floor, legs crossed, elbows up on the coffee table. "Want to hear some truths? The kind that aren't going to make you happy. You can listen and if you don't like it you can leave."

Lauren nodded.

"Wilson Caufeld hired Allan Lassiter out of law school. The relationship was perfect for three years. People I talked to were either jealous of it or amazed by it. Only one person came close to figuring it out. They said "it was love and who could explain that?""

"That was the only explanation," Lauren agreed.

"Then there were the people who said they predicted it wouldn't last. Fourth year. A big falling out and nobody has a clue why. Even Wilson's partners didn't know. One of them told me he suggested Wilson cut Allan loose and Wilson wouldn't hear of it. Told his partner never to mention it again."

"I never heard about a problem."

"It took some digging for me to find it. Right there, that says something. You knew those men so intimately and yet even you didn't know about a crisis." He paused, giving her time to consider what he'd just said. She never took her eyes off him. "I thought that was curious but it didn't raise a red flag. Caufeld was high on the nomination so he was focusing on giving me a professional background. What happened was years ago, and I can imagine that it never occurred to him to say anything. The strange thing is, for some people, this is the only thing they remember about Judge Caufeld. To them, it was a big, big problem. The thing that made me take notice is there isn't one person who has a clue what the problem was and, for high-profile people, that is very unusual. So now I've got a red flag on the pole. It's not flapping in the breeze."

Eli pushed himself up and went to the stack of papers he'd moved. "So I have my interviews but I've also got tax returns from the judge's firm, personal returns, bank records, and correspondence." Lauren slipped off the couch and looked at the papers he put in front of her on the coffee table. "In nineteen eighty-five the judge transferred a lot of money from his personal account to the firm account in one lump sum. The firm was fiscally healthy so there shouldn't have been any need for Wilson to infuse dollars, especially personal bucks. That's what I asked Judge Caufeld about. I asked him why the money transfer was necessary and why his partners didn't know about it."

"And he said?"

Eli went to the floor, put elbows on the coffee table and his hands up to cradle his face. "I thought I'd hear something about a cash infusion, difficulties with the book-keeper, something like that. Instead he was silent and that's telling, Lauren. Then he asked if I would be kind enough to give him some time to confer with someone—a person he cared about—who would be affected by what I'd found. I didn't think I'd really found anything, Lauren. The fact that he thought I did meant I was onto something that wasn't good."

"He could have meant me."

"I chalked you off the list." Eli gave her a crooked smile. "You never worked for him. You've never had a disagreement with him. And I believe you were about six-teen or seventeen at the time. He may have given you an allowance but not thousands of dollars in a big chunk." He couldn't look at her, so he traced the label of the beer bottle. "Besides, Caufeld used the word 'he.' I know he was talking about Allan Lassiter and whatever this is, it can hurt Lassiter bad."

"And you think Allan killed Wilson to keep him quiet?" Lauren laughed outright. "That's crazy! Not only would Allan never hurt anyone but he sure wouldn't get physical to protect himself. That man could crush anyone in court. That's what he'd do."

Eli leaned back, propping himself up with his arms behind him.

"And what if he couldn't bring it into court without implicating himself in something? Come on, Lauren, he's exactly the kind of man who would figure out how to get someone out of the way. He's self-centered, his success depends on his public perception of success, he likes the good life and doesn't want it jeopardized.''

"You make him sound so cold." None of this was funny anymore. Lauren pushed around a piece of pizza, hoping to distract Eli, too. She failed.

"Convince me he isn't," he said.

Lauren put aside the food and sat back. Eli's place didn't seem so welcoming anymore. There was a tightness in her neck, it felt as if someone had shoved a steel rod up her spine. Her head pounded with a deep dull throb.

"I've got to go. I shouldn't have come."

Lauren stood up. She felt confused, unsure if she wanted to leave or stay and talk this out. She stepped around the coffee table. Leaving would be the best. The music had stopped long ago and Eli didn't look quite so charming, nor so sexy, nor did Lauren feel the sense of safety she had when she first walked in.

"Yes, you should have come. You should talk about this, Lauren," Eli murmured. As she passed, he took hold of her ankle. It was a light touch and then his hand closed around it. "If you hadn't had concerns about Lassiter, you would have gone to him. Be honest enough to admit that." Lauren closed her eyes, so very aware of the warmth in the room, the warmth in his touch and the black space in her heart where there was no one waiting for her. His touch lightened. "You want the truth. We're truth seekers right? Just be honest about what kind of man Lassiter is."

"He's handsome, he's smart. He was always there to cheer Wilson up, he ate at restaurants he hated because Wilson liked them. He teases me and gets away with it. He helped me through law school. He cheered when I graduated. He's my family."

"No bad qualities? Not one?" Eli asked. He let her go but she didn't move. Instead, Lauren looked down, right into his eyes. Her heart was so heavy.

"He uses women. He's not above some creative thinking when it comes to his business. He likes his comforts. You have to go to Allan more often than he comes to you. But, in a pinch, he'll pull out all the stops. He really will, Eli."

"I think you should open your eyes," he said softly.

Lauren moved away, needing to be out of his sphere if she was going to stay sane. Eli could make her see green when the sky was blue. That was something Lauren the woman knew; Lauren the lawyer, the friend, wasn't ready to sacrifice history for this new muse.

"My eyes are open. We just don't think alike."

"That can be a good thing. We can compliment each other."

"Not when it comes to believing Allan could have anything to do with Wilson's death. I can't give up years of friendship because you've got a gut feeling."

He was up beside her, his hand clutching hers. "But we do share admiration for Wilson Caufeld. With him gone, are you going to let Lassiter tell you what to do?" Lauren's head snapped his way.

"Wilson never told me what to do, he helped me discover what was right to do. You're not in the same league, Eli."

"I know that and that's why you should help me honor him. You learned the real lessons the judge had to teach and now it's time to use them. You say you want to find out the truth, well here's your chance. Do what he would have done."

"I'll do what I can do," Lauren said.

"No you won't. You'll ignore what I told you. If it bothers you, you'll just shove it away the minute Lassiter smiles, or says something about the judge or does any little thing that makes you believe he's what you want him to be."

"Eli, it's as simple as this. I'm not buying what you're selling and you can't shame me into giving your 'clues' credence." Lauren turned to go but he still had hold of her hand and pulled her back.

Lauren twirled into him and, for the first time, she saw what made Eli Warner powerful. Determination, righteousness, a sense of fair play even if it was defined by his senses. She looked right back at him knowing she was just as strong and just as determined.

"I'm selling the chance to be honest because that's all I truck in. I'm asking you to think about what I've said. You're the lawyer. You look at the evidence. You already know who it isn't." He jerked her closer still until there was nowhere to go but through him. "You told me you know it isn't Henry."

"And there's no evidence that it's Allan. I'm tired." Eli didn't care. He tightened his grip.

"So am I, lady. I can't sleep thinking about this and I want you to lie awake, too." He whispered fast and Lauren was mesmerized by the sound of his voice. "Use your brain. Lassiter acts as if Caufeld meant nothing to him. He was making rain at the funeral for God's sake." Lauren wiggled, uncomfortable with that observation because she had made it herself. Eli held her tight. "Lassiter was the last person the judge talked with the night I brought up the financial discrepancies. The agents on detail saw an angry Lassiter come out of those chambers and a defeated Caufeld hours later. Lassiter told those agents not to bother guarding the judge since he was about to slit his own throat. Those were his words." Lauren turned into him and put her hand on her chest.

"I don't want to hear it."

She was ready to push him away then made the mistake of looking into his eyes. They were hard and bright, the message was intriguing but the messenger irresistible.

"The last call Wilson made the night he died was to Allan Lassiter. Lassiter was pissed at the way Caufeld was handling the Stewarts. Everyone heard him raving. Admit it."

"Yes. Yes. He was mad." She could hardly breathe. The apartment was so hot. Lauren shook her head, desperate to keep on track. "So was I. Do you think I pulled the trigger?"

"You weren't angry like that. You didn't see dollar signs."

"Of course not."

"Pile on a problem from way back. A financial problem that upset the judge to the point of despondency. A problem that would affect someone else with a lot at stake. Emotions start running high. Things were said. Lassiter storms out. You're friends. The three of you were never apart. Suddenly you don't see each other for days. Where was Lassiter?"

Lauren shook her head. "I don't know. I didn't see him. I didn't talk to him."

"And that didn't make you wonder?" Eli almost laughed. "Have you asked Lassiter where he was the night Caufeld died? Do you know that? I don't and I've asked. Just ask him that one question and I'll be satisfied. See if you have the courage to find the answer."

Eli clutched her shoulders. In her eyes he saw that the line had been crossed. Deep, deep down inside her it didn't matter anymore what Allan Lassiter did or how much courage she had or even what happened on the street where Wilson Caufeld was killed. This moment was filled with desire that burned right through her skin. Eli touched her cheek, checking for a fever only to find that what was between them wasn't as simple as sex or lust. There was a need in them both to fill the houses they lived in, big places so vast there were rooms they'd never explored, places too lonely to wander around in alone.

"I haven't wondered . . ." Lauren whispered, her eyes focused on Eli's lips.

She didn't want to hear about Allan or Wilson who she missed so badly. Lauren Kingsley didn't want another word to come out of Eli's mouth. She just wanted him. He understood. It didn't matter what he believed about all the rest, he understood her.

As if to prove it, Eli Warner took Lauren in his arms, pushing her gently back against the wall as he kissed her. No frantic tumbling, no groping, just a kiss. This was just the moment and time stood still during the seconds it took them to realize how right this was. After that, it didn't matter.

Twirling away from the wall, touching and feeling, holding and clutching, they were naked without ever really knowing who had loosened the first button, who had first touched naked flesh. The stereo was silent but music was in their heads. Touches were electric, making connections deep inside. There were sounds but no words, then words without meaning and then glorious silence when they finally fell onto the couch, Lauren atop Eli, his hands at her waist, her breasts pressed against his chest, her lips on his. Eli and Lauren stopped thinking and did what came naturally; they did what they had wanted to do since the first moment they laid eyes on one another.

There were hours between the beginning and the ending and another beginning. Time went by when they didn't say a word and finally a moment when Eli kissed her hair. Holding handfuls of it tight, he thanked her. He was warm, he said and Lauren knew he had just told her something important.

In the last minutes of those long hours, though, Lauren knew that they had begun and finished in that time. When she eased herself away from him, gently putting his arm back onto the couch and the coverlet over him, Lauren was alone again. She gathered her clothes, smiling to see how they were entwined with his. In the bathroom Lauren washed her face and, as the morning light tried to punch through the cracked ice window above the tub, she braided her hair. Beyond the bathroom wall a sudden bang startled her, she paused to listen to the raised voices but they were silent before she could focus. Putting the last pin in her chignon, she walked into the dark living room and got her purse. It was over, this love affair, because there were people she loved more. Wilson, who had left her with the unspoken charge of being loyal to Allan who still lived, would always color the way she felt about Eli. They couldn't survive together when Eli made it clear they would stand apart on the issue of Wilson's death. Lauren closed her eyes and breathed in so that she would remember everything. Then she would be gone.

"You don't have to go." She barely smiled, enjoying the sound of his voice before turning to face him. His eyes were open.

"Yes, I do," she chuckled sadly, "and you know it."

"Second thoughts? Hard feelings? Ashamed?" Eli rolled on his back and propped himself up. "God I hope not, Lauren."

"None of the above. Satisfied. Grateful. Calm. Thank you."

"Think we might try it in the bedroom next time?" He

smiled and she saw his beautiful grin through the dark apartment. He put his hand out to her.

She shook her head knowing he probably didn't see her as clearly. He probably couldn't see that she smiled.

"I don't think so."

He laced his hands behind his head since he couldn't coax her to the couch. "What do you think?"

"I think that we're on parallel lines, Eli." She sighed and picked up her jacket. She gave it a little shake, unable to look at him. "I'll never believe what you believe, and you'll never give up. You'll dog Allan until something happens that satisfies you. We can't live like that."

"You still putting me in the big old FBI pot, huh?"

"Call it baggage," Lauren said quietly. "I've been there, Eli. You are desperate to implicate Allan, and I don't think you can help yourself."

Lauren put on her jacket, she found her purse. Eli was up and stepping into his jeans. The zipper grated. He didn't bother with the snap and the fine line of hair that ran down his belly caught her eye. She looked away for fear of temptation.

"I am desperate to find out what happened to Judge Caufeld, and the only reason I'm even thinking about Allan Lassiter is because something stinks when it comes to him."

"Tell Mark Jackson," Lauren said, trying to control that flare of anger that still burned in her gut.

"I have." His voice rose in frustration only to drop again. He knew to react emotionally would get him nowhere. "I have. He said he'd look into it."

"Then let him," Lauren said as though they had resolved the problem with a compromise unacceptable to either.

Eli shook his head. "Mark wants it to be the militia. Not just for Nick's sake, but because it's politically correct. He'll think about Lassiter, but he won't run with the information and you know it. Please, Lauren, I need your help now that we both know the truth about Henry."

"Stop pushing, Eli. Can't you see that what you call truth is nothing more than a calculated investigation. Your conclusion is preordained. You haven't got anything on

Allan, you've simply decided there should be something. That's the way it was with my mother."

That was the last straw. Frustrated, Eli did a half turn. One hand went to his waist, the other to his hair. He pushed his hair back as if to keep himself in check. He opened his mouth, closed it and finally couldn't remain silent. Eli Warner faced Lauren Kingsley square.

"Take off your blinders, Lauren. I know all about your mother."

"I don't think so."

"You know what I think? I think no one's ever had the guts to tell you that she was guilty as sin."

Lauren's mouth dropped open. In a split second, Eli saw that she was going to run and in that same second she saw he was going to try to make her stay. Eli was quicker. He had his hand on her arm. Lauren tried to shimmy away. Eli made her stay. It might be the last chance he had to make her see what was real and what was right.

"You're despicable and you're wrong," she hissed.

"I've seen the file. I will get it, and I will show it to you."

"Like I'd believe anything you showed me or anything an agent wrote down." With all her strength she pulled her arms down and moved away.

"You want the truth and I'm giving it to you." Eli circled her, inviting her into the ring. "Marta Kingsley was guilty of peddling her influence the same as the other three judges who were going to be indicted with her. I don't think she was a bad woman. She was probably caught up in something that she didn't understand until she was well into it. She might have thought it was politic to do the things she did. I could read it a million ways."

"Shut up, Eli. Shut up right now, I warn you."

Eli shook his head hard, his dukes were up. The truth was hard to take. "Come on, Lauren. You talk about honesty as if you discovered it but you're not willing to hold the people you love to the standards you set. I'm talking about all of them: your mother, Lassiter and even Wilson Caufeld. I'm not saying they're evil, I'm saying they aren't perfect, they weren't perfect."

"I can't believe I'm hearing this."

Lauren shook her head and turned until she was facing the door. Eli moved in. His hand hovered over her shoulder and he spoke without touching her. Lauren was frozen with horror. He was ruining everything, desecrating memories and making it impossible for her to find comfort with the last person living she cared about. Wouldn't she always look at Allan and wonder now? Of course, because Eli was packing her head with questions and innuendo and circumstances that could have meant anything.

"Are you going to live the rest of your life thinking you were cared for by perfect people? The fact that you didn't know about your mother proves they weren't perfect. Lassiter is a charmer. He razzles and dazzles and I bet he kept you entertained so you never thought to ask any real questions. Did you ever ask if you thought he was a good person? Wilson let you think what you wanted to think about your mother and he was right to treat a young girl that way. But you're a woman now, Lauren. If you want to worship truth, and honor trust, then start with yourself. Trust your instincts. Trust me."

"Never! You're part of the problem."

"No, I'm not." Eli embraced her, trying to pull her into him. When Lauren wouldn't budge he moved around her, bending his knees so he could look her in the eyes. "Your mother made a decision and that's what caused her problems. Innocent intentions or not, she screwed up. Maybe one of her friends asked a favor and then someone else was sent her way and she did another favor. Maybe she worried about putting you through college and needed extra money."

"That's ridiculous," Lauren scoffed and shook off his hands.

"Is it? A single parent on a judge's salary? A woman alone. No matter what you think about your mother, in the final analysis that's what she was. A woman alone. She must have been scared. In the dead of night scared people make contingency plans. Sometimes they work, sometimes they don't. Maybe one of those other judges told her how easy it was to pick up a few extra bucks. Maybe he convinced her she could act within the law. Who did it really hurt after all?"

"What do you know about what she thought?" Lauren's voice cracked. She put two fingers to her lips as if that would stop her from shaking.

"Okay, do you want another scenario?" Eli was into it now. He was animated, he was ready with a beginning, middle and end. "She was callous and anxious to use her authority for gain."

"How dare you," Lauren seethed and he caught her arm before she could run.

"I dare because I can make up any rationalization you want. The fact is, no matter what her intent, she did the deed. I tend to think her intentions were good because she couldn't be your mother if she wasn't, at the core, a good person." He gave her a little shake to underscore his belief in the good things. She wasn't buying it, but he tried again. "Neither your mother nor Wilson deserved to die, but Wilson didn't decide to die. You couldn't do anything about your mother's suicide; you can do something about Wilson's death. You owe him something for everything he did for you."

"I can't believe I came here, Eli. I can't believe I thought you would help me work all this out."

"But isn't it interesting that you did when you could have gone to see Lassiter."

That was something to think about. Lauren did so for no more than a second. She looked him straight in the eye and all that she had desired in him was gone.

"Usually I choose better. I suppose I was tired. I suppose I was afraid and I didn't want to disappoint Allan by telling him what happened in that garage with Henry. The thing I can't quite figure out is why you've latched onto Allan? Maybe you're the one who needs to open your eyes and figure out why you're so obsessed with him. Are you going to pull yourself up the ladder by pulling him down? Is there some sort of quota you guys have for trashing prominent people?"

Lauren took one step back and one to the side. She should have left but there was more to say. There was always more to say, that was how she made herself feel well and whole and that's how she ruined herself.

"You might as well give up, Eli. I can alibi Allan the night Wilson died. All you had to do was ask me. I spoke to him at his office that night just about the time Wilson was killed. He was at his office, not gunning down a man he loved so much."

Eli turned his head. His face looked different, harder and his expression more remote from this angle.

"You may have spoken to Allan Lassiter, but I doubt he was at his office."

"I called him there."

"Ever hear of call roll-over, Lauren? Does he have it? Because if he does, Mr. Lassiter could have been anywhere when you spoke to him."

"I don't know what you're talking about."

"You don't watch enough television." The edge to his comment was cutting and mean. He came closer. She could smell her sex on him and it was exciting, or was the excitement in how he challenged her? "Call roll-over is great for busy people—or liars. You see, if it was me, you could call me at my office but I've programmed the call to ring poolside where I'm sitting in a hot tub with a few blondes. You'd assume I was sitting in my office." Eli smiled, ready to let her in on the conclusion. "So if I could be in a hot tub, I'll bet Lassiter could have been standing over Wilson Caufeld's body while he was taking your call and telling you how sorry he was that he was late. So, what do you think, Lauren? Did you see him at the funeral? Do you know if he has call roll-over at his office? Did you know that there were two other people in Lassiter's office that night and neither of them saw him. Lauren?" Eli moved even closer. His fingertips brushed her jacket. Lauren breathed in once. She twisted her head to look at him, her lips parted but he spoke first. "Does he ever talk about Judge Caufeld anymore? Does Allan Lassiter have a gun?"

The questions were still ringing in her ears as she left

the apartment. Down the steps, out into the street, key at the ready to open her car so she could escape. One more look back at Eli Warner. But he was gone, his door shut against her, and for some reason that made Lauren afraid.

Chapter Sixteen

Lauren drove like a crazy woman. She drank the air instead of breathing it, but Eli had knocked the wind out of her and her lungs wouldn't expand. He had come so close, made her feel safe, perhaps loved, then attacked the man she loved like a brother. Didn't she? Lauren shook her head to clear Eli out. Unfortunately, Eli wouldn't be banished. Lauren pressed the gas pedal and decided to damn well leave him in her dust if that was the only way.

She wasn't a coward, Allan was not involved in anything illegal and Eli was not a port in the storm. Wilson was loved. Allan loved him. She loved Allan and those were the permutations that had held her in good stead for her adult life so there was no choice. Lauren went to Allan's home to talk to him, knowing full well she intended to warn him about Eli. She tried not to think about the fact that, with Wilson dead, there was nowhere else for her to go.

Dawn was just coming up over Los Angeles when Lauren knocked at Allan's door. She knocked firmly enough so that he would hear even if he was dead asleep. It was five-thirty in the morning. Lauren rang the bell, but no one came to let her in. Her heart threw itself against the walls of her chest and she put a hand over it to keep it from leaping into her throat. Knowing she needed to see him, Lauren made a decision. She used her key and stepped into Allan Lassiter's home the way she had the night Wilson Caufeld died. This was not exactly the same as that night: this time she wasn't invited.

Lauren eased the key out of the lock and went through the motions knowing she might find something she didn't want to find: a woman sleeping in Allan's bed, Edie Williams coming out of the shower, perhaps Allan, only Allan, angered that she should be so bold, so rude. She didn't consider the possibility of finding something more sinister. Pocketing the key and reminding herself again that she had no right to be there, then Lauren stepped over the threshold.

The first thing Lauren saw was the sky through the huge window. It was the palest peach, the shade that is tinged with gold. Night gray hovered at the very edges of the light as if coveting the morning. Another time Lauren would have admired the world as she stood in Allan's stratosphere, but Allan's universe had changed, or, perhaps, she was seeing it all for the first time.

She was trespassing.

She should leave.

She closed the door and saw Allan Lassiter's home through new eyes.

This was an ominous, empty, forlorn, and deserted place. The furniture, the ceramics, crystal and artwork had lost their sense of purpose. This place had once defined Allan by his taste, his eye for beauty, his flamboyance, his power, money and prestige. Now it seemed to underscore his lack of creativity, warmth and personal connection. There was nothing here: not a picture of Wilson, or of her. There wasn't even a picture of himself with a woman, Edie or otherwise.

There was mail on the side table. She pushed it around with one finger. Bills, professional notices, catalogues. Where were the letters from real people? Friends? His own protégés? People who knew Allan? What about people who liked Allan? Lauren stopped herself. Her thought process was absurd. She was creating problems where yesterday there had been none.

"Allan?" she called softly, listening carefully as she made her way into the living room. Now it was full on day, nature as a quick change artist, and there wasn't a sound in Allan's home.

Lauren took a step toward the bedroom and cocked an ear. The shower wasn't running. How she would have laughed if she'd heard him singing in there. That thought didn't even bring a small smile to her lips.

"Allan?" she called again.

Through the door she could see the shadow of a lacquered chest of drawers she had often admired. From that angel the doorway looked like a portal to another world. The suede-beige walls undulated with shadows cast long and then dispelled as the earth tilted and the sun rearranged itself and then fought to come through the shutters on the windows. The bed was made neatly. It was too early for the daily maid. Allan hadn't slept in that bed the night before. She looked away. That meant nothing. She hadn't slept in hers either. With that thought, Lauren had a vision. Eli and her, naked in the early hours when it was more night than morning.

"Allan? It's Lauren."

By the time the last note had sounded, she was there, in the bedroom. He wasn't; she shouldn't be. Lauren was headed out, urged on by her own sense of propriety, when she stopped. Beside the neatly made bed was the exquisite rosewood chest and atop that was the phone. Sleek, black, silent. Lauren didn't take long to decide that there was something to do before she left. She would do it for Wilson. She would do it for herself. Most of all, she would do it for Allan because no one was there to protect him any more except her.

Licking her lips, Lauren walked slowly toward the bed. She couldn't do it standing up. The mattress gave beneath her. Twice she breathed hard, twice she reached for the receiver, touched it and drew her hand back. On the third

ry Lauren picked it up. Knowing wherever Allan was, he
was not at the office, Lauren calmed herself and dialed
his office number, punching the buttons fast before she
lost her nerve.

She listened with one arm cocked to hold the phone to
her ear, the other draped across her middle. Three rings,
and on the fourth the voice-mail menu announced itself.
Lauren knew the routine. She punched in Allan's exten-
sion and waited again. Three rings and on the fourth she
would get the answering machine.

"Hello there." This was no answering machine. Allan
was at the office.

Air flooded into her lungs. Surprise! Surprise! She had
given Eli's speculation credence and now she had proved
him wrong, wrong, wrong. Her smile was just breaking,
she was just sitting up straighter, ready to chatter when
she heard something that blunted every expression of joy.
Something wasn't right. No. Something was very, very
wrong.

"I always knew you wanted me."

"Allan? It's me, Lauren," she said.

"I know," he whispered and then he laughed aloud.
She heard that laugh in stereo and her blood ran cold.

Slowly Lauren turned her head. There he was. Allan,
backlit by a white gold aura from the huge window in the
living room, leaned against the door to his bedroom. He
was grinning at her and there was a phone at his ear. It
was a small and exquisitely manufactured cellular phone
and he spoke into it. He purred into it. He grinned at her
as he purred into it.

"I've always wanted to get you into bed."

She heard his voice coming through the phone at her
ear and coming at her from across the room. They were
connected and they were together. Lauren's heart stopped.
That's when he snapped the phone shut and came toward
her.

There were three men and a woman in the van with no
windows. They were dressed in black, armed and ready to

go. The house had been surveilled. The hour was good not too early but not late enough for the few neighbors to be up and about. Not that they'd ever really seen neighbors but one had to assume someone was inside the houses where lights went on at night. The man inside the house in question was still asleep and the people inside the van knew what to do. Each one did a last-minute check on his weapon, confirmed communication with the intercept cars positioned at strategic locations and readjusted their body armor. They checked with their commander up front. The word was go, so they went.

The back of the van opened. Four bodies piled out of the car with exceeding grace considering how they were outfitted. The commander stayed at the wheel, radio at the ready, ever watchful for a screw up by his men or unexpected movement from inside. Outside, one of the people went ahead and three watched. The leader called them ahead a second later. They fanned out around the little, ill-kept house on a close-to-abandoned side-street just inside the boundaries of Riverside County. Just outside the boundary line there was nothing but nothing.

Two agents rounded the house in the back. Two stayed in front, laying back against the wall by the front door as they waited to hear that their compadres were positioned. They didn't worry about the sides of the house, the few windows were permanently barred so no one would be heading out that way. The agents in front heard the command to go come through their ear phones.

All hell broke lose.

Front and back, the doors were kicked open simultaneously. Shouts and hollers, barked orders and weapons snapping around each corner, followed closely by the snapper. More barks and roars and heavy boots on the floor as the intruders stormed from room to room. There were only five including the kitchen so it didn't take much time. They found Henry Stewart in the fifth, a small bedroom with a real bed unlike his previous accommodations. They found him much as they expected, paralyzed with fear now that he'd been found out. Poor little Henry was in shock, his expression never changing despite the commotion around him and the sound of assault weapons ratcheting as they were pointed at his head. But Henry wasn't quite what he seemed. He was smarter than they thought. Henry knew they wouldn't shoot because good guys didn't unless they had to. They fought clean, face to face. It was the other stuff you had to watch out for. The people they sent in to make you think there was another choice. That's who you had to be afraid of. People like Nick Cheshire.

So Henry lay with the covers up around his chin watching carefully to see when they would figure it out. They didn't. They were all in the macho mode, even the lady.

"Henry Stewart. FBI. Up. Up. Up now," the first person hollered and the other's followed suit. *Up. Up. Out of bed you sleepy head.* One of them ripped back the covers, all of them ready to rip him right out of the bed.

Instead, they fell silent.

Then they fell back.

Henry was wired.

A bomb was strapped to his middle.

Henry grinned.

That's when they saw the switch in his hand.

"Boy, if this isn't a surprise. Leave one woman's bed, come home and find another in my own."

Lauren jumped and the phone fell from her hands. She fumbled with it, stood and put it back in the cradle. "I wasn't exactly in your bed. I was just sitting on it." Feeling like a schoolgirl caught snooping in the headmaster's office, Lauren stepped away, her hands behind her back.

"Hey, it's a start, right? I mean if you want to get technical, I wasn't really in bed last night either." Allan was jolly. Allan was full of energy. Allan was drunk. Lauren could smell it five feet away. She crinkled her nose and gave him room.

"You've been drinking this early?" Now there was a crack of a smile on her face, a little one of disbelief so he wouldn't think she was making a judgment even though she was. Allan didn't drink. Not that way.

"No, Laurie," he said happily, "what do you take me

for, a lush?'' She forgave him the dreaded nickname because the overly hearty laugh worried her. "I just didn't stop last night, so I don't think that counts as taking a tipple early in the morning. God, I'm tired. Spent the night closing up Michael's. Nice guys. Nobody rushes you. Then I went to Edie's." He thought about that while he loosened his tie. She wondered if he was enjoying the memory or trying to figure out why that's where he ended up. Then he was happy again, teasing her again. "You want to just lay down and take a little nap? I could use one, and you don't exactly look like you got a lot last night." He looked a little closer, and laughed without humor. "Or maybe you actually got some. Fooling around on me, are you, Laurie?"

He tossed the little phone on the chair, pulled off his tie, then stripped off his shirt. Both landed atop the phone. Lauren saw his smile disappear as he turned his face away. His good humor disintegrated on the way to the bathroom. Lauren started to follow but stopped when he glanced over his shoulder. He should have looked rakish, instead he looked sleazy.

"Are you sure you want to come in here? I'm going to get naked and take a shower." He unzipped his pants, forgetting this was Lauren in his bedroom. Or had he? Perhaps this was another prank, a little morning shock to amuse himself.

"No, I don't want to go in there with you, but I will if that's what it takes to get you to talk to me."

"Fine, your choice. Maybe once you see what you've been missing, you won't want to talk."

He disappeared and the water started running. Lauren stood her ground but it was no show of strength. Doubt was enough to render her stationary, no wonder it had never been a favored companion. Lauren had always dismissed doubt as a rabbit hole for a timid mind. She looked toward the bedroom door but walked through the one leading to the bathroom. Doubt was left behind.

Allan could have hosted a party in his shower, and more than likely he had, but now he was there alone. Lauren could see him through the steam that fogged the clear glass, smudging the outline so that he looked like an impressionist painting. There was no doubt Allan was picture perfect. He could have been a model, he could have been a movie star. Form was of no interest to Lauren now, substance was what she needed to determine. She called to him over the noise of the five shower heads that pummeled him from top to bottom.

"Eli Warner thinks you had something to do with Wilson's death."

The water stopped instantly. The door of the shower flew open and Allan stood in front of her, naked. Water beaded and dropped from his hair and body. A rivulet ran into his lips but they were shut so tight it rerouted itself down his jaw. Lauren stepped back. She said again, more quietly, more forcefully:

"Eli Warner thinks you had something to do with Wilson's problems. Maybe even something to do with his death."

Allan looked at her, he looked through her. His eyes were blood shot and bleary. Beautiful though he may be, there were flaws, cracks in his exterior that let Lauren see a molten interior. What he burned for, what burned through him, she didn't know, nor had she known it existed until this moment.

With a snap he grabbed the bath sheet off the electric warmer. Wrapping it around his waist, Allan pushed past her and stopped at the marble sink. There he looked at himself in the huge mirror, picked up a cup and brush and soaped his face. She stayed quiet while he shaved and rinsed and dried his face. A comb was put through his hair and he was almost perfect once more. He picked up his blow dryer.

"Do you have a gun, Allan?" Lauren asked before he turned it on.

"Do you have any brains, Lauren?" He was cruel and he didn't care what he said to her or how he said it. He put down the blow dryer. Lauren moved in front of him.

"Allan, I've got to know."

"I'm not going to answer you." He turned around. They were two real people now, no mirrors, no tricks. "Eli War-

ner is a peon who obviously is just a bit tired of the grunt
work he's been doing.''

Allan swept past her. Lauren followed, standing clear
while he threw open the doors of his closet and rifled the
dusky rainbow of suits: gray, black, blues in all hues. They
were all so expensive. Hand tailored. Great packaging. She
used to think they were the whole picture, now Lauren
knew they were only a piece of the puzzle that made up
Allan Lassiter.

He slipped the wood hangers back: one, two, three. By
the fifth suit he was slapping at them. Finally he threw a
charcoal single breasted suit on the bed. Followed by a
shirt in the palest pink. It was folded, heavily starched, and
it shot like a Frisbee out of his hand. He snapped a tie off
the rack, whipping it onto the pile and he thought nothing
of dropping his towel and dressing in front of her. He
talked as if he'd forgotten she was there. Or, perhaps, she
didn't exist for him any more.

"I hated that guy when I saw him. He's an idiot. Moved
in on Wilson like a torpedo. He was poking his nose into
everything. Well beyond the scope of a normal background.'' Allan pushed his shirttails into his trousers and
zipped them. "Naw, there was something wrong from the
beginning. I've talked to people about him, Lauren. I've
talked to a lot of people. I was going to have him removed.
I had the connections. I could have done it. I told Wilson
I would have him removed but Wilson said no.'' He turned
up his collar and put in gold stays, stabbing them like little
sabers into the holes. He pulled his tie around his neck
and faced yet another mirror. "So what's he saying Lauren?
What evidence does he have that I've done something so
terrible? Lauren, think about this. He actually said I killed
Wilson?''

"No, he didn't exactly say that,'' Lauren backtracked.
He hadn't said that but that's what he meant. "He thinks
there was something wrong between you and Wilson. He
thinks it was something so bad that it could have hurt you
and him. He only has a vague idea, sort of a feeling because
of the way you've been acting since Wilson died and

because of something he found out about Wilson's firm. He's going to keep looking into it.''

"Oh, that's dandy. He's going to run around this city calling me a murderer? Jesus, Lauren, what's with you?''

"Nothing. I didn't say I believed him. I just . . .''

"What? What did you just?'' Whip. Snap. Tug. His tie was knotted.

"I'm just confused. I saw Henry Stewart last night. I talked to him.'' Lauren moved around, trying to look Allan in the eye but he kept turning until he was looking at her through the mirror again. "Allan, listen. I saw him and talked to him and he said he didn't kill Wilson.''

"Oh, now you're making so much more sense. You believe a kid who blew up a building and killed two people. He said he didn't kill Wilson—even though he could have come up with a zillion reasons to do it—you believe him. Then you run off to see a guy who hates my guts because he thinks he's found the scandal of the season and you come here and accuse me . . .''

"I am warning you. I didn't accuse you of anything,'' Lauren interrupted, going to him and putting her hand on his shoulder.

He glanced at her. He tugged at his tie once more, somehow displeased with the way it looked. Finally he positioned it at his throat, stopped and let his shoulders sag. When he turned around he leaned against the dresser, he clutched the end of his tie and his eyes were filled with tears of exhaustion. He took her hand and held it loosely in his own.

"Lauren,'' he said sincerely, "I miss Wilson more than I could ever imagine. Can't you see how terrible I feel about all this? Oh, Lord, sometimes I don't even want to get up in the morning and other times I can't sleep at night. I don't know how to live with this. You know, that guy hasn't got a clue how much salt he's rubbing into the wound. You want to know if I have a gun. Fine. I have a gun. What else? What else do you want to know?''

Lauren moved closer, wrapping an arm around his shoulders. She leaned her head against his, brother and sister, family at last. Allan reached up and took her arm.

His hand was so large, her arm so small. She was so tiny. It occurred to him that he could snap her arm without much thought, and probably do the same to her neck. But that was the residue of the liquor in his thinking, nothing more he was sure.

"Nothing. I'm sorry. I'm so sorry I asked," Lauren said quietly. She moved her head and felt how soft his hair was. It smelled fresh and clean. Eli Warner, who knew so little of what they'd been through, had managed to make her question the bond between Allan and her. Perhaps Allan had not sought her out, but she was equally guilty for not offering a shoulder for him to cry on. She had called to complain, but she hadn't asked about him.

"Allan, I'm sorry. I'm so, so sorry. I should have come to you right away when Eli started talking like that. Now you can talk about it. Just talk about those years he has questions about and get it all out. I'll tell him what he needs to know, and then he'll leave you alone."

Allan stiffened and, as he did so, his hand tightened around Lauren's arm until she squealed in protest. Ever so slowly he pulled her in front of him. Lauren stumbled, disoriented as things changed. "Lauren, before I tell you anything, I have a question." He stared at her, his voice low and threatening. "Did you come here to spy on me?"

"Oh, God, Allan, no," Lauren breathed. Her arm burned but she made no attempt to extricate herself. What he was saying pained her more than anything he could do to her physically. "Allan, don't be ridiculous. I came here to let you know he had questions."

"Did you sleep with him, Lauren?" Allan let her go, and Lauren put a hand to her arm.

"Irrelevant." She stepped back, smarting but unintimidated.

"And there are some things that aren't any of your business," Allan reminded her. "One of them is my relationship with Wilson. You know, you never figured out when to leave well enough alone. Warner thinks I maybe made Wilson miserable. Well, how about the way you made him feel? You're the one that threatened him with a higher court on Stewarts' standing issue. He sure felt great about that. Warner thinks I could have killed Wilson? And what about you? He made a fool of you in court. He was going to ruin your career if he let George Stewart go. Wasn't that enough to kill Wilson for?"

"No, and you know it."

"I don't know any such thing. All I know is that I can make up a story given what I know about you and your relationship with Wilson the same way your boyfriend makes them up about me. You can't see that you're being used, I haven't got the time to teach you how to figure it out. I thought you were smarter than that, Lauren, but you really scraped the bottom of the barrel. He can't do anything for you except bring you down."

"Funny, Allan, at this minute I kind of feel like Eli Warner might be a step up."

"You better watch what you're doing and saying, sweetheart. You don't have anyone to help you, now that Wilson's dead."

"Neither do you, Allan. Or have you forgotten you're where you are because of Wilson," Lauren reminded him.

"I haven't forgotten. The difference is, I've already arrived and you still need someone to give you a push."

"I don't think so, Allan. In fact, of the two of us, I might be in a better position," Lauren drawled. "I may never rise as high as you, but you can fall a hell of a lot farther than me."

Allan glared. Allan didn't move save for a tremor at the corner of his jaw. Lauren watched him, her eyes narrowed, her mind ready to counter anything he could throw a her. She wanted him to talk now. She wanted to hear exactly how much anger there was inside him. But Allan Lassiter wasn't going to be that accommodating.

"Get out, Laurie, and leave the key," he said coldly. "Come on back when you know which side you're on."

Lauren turned on her heel. She tossed his key on the hall table and didn't look back. Eli was right about one thing. Something had happened between Allan and Wilson, and whatever it was, it wasn't a good thing.

* * *

"It's a good thing," Dr. Temple said, sounding like the physician's Martha Stewart. "Come on. He's awake."

Mark walked fast beside the doctor who seemed almost giddy with pleasure that Nick was on his way to recovery.

"How long has it been?" Mark asked.

"He showed some signs of coming out of it during the early morning hours, but we didn't want to call you until we were positive there'd be a chance he could communicate. It's not too late, is it?"

"Too late? For what?" They took a hard left and followed a green arrow that pointed the way to Intensive Care. Mark could have followed it in his sleep.

"For your investigation. I mean, if he can give you the information you're looking for, are you going to be able to put these guys behind bars?"

Mark smiled with pleasure. "Doc, I think they may be where we want them even as we speak. Nick's going to be the icing on the cake. Believe me. Everyone responsible for Nick's condition is going down. One of 'em already bit the dust, and now it's just cleanup time."

A right and they went right by the smiling nurses and in to see Nick Cheshire.

"Nick," Mark said as he walked to the bed, only to readjust his volume when he got there. Leaning over him, Mark talked softly. "You're looking good, buddy. Real good. Had me worried for a minute there."

Nick looked at him, happiness somewhere behind his eyes, drugs and pain still obscuring it. Mark could tell it was there, though, because Nick was trying to smile, too. There was still stuff around his mouth, wires in his jaw but Mark grinned back.

"I know, man, it's been rough. Don't you worry. We're getting them. Every last one. The kid's going down today." Mark tilted closer, trying to talk privately with his friend. There was so much to tell him and Mark was excited. "Yep, old Henry's being brought back to the fold. When you finger the rest I'll give you their heads on a platter. I swear,

I'm going to bury every single one of those militia freaks that hurt you." Nick closed his eyes at the news and Mark grinned. Even in the shape he was in, Nick Cheshire managed to showed his gratitude. That simple act spurred Mark Jackson on. He knew Nick still had a long way to go, but good news would help him recover. Closer still he went, until his lips were right next to Nick Cheshire's ear. His hand grasped Nick's fingertips. "Caufeld's dead, Nick. He put you here with his damned deliberations and now he's dead, buddy. I'm taking care of everything. We're getting everyone who was even remotely responsible for what happened to you."

Nick's eyes opened instantaneously and his head jerked. Mark pulled up, terrified that he had done something to cause Nick pain. Nick was awake, his eyes wide and frantic with terror not pain. He was talking, but the words were garbled from behind his headgear. His fingers clawed at Mark's hand as his eyes flipped back and forth in his head. Mark reached for the buzzer to call the nurse, but Nick managed a tug on Mark's fingers so Mark leaned down again. This time it was his ear near Nick's lips.

Painstakingly, Nick moved his lips beneath the wires. One eternal minute later, Mark Jackson patted Nick's hand. He had two names. It was enough.

"It's okay, buddy. It's enough. You done good. I'll check it out."

He walked purposefully from the unit and down the hall. Behind him, a nurse rushed in to check on Nick Cheshire. The monitor was going crazy. She took his pulse, she looked at his face, she checked the readings. Her patient was agitated, no doubt.

She spoke softly and soothingly, stroking his hand as she did so. The nurse asked him to open his eyes. He did so. There were tears in them. She eased his mind and finally he went to sleep. The nurse left when she was sure he was all right. Back at the desk, she made a note to speak to Mr. Jackson about upsetting Mr. Cheshire. His condition was still extremely precarious.

On his way out of the hospital, Mark Jackson was having a similar reaction. His heart was palpitating and he was upset. Slipping into his car, he wrote down the words Nick had managed to say. Little did anyone know that the situation was this precarious. How, he wondered, had the militia reached so far, and what, exactly, was he going to do about it?

Chapter Seventeen

Mark Jackson sat in the Soft Spot looking death right in the eye. He was tattooed on the bartender's arm and the Grim Reaper was a stunning piece of work. Grand flowing robes were etched from the lady's shoulder to elbow, his scythe and hood were elongated to epic proportions. The look of it gave Mark the shivers, but nothing scared him more than the thought that he'd been drinking out of glasses this woman had touched. She said she'd been tending bar since she was a baby. She looked like she'd been raised from the dead and she loved to talk.

Black hair streamed down her back and looked like something that had come from a river bottom. She was pale and fleshy. Her body was poured into horizontal strips of black leather: a black leather bra from which her huge breasts erupted, a micro-mini so tight at the waist that her gut grew up and out of it, so short at the other end that her bottom poked out when she reached for a brew. Black mesh stockings waffle-printed her legs and her feet rested in well-worn black boots. She had outlined her small eyes with black kohl and lined her fingers with big silver rings. She liked Mark from the minute he walked in. That's why the place was called the Soft Spot. She only let people stay if she knew they would always have a soft spot in her heart. Her name was Wanda. She'd talked to him for an hour, giving him the lowdown on the regulars, telling him how much she loved a man who kept his hair and mustache neat. It was the sign of a man up on his luck. Mark made the appropriate responses and waited for the appointed hour. Just like Wanda said, at eleven the place started hopping and Wanda was too busy to give him her full attention.

"Hey, baby, good to see ya." She called to the woman who came in and slung a saddle bag on the bar. Wanda patted Mark's hand, strutting away with the kind of apology she gave to those she favored. "I hate to run, baby. Be back at you."

"You won't forget me, will you, Wanda?" Mark asked, with that smile he reserved for just such occasions. If his wife could have seen it she would have died.

Wanda turned and winked. Black mascara flaked onto her cheek, "I know who you're looking for, baby. I gotcha covered."

Mark put another buck on the bar just so she wouldn't forget. Wanda came cheap.

She went her way, chatting up the newcomers. Mark downed his Cuervo Gold. That was number three. His limit. He rolled around on his stool, lifting his leg so his jeans wouldn't stick to whatever it was Wanda had neglected to wash off the wooden seat. He lounged against the bar checking out the clientele listening to Wanda's routine. Baby this, baby that, lean over the bar pushing her boobs forward. A kiss. Cheeks, lips, breasts, it was all the same to Wanda. Yeah, they loved her like a mother, ordered their poison and tipped her well. And she talked. Because Wanda talked, he knew exactly who he was looking for.

"Hey, baby," he heard one more time before he tuned her out and slid off his stool, heading for the juke box. He dumped in a buck. Three plays, it used to be four. Absently he pushed the buttons before surveying the scene again. Two at the pool table, three men at the bar. Two women, one chatting up the guys, the other by herself.

That one would be alone until everybody got blinded then she'd go home happy with the guy with the worst optical problems.

Mark settled himself at a table. The woman at the bar gave him the once over and didn't bother to smile. She seemed to know she couldn't convince anyone she was worth a second look so she didn't bother trying. He touched his mustache. He traveled across the worn floor one more time and blessed the dim light when he sat down next to her. A woman like her might have things to get off her chest.

"Can I get you something?" His knuckles pointed toward her half-empty glass.

"Not done yet." She finished up. "Now you can."

"What are you drinking?"

"Wanda," she called in a voice that would have a hard time whispering sweet nothings. "Put a Black Russian on this guy's tab."

Wanda cackled back, "No tabs here, baby, you know that. What'd you think the name of this place was, soft touch?"

Wanda brought the drink and collected the money. From his new angle Mark could see a serpent sneaking its head out from the middle of her bra. Nice touch. He put another five in her brassiere and the snake disappeared.

"Baby, you are the sweetest." Wanda turned to the woman. "Listen, Cory, this nice man here is looking for Udell. You give him the heads up when he comes in. I'm going to be busy tonight, baby."

"Yeah, sure thing." The woman next to him sipped her drink and seemed satisfied. She talked to the glass. "You sure you want to talk to Udell?"

Mark nodded. "I'm sure we've got something in common. Why shouldn't I want to talk to Udell?"

"You don't seem like the kind of guy who'd be friends with that dude." Half the Black Russian disappeared.

"What do I seem like?" He was curious since she hadn't looked at him for more than two seconds.

"An accountant looking to get his head kicked in."

Mark laughed. "Naw, I'm not an accountant."

"What business you have with Udell?"

"How well do you know him?" The vibes were heavy. If she wasn't running interference, he'd change places with Nick. He glanced at Wanda. Could be a setup. Fine. No problem as long as he knew the lay of the land.

"I know him well enough to know that Udell doesn't have much in common with no one." She flicked her eyes his way. "Didn't see you on a hog, so you're no biker."

"Is Udell?"

"Thought you had something in common with him. How can you have something in common with someone you never did meet?" She was facing him now, her arms akimbo, her hand around her glass like it was a grenade. "Cops cut their hair short like that. Could you be that stupid?"

"You prejudiced or something?" Mark didn't bother to sit up straight. She was drunk. He could take her even if she wasn't. She wiggled her head, her shoulders stayed where they were, then she was half lying over the bar again.

"No. Just careful. We take care of our own."

"Yeah," Mark said darkly, "I heard all about how you do that."

The woman backed off, going rigid next to him. She slid off the stool. "Thanks for the drink. I think you're going to be busy now."

"Baby, baby, baby!" Wanda was screeching. In the Soft Spot, that was the equivalent of dimming the lights in a theater. The man had arrived with his entourage. The crowd hushed. The curtain was rising on the first act.

Udell was a big man. Udell was an ugly man. Tattooed from here to eternity, he was a walking advertisement for the US of A. Hoochie Kootch girls danced on his belly, Bugs Bunny wrapped around one bicep, the Marine logo around the other, fish and fauna from the Great Northwest trailed down his back and right in the middle of his chest, big as life, was the American flag. He showed off this splendor wearing nothing but a vest and chaps over low-slung jeans and steel-toed boots. A sweat-stained red kerchief was wrapped around his head Indian style. Two men trailed after him, splitting to check out the room for the right

eal estate. Mark didn't bother with those bozos. It was the
voman—a beautiful woman—hanging on Udell's arm that
ascinated him. Her silky blond hair covered half her face,
he eye in the other half was trained adoringly on her man.
At the sound of Wanda's last "baby" the blond woman
energized.

"Fuck 'n A, Wanda!" she called back, slapping her thigh
and heading for the bar.

Udell pulled her back hard and she shook him off,
pushing her hair away from her face at the same time.
Mark Jackson's insides turned over. That hidden half was
the color of slime, a little darker right under her eye.
Bruises in various stages of heeling ran from her forehead
to her jaw. She must have looked like hell when the things
were fresh; she didn't look too grand now.

"Baby, how's that arm of yours?" Wanda said through
lips that were pursed up with pity.

The blonde slid onto a stool. Her jeans were tight, shred-
ded just below her very fine cheeks. Her skin was beautiful,
her legs long. Her speech foul.

"Fuckin' doctor says it's good as new. Damn prick Udell,
couldn't leave well enough alone. Look at this. I swear,
one of these days I'm just going to knife him and leave
him on the fuckin' side of the road. Who's going to convict
me, huh?" She twirled around on the barstool and kicked
out her long, long legs, laughing with a voice so smoky
one word could have filled a Parisian cafe without lighting
a cigarette. "Shit, nobody'd convict me for doin' him."

"Nobody I know, baby." Wanda perked up. "What's it
gonna be tonight?"

"Udell! Udell! What are you buying me tonight?"

"Beer," he growled.

The blonde turned back. "Shooters are cool. Tequila."

"You sure, baby? I'd hate to see you broken up again?"

"Like I'm shaking in my boots. Did you see them
scratches down his Old Glory?" The blonde gave her a
look and Wanda raised an eyebrow. The blonde slapped
the bar with both hands, drummed out a tune and rea-
soned. "Tequila, Wanda. He'll be so smashed in an hour
he won't know what he's paying for." She giggled and that

hair of hers brushed the bar. Mark wanted to lift it so it
wouldn't get dirty. She felt him thinking. She looked at
him. She wiggled her behind and put her tongue between
her teeth. Wanda, on top of everything, gave her a nudge.
"He's doing shooters, too, baby."

"Maybe he'll put up for a couple of mine." The blonde
put a finger to her mouth. Her hands weren't pretty. They
were the only thing about her that wasn't. She smiled.
"You want to buy a lady a drink?"

Udell wiped that smile of hers away with one quick slap
to the back of her head. She turned on him like a cat,
claws bared. This obviously wasn't anything new. He was
ready for her. Udell caught both her hands in one of his
and pushed her away like a puppy nipping at his toes. The
woman fell hard, crashing her back against the bar before
coming at him again. Udell turned his head. His beard
was long, his hair was long and he looked like a biker god
come down from hog heaven to deal with a pesky mortal.

"Hey, man." Mark didn't raise his voice. "Forget your
old lady. I'll drink with you."

That stopped the blonde in her tracks. "Why you . . ."
She was headed toward Mark until Udell backhanded her.
She gave up. Wanda had a shooter and a bag of ice waiting.
Mark gave her credit. The blonde wasn't slinking away,
just biding her time.

"You want to drink with me?" Udell stood rooted to the
spot. Mark wondered if he had to consciously think about
moving those feet. He smiled.

"Yeah. George Stewart wants you to know something
that's better told over a drink."

"George wants me to know, huh?" Udell grunted. Mark
motioned to a table and got off the stool.

Udell waved away his cohorts. He decided to use his
feet. While they moved, his bare arm scrubbed around on
his face. Mark didn't watch to see what came off on it. He
told Wanda to bring them whatever Udell drank. Mark
took a split second to look the big man in the eye and try
to figure out how in the hell a wimp like George Stewart
managed to recruit him. He pulled out a chair, straddled
it and leaned over the table. It was time for some talking.

This was the place Nick had said he would find out who beat him up; this was the man who supposedly would know. Wanda was right there. Tequila for Mark, water for Udell.

"Don't feel like gettin' mean yet. I get mean when I drink."

"Guess so," Mark said but he didn't look over at the blonde with the black-and-blue face.

"Now what?" Udell was all ears. Mark looked him in the eye and spoke like a man with a mission since that's obviously what this big fella responded to.

"George sent me to tell you that the guy you did a couple of weeks ago . . ." Mark paused for effect.

"Yeah?" Udell narrowed his small eyes.

"He wasn't what you thought." Mark finished.

"Yeah?" Udell's eyes were mere slits.

"George says to tell you he wasn't just a cop. That guy . . ." Mark paused again and snapped his fingers like he was thinking. It was all the time Udell needed.

"Yeah, yeah, I know the motherfucker you're talking about." Udell didn't mention Nick's name but Mark could work around that.

"Okay, so George says to tell you he was FBI. He wanted you to know that everyone in the cell is laying low but to be sure whoever did that guy gets out of town."

"Yeah?" Udell grinned.

"Yeah. It's not going to go down good for you or whoever took him out. The guy's going to die and they've got the whole Bureau on this one.

Udell nodded sagely. He considered this information. He scratched the flag. There were fifty-two states. Someone made a mistake.

"Man, I got a question." Udell took a drink from his tall glass of ice water and put it back down with a thud. He crossed his arms on the table, he tapped Mark's hand with a finger the size of a sausage. His head bobbed. "Who in the hell is George Stewart?"

Days later Mark Jackson would swear a sinkhole opened up, swallowed him and spit him out again. That's what it felt like when Udell asked that question.

"He's the one on trial, man. Heads the Independent Militia? That bombing."

"Oh yeah." Udell's head bobbed harder. "Yeah, I heard about that."

"You jerking me?" Mark demanded under his breath. "George told me I could find more of our people here. You militia or aren't you?"

Udell's head fell back. Initials were tattooed on his throat. They weren't his. Mark didn't ask who they belonged to. Udell finally had enough and clapped Mark on the back.

"Man, you are funny. Funny. Funny. Hey, Wanda," he yelled and his big hand held Mark to his seat. "Bring me a bourbon. Bring this guy another one, too."

"I don't want to drink. I want to know who I'm talking to here. Am I getting myself in deep here or what? Maybe you're a plant, too. Maybe you're in tight with the FBI and you just took out one of your own to make it look good." Mark put on a good face, afraid but not too afraid.

"Relax, man. I ain't no snitch. I ain't no FBI and I sure ain't no militia. Wanda?" He grabbed her rear when the woman came over with her little black tray then he patted it affectionately. "Your friend here thinks we are government hating, baby bombers. He thinks we hate the government."

"No kidding?" Wanda's eyes got as wide as they could, weighed down as they were by her make-up. "Baby, what makes you think that? I don't hate the government. Udell don't hate the government."

"Hey," Udell called to everyone in the Soft Spot and put Mark in one hard place. "Any of you militia? Any of you wanna blow up the government?" A chorus of rude and amused noises answered his question. Udell let Mark go and downed his liquor. He lowered his voice and sounded oh-so-concerned. "Friend, I don't know what beef you got. I ain't never met that guy George Stewart, but if I ever meet him I'm going to take a piece for myself if he's telling tales on me. I don't hate the government. Government and me, we go our separate ways. I don't diss them, they don't mess with me. If they try, I take care of it. And the one thing I don't do is belong to no group. People belong to me. I'm the group."

Mark swallowed hard. "But there's a man in the hospital almost kicked to death. Stewart said he was here. Said you guys beat him up."

"What's his name?"

Mark shook his head, "George gave me a name, but he thinks it's bogus anyway."

"Okay, what's the dude look like?"

"How in the hell should I know?" Mark pushed his chair back. He'd fight and run if he had to. "Don't you know if you did someone? All I know is this guy's in bad shape. Almost dead. That's all I know."

"Okay, buddy. You got me. We did a number." Udell pushed his chair back and planted his feet hard on the ground. He raised his voice. "Hey, Cindy." The blonde looked up, she had a scowl on her face and love in her eyes.

"Don't you come near me," she said, and didn't mean it.

"Aw, you'll be begging me tonight." Before she could answer, he laughed hard and said, "Sugar, you know that guy you were doin' a few weeks ago. The one I caught with you in the trailer? That measly little wimp?"

"He was a gentleman, Udell. No need to have done all that. Did you hear how he's doing?"

"Yep. Looks like he's going to buy the farm. But here's the thing, Cindy. You were screwing a Fed!" Udell was still laughing when he gave his attention back to Mark. The minute they locked eyes, he became deathly serious. "Cindy's my woman. We may not see eye to eye and we may play rough, but I love that broad. Ain't nobody going to take my place. So you go on and find whoever it is you work for and you tell 'em you're damn lucky to be alive. You tell 'em the government don't scare me none. FBI or anything else. Now, 'less there's something else I can help you with, I think it's time you be going."

Mark's jaw worked. There were things he wanted to say, questions he had to ask. More importantly, there was a scream deep inside him that had to come out. He dug in his pocket.

"Keep your money, man." Udell was disgusted. "You government types don't make enough anyway. Guess that's why you're so stupid, huh? Always tryin' to screw whoever gets in your way, and always fuckin' it up."

"Mr. Jackson, it's after midnight. Mr. Jackson, please."

A nurse hurried after Mark Jackson, stopping when he turned on her, raising a finger to silence her. "I'm going to see Nick Cheshire and I'm going to see him now. You got that? You call anyone—a doctor, another nurse or security—and I will have your job. When I leave you can go in and see if he's still alive. You got that?"

He didn't bother to wait for her answer and there was no doubt in his mind that he would be left alone with Nick long enough to say what was on his mind. He made it to Nick's private room, walked straight up to the bed and kicked it.

"Wake up, Nick. Wake up you shit."

Groggy, Nick opened his eyes. He was awake in the next instant, understanding the look on Mark Jackson's face.

"You gave me the name. You gave me the place. Why in the hell didn't you tell me you nearly got yourself killed for a biker's woman. You jeopardized two years of work, the Stewart trial, and for what? A piece of ass. What in the hell were you thinking? I oughta kill you myself."

Mark threw himself away from the bed, understanding Udell's desire to kill. He took three fast breaths through his nose and put his hands on his hips. He didn't feel any better. He twirled back, staying close to the bed so he wouldn't be tempted to raise his voice and let the whole world know what happened.

"I'm out of here, Nick. I will not be back. I will not even know you when you finally get out of this place. You will not have a job. You will not have a friend in the Bureau. You will not have a reference. You will not exist as far as I'm concerned." He went closer still, his voice molten, the words burning into Nick's head. "You should have died, buddy. You should have died if this is the way you repay me."

Mark stormed down the hall just as the nurse, finally having decided to try and save her patient, was hurrying in with a security guard. The man in the rent-a-uniform backed up against the wall when he saw Mark. Mark didn't give them a second look. For him, this place and all the people in it, didn't exist anymore.

At home, Mark sat in the dark in his garage considering his options. They were limited. Putting a hose on the exhaust seemed an excellent one. Mark let his head fall back against the seat and his mind wander. It went to the good times with Nick, to the excitement of the Stewart arrest, Caufeld, dead because Nick couldn't keep his pants on and Mark's little vindictive mandate. Sometime during the night, as he dozed and worried and finally gave up, it dawned on Mark Jackson that there was one person who might help him out. He was showering when his wife woke up. He kissed her, inquired about the children, made a phone call and headed for the club.

Chapter Eighteen

"My word, Jackson! Where in the hell did you learn to hit a passing shot with a left-handed spin?"

The man on the other side of the net had aged a good ten years during the last set. Shaking hands over the net, the two men made small talk as they went toward the clubhouse. Mark wrapped a towel around his neck and was headed for the showers when he saw Abram sitting alone at a table. He had almost forgotten. That's what a good hard, killer game of tennis could do. It could wipe away all your problems. Unfortunately, they came back.

"I'll see you next week," he muttered to the man he had just pounded.

The man, whose ego was so sorely bruised, nodded and hailed a waitress as he fell into a chair. Mark ambled over to Abram and pulled out a chair of his own. Abram smiled. It was interesting to see Mark here, dressed as he was. In the office he seemed to tower. Here he seemed quite normal.

Upon closer inspection, though, Abram decided it wasn't just the tennis whites that diminished Mark Jackson, nor was it the smell of sweat. What Abram finally identified was the scent of fear, and that gave Abram the creeps. He hoped to God it was just his imagination.

"That was a wonderful match," Abram commented convivially.

"How long have you been here?"

"Long enough to know that if I played tennis I would opt for doubles and I'd be your partner." Abram sipped his drink and watched Mark. He tried desperately to keep this social. Abram always believed if you didn't hear about a problem, it didn't exist. "Do you want something? I can't recommend the soda. Too much syrup."

"No, I'm not thirsty. I just need to cool down. Sorry to get you all the way out here, but this isn't a conversation we should have in either of our offices."

Abram slipped on his sunglasses. No sense in facing the glare of whatever had brought him here.

"We've got a problem, Abram, and I want you to listen close." Mark used the towel once more as if to wipe away any confusion before he began.

"I don't quite know how to say this." His short laugh told Abram they were both in hot water. "I took Caufeld's guard off him the morning of the day he was killed. We'd had him covered until then, but I'm the one that gave the order to leave him open."

"I'd assumed Caufeld had dismissed them," Abram said cautiously, knowing there would be more.

"Yeah, well. The guys on watch know. They won't say anything. I don't think anyone will ask about it but I thought you should know."

"Eli Warner asked," Abram said.

"When?" Mark looked sick.

"A few days ago, Mark. Again, I assumed he was investigating the murder since he'd already done so much legwork on Caufeld's background."

"Wrong again. I wish I had done something about him earlier." Mark waved away that wish. "It doesn't matter. I'll reassign him now. I've got a background that will take him out of the state if he does it right." Abram grimaced. This was sounding worse by the minute. "Now, I'm not real worried, but under oath my men are going to have to testify that I pulled them off Caufeld, then somebody's going to ask me why I did that."

Abram sighed. "Okay, I'll bite. Why did you do that?"

"Nick Cheshire had the crap beat out of him. He lost a testicle for God's sake." Mark allowed a moment of silence. "I loved that kid. I'd invested years in him. I brought him along through the agency."

"That's nice, Mark, but I must point out, the question is, why did you remove Caufeld's guard?"

"I figured Nick got done because I'd left him with the militia boys too long while Caufeld deliberated. I was ticked at Caufeld for putting Nick in that position. I figured I'd give those militia boys a chance at him. I never really thought they'd take it."

"Kudos, Mark. It's not something I would have done, but obviously it was effective. I hope you can sleep at night." Abram was appalled, but not surprised. Speak in haste, repent in leisure. Still, Caufeld was dead, the agents silent, there was nothing to worry about for the time being.

"I could sleep if that was all there was to it." Mark put a fist to his face as if he could punish himself. Instead he put it against his lips then finally let Abram in on his secret. "Caufeld didn't have anything to do with what happened to Nick. He was screwing a woman married to a biker who gets mean when he drinks. They went easy on the woman." Mark took a minute for himself. "I can't believe it. I taught him better, Abram, and he disappointed me. Then I disappointed myself."

"How did you find out?"

"Nick could hardly talk. I asked him who did it, because I wanted a piece of them. He gave me the name of a bar, the name of the man and I figured George Stewart had a cell at the place. I went to check it out, found out there's no militia action, just this big guy with a bad temper. The woman's a witness if it comes to that."

"That's a gruesome story, Mark, but why are you telling me all this?"

"Because we are both in it, Abram. Think about it. I'm pissed at Caufeld because he's endangering my agent. You're ticked off at him because he's taking away half your case. You played politics when you assigned Kingsley and everybody knows it. Now you've pulled her off 'cause Caufeld isn't hearing the case anymore. All the press needs is a whiff of our extracurricular activities and we're going to be burned at the stake. They'll talk conspiracy, Abram, obstruction of justice, endangering a life, tampering with . . ."

"Yes. I get the point. Fine." Abram was sitting close now. Their heads were together and their minds were running a mile a minute. "We'll have to indict Henry Stewart fast then. Whoever I assign to that prosecution is going to ask questions about Caufeld's guard. I'll work to minimize it on my end and you work on yours and we'll do it all most expediently."

"I agree things need to happen fast, but there's another problem. Henry Stewart didn't do it."

Abram groaned, putting his face in his hands. Mark touched his arm. It looked like a friendly gesture but he growled his orders. "Don't do that. You look like it's the end of the world."

"It's my opinion that we're close to it, Mark," Abram suggested, but lowered his arms anyway. "I made the short list for Caufeld's vacant seat and I'm not going to lose it because your fraternity brother was on a panty raid. I want to prosecute Henry whether he did it or not. No one will question the indictment. It's a foregone conclusion, especially now that he's become so vocal. He's determined to self-destruct. We'll help him along."

"Public opinion won't put him away. Caufeld was shot with a twenty-two and Henry was found with a thirty-eight. Everything the kid told Lauren was true. We corroborated his story about the fast food. We even found someone who saw him arrive back at the house. No way you can get around that."

"We can get around it."

"Only if the defense is brain dead, and Joe Knapp doesn't fit the bill. Don't knee jerk, Abram. That's what got us into trouble in the first place. Chill for a little bit. I've got other things happening and hopefully I'll hand you someone soon, okay?"

Abram pushed his chair back. "What choice do I have? You have made me an accessory after the fact, so to speak. I could have defended my assignments, you know."

"Bullshit. I know what you did, you know what I did and a federal district judge is dead. Our intentions may have been the best, but who's going to agree with them? They'd say we're the reason the militia is blowing up buildings. It's the two of us, buddy, and that's it."

"All right. What exactly is it you want me to do?"

"When I bring you a suspect, I want him prosecuted fast. If I can't find anything that looks airtight, I want you to back me when this case is closed for lack of evidence. We'll make it disappear and put Caufeld's death down to random street violence. No questions asked."

"Yes, yes. All right, but we've got to analyze every step, Mark. I mean every step. There are more people to consider than us, Mark. I don't think it will be as easy to make this disappear as you think. I consider Lauren to be at the top of the list of those who won't let it die. I do believe she hears Caufeld's voice from heaven."

Abram pushed his chair back yet he still sat as did Mark. Mark stared at the table.

"Don't I know it, Abram. I wish I hadn't been so pissed at Caufeld. I swear, I could have killed the man for being so stupid when he decided to sit on that issue. I could have just killed him for that."

Slowly Abram raised his head. There was a thought coming to him with equal leisure. He'd heard Mark say that before. Mark had said the same thing in front of Edie and Lauren and him, right there in Abram's office. But now it was the two of them. Mano a mano. Abram licked his lips.

"And did you, Mark?" he asked quietly.

Mark returned his gaze. "Abram. Really."

There was nothing more to say, nothing more Abram wanted to hear. He got out of his chair. The sound of tennis balls, the indecipherable yelps and hollering from the club courts, made him shiver. On a dark night, somewhere else, there had been a pop, perhaps words, perhaps a cry of pain and a man was left dead on the street. Someone did it. Someone who had a reason.

"Call me when you have something, Mark."

"I shall, Abram. I feel better for just talking about it."

Abram walked away and Mark Jackson picked up his racket. He had a wicked touch. He could demolish any opponent with a well-placed shot. It was because he reacted well. Fast. Definitive. Without thinking. His reactions couldn't be matched by anyone on the court. In real life they had created a problem, but he could handle it.

Mark took a modified swing and watched the muscles stand out in his forearm. Yeah, he could do it. Not a lob into Abram's court, but something that would end the game fast. He would do it.

"Edie, I've got a problem and it's very sensitive."

Abram practiced his pitch all the way back from the tennis club. Now that he had actually said it, there was no doubt it was the wrong approach.

Edie flopped herself in the chair opposite his desk. "Go ahead, ruin my day." She reached into her pocket and pulled out a pack of cigarettes. Eyes on Abram, she lit one and shook out the match. He hated the smoke but if he was going to burst her bubble after the great day Edie had in court she could ease the pain with a cigarette. She pulled the potted plant on the side of his desk toward her. "Now I'm ready. But I'm going to warn you, I'm really tired and I want to go home before Lauren catches me and tries to tell me that she's been doing some research on her own on the Caufeld thing."

"Well then, this may solve that problem, Edie."

"I'm all ears." She took a drag and, indeed, looked more attentive.

"Mark Jackson personally pulled the guard off Caufeld. Caufeld's dead. Jackson swears if he's questioned about any of it, he's going to bring this office into it and talk about playing politics with our case assignments, etc."

"So, he wants us to cover up his mistake. No big deal."

"It might be."

"I'm listening."

"He would prefer to make the Caufeld matter go away. No arrest, lack of evidence."

"Lauren will make a stink. Why not Henry?"

"He didn't do it. Mark checked it out himself. We'd never win and we need to win. Second option. If he can bring us a suspect with a good chance of a case he wants us to push it through. Can I count on you?"

"Can it wait until the Stewart trial wraps?" Edie seemed to have forgotten her cigarette. It burned down to the filter and the smell reminded her to put it out. She did so under the little potted palm.

"I don't know. I suppose it depends on when and who he's got."

"I can manage. I can't manage if Lauren's going to second-seat this." Edie licked her lips and tried not to smile.

"No. I don't want her anywhere near this," Abram agreed. "We could all have quite a bit to answer to if this backfires."

"You wouldn't be a federal district judge."

"You would never be Los Angeles' U.S. Attorney."

"There's more to consider even than that," Edie mused. She stood up. "I think administrative leave would be in order for Lauren if we're going to work effectively to prosecute Caufeld's case. She is too close to this one."

"Fine. I'll leave it to you."

"Yes, Abram. Leaving it to me is a good idea."

Edie was gone, only to pause and lean against the door she just closed. She lowered her lashes and composed herself so she wouldn't walk down the hall grinning.

Chapter Nineteen

"She was the most beautiful girl you had ever seen. She made her clothes and went to school at night to study on the computer. My daughter was going to be somebody someday, and now she's dead. I buried my beautiful daughter, and I couldn't even kiss her goodbye. They said half her head was gone. Half her beautiful head . . ."

The woman on the stand wept quietly, her cheek resting on the frame of a huge portrait of Cora Constanza Hernandez, the first victim of the Stewarts' bomb, her mother the last witness in the prosecution's case. The woman was a perfect blend of grief and dignity. A lady who cleaned houses to care for the six children after her husband ran off. This was a proud woman who spoke of how Cora Constanza's salary helped her feed and clothe her little brothers and sisters. Mrs. Hernandez didn't know about Cora Constanza's use of recreational drugs and the gang affiliation of her daughter's boyfriend, and that made everything perfect. She would leave the jury with this saintly image of the victim.

"I'd like to request a recess, Your Honor, to give Mrs. Hernandez time to pull herself together," Edie said.

Judge Martinelli looked at the witness, then at Edie. "Do you have more questions for this witness?"

"No, Your Honor."

"Mr. Weitman? Will you be asking Mrs. Hernandez anything?" Eric Weitman shook his head. He wanted Mrs. Hernandez gone. "Mr. Knapp?"

Joe shook his head, too.

"I'll ask her something! I'll ask her something! I want to know what proof she has that we did anything to her daughter. Her daughter worked for a blood-sucking institution that half the people in the United States want to destroy. I'll ask her something. Hey, you. Mrs. What's-Your-Name."

Mrs. Hernandez wailed in fear then cried harder as Henry Stewart hollered at her. The spectators oohed. This was exquisite drama cut short with swift retribution. Martinelli had seen two judges before her pulled down by this albatross, she didn't want to be the third.

"Remove the defendant," Judge Martinelli ordered and the marshals did just that without concern for the bandages on Henry's hands or the hideous scabbing on the side of his face.

Poor Henry was not good at blowing himself to kingdom come. The fizzle when he detonated the bomb strapped to his chest had put him in the hospital for four days and sent the agents to the bar to talk about the amazing thing they'd seen. The doctors released Henry just in time so Martinelli didn't have to sever his trial and deal with George alone. Martinelli looked at George. She was cool, it was impossible to tell that he scared her to death. The only sign of her fear was that she was moving this trial along with the speed of light.

"Let's get this all over with. Do you have anything to say, Mr. Stewart?" George remained silent. "Fine."

Martinelli denied the recess and on they went, starting the defense case, minus Henry and minus Lauren Kingsley who quietly exited without looking back.

* * *

Lauren was a specter. When she stepped into Judge Martinelli's courtroom people looked right through her. Weeks ago she had been sitting where Edie sat. Weeks ago she had been in Abram's office discussing strategy. Weeks ago Lauren Kingsley had been hailed in the press as a bright young star, a hard-hitting prosecutor dealing with the Stewarts with an energy seldom seen on the government's side of the courtroom. That clipping was now put in a drawer, instead of left with pride on the bedside stand.

Now nobody cared if she came or went, because Lauren Kingsley didn't really work for the U.S. Attorney's Office anymore. She was on administrative leave pending an investigation into the incident in the parking garage, her continued harassment of the LAPD and FBI regarding the investigation of Wilson Caufeld's death and insubordination. She talked too much and nobody wanted to hear it anymore. Wilson Caufeld might be the only thing on her mind, but everyone else's mind was full of other things that needed attention.

Lauren hadn't meant to stop in Martinelli's courtroom but she did. Once inside the doors, she knew she had been wrong. If not leading the prosecution, she should have at least been part of it. Perhaps she was punishing herself for her own stupidity by stepping into that courtroom. Perhaps she was curious to see what had become of her late-night caller, Henry. Perhaps she just wanted to assure herself that Wilson had been the superior judge despite Martinelli's best intentions. When Edie rested her case, Lauren decided she had punished herself enough that day.

She left as the new and improved Henry Stewart was escorted out of the courtroom. The last thing Lauren saw was the proud smile his parents shared. Henry had got religion and George was now his one, true God. Lauren pushed through the door, went down the hall and walked through Wilson's courtroom to his chambers. It was getting easier all the time because so much of Wilson was gone. The place was beginning to look like any other office in any other building.

"How you doing, Barbara?" Lauren smiled and got one in return.

"Do you want these plates that Judge Petersen gave to Judge Caufeld every year? You know, the ones with the horses on them?"

Carrying a few of the plates, Barbara followed Lauren into the judge's inner sanctum. Lauren went around Wilson's desk and looked at them as she turned on the computer. She crinkled her nose. Wilson could serve a dinner party for the royal family there were so many.

"He never said, but I don't think he really liked them. Is there anyone we've forgotten who might like something from chambers?"

Barbara shrugged, tilting the plates as if that might make them more attractive. "Maybe the secretary in the clerk's office who remembered his birthday every year."

"That's a nice thought." Lauren nodded and stashed her purse. "Go for it."

"I think I'll just take one down. She'll have to figure how to get them all out of here." Barb hefted the plates, then asked the question she asked every day. "How are you doing?"

"Not bad." Lauren logged on. What else could she say, after all? *Allan is acting like a jerk, but maybe that's my fault. Eli Warner is concocting conspiracies and dredging up old news to use in new ways. I'm so lonesome I could die.* Great office chit-chat. She settled herself in the big chair and put a bit of perk into her voice. "I didn't know the judge was so into this computer. He has more records on disk than anyone I know."

"Neat for a man his age to jump right into cyberspace, huh?" Barbara looked over her shoulder. "I'll never forget when he got that scanner. Sat in here for hours on end scanning in his old records. The man was amazing. Well, I'm going to run these downstairs then take off, if that's okay with you?"

"Sure, I've got all the time in the world," Lauren laughed ruefully and Barbara pulled a face.

"Their loss, my gain," Barb quipped and just as suddenly sobered. Though Lauren seemed unruffled by everything that was happening, Barbara offered her a shoulder to cry on just in case. "You know, the judge would have been so upset by all this, to see you investigated and everything. If you ever need to talk about it, I hope you'll let me know."

"You'll be the first one I call, I promise." Lauren gave her best stiff-upper-lip nod. "I'll see you tomorrow."

Barbara was gone and Lauren started to work again, discarding the diskette in the A drive. Car repair correspondence was of no interest unless she could use it to get her car out of the shop. The next disk contained personal letters. Judge Caufeld had kept up a correspondence with so many people. She scrolled past names she didn't recognize, and lingered over those she did: the letter of recommendation Wilson had written on her behalf when she applied to the U.S. Attorney's Office, the one recommending her to law school, letters lauding Allan to various businesses and individuals. She and Allan had been incredibly privileged, and both of them had lost sight of that. Lauren pocketed the disk. She'd show it to Allan. He would remember the good things. They would be friends again.

Next, bank records. She leaned down and popped it out. Still bent over, disk in hand, Lauren had second thoughts. Slowly she put it back in and looked once more. This wasn't a record of personal transactions, nor a scanned disk full of monthly statements. There was one extensive file, untitled, with debit and credit information. She scrolled. The entries were unique in that they were almost exactly alike, month after month. Initials followed debit entries and the initials changed every year or so. Scrolling back up, Lauren checked the dates and notations again. The first credit entry was the latter part of 1985, a year that had captured Eli's imagination not so long ago. The last year Allan worked for Wilson's firm. A year that . . .

"Hi."

Lauren looked up. Eli was there, right there in front of her. Eli who she had just been thinking about. Eli who was the one who had wanted her to talk to Allan about the year 1985.

"Hi," she said back.

"Mind if I come in?"

She shook her head, even though he was already in. He looked wonderful, like a friend.

"Looks like you're busy."

He was dressed in dark green khakis, a tweed jacket, a button-down shirt the color of sand. Today he sported loafers, the bucks had been left at home. Eli hadn't lost any sleep over her. Then again, she hadn't lost any over him. She just didn't sleep anymore so it wasn't there to lose.

"It dawned on me that nobody would think to clean up the office." She reached down and popped the diskette out of the drive pocketing it just to have something to distract her from Eli's smile. "Then I finally figured out there wasn't anyone else to do it."

"Lassiter might want to help you," Eli suggested. Lauren stiffened, and Eli was quick with an apology. "Sorry, I didn't mean it that way. Bad move."

"Yeah," Lauren agreed. "I thought you were supposed to be the one who's so sensitive."

"I guess chatting about how you got canned from the Stewart case is kind of a taboo subject, too, huh?"

"You wouldn't make any points," Lauren warned, still not sure she was going to let him redeem himself. "So, what do you want?"

"Mind if I sit?" He motioned to a chair then didn't take it. "On second thought, mind if I take you to lunch? I'd rather apologize with food between us. We seem to do best that way."

"That's kind of dangerous. If I don't like the way you apologize for trying to bring Allan into this I might start a food fight."

"Then we might as well not go to lunch," Eli said, looking suddenly sad. "Because I'm not going to apologize for that. I just wanted to tell you I was sorry I didn't listen to you the other night. I had an agenda, you were there, it seemed the thing to do. Maybe the way I feel about Lassiter is personal. I'm working on figuring it out, I swear."

"Does that mean you're investigating or soul searching."

"I plead the fifth." Eli grinned. "Do you want to go to lunch?"

"Did you bring me any M&Ms?" He reached in his pocket and tossed a bag on her desk. "Okay."

"Okay." He put his hand out. She took it and couldn't imagine why she ever thought of letting it go.

Lunch was nice, and longer than Lauren thought it would be, but that was only because Eli was a perfect gentleman. He didn't make a move on her, didn't allude to their night together, didn't say anything suggestive, all the while letting her know he treasured the time they'd spent together. They talked about everything except the Stewarts, the office, the FBI, her mother, Wilson or Allan. It amazed her to find that she could carry on a lucid conversation while skirting those particular topics. It was three o'clock when he walked her back to Wilson Caufeld's chambers and Lauren was sorry to go.

"So have I done well enough to suggest we could start from scratch again?" Eli asked.

"I think my calendar has a few openings. How about tonight?"

"Wow, lift the yoke and you really let your hair down." He opened the door and held it for her. She slipped past him feeling positively giddy.

"You haven't seen anything yet. I've got a couple more things to do here. Can you pick me up around six-thirty?"

"I can do that. Mind if I use Barbara's phone? If I don't check in they'll report me missing in action."

"I don't think she'd mind." Lauren motioned to the phone. Eli didn't move toward it. He just kept looking at her.

"Think I ought to risk kissing you goodbye?"

"I thought we were starting from scratch," she flirted.

"You drive a hard bargain." He ran a finger down her cheek just to remind her they had already gone beyond the beginning. "I'll poke my head in before I go."

Lauren opened the door to Wilson's chambers and backed in. She was grinning like Doris Day backing into Rock Hudson's bachelor pad. But when the door closed, Rock Hudson wasn't in chambers. Allan was.

"Hey, hey, Lauren. What a surprise." He was sitting at Wilson's desk, the computer was on. She had turned it off.

He had his hands in the cookie jar or, more specifically, the drawers of Wilson Caufeld's desk.

Lauren blinked, then smiled. "Well, this is a surprise. I thought you were too busy to help clean out Wilson's office." Lauren dropped her purse. "What changed that hard heart of yours?"

"You're not going to give an inch, are you?" Allan sat back, closing the drawer to his right as he did so. Lauren's eyes flicked to it, he pretended he didn't notice. "I was a jerk the other morning. I wasn't in the mood for visitors, and you have to admit it's pretty weird finding someone in your place when they weren't even asked."

"Since this seems to be a day for apologies, I'll do my part. You're right. That was rude of me. I'm sorry."

"Great. Friends again?" He was smiling but his fingers were drumming the arms of the chair.

"Sure, but I still don't know why you're here."

"Edie was asking how you were. No, really," he insisted when Lauren looked skeptical. "She knows how she'd feel if it was her, and she wanted me to make sure you were okay."

"That's why she fought so hard to have me retained," Lauren muttered as she moved a stack of manila folders from the floor to the credenza. Allan's eyes followed—the folders, not her. "Forget I said that. It's nice she's worried, but I'm doing just fine. Since you'll probably see her before I will, tell her I'd love to get back to work. I really would." Lauren surprised herself with her candor. "Sorry, this has nothing to do with you. Maybe you and Edie should just leave me out of your conversations. Much as I appreciate your concern."

"Okay, so what can I do here? I thought there might be some things you wouldn't know what to do with. Business things that were in play before you were part of the fraternity." Allan was anxious to get on with business.

Lauren raised an eyebrow. She leaned casually against the credenza and eyed Allan carefully.

"Did you decide that, or did Edie?" she asked. "Maybe she thought you should keep an eye on me so I don't do anything stupid." Lauren laughed he looked almost hurt.

"Okay, let's get to it. I was just tossing most everything that related to business before 1995. I'm forwarding anything after that to the appropriate divisions or parties. Anything I can't identify I put in that pile." She pointed toward a stack in the corner. "Maybe you want to start with those things." Lauren headed for the desk and was by Allan's side before he could move. It took ten seconds for her to see what was going on. Every drawer was open except for the small one he'd managed to close. Not one file was out, packed or culled, but everything had been moved. She closed the drawer near his knee then the one by his foot just in case he decided he didn't want to stay and help after all. "It kind of looks like all you're doing is looking through Wilson's stuff, which won't be helpful at all. Maybe if you tell me what exactly it is you're looking for, I could find it. Then you can get back to the important business you do."

"Jesus, Lauren, you make me sound like a criminal," he snorted, smiling for her, not at her.

"Are you? Is there something Wilson might have kept that you don't want anyone to see? Not even me?"

Allan stood up and walked past, unflappable when he was alert. "Lauren, give it a rest."

"I would have except that you keep piquing my curiosity. You've been acting edgy, Allan, and I'm not the only one who's noticed it." Lauren was giving him every opportunity to explain himself, but Allan was smooth.

"Curiosity killed the cat, Lauren. In your case, I do believe you did yourself right out of a job if I recall." He flipped through the stacked files and turned back to her.

"That's unfair. At least I'm trying to do something. You buried Wilson and forgot he ever existed. Now I find you here rifling through his drawers. I'm beginning to think something is really wrong. Now, you either want to confide in me . . ."

"Hi, guys, what're you doing?" Allan and Lauren looked toward the doorway where Eli was grinning at them both. Allan started nodding. His head went up and down in big gestures as the light bulb flickered on above it.

"Okay. This makes sense now. You two are still playing games. Very funny, Lauren."

"I don't know what you're talking about."

"This!" Allan slapped at some of the papers on the desk. "You're sitting in here pretending you're wrapping up Wilson's business and instead you're helping him investigate me. This is getting so ridiculous. Lauren, I feel really, really sorry for you. I don't know where Wilson and I went wrong that you can't see what's happening here. Mr. Warner is playing you for a dupe."

"We're not the ones who were sneaking around in here. Eli just came to take me to lunch."

"He was here to soften you up because he knows that he's at the end of his rope." Allan looked at Eli. "I hate to tell you, but that big, sinister falling out Wilson and I had was just about money. That's it. It was about my salary and so you can quit your little treasure hunt." Allan walked a few paces but didn't come as close to Eli as he had intended.

"I got the feeling there was something more to it, Mr. Lassiter," Eli said evenly. "I'd really like the details so I can finish the file on Judge Caufeld. I like my work to be as complete as possible."

"Wouldn't you just." Allan put his hands in his pocket, pushing back his jacket. Today he wore paisley suspenders. "Look, I know what you're trying to do and I'm really sorry to disappoint you. The problem I had with Wilson was private. We sorted it out and anything that happened between us then is irrelevant now. He's dead, Warner, and I think it's time you stopped your little renegade investigation because it's over and done." Allan shook a finger. "You know what I'm talking about, don't you, Warner? You didn't bother to tell Lauren, did you?"

"What are you talking about, Allan?" Lauren demanded.

Eli opened his mouth to answer, but Allan held the spotlight. He paced. He rounded Lauren and leaned over her shoulder as he watched Eli. "He's looking for a spectacular bust Lauren and he's not going to let up even though everything has been settled. He didn't tell you that, did he, Lauren? He didn't tell you everything's being wrapped up."

"Eli?" Lauren turned wide questioning eyes his way but Eli wasn't looking at her. He was looking at Allan.

"I didn't keep anything from you, Lauren. I just found out," Eli said evenly.

"So, ends the mystery of who killed Wilson Caufeld. There was no militia conspiracy. I did not skulk down the street and lie in wait for Wilson Caufeld and then shoot him. There were no surprises to uncover, nothing in the near or far past. Tell her who killed Wilson Caufeld, Mr. Warner."

Eli turned his head, speaking to Lauren. "They arrested a gang banger by the name of Damien Boyd."

Lauren put a hand to her forehead. She thought she might swoon. She had been right about Henry, and Eli had been so wrong about Allan. She blinked and watched Eli. "You really just found this out?"

Eli nodded. "Yes."

"I heard it yesterday. I'm surprised you didn't."

"I wasn't part of the investigating team, and Jackson had me in Oklahoma for three days following up on a background investigation that hit the skids. I came right here from the airport."

"Now, I will assume that there won't be any more talk about the difficulties I had with Wilson being so serious that I might be considered a suspect in his murder."

"I didn't realize you had been told," Eli said.

"I thought it was fair," Lauren muttered guiltily. "He needed to know what you thought."

"I don't understand a whole lot of this," Allan fussed, "but I hope you're both satisfied. I think we all have the answers we need. We can put this behind us."

Eli still looked at Lauren. He wasn't hurt. He didn't feel betrayed. He understood her loyalty to Allan Lassiter. Loyalty was a hard thing to leave behind.

"Are you satisfied, Lauren?" he asked.

"If Mark and Abram are satisfied with what they've got then, yes, I am. Are you?"

Allan stepped between them. "I'd suggest you decide

right now whether or not you're going to let this go, Warner. Anything you do, or say, that in any way harms me or my reputation, will be considered harassment at the very least if you persist. You won't have a job if you keep this up. Make no mistake, I can, and will, see to it."

"Allan, stop." Lauren took hold of his arm. "That isn't necessary."

"No, that's all right. It's good to know where I stand," Eli interjected. "I think I'll just go ahead and do my job."

"As long as you know exactly what your job is, I think that's a great idea," Allan said.

"My job is to find the truth, Mr. Lassiter. Always has been, always will be. Lauren, I enjoyed lunch." She saw him to the door and then closed it.

"Good riddance," Allan mumbled, but his victory was short lived. "What? You look like I'm the one acting like an idiot."

"You are," Lauren said quietly. "Now, I've got something to say to you and I want you to listen. I've thought a lot about what Eli has to say and I've defended you with everything I've got. But your own actions are making it more and more difficult for me to look at you and say that this is just your way of handling your grief. I don't think you have any grief, Allan. I think you feel something, though, and I want to know right now what it is."

"I can't believe I'm hearing this from you!" Allan said and held out his arms to her.

"Don't!" Lauren ordered. "I'm not stupid. I've played the little girl in our trio for too damn long. Wilson is dead, Allan, and I want to know why that doesn't bother you very much."

"I feel relieved that someone's been arrested for his murder," Allan said coolly.

"That wasn't the question."

"Don't try to best me. I've been in more courtrooms, I've asked more questions than you have."

"What about lies? Have you told any of those, Allan?" Allan's tongue rolled inside his cheek. He was swallowing words Lauren desperately wanted to hear. In the heat of the moment is when truth was told. She wanted him at the boiling point and she wanted it now. "What were you looking for in here, Allan? What's so important that you had to sneak around to find it? And, Allan, if you knew about Damien Boyd when you walked in here, why didn't you tell me yourself?"

Allan raised a hand, made a fist and brought it down through the air. Without another word, Allan turned on his heel and left, the outer door slamming behind him. Lauren followed a minute later.

She didn't know it all. But now she was going to do everything possible to figure it out very, very soon.

Chapter Twenty

"Monique."

Lauren walked past Abram's secretary and into his office without waiting to be announced. Abram was working, his little toy soldiers sat forelornly on their raised battlefield.

"Lauren?"

"Sorry for bursting in on you, Abram, but I really think there are some things we should talk about. I figured if I asked Monique to announce me there was a good chance she might lie about whether you were here or not." She looked over her shoulder. "Isn't that right, Monique?"

The woman who had come in with the express purpose of making up an excuse for her boss ducked back behind the door leaving Abram Schuster to take care of himself. It was almost time for her to go home anyway.

"You're probably right. I should object, but I'm not going to. I think we've all been reacting far too quickly to any little thing that comes our way. Our nerves are stretched thin by the ridiculous scramble recently." Abram sighed. "Sit down. Tell me what's on your mind. I've been hearing what's on everyone else's."

Abram laced his hands over his middle. He was pale and drawn, as if he'd been working long hours. Then the look on his face became hopeful, his eyes were raised toward the door. Lauren looked, too. There in the doorway stood an equally exhausted Edie Williams.

"Sorry. You're busy." She hadn't seen Lauren since she'd been put on leave; she didn't want to see her now.

"Come on in Edie. I have a feeling Abram wouldn't mind if you joined in the conversation." Abram raised his palms as if to say it was her game, she called the shots. Lauren didn't smile when she asked, "Do you have a few minutes, Edie?"

Edie slipped inside the room and settled herself near the window. She crossed her arms as if to hold herself together. The long hard day she thought might be coming to an end just looked like it was going to extend itself.

"Lauren?" Abram opened the floor.

"I'll keep this short. I heard there was an arrest in Judge Caufeld's murder. I heard it happened yesterday, and I want to know why I wasn't informed."

Abram glanced at Edie and she at him. Only Abram looked back at Lauren. Edie found the floor more interesting.

"Edie and I decided it was best to keep the arrest rather quiet since we don't want the press making more of it than it is. Mark concurred, of course."

Lauren almost shot out of her chair. "More of it than it is, Abram? Wilson was a federal district judge, he was the first federal district judge to be nominated to the Supreme Court, and you don't want to make more of it than it is? Do you hear yourself?"

"Abram means he doesn't want to have this case tried in the press. We controlled the Mexican Mafia and the Stewart trial to a great extent, and we'll do the same on this." Edie jumped to Abram's defense. "One thing at a time is what we're shooting for. The Stewart prosecution has given us more headaches than it was ever worth. Our strategy is to focus on it, finish it, and get it to the jury before we give the public something else to chew on. It's an administrative decision. Besides, if we do our job right, when we get to trial on the Caufeld matter, the case will be airtight. That's what we want, isn't it? We want someone to go down for that.''

"I don't just want someone to go down, I want the killer to go down." Lauren backed off, curious to find that Edie was speaking like she was the U.S. Attorney. She picked her way through this unknown territory. "Okay, semantics. I can even accept there might be public perception problems if both cases aren't wrapped up properly. What I can't understand is the other end of this whole thing. I would have thought common courtesy would dictate a call to me. Not only am I a federal prosecutor, I was part of Wilson's family and . . ." Lauren fought back tears. She hadn't anticipated this. The tears, she'd imagined, were gone for good. ". . . and Allan Lassiter was told. I'm not sure I understand why his relationship with Wilson Caufeld is considered, by some, to be of greater importance than my own. I find it not only unprofessional, I find it appalling." Lauren sat quite still even though there was really nothing more to say.

Edie pushed herself off the window ledge and stood closer to Abram. She actually put her hand on the back of Abram's chair. Everyone, it seemed, was getting friendly, the further Lauren was pushed from the circle. The sad thing was, she didn't want to be pushed away.

"I'm responsible for that oversight," Edie said evenly. "I'm sorry. I simply had more opportunity to disclose that information to Mr. Lassiter," She gave a nod toward Abram to explain her formality. "I suppose, given everything I've been thinking about lately, I assumed he would tell you."

"No you didn't, Edie. You didn't even think about me because I'm out of the loop."

"Professionally that's true and you know why that is." Edie didn't give an inch. "Nobody is responsible for your credibility rating but you. If we were to bring you back into the loop because of a personal link to the Caufeld case, there might be even more questions about who exactly is making the big decisions in this office."

"Now that is funny." Lauren rearranged herself until she sat on the edge of her chair, hands clasped together to keep from using them in a gesture that might be construed as disrespectful. "The reason that last statement is so funny is that it wasn't long ago you were happy to let me call the shots. My personal relationship to Wilson Caufeld was considered more than a plus. As I heard it, my relationship with the judge was considered vital to the prosecution of the Stewarts. I believe I was advised to tiptoe up and look over the top of Caufeld's fence. Wasn't that what I heard?"

"Players change, Lauren, and so do strategies," Edie said quietly.

"I have a feeling things might change even more if I were to start talking about how things work around here," Lauren responded in kind.

"It wouldn't be anything new," Abram scoffed, but Lauren could see his indifference was a bluff. Common sense dictated he should be worried.

"No, I suppose it wouldn't be anything new. In fact, it probably wouldn't be more than a paragraph or two in an editorial in the *Times.*" Lauren sat back, more relaxed now that she knew how things were and where her strength lay. "But I suppose there are other things to consider."

"For instance?" Abram was getting paler as she talked.

"The pendulum could swing the opposite way. Politicizing the U.S. Attorney's office could be fodder for a movement to reassess the people who make policy. If you're playing games with prosecutions, you're endangering the public. The right person could make a case for that. And, even if there isn't a hue and cry, some of the movers and shakers might be very curious about the way you made a young attorney lead on a case as important as a militia bombing. They wouldn't think twice about why I accepted it, but they might wonder whether a man who dismissed a seasoned prosecutor in favor of someone like me, is the kind of man who would make a good federal district judge. He might seem rather indecisive." Lauren looked at Edie. "They might further wonder whether a woman who was willing to take second seat in such a trial would be an effective U.S. Attorney. I could call some of those people who might be interested in this story. They were all friends of Wilson's. What do you guys think?"

Lauren smiled. The expression on Edie's face was a curious mix of admiration and concern, but not fear. Lauren gave her high marks for that. Abram, on the other hand, wasn't pleased.

"I think you overestimate your power, Lauren. You were a protégé, not a designated successor to Wilson Caufeld's respect, power or position. Do you understand that?" Abram asked.

"Yes, I do. I want to be clear, this is not a threat. But I do remember the lessons Wilson taught me. He always said that those in power should be the ones who know how to use it properly. I'm not sure any of us deserve to be doing what we are doing."

"We do deserve what we have, Lauren. We are the best there is." Abram laughed with actual delight. "I can't believe you haven't figured that out. Government service is only a brief stop for most lawyers. Trial experience means bigger salaries in the private sector. Edie and I, and you of course, are the exception. Government is our life and we are as good as you're going to find here. So, Lauren, whatever dreams of ethical grandeur Wilson Caufeld put in your head, you can just put them right out again. Deserving of power, indeed."

"That may be the case, but I could make it a topic of conversation, Abram. A call to the broadcast news, a lunch with a reporter from one of the weeklies. Perhaps talking about it would make me feel better."

"I doubt Wilson Caufeld taught you how to bargain like that," Abram said as Edie wandered back to the window. "I haven't the energy to fight you, so let's get to the bottom line. What is it you want, Lauren?"

"I want to prosecute Caufeld's murderer." Lauren pushed, now that she had him where she wanted him. "I want to be in from minute one. I want to be the one to handle the grand jury and get this bastard indicted and then I want to witness the execution. Let me do that and I won't make any trouble."

There was silence in the office. On the street below, a horn honked and then another. In Abram's office a clock ticked. Edie looked over her shoulder and then out the window, as if jumping was a consideration. When she looked back, Abram was waiting for her to speak. She took a deep breath and steadied herself, palms against the ledge, shoulders hunched, her gaze fixed at a point in Lauren's middle.

"Damien Boyd's already been indicted, Lauren," Edie said quietly. Edie Williams had Lauren Kingsley's full attention.

"That's impossible. I thought he was picked up yesterday?"

"He was. We got him in the morning and had him in the grand jury yesterday. Mark Jackson is the case agent and he testified as to hearsay. Assignment's been made to Judge Petty. We're set for trial in three weeks." Edie paused then added, "I'm prosecuting."

"I want to know everything." Stunned, Lauren sat paralyzed in front of them.

"No." Edie was firm. "You won't be part of this. Abram, would you excuse us for a minute?"

"Absolutely." He got up. Lauren blinked at him, unable to understand why he would relinquish his chair. "Take as long as you like."

When they were alone, Edie sat close and put her hand on Lauren's. A most personal gesture and Lauren was distrustful of it.

"I'm going to be straight with you, Lauren. Nobody wants you on this one. No matter how you think you'd act, the truth is you couldn't help making this extremely personal." Lauren took her hand away from Edie's. Edie looked almost sad. "Don't try to tell me it wouldn't be. We screwed up from the minute Caufeld was assigned. We put you in front of him, we put the pressure on you to perform and we were wrong. We won't do it again." Edie reached in the pocket of her skirt, found a pack of cigarettes but decided against lighting one. "Abram and I've had extensive talks about you. We don't want to lose you. We've already decided that you'll be reinstated at the wrap of the Stewart case. It will be quiet, so there won't appear to be preferential treatment. There will be no discussion of the inquiry as to your involvement in Henry Stewart's escape in the garage of this building."

"There never should have been any discussion in the

first place," Lauren objected quietly. "If I called for help he could have killed me."

"Your opinion. Look." Edie put a hand to her forehead, obviously tired. "I think you are extremely talented, I think you've suffered a great loss and I think this office is having a hell of a time holding things together at the moment. I'm tired, Lauren. There are administrative concerns that Mark and Abram have expressed."

"What administrative concerns?" Lauren insisted. "You know, I just don't get that line of reasoning, Edie. Publicly prosecuting Wilson Caufeld's murder will do more good than harm. Let people see that you are taking care of business."

"There's more involved than that."

"Tell me what it is, and I'll work with you," Lauren pleaded.

"No!" Edie yelled. She yelled and stood up so quickly Lauren fell back. Edie walked away, closing her eyes as if she could ignore everything that had just happened. "Stop pushing, Lauren. I am tired. I will do my best to prosecute both these cases, but I'm not going to get into all the reasons why I'm the one handling these things. I'm not going to argue policy with you because, truthfully, I don't have the time or the energy, okay?"

Quietly, Lauren rose from her chair. She hadn't been able to do anything about her mother. Now she was being denied the opportunity to bring justice to Wilson Caufeld. She looked at Edie and saw true sorrow in her expression. Lauren appreciated that, as far as it went. Well, she was tired, too. Tired of letting Allan, Edie and Abram decide how far anything should go. Nodding to Edie, Lauren walked to the door, but Edie had one more thing to say.

"Lauren, I want you to know something. I want Damien Boyd in jail just as much as you do. Maybe more."

"I doubt that, Edie," Lauren answered ruefully and left.

Alone, Edie stared at the half-open door then snorted a little laugh.

She did so want Damien Boyd in jail.

More than anything in the world.

Chapter Twenty-One

The outcome of Eli's work depended on three things.

The first was patience. When he was serene and silent, other people became agitated and talkative. Few people truly listened and fewer still could endure a silence, no matter how companionable.

Reason was next. When Eli sat in his chair or drove in his car he could make the most interesting connections between word, deed and any two people's perception of both. After years of methodical, meticulous, puzzle-like work Eli knew that two people might think they were saying the same thing. More often than not, they weren't. Always there were subtle differences, strange little bits of information that, if put together correctly, made a wonderfully clear picture out of any up-at-night problem.

Finally, there was instinct. Instinct, above all else, made Eli good at what he did. Right now, instinct was on overdrive, reason was working overtime and patience had been overindulged.

So after his lunch with Lauren and his face to face with Allan Lassiter, Eli had gone back to the office and listened quietly to the scuttlebutt about Damien Boyd. What struck him as odd was that everyone seemed surprised by the

arrest and few knew a great many details about what had
gone down.

Two days after that, Eli considered the facts as he knew
them and found a few holes that needed filling in. A
weapon, for instance. No one had mentioned it. A suspect
indicted faster than Eli could say "this is curious" and an
arraignment following hot on its heels. Mark Jackson taking a personal interest when he hated Wilson Caufeld
looked like a piece of the sky in Eli's puzzle but he had a
feeling it really belonged right in the middle of the board
where the big picture was. Edie Williams prosecuting when
there were two hundred others who could do it, added
another piece and the fact that Allan Lassiter was acting
as if the case was closed gave Eli just enough to drive him
on.

Today, the third day after Eli's lunch with Lauren, his
gut was churning. Instinct said the whole thing smelled.
It could come from a bit of trash clinging to his collar or
an entire heap of garbage dumped on someone named
Damien Boyd. With all his criteria for action met, Eli Warner got his act together and took it on the road.

The first stop was the Federal Detention Center where
Damien Boyd was incarcerated. Eli went to see him without
expectations and armed with certain assumptions. He
assumed that Mark Jackson's arrest was solid and he
assumed Damien Boyd would be hostile. These assumptions made the scales of justice level, so that now anything
he heard or saw that convinced him to tip those scales
would be a truth.

When he came face to face with Damien Boyd, those
scales shivered at the discrepancy in the weight of Eli's
assumptions. Damien Boyd was not hostile and if there
was solid evidence, Mark Jackson was holding it close to
the vest.

Damien Boyd was a young man who had never made it
out the other side of the dark tunnel of puberty. His face
was clean as a baby's bottom, and with a long hangdog
look. His ears stood out, his hair stood up, and his body
had the look of a marionette strung together with rubber
bands. Damien Boyd tripped over the lines etched into

he linoleum, he ran into imaginary walls that seemed to
spring up in front of him in the stale air. Damien Boyd's
face was a play of surprise and fear inspired, of all things,
by Eli Warner himself. Eli half stood when Damien sat.
Damien almost missed the chair. He was a boy with big
features on a thin face, a tall guy, a confused kid in mini-
braids.

When their talk was over Eli left, carrying all he'd heard
down in his gut where instinct was on alert; Damien Boyd
went back to his cell never questioning who Eli Warner
was.

Eli's next stop was Edie Williams's office but she was
busy. He only managed a short walk down the hall with
her. He only managed to tell her he thought there were
some hinky things going on. She was sympathetic, in that
rushed, clipped Edie sort of way. She was satisfied, given the
information on her desk. Edie said everyone was satisfied,
including the family. That's when Eli stopped following
her. He filed away the reference. Allan Lassiter, he
assumed, was the family Edie was talking about. Nice that
he was being kept appraised of all the details.

Eli went back to the Westwood building and straight up
to Mark Jackson's office on the off chance the man was
there. Today, Eli was surprised. The Special Agent in
Charge was there, behind his desk and willing to take a
few minutes to talk to Eli.

"How's Nick?" Eli asked as he settled himself.

"What's up?" was the only answer Eli got. Mark's mustache twitched then his expression settled.

"Wilson Caufeld."

Mark Jackson's head went west, his shoulders rotated a
little north and south. Eli had his attention.

"What about him?"

"He's dead and I think you may want to take another
look at Damien Boyd. He didn't do it."

Mark Jackson laughed. "Eli, you are a piece of work."

Eli was smiling. Mark Jackson's shoulder came back to
roost and one hand found its way to the desk. His fingers
fidgeted, but ever so slightly. That was a surprise from an

agent who knew about patience and reason and instinct Mark Jackson seemed to have forgotten his trade.

"First, Eli," he said quietly, "why in the hell were you talking to Damien Boyd? Last I heard that was my assignment, and I don't remember asking you to help out."

Eli grinned and his eyes curled into the half-moon shape that Lauren found so intriguing. Mark Jackson wasn' affected in quite the same way. Eli wasn't offended.

"I'm wrapping up Caufeld's background. Just want to put it to bed the right way. When I heard what happened I realized talking to Damien Boyd would be the way to do that." Eli lied easily when necessity demanded. He played the game, concerned and deferential, and knew that Mark Jackson was playing one of his own. There was only one problem. Eli was playing blindfolded. "I know how sensitive this is. Our office is going to come under scrutiny and I don't want anyone vulnerable. Especially me." He chuckled. Mark wasn't moved.

"No harm done. Finish with that file and get it on my desk. I'll include it in my case file. Anything else?" Mark picked up a pen. Tip down on the desk, he slid it through his fingers, turned it, put the top down and repeated the motion.

"Not really. Just wanted to give you my impressions of this whole Damien Boyd thing. He doesn't seem like he could pull your leg much less the trigger of a gun."

"We have him placed at the scene. Time is right. Eye witnesses. Not to worry." Down went the pen. "I think I've got my bases covered. I'm on top of it."

"Yeah. I know you've taken a great personal interest. I talked to Jim Walsh and he told me you were the one who relieved his protection detail the morning before Caufeld died. Guess you feel kind of responsible."

"The judge didn't want protection. It happens. I'd be less than human if I didn't feel some responsibility," Mark said.

"I wouldn't want to be in your shoes." Eli let his head roll side to side commiserating with his boss.

"Then it's a good thing you aren't." Mark gave the pen

his hand a click. "When do you think you'll get me the Caufeld file?"

"Well, that's a problem. It's going to be hard to finish considering the way I feel about this kid. He's scared and he tells me nobody's really listening. He's says nobody's bothered to take a full statement, that his lawyer is always in a rush. You know, stuff like that."

Mark laughed, thoroughly amused. "I've taken a statement. I've taken a couple, if you must know. The guy is good. He looks like a sitcom comedian, but believe me he's not."

"He must be a heck of a liar, or I'm losing my touch. I had him pegged as afraid, confused, not too bright. He swears he was with his homeboys . . ."

"A gang. A blast. Nothing to it. Happens every day in Los Angeles."

"But Damien swears they don't carry weapons since the truce. He told me nothing was found at his house. His mother hadn't washed his clothes so I guess my next question would be was there any residue on them. Then he told me about someone else on the street that night. It was hard for him to see because everything happened to fast, but he says the car was dark. Gray maybe. The person was white and tall."

"Hey! Whoa." Mark was back on track. His face had transformed from curves of discomfort to planes of exasperation. "That's enough. You're so interested in Damien Boyd, sit in on the trial on your own time. I heard the same story. A lone Caucasian in that neighborhood is a stretch but I'm checking that, too. Now, if you don't mind."

"Actually, Mark, I had some thoughts of my own. I don't know if you're aware of it, but something came up during my investigation. If you really want to find out what happened to Wilson Caufeld, I think you've got to look into . . ."

"Warner. Listen carefully." Mark got cozy with his desk. "Until you sit in my chair don't try to do my job. You got it?"

"I'm not, Mark. I'm trying to do mine."

"Bull." Mark threw the pen on the desk. "I don't know

what's gotten into you. You're one of my most reliab
agents. I can always count on you to get just what you'
supposed to get, now you're muddying the water on th
Caufeld thing. I don't get it.''

"I guess it's semantics. You say muddying, I say I'
moving things out of the way. I'm telling you, Boyd's ge
ting railroaded.''

"And you want to point the finger at one of the mo
prominent attorneys in the state.''

"I don't think I mentioned any names," Eli said casuall

"Maybe I've been keeping my ears open, too. I've hear
from Mr. Lassiter about your harassing questions. I'
heard from Edie Williams, who has also heard from M
Lassiter. How many other people do you want me to hea
from about this little theory of yours? There are a fe
reasons it's not smart. First, I want this thing closed an
off the books. Second, Judge Martinelli is the third judg
on the Stewart case. It's time to finish that one. Nobod
wants Caufeld's murder outshining a militia trial. They ar
more afraid of the militia effort than random street crim
Third, Edie Williams can make a case. Everyone excep
you is happy and, if you don't mind me pointing this ou
you weren't asked.'' Mark was winding up. "Your concern
are noted. It's in Edie's hands now, if she wants to talk t
you make yourself available. Other than that you're don
Turn in the Caufeld file and attend to your new assign
ment.''

Eli nodded. The discussion was over, the investigatio
wasn't. Eli didn't even have to think twice about that. H
left Mark's office and Mark, who waited just long enoug
to be sure Eli Warner had cleared out before picking u
the telephone. He never dialed. Who was there to cal
after all? He'd have to rely on himself. If Eli meant t
overstep his bounds, Mark would have to create som
boundaries he couldn't step over. Thankfully, as Specia
Agent in Charge, creating them wouldn't be too tough.

Chapter Twenty-Two

"Thanks for coming."

"I haven't got a whole lot of better things to do," Lauren said as she slipped into his car and pulled the door shut behind her. They were parked in the red zone in front of the courthouse. Neither worried. Credentials were effective little items that warded off all sorts of evil. Besides, Eli wasn't going to stay long. He was going with or without her.

"Are you making headway on the judge's office?"

She threw her purse at her feet and shook her head.

"There's still a lot to do." It was as good an answer as any for now. "I've been monitoring some other things."

"Can you take a break?" Eli asked. His left hand was on the wheel and his shoulders were turned toward her. It was warm outside but he had on an argyle sweater done up in golds and browns. It looked good on him. She thought of how good he looked wearing nothing at all. He cocked a wry smile. He laughed, "What?"

"Never mind. It's one of those things you should discuss in the middle of the afternoon, in public, in a car. I'm glad you came back after that disaster with Allan."

"Thought you'd figured out I keep turning up like a

bad penny." Eli moved around a bit more. His hand w
off the wheel and both were planted on the stick shift. F
looked like he was praying or begging. She doubted I
was begging. "Here's the thing. I saw Damien Boyd toda
I'll be really honest, Lauren, I went to see that kid becau.
I thought he would implicate Lassiter in a conspiracy.
figured Lassiter hired Boyd to do the hit."

"And?" Lauren asked straight on.

"And I don't know what to think. The only thing I c
know is if that kid killed Wilson Caufeld then it's time
quit this job because I'm missing something big." Laure
nodded, and she stayed and that made Eli bolder. "I war
you to come with me to see Damien Boyd's mother."

"And the reason is?"

"I don't know, Lauren. I only know that if I leave th
to Mark Jackson this guy might be convicted of a murd
he didn't commit. Judge Caufeld wouldn't want it either.
He touched her hand. "Will you come with me? Will yo
listen to her and see what you think? Will you do it f
the judge?"

Lauren slid in her seat until she was facing forward. H
eyes were narrowed as she scanned the streets. Everyor
was back from lunch long ago but the streets were st
busy. She wondered how many of their lives were in shar
bles. Which one of them had lived through the unthinkab
and which had given up, who had gone on? Had the
come a moment in their lives when one choice would mak
the difference between a bright future and despair? Ha
any of them sat where she sat now?

She turned her head toward Eli. He hadn't moved a
inch. It was funny that after all the tragedy it should I
him, someone without a grand title, an FBI agent of a
things, who would be the one to call on her to prove wh.
she was made of.

"I'll do it for you," she said and slipped on her su
glasses.

Chapter Twenty-Three

"Violetta Boyd?"

The woman was tall and thin like her son. In fact, she was tall and thin like the three other children who were playing outside and the one that could be seen through the window of the small house with the chain link fence surrounding it. She was stitching jeans, closing a hole in a knee that had already seen a patch or two. Her fingers never stopped but her eyes did. Those eyes pegged Eli and Lauren and kept them skewered where they stood on the street side of her fence.

"I already told you everything you need to know. Leave me alone, or it's harassment. I know a lawyer."

Violetta did lower her eyes, but only to tie off the thread and snapped it with her finger. She was well practiced and probably had eyes on top of her head.

"I am a lawyer, Mrs. Boyd and believe me we're not here to harass you," Lauren called.

"What about him?" She raised her chin toward Eli.

"FBI. Would you like to see our identification?"

Violetta laughed. "Naw, I already knew he was something like that. Just wanted to see what you'd say." She sobered quickly and stood up. Tall and lanky, she was joined with rubber bands like her son. "We still don't have anything to talk about."

"We think Damien's being railroaded," Eli called, lifting the latch on the fence. Violetta planted herself on her porch and the children stopped playing. Obviously they'd seen this stance before.

"That's a new way of getting past the front door. More polite than bustin' it down."

"Is it going to get us in?" Eli called even though they all knew he wasn't going to take no for an answer.

"I guess. Come on in."

The gate was opened. A dog came round the side of the house. It was a big black thing that looked to Violetta for a clue. Obviously he got it, because he dipped his head and sniffed his way out of sight again. Violetta didn't wait for them. Lauren said hi to the kids in the yard as they walked up the path. Eli lagged behind, bags of M&Ms passed from him to the kids. Lauren thought he had redefined the concept of deep pockets. Inside, the fourth child was nowhere to be seen. By the time Eli came in Lauren was on the couch. He sat beside her facing their hostess. Violetta was in a chair.

"I'm not going to offer you anything to drink or eat. I don't want you to stay that long. I've gotta go to work at seven anyway." Violetta's eyes flicked to Lauren who looked right back. "You don't look like you want to be here."

"Eli was heading here so I came." Lauren said honestly.

"Eli, huh? Eli comin'." Violetta laughed again and it was a hearty sound. "Well, Eli, what's on your mind?"

"I want to know about Damien. I want to know about the night Judge Caufeld was killed. I want to know anything you can think to talk about: that night, Damien, yourself."

"Why not talk about the judge?" Lauren raised a brow and Violetta enjoyed her little surprise. "Nobody thought to even ask that one. Not even you. You didn't know we knowed who he was, did you? That's why there's something to laugh about here. God is playing a good joke, Mr. Eli. That judge, Caufeld, he's going to take two of my men from me. Oh, Lordy, that's a pity."

Eli sat back. Patience time. Lauren was on the edge of the couch. Violetta lost her humor and then lost herself in some memory. Lauren had the sense that the woman was rocking but it must have been a illusion. The chair sat on four big legs solidly planted on the worn carpet.

"I'm tellin' you, when I heard who it was been shot, I figured there'd be trouble for my family. I didn't know how it would come, but I knew it was on the way. Judge Caufeld put my man in jail. Put him away in the penitentiary because he murdered a man." The woman's dark eyes came up. They weren't as hard as they were before. "I'm not saying he didn't murder that fellow, but I'll tell you I don't know he deserved hard time like that. The man he killed was bad. Not that it mattered in the end. He died in there not three years after he started serving that time."

"Did Damien know about this?" Lauren asked.

"I don't keep things from my children," Violetta scoffed.

"I think that's wise," Eli said, "but I also think that kind of history could be a perfect motive for murdering Wilson Caufeld."

She laughed again. "Yeah, could be. Then I say, After all this time? Have you met my Damien?" Eli nodded. "Then you know he isn't exactly the type to focus now, is he?"

"He seemed to be very nice. He was afraid."

"He should be because this law uses boys like him. They make them examples or they make them causes. They don't look at the boy. I thought they did once, but Damien didn't quite make it out. He got arrested for burglary when he was thirteen, not quite fourteen."

"Did he go to Youth Authority?" Lauren asked.

"Naw," Violetta answered, "they did him like an adult. Got him a fancy court-appointed attorney. This man was so slick. He was just a good-lookin' man. Even made me think twice. He made Damien a cause. Said all the right things and did all the right talkin' in court, but I'll tell you I sure do wish he'd left well 'nough alone. I did pray he'd have a regular PD then he'd probably be sittin' in jail doin' his time for burglary. If he'd been doin' his time, he wouldn't have been on the street, then none of this would have happened."

Suddenly the living room erupted. Two of Violetta's children tumbled through the front door. She was up like a flash, marionette arms flailing as her voice rose an octave. She chattered so fast Lauren couldn't understand a word she said. Violetta swatted the biggest one who put his dukes up and danced around her before running off laughing. A few more words tossed at the smaller one and she ran, too. Violetta sat down as if nothing had happened.

"Look, you can tear this house apart and I'm tellin' you, there isn't nothin' to find. Not a syringe or a nickel bag. There ain't no drugs here. You won't find a gun 'cause I won't have it. I ain't sayin' Damien's an angel 'cause if he was he wouldn't be in court in the first place, but he's no bad criminal and he ain't no murderer. That boy couldn't do it, and he wouldn't do it, for a man he never did know. He'll fight for me," she said proudly, "he might even fight for some of them." She jerked her head toward the sound of children. "He'll steal for us, that's sure. He wouldn't kill for nothin', and if you've seen him you know that."

"I do know that," Eli answered.

"Why you here then?" Violetta seemed to accept Eli at face value but Lauren still bothered her. "You're not a public defender. You got that smart, rich look. You would have done the same as Damien's pro-bono man. He was a fancy lawyer, thought he was doin' some good but all he was doin' was makin' things worse." She ended in disgust, "Mr. Las-si-ter didn' know what he was doin' when he got my Damien off."

Lauren was standing and she didn't quite know when she had managed to do that. Violetta was looking up at her. Eli was touching her hand that hung at her side. Lauren was out the door without a word. Behind her Eli was talking sweetly, probably shaking that woman's hand and thanking her for her time, but Lauren couldn't breathe in that big room. The dark had come so suddenly it spooked her. She was holding onto Violetta's fence when she heard the screen door open and close. Only Eli came out.

"You okay?" He touched her arm. She shook him off gently and hugged herself. They started walking, Lauren counting the times she saw the tips of her shoes as they went.

"I'm sorry. I just wasn't thinking," Lauren finally said.

"I wasn't exactly suave myself." Eli walked with his hands in his pockets and his eyes on the sidewalk. "So, what are you thinking?"

"Probably what you are. That was damned odd." Lauren's eyes slid his way. "Did you know about that?"

Eli shook his head. "No. I was hoping I'd find something that might give me a link, but I never expected it to be that blatant. Now that I've heard it, I have to tell you it makes my skin crawl."

"Okay, so you're considering a murder for hire," Lauren stopped and her face was serious when she looked at him. "But I thought you said you didn't think Damien could have pulled the trigger."

"I still don't. Maybe Damien just put Lassiter in touch with one of his homeboys. Maybe one of them did the deed. There was a gang of kids that night, it could have been any of them." Allan let her think about that for a moment. "This is where he died, Lauren. Right there. Wilson was shot right there. Men like him don't grow on trees. Even if it hurts you to find out the truth, at least help me find it."

"Eli, I want to tell you . . ."

Lauren couldn't finish. They weren't alone. Men materialized out of the gathering gloom of twilight. They were young men in shorts and jeans so loose, so huge, they seemed to magically hover around their thin hips. On their heads were caps pulled low until eyes were only hinted at, hairnets or heads completely shaved. They wore big shirts open to show tattoos and they moved with big, deep steps. They were in your face, taking the space. They had Lauren's attention and Eli's too.

"Yo, man." They closed in. Two steps. Two words. Two steps. Lauren did a half turn either way to get the lay of the land.

"My man," Eli said back.

"You bein' gettin' killed down this way, know what I'm sayin'? Folks get killed down here, right where you're standin', know what I'm sayin'?"

"I heard. You Damien's homeboys?"

The talker ignored the question and checked out Lauren. "Your woman, too? You bring your woman on our turf and you gotta be crazy, man."

"I came for Damien, know what I'm sayin'?" Eli parodied. Lauren almost raised an objection. She thought better of it.

"You seen Damien? He's our boy, know what I'm sayin'? He don' be doin' nothin'."

"We know that," Eli moved closer to the headman and he didn't back off, neither did he move forward. "We talked to Violetta. We talked to Damien. So we've got to go back with something that's going to help him. Anybody talk to you about this?"

They all laughed, giggly laughs and snickering. Heads turned to view one another and the friend's eyes mirrored that they were cool. Very bad.

"Yeah." Another boy stepped up. Shorter than the first. A scar on his cheek and four fingers on one hand. He threw a sign and Lauren wondered if it was one only he could throw. "They let us have coffee so we could tell 'em what went down while we was comfortable, know what . . ."

More laughing. The leader waved away this new man before he could ask Eli again if he had a clue what he was sayin'.

"What you take this for? They wanna find out who offed that guy they shouldn' be pointin' to us, man. Them bros should talk to us 'cause we saw the car, we saw the dude that done it, know what I'm sayin'? A tall dude and one of them cars. You knowed the kind."

"What kind?" Eli reached into his pocket. Beneath the baggy clothes, bodies went rigid, fingers moved for weapons but none appeared. Lauren stayed alert. Eli said, "Hey, man. I'm cool."

Eli talked slowly and calmly. When his hand came out of his jacket, Eli was holding up a fifty that was snatched in a flash.

"I don't know what kind," the leader said. "I ain't one
o tell you how all them cars are. Every one look alike,
now what I'm sayin'? You know, like an egg, you hear me
alkin'?"

"An expensive egg? An old one? Damaged?"

"New. Looked new I mean no holes or nothin'." He
ooked around. Heads nodded. "Look, man, we don't
vanna see Damien go down. He's my man. He's cool,
inderstand what I'm sayin'?"

"Yeah, I understand what's going down." Eli nodded.
"What about the man you saw."

He shrugged, "I don' know. It was a tall dude. Moved
ast. We was way back and it was dark. Man, we was just
aangin'. We come around that corner, know what I'm
ayin'?" He pointed behind him and Eli squinted. Lauren
ooked, too. It was a long block and, even now as the light
aded, it was hard to see. Overgrown bushes, a street lamp,
ousted and hanging by a thread. And then there were the
vitnesses. High on life or otherwise, they wouldn't have
oeen sharp until . . .

"Man we heard . . . bam, bam . . . man, we're gone. Shit,
here be no hardware here. We be goin' with the truce,
ny man?"

"I know. Damien said you were cool on that. No guns.
We got it. Could you identify who you saw?"

They all shook their heads. "No way. We feel bad for
hat. Damien's gonna fry. A judge, man. That's not cool.
3ut he ain't got no gun. We ain't got no reason to kill
inyone 'cept gang, and we're not doin' that. You know
vhere I'm comin' from?"

"Listen, my man. Do you know anybody who came to
.ee Damien? A white guy? Tall? Any of you seen a guy like
hat? Or anybody who might have seen what you saw?"

"Maybe, there," the boy pointed to a house they had
oassed three doors back. Lauren looked up and eyed the
olace, well-kept, a nice place in this very changed neighbor-
1ood. She was checking out the house number when her
urm flew up as a car sped toward them, brights on.
Damien's homeboys scattered. Eli threw his arms around
Lauren as the car swerved then turned hard, the front

wheels flying over the curb, the giant piece of metal comin
to a stop five feet in front of them.

Alone on the street, they clung to one another in th
sudden silence. A dog barked. A woman called. The fron
door of the house Lauren had been looking at opene
and a woman peered out. But mostly Lauren felt peopl
cringing behind their doors, turning away, pretending fou
big men were not opening four big doors and going a
the two white people standing together in the glare of th
headlights.

Unhurried, they came toward Eli who handed Laurer
back and behind him. He went to meet the men. Thei
faces were dissected by the headlights and Lauren, tryin
to memorize those faces, only had vague impressions o
each of them. Collectively she had no problem describin
them. They were muscled and tight. They walked as if the
never walked on any ground that didn't belong to them
They formed a semicircle.

"Eli," one of them said. His voice was surprisingly high
pitched and friendly. Lauren felt the breath come bac
into her. They were friends. They talked as if they'd know
Eli forever.

"Yeah," Eli said.

"We got a message." This person's voice was deeper bu
not as friendly.

Clearly illuminated in the bright light, Eli raised his heac
recognizing these men with a half smile. Lauren almos
expected him to offer a bag of M&Ms. Before he could
the smallest of his new playmates buried his fist in Eli'
middle and the man grunted with pleasure.

Eli didn't cry out as he was doubled up and half raisec
off the ground by the force of the blow. Lauren cried ou
for him, only to silence herself as another man made a
move toward her. Another snapped his fingers and Laurer
was safe. Like a cat she skirted around them all and threw
herself over Eli only to be grabbed, her arms pinnec
behind her.

It was over in another second. A clip on Eli's jaw. Anothe
on the back of the neck. The fourth gave him a kick along
with a few words of advice.

"There's a man who wants you to shut up, Eli. We think you should listen to this man. We think you should listen now." The man who had kicked Eli leaned down close. "We think you know who you're supposed to be listening to, right, Eli?"

That was it. There was no more.

Lauren was released, thrown forward to her knees. She stumbled and crawled until her arms were thrown over Eli who was rolled into a ball of pain. One. Two. Three and four doors slammed shut. The engine was fired, the car slammed into reverse and then the street went dark again.

"Eli?"

Lauren cried gently. She lay over his body, knowing there was nothing she could do for his pain, praying it was not so bad that he couldn't get up and out of there. "Eli?" She raised her head and then her voice. "Someone! Help us!" But Damien's homeboys were gone, off into the night, enough trouble chasing them already. "Someone?" Lauren whispered knowing that no one would come.

They stayed there, curled together, licking their wounds. Lauren and Eli rocked, alone on the spot where Wilson Caufeld died and Damien Boyd had run from the sound of gunfire. Backs had been turned on Wilson that night, eyes closed, hands were put over ears. As Lauren lowered her cheek to Eli's back, she knew that ended as of now. She'd watch her back, but she'd never turn it to Eli Warner or Wilson Caufeld again.

Chapter Twenty-Four

"Your kitchen is so neat. The ice trays were actually filled."

Eli heard Lauren from the other room but he didn't open his eyes until she was standing over him. Even then, opening his eyes was a chore.

"Don't. Don't do anything that hurts." She slipped onto the sofa and put her fingers over his eyes, closing them. She felt him relax at her touch only to brace himself as she shifted her weight on the sofa. "I'm sorry. I'm sorry. Shhh. Here."

Ice pack. That went on his jaw. Fingers. Those went through his hair. Soft, wonderful hair that wasn't quite wavy, nor quite straight.

"What do you use on your hair?" She pulled her fingers up and let his hair sift through them. "Most women would kill for this hair you know."

"Better than . . . guys who tried . . . tonight," Eli mumbled.

Lauren chuckled. "Oh, I don't know. Ever been stomped with high heels?" Eli shook his head carefully. There was no way he didn't hurt like hell and she thought

e was crazy for trying to act like he didn't. "You know,
ou don't have to be brave for me."

"I not." He swallowed hard. He seemed to have a two-
word maximum per breath and contractions weren't part
f the deal. He adjusted his ice-pack, his hand over hers.
"Brave. For me."

Lauren laughed out loud and leaned down, burying her
lips in his hair, talking against it because it felt marvelous
on her mouth. "You're a funny man, Eli. In more ways
than one." She sat back up again. "I have a warm bath
ready. You sure your ribs aren't broken?"

He shook his head. "Okay."

"Ready to try to get up?"

Lauren eased herself off the sofa, barely moving the
cushion as she did. Gently she snaked her arm under his
back and lifted. He did his part but she didn't let go even
when he was on his feet. He could have actually found his
own way, but Lauren couldn't let him go, and Eli had no
good reason to ask her to.

The bathroom was steamy and she shut the door quickly
so it would stay warm. With exquisite care she undressed
him, kissing him now and again, comforting him the way
she should. Tonight she was caretaker, magician, someone
stronger, but only because the hurt was on the inside. She
hurt because she had let him stand alone so long.

"Careful now," she said, helping him step into the tub.
She steadied him as he lay back. Wordlessly Lauren minis-
tered to him. Soap on a cloth, she washed his body, cloth
dipped into the water and water dripped and waved over
him until she saw the pain wash away. Lauren smiled,
seeing she cared for him well. It was a new experience.
There were people in her life to lean on, to bury, but no
one to care for. Wilson needed nothing but her company.
Her mother had been so young and competent when she
died. Allan . . . Lauren shook her head. She'd rather think
of anything but Allan.

"You didn't lie about my mother, did you, Eli?" Another
wave of warm water over his shoulders and another. His
eyes were closed so he didn't see the melancholy smile on
her lips when he stayed silent. "I didn't think so." The

sound of the water lapping over his aching muscles as she moved methodically soothed her too.

"Sorry," he mumbled.

"It's okay. Really." More soap, but this time she used her hands. Small hands running over his broad shoulders. Slipping down across his chest while she talked. "After tonight I don't think I'll be talking about it anymore. You were right, Eli. People just do things. Sometimes they think about the things they do, sometimes they don't, sometimes they punish themselves for their mistakes."

"Sometimes they punish," Eli swallowed. The bath must be working. He got four words out. ". . . others."

Lauren nodded. Yes. Sometimes people who had done wrong hurt others, and there was a possibility that Allan Lassiter had done just that to Wilson Caufeld. Though those reasons were still unclear, Lauren had no doubt they existed.

"What about you? Remember you told me you lived with someone who taught you about honesty? What was that all about?" She rinsed her hands and dried them, sitting with her back to the tub while Eli lay quietly. "A wife? Did she cheat? Did you? No, never mind. None of my business. I just want you to tell me your war stories so I'll feel better about mine." She tilted her head back and smiled. He was watching her. Eli lifted his hand from the water and touched her face. Lauren took that hand in hers and held it there, tight, cupped against her cheek though water trickled onto her shirt.

"Mother, too." Eli let his hand drop. Lauren turned, slipped to the floor and put her back to the tub. She rested her head against the porcelain and closed her eyes. Tired but not too tired to listen to the story he told so slowly and painfully. Perhaps that's what made the tale so poignant. Tears came to her eyes imagining Eli the boy, so desirous of warmth and love, so rejected. She sighed deeply.

"We're a pair aren't we, Warner?" Lauren pushed herself off the floor.

"Orphans."

"Nope." She set her jaw, that square jaw Wilson found so attractive. "Not anymore, Eli."

"Believe me . . ." He swallowed, "now?"

"Yes, Eli," she said and reached for him, supporting him until he could stand, helping him back out of the tub. She rubbed him with a huge towel. She kissed his back and wrapped him in his bath sheet. He pushed it away and wrapped his arms around her as if that was the only comfort he needed. He didn't shiver, and Lauren closed her eyes.

"Warm. Thank you," was all he said and Lauren knew she had accomplished something magnificent.

Finally, she had him in bed. Aspirin was administered. Covers were pulled tight. The lights were off.

"Will you stay?" he asked while she still bent over him.

"Yes," she answered. She kissed his lips and that kiss was lingering. He smelled of soap and sorrow.

"Sorry."

"About what?" she whispered against his lips.

"Your mother. Caufeld." He hesitated. "Lassiter."

"I know. But it's all right. It was time for me to know, Eli." Pulling back, she smoothed the covers on his bed. So many, many covers to keep him warm. Lauren stood back. She saw his eyes glitter through the dark. She didn't touch him when she said, "I was going to tell you something before your friends came. I went to Damien Boyd's arraignment. Indicted in a day, arraigned in four, Edie pulling out all the stops. Mark Jackson was looking so damn smug."

"Lassiter there?"

Lauren shook her head. "Nowhere to be found." Eli's eyes closed. That defeat hurt more than anything those men had done to him. This, though, Lauren could cure. "But Damien Boyd is being defended by Bernard Goldracknian." Eli's eyes opened. Lauren gave him a huge dose of medicine. "Bernard used to work for Allan. He never made partner. Allan said he was incompetent. He couldn't get another job, so he hung out his own shingle. He was barely making it until Allan kindly recommended him to Damien's case. Bernard's thrilled. He's sure the publicity alone is going to shoot him right over the top. Bernard may have his fifteen minutes of fame on this, Eli, but consider this. With an incompetent attorney defending him, Damien's bound to go down fast."

"Think that's interesting?"

"Isn't it? Considering that Allan handled Damien pro bono."

"Too much coincidence."

"I'm still not sure he pulled the trigger," Lauren said and smoothed his hair.

"Probably didn't," Eli said and turned on his side. Lauren knelt on the ground so she wouldn't disturb him as he drifted off to sleep. He murmured, "Gotta prove it."

"Gotta figure out why," Lauren whispered back, kissing him once again before she left him to mend.

Back in the living room, Lauren covered herself with a blanket and settled herself in Eli's chair. She curled up and lay her head back hoping to rest. Instead, she stayed awake for hours listening to the sounds of a different night than she was used to. Not so quiet. Not so secure. When sleep came, it was deep and satisfying because she knew exactly where she stood. When morning came and Eli still slept, Lauren let herself out of his apartment.

God help her, she knew exactly what she had to do.

Chapter Twenty-Five

Traffic had been bad from the minute Lauren turned onto the San Diego Freeway. Three cars and a packing crate of toilet paper had done battle. The toilet paper won. When Lauren inched past the scene there were two police cars, an ambulance, the three damaged cars and the undamaged crate on the side of the road. At least one news helicopter hovered overhead and gave those not involved the option to look up or over and hopefully ahead so there wouldn't be another mishap anytime soon. A car length after she cleared that crash, four lanes opened, the pace picked up and she flew until she hit the Santa Monica Freeway. There it slowed again for no good reason. Lauren crawled along with everyone else and tried to keep her anxiety under control. Finally she transitioned and exited on Broadway.

She parked on Temple at an outdoor lot that charged thirteen dollars a day or a dollar-fifty for every twenty minutes. She locked up, took her ticket and started to walk. Yesterday seemed forever ago. She had slept in her clothes—jeans, worn cowboy boots, and a shirt over a tank. She had showered and let her hair dry on the way downtown. Now she pulled it back and slipped a rubber band around the cloud of curls. Wisps and tendrils had crimped around her face and over her shoulders. She looked gorgeous. She tried not to look scared.

Walking tall, or as tall as she could, Lauren hurried keeping her eyes open for anyone who watched, searching for anyone who waited ahead. But no one was interested in her. Lauren passed a diner, so small it could seat only four at the counter and two at a table near the window. Eggs were cooking. They smelled good. She passed by, half standing on tiptoe as if that would make the red light change faster when she reached the corner. Three cars made right-hand turns. She looked the opposite way, saw a clear path and darted across the street only to slow as she cut across the park. Something was going on. People were gathered outside the Federal Courthouse. They milled about, some lounged, most complained. Two news screws were on scene.

"What's going on?" Lauren asked a woman whose nose was buried in a paperback novel. The woman looked up and pushed on her sunglasses. Lauren had the sense that she was surprised not to find herself alone.

"Bomb threat," she muttered.

"Independent Militia?" Lauren asked.

"Don't know. Maybe. I work in the cafeteria." Lauren nodded, accepting that as an excuse for ignorance. It seemed as good as any. Checking her watch, Lauren wandered to the far edges of the crowd to watch.

The vantage point was excellent. The LAPD bomb squad was there. Lauren tagged at least two FBI agents but knew there were probably fifty more inside the building. She saw dogs restrained by their handlers and wished she had thought to bring a hat, more to hide her face than shade her from the sun. She looked for Edie but identified only a smattering of assistants from the U.S. Attorney's office. Lauren steered clear of them all.

Leaning back against the wall behind her, she let her gaze wander and that's when she saw her. The one woman Lauren hadn't really thought about in all this, the woman who, for a while, had been the only one to interest Lauren. Slowly, she pushed herself away from the wall and made her way diagonally through the crowd, cutting north again and coming around the woman she wanted to talk to.

"Mrs. Stewart?"

To her credit, Carolyn Stewart didn't startle easily.

"Ms. Kingsley." She seemed on the verge of saying something more but thought better of it. Lauren moved beside her, standing shoulder to shoulder. It was a calculated risk, but given the bomb threat, Lauren imagined surveillance on Carolyn Stewart had been relaxed for the moment. She prayed she was right.

"Did you call it in?" Lauren asked.

"I don't know what you're talking about," Carolyn said evenly.

"Sure you do," Lauren laughed. "Look, I don't really care. You know I'm not assigned to your case anymore. I just need to know if there's really something in there. If there isn't, then I can go do what I came to do. If the threat's bogus, tell me. Nobody else has to know. I need to get into that building and I'd like to know if I can do that without getting blown to kingdom come."

There was the beat of a two-step before Carolyn answered. "No. You won't meet your maker."

"Thank you," Lauren sighed. "Okay. Anyplace I have to worry about your people being? Hostage stuff, anything like that?"

Carolyn Stewart laughed ruefully. "My people." Carolyn shook her head. "The only people I have are my husband and my son. The Independent Militia has exercised their right to be completely independent. They've all gone, denied they even know us, all my great and brave soldiers."

Lauren turned and faced Carolyn Stewart. The other woman only turned her head.

"When?" Lauren asked.

"It started after Caufeld was killed. Nick Cheshire didn't help. They thought the FBI had taken him out, then Henry told us he was a plant. More of them got nervous." She shrugged. "There's been a steady decline ever since. I think George knew it would happen. I think he knew they didn't have any guts and that's why he took Henry with him that day. That's why he changed plans. He knew it was just us against all of them."

"God, that's so sad," Lauren whispered.

"What? That the three of us are willing to stand alone?"

"No, it's sad that everyone turned against you. And it's sad that in the end you and I are just alike. All this work, all this heartache, and we're just alike."

"I don't know how you figure." Carolyn looked away again, fascinated probably that one phone call from her could still disturb the equilibrium to this degree.

"Alone. People we care about dead," Lauren looked to the courthouse, "or close to it. I suppose I should be grateful that Judge Caufeld went fast. What you've got ahead of you will be ten times worse. Maybe you should stop fighting."

"Are you going to?"

Lauren shook her head. "No."

"Are you going to hurt people doing what you've got to do?" Carolyn asked.

Lauren nodded. "Probably."

"Then you're right. We are alike."

"But I wouldn't have let my child get involved. I would never let my child be hurt." Lauren took off her glasses. She put her hand on Carolyn Stewart's arm. "He's a good kid, and he's torn apart by loving you and your husband. I talked to him, you know."

"He told me," Carolyn answered.

"Then you know he just wants you to love him. Help him if you can."

Carolyn's chin tilted downward. Lauren thought she shook her head once, but the movement was almost imperceptible. Her voice was strong, yet somehow dispirited when she spoke again.

"Henry's suffering. I won't let him suffer much longer. I promise I'll help him get to where he should be if I can."

"I wish there was something I could do to help. I really do."

"Thank you." Carolyn looked toward the bomb squad van. There were more men than there had been a minute ago. They were giving up. "It won't be much longer now."

Lauren thought about touching Carolyn Stewart. Instead, she melted away, becoming part of the crowd as the go-ahead was given for the building to be opened. She kept her head up and her eyes open and forgot that if she could see them, they could see her.

Wilson Caufeld's chambers were cleaned out. Not a scrap of paper, not a book, not a paper clip remained. The computer was still on his desk and Lauren ran for it. She flipped the switch. It seemed to take forever to light but finally the menu pulled up. Thankfully, they'd left the chair too. She sat down and began to type. Nothing but the software. All the files had been erased, or copied then erased.

"Damn!" She slapped the desk and pushed the chair back hard.

"What are you doing here?"

"Barbara," Lauren exclaimed. Weak with relief she ran to the other woman only to stop short. Barbara hovered in the doorway as if she wasn't sure if she should come or go. There were no welcoming arms held out, no smile on her face. Lauren regrouped. She forced a smile to her face. "I wondered where you were. I came to help. I thought we'd left quite a mess in here. Looks like you've been working overtime."

"I know you didn't come to help, Lauren. I think you better go right now." Barbara looked down and then threw her head back. "Look, I know what's been going on and I just can't believe it. I really thought Allan was the one I had to worry about all these years."

"Barbara, please." Lauren moved cautiously away from the desk and toward Wilson's secretary. She held out her hands to show she had no tricks. "I don't know what you heard, but you don't have to worry about me at all."

"How can you say that? You've been telling people that Allan killed Judge Caufeld. Lauren, Allan was as dear to the judge as life itself. How can you betray either of them that way?" Barbara looked ill, her face stretched in an expression of such despair and disappointment Lauren thought her heart would break.

"Wait a minute." Lauren pumped her hands against the wall Barbara was putting up. She kept her voice low. "I don't know who told you that, but I never said Allan killed Wilson. But things aren't as they seem, Barbara and I'm trying to figure out what the truth is."

"The truth is you're trying to bring Allan down because Mr. Warner wants to. Lauren, it's all over the place. Can you honestly tell me that you aren't turning against Allan because you've been sleeping with Eli Warner? Is that what this is all about? Have you been brainwashed?"

"I suppose that's how Allan would see things," Lauren lamented, "but it's not true. Eli told me certain things, I've seen other things for myself. The only thing I know for sure is that Allan has something to hide and if you give me a minute I can tell you what I know." Barbara shook her head and backed away. Lauren hustled after her, insisting, "Can you just listen?"

"No," Barbara said, her purse held in front of her as she backed through her own office. Lauren stopped halfway across Wilson's office. The two women faced off.

"Why not? Please, Barbara, please! You listened to Allan. You believed Allan. Wouldn't Wilson want you to give me a chance, too? Please, Barbara. Please?"

Lauren closed her eyes and prayed. She only opened them when she heard the door close. She opened them to see that Barbara was standing on the right side, with her.

Lauren paced, she stood, she postured as the words poured out. Her arguments were concise, the evidence beyond reproach. She knew she was arguing the case of a lifetime for a jury of one, and the consequences of losing could be devastating, if not lethal. She talked about Eli's investigation and the years before Barbara had come to work with Judge Caufeld. She expounded on Allan's reactions to her questions, to his odd behavior at the funeral. Lauren held the desk as if it was the lectern in a courtroom.

She ticked off a list of every instance where Edie Williams had known something, done something or rerouted something to make it more expedient for Allan. Lauren talked about Damien Boyd and his defense counsel. She told Barbara about Allan's pro-bono defense of Damien Boyd all those many years ago. She told Barbara slowly and surely about the attack on Eli the night before. She told Barbara she was afraid to find out what lay ahead and more afraid not to. There was no going back for her or Eli now because someone was angry enough to hurt them.

"I don't know what to think," Barbara said when Lauren was finished.

"You have to think something," Lauren pleaded.

"No, Lauren, I don't. I adored Judge Caufeld and it pains me to say I don't have the courage to find out the truth, but I don't. That's the way it is." Barbara stood up and retrieved her purse. She had aged in the last hour but it had nothing to do with the passage of time. It had to do with a conscience that was called to task and refused the challenge. "I've been offered another position, and I'm going to take it. Where you're headed can't help anyone, Lauren, it can only hurt."

Lauren's bottom lip disappeared between her teeth. She bit down hard to keep from screaming. She needed help. Eli needed help and Barbara was turning her back. She bit one notch harder and knew that she couldn't blame the woman.

"I understand. Really, I do. But if you can't believe in me, please don't turn on me. Let me work this out and don't say anything to anyone. Please, Barbara. I understand if you can't do more than that."

"Okay, Lauren." Barbara was ready to go. Lauren stepped back then changed her mind. "Wait. Wait just a minute, please."

Quickly she found her purse and one of her cards. She scribbled Eli's address and phone number on it and gave it to Barbara.

"Just in case. I don't know. You might need to find me." She stepped back. "Good luck on your new job."

"Thanks."

Barbara had the door open when Lauren thought to ask.

"Where will you be?"

"Westwood." She chuckled almost mournfully. "Another federal building. Mark Jackson offered me a job as his special assistant."

"I didn't know he was looking," Lauren whispered.

"Allan was worried about me. He put in a good word," Barbara said and the undertone was a guilty one. "Bye, Lauren. Take care."

Lauren nodded.

Care was exactly what she'd be taking.

"Oh, my God!" Cheryl squealed and put her hands to her lips when Lauren stuck her head into her cubicle.

"Nice to see you, too," Lauren said to her secretary. "Is everyone still in the morning meeting?" Cheryl nodded. She looked sick. Lauren smiled, hardly noticing. "Okay. Listen, I've got to get my things out of my office but it's locked and I don't want to make a big deal out of this. Give me the keys. I've got a zillion things to do today."

Lauren stuck out her hands and wiggled her fingers waiting for the keys. Cheryl didn't move. Cheryl looked scared to death.

"Okay." Lauren laughed. "I haven't been around for awhile, Cheryl, but I'm not exactly a ghost."

"Lauren, they told me to call GSA police if you showed up. They told me I was supposed to keep you here as long as I could, so you wouldn't get away before they could talk to you."

"Who? Who told you that?" Lauren demanded. "And why? I'm not a criminal."

"They told me you were, Lauren," Cheryl breathed, taking Lauren's hand and pulling her into the cubicle with her. "Listen, you better go now. They said you were trying to steal files on the Stewart case. They said you were going to try to sell information to the tabloids. Did you really try to do that?"

"Jesus, Cheryl, no!" Lauren couldn't believe this. "Who told you that? Edie? She is so out of hand."

"No. It was Mr. Schuster and Mr. Jackson. They came around and told us all, but I got a private talk because I handle your stuff, I guess. They just put the fear of God into me, Lauren."

"You don't think what they said is true?"

"I don't know. I mean you were acting kind of weird right after Judge Caufeld died." Cheryl didn't look quite so beautiful anymore. She looked fairly stupid.

"I was not," Lauren objected and then fell silent. What was the use? She could talk herself blue in the face and a secretary worried about her job wouldn't change her mind about anything. "Okay. I understand things are a little weird around here right now. But I promise, I wasn't going to do anything like that. Listen, I won't even ask you to let me into my office, but I want my things. You just go in and get my briefcase and the picture of my mother. You can check it if you want . . ."

A door slammed and Lauren ducked. Cheryl's eyes widened with fear. No one came their way.

"I can't, Lauren. You should just go back home and wait until everything's over. Then maybe you can talk to Mr. Schuster and figure all this out. But I can't take the chance." She looked at the clock on her desk. "God, Lauren, the meeting's going to break up in ten minutes. Please, just get out of here, and I won't tell anyone I saw you. How's that?"

Lauren backed away. There was no way around this. She gave Cheryl a thumbs up and mumbled something that sounded like thanks anyway. Quickly she walked down the long, gray-carpeted hall heading toward the elevator then she had a change of heart.

Edie was not only in trial on the Stewart matter, she was now handling Damien Boyd. She just might be in her office dealing with last minute preparations. It was early enough, and Martinelli wasn't a judicial early riser. Lauren rushed, looking over her shoulder as she went and catching her breath as she opened the door to Edie's office.

"What a surprise," Edie said, hardly seeming surprised at all.

"I know what's happening," Lauren blurted out.

"Really?" Edie threw her pencil on the desk.

"Cheryl says Abram concocted some story about me trying to pull my files and sell them to the media. You know that's not so, Edie."

"I thought it was a rather ridiculous story. But it still doesn't mean that I want you anywhere around here either. You're bad news these days, Lauren, and I've got prosecutions to take care of that outweigh any problem you've got."

"No, that's not true. Look, I don't want anything from you, okay? I just want my stuff. My briefcase is in my office and I want the picture of my mother then I'm out of here until I hear there's a verdict on Damien Boyd. Okay? Is that a deal?" Lauren lied easily. She'd be back in a flash if she got solid evidence that Damien Boyd had nothing to do with Wilson's murder. But Edie seemed willing to believe she'd leave quietly.

"I don't care. Go get it," Edie picked up her pencil.

"Cheryl won't let me in. She thinks she's got to call GSA police. I need you to get it for me. Please, Edie. Please."

"What's in it for me?" Lauren almost laughed. Allan. The woman had absorbed so much of him.

"Nothing, Edie, but I'll tell you some things I know. I know that Allan defended Damien Boyd pro bono years ago. I know that he's got Bernard Goldracknian fixed up to defend Damien and that Paul couldn't litigate his way out of a paper bag. I know something is terribly, terribly wrong with Allan, and the only reason I'm telling you any of this is because I think you really do care about him. In fact, I think you love him, Edie, and if you do you won't blow this off. You'll help him, because you know you're the only one who'll be able to. Just help him, Edie."

"Do you think he killed Caufeld, Lauren?" Edie asked coolly.

Lauren looked at her. She turned on her heel and took three steps across the room. She was almost at the wall before she gained her perspective. She looked at Edie when she asked.

"You know him better than I do. Do you think he did?"

Before Edie could answer, the door to her office flew open, almost pinning Lauren against the wall. She didn't breathe, she leaned away so that it wouldn't hit her. Lauren froze and said her prayers. First she prayed whoever it was wouldn't come in. Then she prayed that, if they didn't, Edie wouldn't give her away. Both prayers were answered simultaneously.

"Abram, you scared me to death." Edie's hand went to her heart as she stood up and floated toward the half-open door. She reached for it and Lauren prayed again. Instead of pulling the door back, Edie held it. "I was just coming to find you. I think I left the Grand Jury transcripts on your desk, and I need them before I go to court this morning."

"I didn't see them. Besides, I have something more important to talk to you about," Abram snapped. He wasn't in a good mood. Perhaps lying didn't set well with him.

"Tell me while we walk. I'm due in court in twenty minutes and I've got to have those transcripts. Brendan's out handling the cross on the Stewarts' and I promised I'd be in Martinelli's court . . ."

That was the last Lauren heard as Edie walked out the door with Abram Schuster. Finally breathing again, Lauren twirled slowly so that she faced the wall. There she stayed, hugging the bad paint job, waiting to see who it was that would walk through next and wondering if she could possibly make it out of there before anyone did. Five minutes later Edie stepped back in.

"Here." Lauren's briefcase was passed to her. "Mark's men saw you outside talking to Carolyn Stewart. You are an idiot, Lauren."

"Maybe. But thanks."

"The stairs would be a good choice."

"Okay. I promise. This is it. I won't ask you for another thing."

"We're even. You didn't screw me when it came to the Stewart prosecution and I appreciate it. You could have knocked me out of the process completely." Lauren nodded. She was opening the door when Edie put her hand out and held it shut. "About the other thing? Allan? He couldn't have killed Caufeld. I want you to know that. You're only going to hurt yourself if you keep going after him."

Lauren gave a curt nod. Edie cut her loose. Lauren had already run down six flights of stairs when it dawned on her that Edie's assurance hadn't made her feel any better.

She hit the ground running and was back to her car in record time. Unlocking the door, she threw in her briefcase and followed fast. Breathing hard, she unbuckled the straps, unzipped the main compartment and stuck her hand in but she didn't find what she was looking for. The *Daily Journal*. Notes on the Stewart time line. Pulling the case on to her lap, she unzipped the other compartments and shook out the contents until the briefcase was empty. Agitated, she pushed through the pile: papers, pens, business cards. The things she was looking for weren't there. Defeated she sat with her head back, thinking about the last week and every movement she made in Wilson Caufeld's office. Then, like a miracle, the heavens of her mind opened up and she knew exactly what she had to do to get what she wanted.

Chapter Twenty-Six

"I'll be there as soon as I can. I'm glad you're feeling better. I was worried. Okay. Right. Don't move around too much. I'll be back in forty minutes. I have a surprise for you. No, not pizza. Better than that." Lauren held the computer disks between her fingers and dropped them into her purse. "See you soon."

Lauren hung up the phone, relieved on two counts. Eli was feeling better and she had remembered which jacket pocket those disks were in. Personal letters and the annuity log. They may not be much, but, then again, they may mean finding an end to this nightmare.

Quickly as she could, Lauren packed clothes into her overnight bag then went into the bathroom to scoop up the first things that came into view. She dumped them in with the clothes. Finally ready to go, she slung her purse over her shoulder and hefted her overnighter thinking about their next move as she walked into the living room and into Allan Lassiter's line of sight.

"You aren't the only one who watered plants." He smiled at her as he tossed her house keys on her coffee table, sat back on her sofa, laid his long arms across the back of it and crossed his legs. "Now, I do think it's time we had a heart to heart, Laurie."

"How did you know I was here?" Lauren asked quietly, taking her steps cautiously now.

"Easy." He was so pleased with himself. "Edie called. Said you looked like you'd slept in your clothes. Said . . ."

Lauren didn't wait to hear one more traitorous word. With all her strength Lauren swung her overnighter and crashed it into Allan's face. Without thinking, she bolted for the door. The gods were with her all the way down the hall and into the open elevator. Even as the doors closed she heard Allan's howling. Safe inside, Lauren fell back into the corner of the metal box and prayed it would go faster. *Please, please, please.* The prayer became so mesmerizing it took on a life of its own. What on earth did she pray for? That she hadn't slashed Allan's face with a zipper or a wheel? That she would wake up and find this all a nightmare, herself caught in the throes of some disease that caused hallucinations? Perhaps, she prayed for something small. To make it through the next five minutes, to make the right decision when the doors opened, to make it back to Eli who was now a world away.

The elevator jerked. Lauren lost her footing, skidding forward only to right herself as the doors slowly opened. Head down, she eyed the opening. It grew in proportion to her terror. Was he there? Had he managed to run down all those stairs, bloodied and angry enough to kill? No, thank God. No one was waiting, and there was nothing to stop her. Barely able to control her trembling, Lauren found her keys on the run, opened the door and started the ignition.

She was almost home free. Quicker than lightning, she pushed the remote and the gate started to open. Christ it was slow. Sluggish like a snail, the mechanism grinding. Anyone could hear it. They would know what she was doing. They would find her. He would find her.

"Hurry. Hurry," Lauren whispered but the iron gate did only what it could.

Lauren shifted, glancing over her shoulder, looking at the elevator nook. Allan hadn't followed, or if he had the

levator was slow. She'd be gone by the time he got to the
arage. Lauren smiled, laughing as hysteria tried to grip
er. She shook it off. The gate was open wide enough now
or her to get through. She gunned the motor and the car
urched forward, the front fender catching the gate so that
t paused, as it was programmed to do. Lauren slammed
nto reverse and closed her eyes, waiting out the safety
mechanism. It moved again, trying to close. She grabbed
he remote and hit it. The door stopped. She hit it again.
t began to open and now she could make it through.

Half out of the gate, speeding for the street, Lauren
lammed on the brakes just as Allan pulled his Lexus in
ront of her. Tires on both cars squealed, drowning out
he cry of terror that came from Lauren. She smelled the
tench of burned rubber and saw the fury in Allan's eyes
s his door flew open and he rose like a Phoenix from the
ar. He screamed at her.

"For God's sake, Lauren. I want to talk to you. I just
vant to talk to you."

He bled. He bled and he was enraged and Lauren was
paralyzed with fear. That lasted only long enough for her
o realize there was no one to save her except herself. With
hat thought she threw the car into reverse, back into drive
nd, as the tires cried, she did too, and aimed the car
hrough the only open space. Allan moved fast, pirouetting
ut of the way and grabbing for the door handle. The
ar jumped forward, shaking Allan off like a bug. Lauren
rappled with the wheel, turning right when it seemed it
ad a mind of its own to go left. She jumped the brick
urb separating the flower beds from the sidewalk. Fighting
or control, Lauren held steady then swerved again, barely
nissing Allan's car as she went around. Or did she? Did
he hit it? Did she kill him?

Tears flooding her eyes, arm raised to wipe her nose as
he cried, Lauren looked ahead. Oh, God, she could have
illed someone on the street, someone she didn't see.
Lauren cried harder and looked in her rearview mirror.
She leaned close as if she could hurry the car along if she
hould suddenly find Allan running after her, holding
er car, pulling her back. But Allan wasn't near. He was

standing in the street, far from dead. Lauren only glance
at him because there was something far more horrifyin
to look at.

Lauren slowed, almost stopping the car. With one han
on the steering wheel she used the other to wipe at he
eyes, hitting them hard with the back of her hand so tha
all the tears would be gone when she looked again at th
egg-shaped, gray car that Allan drove. A car so like all th
others, the way Damien's homeboys said. Lauren set he
foot on the gas. Her car careened around the corner a
she headed to the freeway and safety.

Even Allan had said all cars looked alike on the outsid
He had told her it was what was inside that counted. Allan
of all people should know. He had mastered the art c
camouflage.

Chapter Twenty-Seven

"I'm so happy to see you. I'm so happy to be here." Lauren kissed him hard. She threw her arms around Eli Warner and when he groaned she backed away. "I'm sorry. I'm so sorry. I was just so scared, Eli. He was coming at me like he wanted to kill me. It was the middle of the day. I couldn't believe it."

"It's okay. You just kind of hit one of those bruises hard." He pushed her hair back. She'd never looked more beautiful and he wished there was time to tell her. "You okay now?" He held her face between his hands and kissed her when she nodded.

"Yeah, I think so. Oh, Eli, I really hadn't believed. Not really." She talked the way people raised from the dead will. She wanted him to know about her near death experience. "I just didn't want to believe that Allan could do anything like that to me. But I guess if he can. He could have killed Wilson, couldn't he? Do you think he'll come here? Do you think he'll come after us?"

Eli shook his head, "No. He won't do anything to you, and he doesn't have the guts to come here. I don't think he had the guts to kill Judge Caufeld face to face either."

"Oh, Eli. Wilson loved him so much." Lauren's head

fell onto Eli's shoulders and her own convulsed with silent sobs. He held her. He pulled her closer still.

"I know. But now we have a lot to do. We've got to find out why, because we can't do anything unless we know why. Okay?"

"Okay. Okay."

"Go wash your face. Can you do that? Do you want something to eat or drink?"

Lauren nodded. In the bathroom she did as he asked and washed her face, sticking her head out to ask for a clean shirt. He handed her a long sleeved one that smelled like fresh starch. It engulfed her so she rolled up the sleeves and tied the tails at her waist then went back to where he was waiting. He was sitting on the couch. His bag was packed and near the door.

"Are we going somewhere?"

"To a friend's for a few days. I've got Wilson's financial records. My buddy's an accountant. I think he can help us put some of the pieces together."

"I've got something, too." Lauren fetched her purse. "Computer disks. Financial information on one, personal letters on the other. Both go way back. I tried to get some of the other things out of Wilson's office, but Allan had cleaned it out." Lauren sat beside him and handed over the disks.

"Thanks. Feeling better?" He took her hand in his while he asked.

"A little. Not really. How can I? Allan could be a murderer or at least a conspirator. And, if he is, does that mean Wilson did something that made Allan think he deserved to die? Does it mean that?"

"I don't know, Lauren. I can only try to find the answers."

"You're the only one that cares to. Edie called Allan the minute I left. Barbara was ready to call security. She believed what they told her about me."

"I don't know that's true," Eli said and let her hand go.

"You weren't there. You didn't hear her."

"Whatever she said today, I think she changed her mind

Here. This arrived late this morning by messenger." He wiggled it in front of her when she looked at him, a question in his eyes. The envelope was plain, but inside there was gold. "Oh, Eli. It's her office calendar."

"There's a note."

She read aloud, "It may not hold up in court, but I'd bet my life it's as good as the judge's own. Good luck. Barbara." The color flooded back into her face. "She didn't believe them."

"How could she?" Eli said softly before raising his eyebrows. "Now, if you don't mind, on the outside chance anyone might come over here to give us another lesson in deportment, can we get our rears in gear?"

"Sure. I'm ready."

Eli followed her down the stairs and out to his car. He only had one thought. He wasn't sure he was ready for where they were headed.

"Eli! Eli! Eli!"

The decibel level rose with each screech of his name. Lauren was sure she'd find a seven-foot banshee when she got out of the car, instead it was a three-foot mite, her blond hair serrated rather than cut, her face smeared with something green.

"Annie. Annie. Annie!"

Eli did his best to return the greeting but the hand at his jaw was a dead giveaway that the spirit was willing but the flesh was weak. Unfortunately, Annie was not adept at reading the signs of pain in suffering adults. She threw herself at him, knee level. Eli looked to Lauren who raised her shoulders. This was new to her. The last time she'd interacted with a child was when she talked to herself when she was five. The little girl disappeared as quickly as she had appeared and Eli reached out for Lauren, more to support his aching body than anything. They hadn't gone far up the walk when a horizontally imposing but vertically deprived man came out to greet them with equal joy.

"Hey, my friend," Eli called, abandoning Lauren for the other man's gentle hug.

"You look like you've been beat up," the man said.

"Perceptive as always. Lauren." He held out his hand and pulled her into the circle. "This is Fred. Fred and I go way back. All the way to high school. A better friend no man could have."

"And a psychic, too," Lauren laughed.

"Nah, Eli called and told me what happened. You've come to the right place. We'll get him fixed up in no time, maybe even see if we can come up with some kind of gruesome conspiracy and sell it to the movies."

Fred took their bags, and Lauren relinquished them happily. Inside Annie popped about, there were new toys to show, tales to tell of school, kisses and hugs to administer. In between those wondrous moments, and while Fred was putting their things in Annie's room, Eli managed to fill Lauren in. Fred's wife had taken off with a thinner guy. She squeezed his hand acknowledging the sadness of it all. Her lips were sealed and her admiration for Fred and Annie intense.

"Daddy cut my hair. I love my hair. Do you like it?" The last was directed to Lauren who seemed to make noises appropriate to the situation.

The afternoon went, and the evening too. They feasted on real food. Fred managed steaks and salad, potatoes. Food, he said, to heal anything. Annie served the dessert, Oreos and ice cream. It wasn't until eight—8:05, to be exact—that Annie suddenly and inexplicably stopped chattering and fell asleep. Fred put her in his room in her Barney sleeping bag and came back out rubbing his palms together.

"Now, how about a little adult fun." They followed Fred to a closed room down the hall, which, when opened, proved to be a haven of sorts. "My playroom," Fred said with great pride.

Paper, computations, e-mail messages and three computers comprised Fred's idea of heaven. He and Eli seemed to know where to stand and where to sit. They were settled in no time. Eli passed over their disks then unpacked his paperwork, stacking it on the one free space Lauren could see; the top of a mini-refrigerator. Lauren was on her own.

"Here, Fred, I'll take the one marked correspondence,"
Lauren held out her hand, ready to work. "Which one of
these things do you want me on?"

"You can take the old warhorse over there. Better get
a chair from the dining room though."

Lauren was dismissed, Eli was relegated to passing
paperwork and Fred chatted up a storm while he worked.
Keys clicked and he was fascinated by Wilson's financial
records on the disk.

"This is easy. It's an annuity. If you go way back—see
here we're looking at the latter part of 1985 and the early
part of 1986. A year period in which money was paid in.
Nothing pays out until about two years after the money's
been paid in and earned some interest."

"What kind of funds are you talking about?"

"Total is $150,000," Eli said over his shoulder.

Average payback on the investment is twelve and a half
percent. So the judge wasn't making a profit. He was handing out the interest as soon as it came in. He was giving it
out quarterly to these people." Fred pointed to the names
that appeared after each payout.

"Okay. So that buys us . . . ?" Lauren led and Fred followed.

"Nothing right now." He smiled.

Eli leaned back in his chair and stretched. Lauren saw
him wince and then he smiled, too.

"Too bad you don't know who they are."

"Maybe we could just ask the person who's writing the
checks."

"That would be nice," Lauren laughed. "Which hay-
stack do you propose we look in for that information."

"Well, these documents were scanned from original
statements. Look, there's an initial after each payout. Same
initial on the original deposits. Vanguard is the brokerage.
I bet if Eli flashed his little badge he could get them to
tell him who they've been talking to all these years."

"That's a possibility." Eli grinned and the men high-
fived their ingenuity. Lauren, on the other hand, was
thoughtfully flipping through Barbara's calendar.

"I think the woman is on to something," Fred laughed.

"Could be." Eli stood up and hunkered down beside her, a hand on the back of her chair. "What have you got?"

"I think I've got the person who's been handling the money, and if money was what made Allan crazy, then this is the trail we're going to follow."

"And just where are we going to follow it to?"

"Right back to Baldwin Hills, Eli. Right back to the scene of the crime. First thing in the morning."

"Maeve Samuels?"

"Yes?"

"We apologize for the early hour, but we need to talk to you."

"No need to apologize. I don't sleep as much as I used to." She was accommodating, even gracious, and she held the door unafraid of strangers as long as it was daylight.

"I'm Eli Warner. This is Lauren Kingsley." The woman's eyes flicked to Lauren. She smiled.

"Yes. I know. It's nice to finally meet you." The woman put her hand on Lauren's arm. Her fingers were gnarled with arthritis. Lauren was glad she hadn't offered to shake hands.

"Do you know why we're here?"

"I suppose I do. I just wonder if you know why you are," she said, and there was a touch of tragedy in her tone. "Won't you come in?"

"Thank you." Eli went first, ever cautious of what might be found in new places. He looked around. The house was neat, the furniture in good repair. There was a picture of Maeve Samuels and Judge Caufeld at his swearing in. It was prominently displayed on the mantel along with pictures of children and weddings. Lauren made a beeline to the exhibit.

"He was very young. This must have been when he was appointed to the Superior Court," Lauren said.

"Yes, it was," Maeve sat on the sofa, using a cane to help lower herself. "I'd known Wilson a good many years when he was killed. He died just where you were standing the ther night when you had your troubles. That was you, asn't it?"

Eli nodded and sat in the chair next to her.

"Do you know who killed Judge Caufeld?"

Maeve shook her head sadly, "I couldn't swear to anything in court. That's one of the reasons I didn't call anyone. I don't think it was that boy. He and his friends were too far away. The papers said the judge was shot at close range. They were more than half a block from Wilson. He was talking to someone else just before he died."

Lauren came back. Putting her hands on the back of Eli's chair she considered Maeve Samuels. She was a handsome black woman, her gray hair coifed, her nails buffed. She wore a housedress, not slacks. It was as if Maeve had been frozen in time.

"Did you know it was Wilson at the time?"

Maeve turned her head and smiled, her eyes sparkling as she looked at Lauren. "You are so pretty. Wilson always said how pretty you were. And smart, too. I should have known it would be you who showed up here." Maeve seemed to hold onto that thought, then she remembered that the question was. "Yes, I knew it was Wilson out there. He came the same time, third Thursday of every month. But I never went further than the door. I need a new hip. Walking's kind of hard. And my eyes aren't what they used to be and, heavens, neither is this place. This used to be the most beautiful neighborhood. Now it's what it is. I haven't the energy or the money to move. Where would I go?" She shook her head. "I haven't offered you refreshments. Would you like something?" Eli and Lauren politely declined. "Then I'll ask you a question. How did you find me?"

"We found records of the Vanguard annuity. We saw your initials. Barbara, the judge's secretary, she kept a duplicate calendar for the judge. Your name was there, once a month. A standing appointment."

"That's a good job of sleuthing."

"The judge also kept records of all his correspondence. There were letters to you. Add the police report, the name of this street. It wasn't hard after that."

"No, I suppose it wouldn't have been hard to find me
I just thought it would be Allan coming here. I figured he
was scared enough by now."

"Why, Mrs. Samuels? We know there was money trouble
between the judge and Allan, but we don't know what it
was. I believe it had to do with some transactions in 1985
that . . ." Eli was on a roll. He was picking up speed when
Maeve laughed and held up her hand.

"Yes. I know," she said and suddenly her voice sounded
weary. "I wonder though, what will you do with the story
once I give it to you?"

"I suppose it depends on what it is." Lauren came
around Eli's chair and sat next to Maeve on the couch. "I
loved Wilson, Mrs. Samuels. Nothing will be the same for
me if I don't find out why he died, and try to do something
to bring his killer to justice. Can you understand?"

"Oh, sure, honey, I understand. I thought about it, too.
But what if, by doing that, you're going to bring down the
person who already paid the price. What if you bring down
Wilson with what you find?"

"Then that's what will have to happen," Lauren answered evenly.

"All right, then. I'll tell my story and you decide what
to do with it. Poor Wilson, he called and told me about
you, Mr. Warner. I told him not to be an old goat. I told
him to let the past rest. But Wilson thought God was sending him a message to make his life right because you'd
found out about all this. Guess he knew what he was talking
about because he's with the good Lord now."

Maeve sighed and patted Lauren's hand.

"Yes, yes. I'll get to the point. I was Wilson Caufeld's
secretary in the earliest days. He trusted me with everything, and I stayed with him until he went on the bench.
When he did that, I came home and I worked for him
here but nobody ever knew about it. What I did was very
special. What I did was watch over Wilson Caufeld's
shame."

Maeve picked up her cane and pointed it at Eli.

"Ever had anyone believe in you so much they'd do
anything for you?"

Eli gave her a half smile, "Can't say that I have. Wish it were so."

"No you don't. That's what got Wilson and Allan into trouble. Wilson loved that boy and thought he'd teach him how to be a great man. But Allan didn't have the makings of a great man. Allan had the makings of a man who wanted to look great. When he started working for Wilson he made big money for a kid who came from next to nothing. But that wasn't enough for Allan. Always, always he wanted more. Wilson would try and tell him the big money would come in time, but I suppose Allan never really believed it. He just seemed to be listening. What he was doing was scheming."

"Did he steal from Wilson?" Lauren asked quietly.

"He stole from the partnership. One hundred and fifty thousand dollars. We almost didn't catch it, but the accountant came to me and I went to Wilson. Wilson went to Allan. There was a big fight between the two of them. Late at night. Wilson asked me to stay but everyone else was gone. Allan was a mess. He was crazy, beside himself. Crying and apologizing and telling Wilson he'd never do it again. He begged Wilson not to ruin him. That boy made such a scene. Either he was a darn good actor, or he was really terrified of the consequences."

"But Wilson couldn't turn him in, could he?" Eli asked. Maeve shook her head.

"You know Wilson, don't you? He would have gone to jail himself. No, he couldn't bring charges, and he knew if the other partners found out they would. They all liked Allan well enough, but embezzlement would have ruined the firm if it got out. Then there was the matter of Allan breaking the law. 'Course that was never talked about out loud, but that's what hurt the judge so bad. Funniest thing about Allan and the judge, the two of them were like oil and water." Maeve shook her head remembering that night. "Lord, it was dramatic. No television show could be better than what happened that night."

"What did happen?" Lauren asked, almost afraid to hear.

"I was sent home when things calmed down. To make a long story short, Wilson came in late the next day. He'd

met with the accountant. Told him that he had borrowed
the money and there had been a mix-up in transferring
funds from another account. I don't know if the accountant believed him, but the money was back where it
belonged. All one hundred and fifty thousand dollars.
Allan wouldn't be going to jail, he'd keep his license to
practice law. There'd be no charges because Wilson wasn't
going to bring them and nobody else but me knew what
had happened."

"But Wilson covered up a crime," Lauren breathed.
"Wilson did the one thing that he couldn't conscience in
anyone else."

"That's it. Poor man was never quite the same after that.
Nothing anyone who didn't know him would figure out.
But I knew him. I knew it near killed him to do what he
did. He thought a close call would keep Allan on the
straight and narrow. All those visits we had over the years
he only admitted once that it had been wrong. That was
out loud. I bet you anything, he talked to himself about
it every night of his life."

"So did Allan pay him back? Is that what this account
was all about?" Eli pressed for more information.

"I'm getting there," Maeve said, happy to have someone
to talk to and taking her own good time. "So, I didn't
want to work with Wilson when he went to Superior Court.
Too far away. I was ready to retire and he knew that. He
asked if he were to pay me to take care of a special project
would I do it? That's what you were looking at. My special
project. Did you see all the initials?"

Eli nodded. "We did. Haven't got a clue what they mean."

"Those are the young people who got scholarship
money for college. You see, Wilson set up the account.
Allan's salary was attached for almost a year, plus what he
saved, until the entire one hundred and fifty thousand
dollars was paid back. But Wilson couldn't bear to think
about that money. He wanted nothing to do with it. He
never put a cent back in his personal account."

"So you became the executor of a trust, watching over
the investment and doling out the interest as scholarships,"
Eli finished for her.

"That's right, Mr. Warner. That was the judge trying to make up for doing something so bad it almost killed his spirit."

"What did Allan do? Did he ever refer to it?"

Maeve pulled her lips tight and closed her eyes as she shook her head, "No, ma'am. That boy acted like nothing happened. I didn't expect anything more. There's always been something missing in Allan. He loved the judge best he knew how, but he loved himself more than anything. He always figured he could weasel out of anything, until Wilson decided he was going to answer any questions your report brought up, Mr. Warner. Only he wasn't going to answer you, he was going to do it in front of the whole Senate if they asked. That was the punishment Judge Baufeld gave himself, a public confession and acceptance of the consequences."

"Do you think Allan killed the judge?" Eli asked.

She shrugged. "I don't see good without my glasses."

"Why didn't you go to the police or the FBI with this information?"

"Lauren, honey, I thought Wilson was a fine man. What good would it do to tell people he wasn't?"

"It would keep Allan from getting away with murder twice and the last time literally."

"You don't know that." Lauren shot off the couch as Maeve reached for her. "You don't," Maeve insisted and looked to Eli for help. He had none to offer so they let her talk.

"Yes, I do know. Beyond a doubt, I know that he did it," Lauren said in a fury.

"Then," Maeve said simply, "you have to do what you think is right. Isn't that what Wilson taught you? That's what he said he tried to teach you."

"Yes, that's what he taught me," she muttered.

"Isn't that what he was doing at the end of his life? Wilson was doing what he thought was right?"

"Yes," Lauren whispered.

"Then you don't have much of a choice do you? Guess you've got to do what you've got to do."

Chapter Twenty-Eight

"Twenty minutes from Baldwin Hills to Century City." Lauren noted the time as they parked.

"You can also assume he was driving like the devil was after him. Cut off five or so for that. A Lexus can fly and everyone gets out of the way."

"He could have done it, Eli." Lauren didn't move even though Eli had already pocketed his keys. "God, that's so awful. I mean, this is like turning in my brother for murdering my father."

Eli stayed quiet, letting her think about that one and knowing it would be a good long while before she actually came to grips with it.

"Which one is it?" He scanned the high-rises and asked only when enough time had passed.

Lauren pointed to the glass building rising out of the ground and reaching for the sky. "What if he's gone already?"

"Then he's gone. We wait until he comes back."

"We could try to find him at the club. That's usually where he goes on Saturdays." Lauren swiveled her head. Eli had his chin cradled in his palm, his arm cocked against the window as he looked up.

"No. I don't want anything that public." Eli muttered. He took a breath and mused, "I was just thinking that even though he had a lot to lose, there had to be another way. Murder seems so out of character for someone like Lassiter."

"Yes," Lauren whispered. "I would have thought so too—until he pulled in front of me the other day. I swear he looked like he would tear me limb from limb."

"He'd be more subtle about it. Ready?" He dropped his arm and looked at her.

"Ready as I'll ever be. Are you sure you don't want to call the office? Maybe we should have some backup."

Eli shook his head, "Mark Jackson would probably call Lassiter himself and tip him off. I don't know what the connection is there, but I'll tell you, he and Edie and Abram, they are thick as thieves. Even if they don't know about this, they don't want to know the truth. For whatever reasons, they really don't want to know."

"I guess not. I don't get it. I used to think I knew what this job was about. You know, put the bad guys away. Seemed fairly straightforward. Now I feel like everywhere I look everyone on our side has an agenda equally despicable as the bad guys."

"Welcome to my world," Eli laughed. "Good Lord, woman, why do you think the government does background checks?"

"To see if anyone has a personal agenda." Lauren laughed and pointed a finger at him. "Oh, Lord, Eli. Everything is about to change."

He took her face in his hands and kissed her lips. She tasted good, sugar from the donut they ate on the way still clung to those lips. When he sat back he wasn't smiling.

"It changed the minute Wilson Caufeld was shot, Lauren. Never forget that's what this is about. Not money, not reputation. It's about one human being taking another's life."

Lauren nodded. "You're right. Let's go."

It took no more than a wave at the doorman, a finger to her lips and an admonition that they were there to surprise Allan, for Lauren and Eli to waltz past the man who was supposed to announce their arrival. Caught up in the fun, he called an elevator for them and ask that he be remembered to Mr. Lassiter on his birthday. They promised to do so then stood silently in the elevator, Lauren's fingers fidgeting with the strap of her purse as they hurtled to their destination.

Eli looked left and right when the stepped off on the twenty-sixth floor. Lauren cocked her head and led the way. She swallowed hard and took a minute to collect herself before she rang the bell. The minute she did so, she stepped back and put her shoulder against Eli's. The door opened and Allan, the cut on his head still red and raw, looked them over. Lauren would have liked to believe he sensed betrayal. Instead, she decided, he knew the end was near.

"Lauren, you are such an idiot."

He walked away, leaving the door open and the insult hanging there like a curtain to keep them out. Eli parted it. He stepped over the threshold and into Allan Lassiter's world. He scanned it. That was that. Lauren closed the door quietly behind them. When they found him, Allan was in the kitchen tending to his coffee. He wore sweats that hung off his slim hips at just the right angle, a muscle shirt, too big to actually fit and just big enough to emphasize the lean proportions of his torso.

"I hope you'll forgive me if I don't offer you coffee."

"No problem." Eli slid onto a high leather stool near the marbled counter. He was about to go on when Lauren stepped in.

"Wasn't there some other way? Something you could have done to work this out. But to kill Wilson, Allan?"

Allan didn't do her the courtesy of looking her way. He measured out his coffee while he spoke coldly. "Do you ever get tired of listening to all your righteous bullshit, Lauren? I don't know how Wilson put up with it all the time. You and your stupid pronouncements." He plugged in the coffee, glanced at Eli and walked past Lauren. "I didn't kill Wilson. I was at the office the night he was killed. You were here. You're being absurd and if that's all you came for you can leave right now." He paused and looked back. "Unless your friend there wants to put me in irons and drag me through the street."

Eli swiveled, balancing his elbows on the counter behind him. "I was kind of hoping you'd just come peacefully."

Allan laughed. He flopped himself on the couch and grabbed the paper. It lay in his lap while he glared at his visitors.

"You have call rollover at the office, Allan. When you found me here that day that's what I was checking."

"Big deal. Half the people in this city have that. I'm telling you, I was at the office. I could probably find half a dozen people who'd swear to it."

"No doubt," Eli mumbled. "But I couldn't find one."

"I was there. My partner saw me," Allan said. "What other stunning evidence of my murderous intent do you have, Laurie, dear?"

"We know about the money you embezzled from Wilson's firm. Maeve Samuels told us."

"Maeve Samuels? Now there's a name from the past. What does she have to do with any of this?"

"She's been administering a trust. Wilson took the money you paid him and put it in a trust. The interest has been paying for scholarships for kids all these years."

"Oh, my, my, my." Allan puffed up his chest and puffed out his breath. "Can you believe that? Wasn't Wilson just so righteous. Didn't want to dirty his hands using any of it, huh?"

"Oh, Allan, give me a break," Lauren lashed out. "Your the one who committed a crime."

"And he's the one who covered it up, so we were even. Why is he the saint and I'm the bad guy?"

"Because he's dead. And you had good reason to kill him. Why else would you have all the papers removed from his office? Why would you have tried to run me down outside my apartment?"

Allan slapped the couch. He stood up so fast the papers went flying. "That's it! You are certifiable, Lauren. I wanted to talk to you. Do you know how many people called to let me know that you and this person here," he waved Eli's way, "were stirring up trouble? If you kept it up there was going to be an investigation into my finances and then where would I be? The same place I was before Wilson died. So I filed a complaint with Mark Jackson.''

"Did you have me removed from the Stewart case? Did you ask Edie to do that?''

Lauren was aghast. She hardly noticed that Eli had moved, wandering past the picture window with hardly a glance at the view.

"You did that yourself, Lauren. I didn't have anything to do with it. Look, I know people, I have a thriving practice. You and this bozo here were starting to make waves that were coming my way. I felt just as bad as you about Wilson biting the big one, but I'll be honest, I was relieved too. There, happy? He was going to tell everybody that I'd embezzled those funds. Now, take a look at what's going on out there today. I mean if the president's chief of staff goes to federal prison for embezzling two hundred thousand do you think anyone's going to give me a break because I only managed a hundred and fifty?'' Allan threw up his hands. "If you would just keep your mouth shut once in a while Lauren. That's all you had to do and all this would have gone away.''

"Don't you dare lay this one on me. I'm not the one acting like I have something to cover up. Don't you dare. You're the one who got Bernard Goldracknian to defend Damien. Are you going to tell me that was a coincidence? You represented Boyd pro bono years ago . . .''

"Because Wilson had me wearing sackcloth and ashes whenever he could. He felt bad about Damien Boyd's father, so I get saddled with a crappy defense for burglary. After the money thing I couldn't very well tell him no. It took him six years to stop calling me with every hard-luck case that came around.'' He came at her in three strides, his hand raised. She didn't move. He wasn't going to hit her, he only raised that hand in frustration. "Why is it that you assume Wilson and I told you everything there was to know about our lives? You know, you're just a crazed person. You never really wanted to know the truth about anything. All you wanted to do was prove how lily white you and your mother and Wilson were. You weren't too sure about me but you figured if Wilson liked me I was okay. Well, baby, life ain't like that," he sneered, "everybody jockeys for their position and everybody's got sins. Your mother, Wilson and me. That's why you're being buried, for no other reason than you keep trying to make everyone play by your rules." Allan looked as if he couldn't stand the sight of her. "Get out of here, Lauren."

"Not until I see your gun, Allan. I want to see your gun."

"I don't think that will be necessary, Lauren," Eli said quietly.

"Yes it is. I want to see if it's a twenty-two." Lauren whipped toward him, the rest of her sentence lost in her shock.

"Edie?" Allan seemed surprised, too. Not by her presence but by the fact that she was standing in the doorway of his bedroom pointing a gun their way.

"Here's a twenty-two, Lauren," she said evenly.

"Is it Allan's?" Lauren whispered, unsure what was happening.

Edie, ever in control, neither smiled nor looked concerned. Her dark hair, as usual, covered one eye. The other, though, glittered intensely and she moved into the room like a cat, one foot crossing over the other, steps silent on the carpet. She wore a blue cotton shirt, one of Allan's, her long legs were bare, her feet shoeless.

"Yes. As a matter of fact it is."

"Edie, be careful with it. That's the gun that killed Wilson. We'll need prints." Lauren held out both hands as if she could ease the weapon out of Edie's hands, preserving precious evidence.

"It's all right, Lauren," Eli said easily. "This isn't the gun that killed Wilson."

Lauren looked at him then back to Edie. Allan moved around until he stood almost between the two women.

"I love a man with experience. My job would have been so much easier if I had case agents like you." Edie paid the compliment sincerely and Eli accepted with a nod of his head. "That's the one thing Lauren really lacks, you know. Experience. I don't think it will ever make much difference, though, when she gets it. She'll always want to rush right in and muck things up without thinking about the consequences."

"No matter how experienced she is, she'll always want to find out the truth, though," Eli noted.

"Then hopefully experience will tell her there are two kinds of truth. The one she thinks is real, and then the real one. That's the one that keeps everything on an even keel. It's a little shaded, a little tarnished, but it's basically the truth. Isn't that right, Allan?"

Edie's eyes flipped his way. She shook her hair back and smiled, but something was different. Then Lauren knew what it was. For the first time ever, Edie Williams looked superior to Allan Lassiter.

"Edie, put that thing away. This whole thing is getting out of hand."

"I don't think so, Allan. Things are still under control and those two aren't stupid. Tedious, maybe," she tagged Lauren with her hard eyes, "but not stupid."

"Edie, where's the gun that killed Wilson?" Eli asked. He had moved up a half a step but only Edie seemed to take note. She took a half step toward Allan.

"In my purse," she answered lazily.

"Oh God," Lauren breathed.

"Edie?" Allan was incredulous and that seemed to anger Edie more than anything else possible could.

"Don't look at me like that, Allan. Don't look at me like you're appalled. You have no right to be. You didn't care what happened to that old man, you just wanted him taken care of before he said anything that would hurt your precious reputation. Well, I took care of it for you. You should be happy. You should be thrilled. You should be kissing my feet." She spit the last words out like venom.

"Edie, I never asked you to kill him."

"Do you think I meant to?" she snapped. "I don't know anyone who isn't a sociopath who wants to kill someone. I didn't want to hurt him. Her voice shook ever so slightly. There was fear, too. Lauren could see it.

"Edie, don't say anything now." Lauren stepped forward, reaching out woman to woman for Edie. Edie was quick. The gun turned toward Lauren smoothly and surely.

die was in a firing stance and there was no doubt she ould use her weapon.

"Why not? If I don't say the words you'll put some in ny mouth. I'm telling you. I didn't mean to kill him. I'd one to talk to him. Allan, I'd only gone to talk to him, nd I want you to understand that."

Her eyes were trained down the barrel into Lauren's hest. From the corner of her eye Lauren could see Eli eady himself. Allan, wisely, said nothing.

"I want you all to understand that," Edie said, her voice oftening and shaking just a bit more. "I went to talk to im at his home because it was becoming increasingly mbarrassing to try to do so at the office. Caufeld came ut of his driveway before I could get to the door. When ne car parked on the street didn't move I realized Mark ackson didn't have his bodyguards on Caufeld anymore. don't know," she shook back her hair, "I just followed im. I drove and I wasn't thinking about anything except vhat I'd say to him when he stopped. But he didn't stop ntil he got to Baldwin Hills."

Edie shivered. Her arms relaxed. Lauren could see she vas forcing herself to loosen the muscles that kept the gun evel and at the ready. Lauren's heart pumped once, twice. t was starting to work again.

"And you got out?" Eli urged her to keep talking. Edie ooked beautiful when she was surprised. She had almost orgotten Eli was there. Edie looked at him. She relaxed, eeming to like him there, as if he was the only sane one o talk to.

"Yes. I got out. Why turn back after coming all that way? ran across the street. I called to him. It took him a minute o recognize me. Can you believe it? I mean we're in trial, nd he doesn't recognize me."

Edie snorted at the absurdity of that; at the insult of hat. Who, after all, was she really? She shook her head nd let the gun fall to her side. Edie leaned back against . low chest of drawers. She was tired and she talked to the loor. "I told him that I knew what he was going to do. Ie told me to get out of the way. He actually put his hand ut to push by me. I don't know, I guess that did it." Edie ran a hand through her hair, pushing away all that dark hair but not the memories. "I ran in front of him again and put my hands out. I'd come all that way and I had something to say, he could at least do me the courtesy of listening." She shook back her head and looked at all of them to see if they understood. Allan turned toward the window. Edie's expression soured.

"That's right, Allan. Turn away. You always do. You always expect other people to do your dirty work. Well, baby, I did it. Yes, I did and I thought that would clear the way for us. What a fool I am."

Edie breathed deep. "I took out my gun. I showed it to him. I told the judge he might as well take a gun and shoot you through the heart if he was going to ruin your life. I told him that, Allan. I told him he should love you more than that."

When she finished, the silence in the room was deafening. Allan's clocks were state of the art, there were none that ticked away the minutes. The situation demanded courage from someone. It didn't come from Allan.

"I never asked you to do anything like that, Edie," Allan whispered.

"No, you're right," she said in defeat. "I suppose I always wanted you to though. I would have killed for you, Allan. But this was an accident. Caufeld started to shove past me again when a gang of kids came around the corner. I knew where I was and it was no place for me at that time of night. I reacted. It was a reflex. I put my finger on the trigger just in case I had to defend myself. Caufeld pushed. I fired. It happened so damn fast, Allan."

"That's why the entry wound was at that angle. You were taller than the judge," Lauren said.

"Nobody even looked at that evidence when we were trying to bring Henry in on this. Boyd was better. He was taller." Edie wasn't showing off. She had thought of just about everything before the rest of them. But work didn't interest her anymore. She wanted them to know about that night. "I thought maybe Caufeld was wounded, but I ran. I came here wanting to be with you when they found out I'd shot him. I knew he'd tell it was me. My life was

ver and I wanted to be here, with you. But Caufeld never
oke up, did he? He died. I killed him. Your problem was
ken care of. You were safe, I was safe and that's all that
attered."

"How did Damien Boyd get into all this?" Lauren asked.

"If you had just let that go, Lauren, I wouldn't be telling
ou any of this, you know?" Edie laughed. "I can't believe
ou and Mr. Background Checker here were the ones who
essed that one up. It was the perfect ending."

"Was he a random choice, Edie? How'd you manage
?" Eli asked, enthralled by the story and knowing there
asn't much time before Edie got tired of telling it.

"I wish I could say that was my idea. Mark found him.
e had his own problems. He ordered the guard off
aufeld. So, in a way, he was just as responsible for the
dge's death as I was."

"Why would he do that?" Lauren put a hand on the
ack of a chair just to connect to something.

"You're not going to believe this. Nick Cheshire? The
I we were all counting on to testify against the Stewarts?
e was having an affair with a biker broad and that's what
ot him beat to a pulp. Mark thought the militia had
ncovered him and blamed Caufeld's procrastinating for
aving Nick exposed. Mark knee-jerked, pulled the guard
nd that was that. When Mark found out the truth he tried
o cover his bases because he knew he couldn't convict
lenry Stewart."

"He looked in his files and found Damien. He's got
history of sorts with Judge Caufeld, he's in the right
eighborhood and a few well-placed questions puts him
n that block at the right time," Lauren finished for her.

"It sounded good. We told the papers you were out on
rief leave. All we had to do was wrap up the Stewarts,
end someone down for Caufeld then you come back when
his mess is finished." Edie twirled the gun, pleased with
he grand proportion of the circle of events. "Actually,
onsidering that everyone was acting out their own little
cenario, things didn't turn out too badly. All you had to
o, Lauren, was let Mark investigate Caufeld's murder.

And you," she turned toward Eli who gave her a smile. She smiled back. "You just had to close the file."

"Guess I can do that now, can't I?" Eli was charming. Eli didn't move. Neither did Lauren. Allan walked to the couch. He touched the back of it and looked at Edie's profile.

"I want you to know I'll do everything I can for you Edie. It will never go to first degree." Allan spoke slowly. For the first time since Wilson's death, Allan was finally feeling the impact.

"Oh, Allan," Edie sighed and in those two words Lauren heard all the love, the forgiveness for his shortcomings, the patience Edie Williams had lavished on Allan Lassiter all these years. She almost looked away to allow them as private a moment as possible. Then she heard, "I'm so sick of you."

With that, Edie turned the gun and fired. Lauren put her hands over her ears. The retort was deafening. She crunched. Allan hollered and Eli fell.

"Eli!" Lauren screamed. She rushed to him but Edie didn't want her there.

"Get away, Get away?" Edie seethed. She stalked toward Lauren.

"Edie, what are you doing? Are you crazy? Edie, for God's sake," Allan called. Edie swung back toward him, her arm still out to the side, the gun still pointed at Lauren.

"Shut up, Allan. We've got to do this. They came here threatening you. Get his gun, Allan. Get his gun and put it in his hand. We were defending ourselves." Allan was paralyzed and Edie's rage grew until she shook from head to toe. Both hands were on the gun now. "Get away." She screamed at Lauren who scrambled toward the corner of the room. "I'll do it!" She screeched to Allan. And she bent to rip at Eli's jacket, bloodying her hand in the process. Finding his gun she pulled, but it was caught in his shoulder holster. Edie pulled again and that's when Eli, not quite dead, grabbed her ankle and sent Edie Williams crashing to the floor.

The next minutes were nothing more than a collage of color and sounds, pleas and threats. Lauren threw herself

to the fray but the gun was spinning away from her
s Edie slapped her across shoulders. They grappled, Eli
olling away, trailing blood from what part of his body
auren didn't know.

"Stop! Stop!" Allan hollered.

Lauren and Edie did just that. Tangled together they
eard something in his voice that told them it was time to
sten. Panting, they looked up at him. The gun was in his
and. Edie threw her arm over Lauren's chest and held
er tight.

"Do it," she commanded, "do it now, Allan. Kill her.
's the only way out of this mess. I'm your witness. Everyone
nows what they've been doing. Kill her now."

Terrorized, Lauren lay in Edie's arms looking up at the
aan she had counted as family, remembering the man
ho had loved Allan the most.

"Allan?" she pleaded.

That's when he made his decision. Allan Lassiter took
wo steps, leaned down and pressed the barrel of the gun
gainst the head of the woman he knew must not survive.

She closed her eyes.

There was no one to help her now. But then, there never
ad been.

Chapter Twenty-Nine

"Ms. Kingsley, was it hard to take up closing arguments against the Stewarts?"

Lauren looked out on to the sea of faces. Lights blazed, microphones were shoved in front of her, people she couldn't identify screamed questions at her. She wanted to answer each and every one of them. She'd do it truthfully. It was time people knew.

"No. I knew that case inside out. Judge Martinelli wisely did not declare a mistrial. It was time to finish this matter and, since she only gave our office a week for someone to come up to speed, I was the logical choice. I'm delighted that I played a part in their conviction."

"Are you sorry they didn't get the death penalty?"

Lauren looked left. A man had spoken. She didn't see which one.

"No."

"What about Edie Williams?"

This time it was a woman.

"What about her?"

"Do you think she deserves the death penalty if she's convicted of killing Wilson Caufeld."

"That's for the jury to decide. I won't be handling the prosecution."

"Will you be working on the Stewart appeal?"

"No," Lauren said quickly. "No. I've turned my resignation into Abram Schuster." The reporters went nuts. There was going to be more to this than they thought. Lauren waved her hand, smiled without humor and started to push through the media only to change her mind. She stepped back and looked at them until they fell silent.

"I have a statement to make. I went to work for the U.S. Attorney believing that I could make a difference. I wanted to be the voice of the people. I wanted to act on the people's behalf. I wanted to emulate a man who taught me so much. I wanted to serve the people like Wilson Caufeld. I wanted to make sure that those who threaten all of us by their actions, were taken to task for those actions."

Lauren lowered her eyes. When she looked back up she tried to look at each one of them in turn.

"I'm quitting today because I've found out that those who threaten us are not always on the outside of the system. Today I spoke to the Attorney General of the United States. I told her that the Stewart prosecution had been manipulated by the U.S. Attorney in the hopes of swaying Judge Caufeld's opinions and rulings. I told her that I believe the FBI, and Mark Jackson in particular, was not only indirectly responsible for the murder of Wilson Caufeld but directly responsible, in conjunction with the U.S. Attorney's office, for railroading an innocent man in order to expedite that prosecution and cover the ineptitude of that office." Lauren hitched her briefcase. "I'm quitting, and I'm not sure that's the right thing to do. But I hope you won't. I hope you'll be there reporting it all so that the people we say we represent will understand how this system works and, hopefully, do something to make sure the right people are running it."

With that, she pushed through the crowd, losing the hangers-on about a block down. By the time she got to her car, only one young reporter was tenacious enough to follow. Microphone out, her cameraman huffing and puffing behind, the woman was there when Lauren fastened her seat belt. Lauren attended to her. Persistence, she had learned, needed a reward.

"Ms. Kingsley, Mr. Jackson, Mr. Schuster, and Mr. Lassiter have issued statements accusing you of slander. They say they are preparing civil suits. How do you feel about that?"

"Sad," Lauren said with a grin then added, "For them."

"Why?"

"Because I tell the truth and they don't."

"Did you know Mr. Lassiter's bar ticket has been revoked?"

"Yes."

With that, Lauren backed up and headed West. Behind her, the reporter was trying to figure out what on earth she could do with an answer as simple as that.

Lauren unwound her braids as she went and let her hair blow itself out in the wind now that she'd put that old rag top down. Wilson was gone but not forgotten. Allan was a part of her past. Edie Williams, Abram Schuster, and Mark Jackson had never meant anything to her. Not really. There was really only one thing that had ever mattered and that was the truth. And the truth was, Eli was waiting, and that was all that mattered anymore.

If you enjoyed the riveting legal suspense

of R. A. Forster's *The Mentor*

then please turn the page for

a sneak peek of R. A. Forster's

Keeping Counsel

on sale at bookstores everywhere

Prologue

He hung his head out the window like a dog on a Sunday drive. The whipping wind roared in his ears and slicked ack his long hair, baring a wide high forehead. His eyes arrowed, squinting against the force of hot air hitting 75 iles an hour.

Sinister, that's how he looked. Like he could take anyone own.

Women could fall at his feet and he wouldn't give two nts even if they were naked.

That's the kind of man he was.

But if they were naked, he'd give 'em a grin for sure.

"Hah!" he laughed once, but it was more of a shout, st to make sure he was still alive and kickin'.

He was feeling neither here nor there. He had a woman. he didn't make him happy. Thinking about her, he epped on the gas and the ribbon of road blurred, turning olten under his wheels. The asphalt was hot as hell; still eaming, though the day had been done for hours.

Hot! Hot! Good when you're with a woman, bad when you're the desert.

Lord, that was funny. True things were the biggest kick f all.

But damn if this wasn't the most lonesome strip of lane
in all New Mexico and him a lonesome cowboy ridin' i
on the back of some hunkin' old steed. Cowboys were th
good guys. Had a code to live by, guns to carry. And cow
and horses, they just needed a stick in the ribs, a kick in
the rear to get 'em going. No need to talk. No questions
No answers.

*Do you feel happy? Sad? What are you feeling now? Good
Good. You'll be going home soon. Do you feel anxious? You're s
quiet. Do you feel? Good. Good.*

He was hot like a stove top. Hot like a pot about to boi
and damn if he wasn't sitting right on the burner, all these
thoughts in his head making his lid start to dance. He'
blow the top of his head right off and out would tumble
all those good jokes, and lines that would make women
weep. Hot damn. Make 'em weep.

He shook his head hard and wrapped one hand tighte
around the steering wheel while he pushed farther out th
window, head and shoulders now. The old car swerved bu
he got it back on track, straight on that dotted line.

He loved those dotted lines. Man perforating the world
A place to rip it in half. Tear here. Send the part with him
on it back for a refund.

He shook his head like the dog he was pretending to
be. His lips went slack and he heard them flapping, ever
over the noise of the wind. What an ugly sound and he
wasn't an ugly guy. So he turned into the wind and it blev
his head empty. When he turned it back, the hot air ran
straight at him and made his eyes tear.

Life was wonderful again. Television is a blessing. Doc
tors cured themselves of cancer with a thought. Smart and
fancy women could be had with a smile and a wink.

Damn, life was good. It had taken a while but he wa
cookin'. He was the most scrumptious thing on the menu

"Whoeee!" he hollered, and the wind lashed that sound
around and threw it right back at him as he hung his head
out the window. He pulled it back inside just a snail's trai
before the semi whizzed by.

He thought about that close call and making love and
a cigarette all at the same time. The close call was past so

e tossed aside the image of his head rolling around on
ıe asphalt. His lady was a pain in the ass, so thinking
bout her was idiotic. The cigarette, though, he could do
ɔmething about that.

Two fingers burrowed into his shirt pocket. He was
lready tasting that first good drag and swore he could
ɛl that swirly smoke deep in his lungs. But the pack was
mpty and crinkled under his fingers. His smile was gone.
Ie didn't feel like hollerin' anymore.

Two hands slapped atop the steering wheel and he drove
ith his eyes straight forward on the lonely road. He just
anted one lousy cigarette.

But anger wasn't right. He plastered a grin on his face.
he new him. New and improved. He accelerated down
ıe four-lane, singing at the top of his lungs in a voice that
e was almost sure didn't belong to him. It was too smooth.

Smooth like the turn of the wheel, the slide of the stop
e made four miles down. He was still singing when he
almed the keys and unwound his long legs, and stood
ke a rock 'n' roll god in a pool of fluorescent light at the
ircle K convenience store.

He took a minute to admire himself in the side mirror.
Ie didn't like the way his dirty ice eyes looked, so he
dmired the night sky. Nothing like these black New Mex-
ːo nights. Stars as plentiful as rice at a weddin'. He tucked
ı his shirt so he looked really good. Handsome. *Damn,*
ɛe was fine. Whistling softly, he moved on.

Pushing open the glass door, he stepped inside, sur-
rised at how vibrant everything seemed now that he was
raight. Michelle Pfeiffer looked like she could just walk
ght off the cover of *People* and give him a little hug. The
urpy machine's neon blue and pink letters quivered as
' overjoyed to be colored pink and blue.

He ambled over to the register. Little Fourth of July
ags were taped all over the place: flags next to the Smokey
ɔe Hot Salami Sticks, flags wavin' over the stale donuts
nder the Plexiglas counter box, flags pokin' out of the
lmost-hidden condom place on the shelf behind the
ɔunter.

Hot damn! Independence Day. He almost forgot. Good

day for him. He did what he liked, when he liked. No on
around to tell him anything. Only his cowboy conscience
only his roamin' man code to keep him in line.

The smokes were neatly stacked on a metal thing abov
the counter. He looked for the Camels. Left, third ro
down. Filters one row lower than that. It was the same ?
every Circle K. What a mind! He could remember ever
thing.

He wandered toward the counter, laid his hands ato
it, and peered over, half expecting a pimply-faced clerk t
pop up like a stupid kid's toy. Nobody. Just worn linoleun
a wad of gum stuck to it turning black. Great. He coul
take a pack. Just reach up and be on his way.

But he knew right from wrong. He wanted to follow th
rules and felt bad when he didn't. It took a while sometime
for that feeling to happen, but it always did.

Then he saw her.

She was fixing coffee at the big urn right next to th
two-for-ninety-nine-cent burgers in those shiny gold an
silver wrappers behind the glass, under the red lights tha
never kept the damn things hot. Whooeee, he loved thos
burgers.

The woman was another matter. He could tell what kin
of woman she was right off: fat and fussy. She was wearin
a stupid little Uncle Sam hat that didn't fit. The stor
manager probably made her wear it, but he still hated i
She should have some pride.

He hated her. She didn't even care he'd come in. Sh
was supposed to care. *Hop to it. A little service here.*

With that thought, the heat caught up with him. Jus
exploded his head like a potato too long in the fire. Thi
time it wasn't funny. This time he felt sick. The lights wer
too bright. Too much pain inside his head. Hand out, h
found the door and pushed it hard, his other hand hel
tight to his temple.

The heat smacked him good when he walked out of th
white light and frigid air of the store and back into th
desert night. He pressed his temple harder as he walke
to the car and got in.

He checked himself in the rearview mirror. His hair wa

ness. He'd feel better if he looked better. Get the comb.
e leaned over to the glove compartment thinking his
ad would split wide open, and laced his hands around
e first thing he found. It was cool and it was metal and
held it to his head.

No comb. He needed a comb. Maybe that damn clerk
uld notice the second time he walked into her store
d sell him some smokes and a comb. Then he'd feel
tter.

He looked through the window of that Circle K again.
e was still making coffee. Ignoring him.

He needed a cigarette bad. He needed a comb and now
needed some aspirin. He hurt so bad he could cry and
e was just standing there making coffee.

Inside again he turned right, and walked up to the
man who was putting the big lid on top of the huge
el urn that would brew coffee for whoever it was that
ght come to a godforsaken place like this in the middle
the night. He walked right up to her and she felt him
ming because she turned around. Her eyes were hazel
d real clear and he saw himself in those eyes, reflected
ck the way people saw him.

Hot damn, he was a good-lookin' cowboy.

And when he smiled at himself, she smiled right back.
e didn't have a clue. They never did.

One

Tara Linley was the last of a long line: a family that had started with the Indians and bred with the Spanish until the Anglos put in their two cents over the course of a hundred years.

Her cheekbones and blue-black hair were a legacy of the ancient pueblo dwellers. Her tawny skin was a credit to her great-great-grandfather, Juan Montero. The blue eyes were Irish, but had never gazed upon the Emerald Isle. Old family photos showed a succession of handsome women to whom credit could be given for her height and slim-hipped, lush-chested figure.

From her mother, an artist, came Tara's spare sense of style and her love of home and hearth. From her father came Tara's confidence, but not his fondness for power and prestige. Her mother had died before Tara could talk. Her father had raised her until his death. The law was her sister, politics her brother, and both were poor excuses for family, but Tara hardly noticed.

Now her father was dead, and at times like this, she felt his absence so keenly it hurt. He would have been sad to see her alone. For all his success, the most important thing in his life had been his daughter. She missed his friendship

and his counsel, especially now when Albuquerque wa
changing and she was standing still.

On the North Rio Grande, horrid East Coast clapboard
mansions were being constructed by immigrant yuppies
springing up faster than Tara could blink. The interloper
planted trees and bushes imported from parts of the coun
try where water was less valued and more readily available
They complained of the heat in the summer and the cole
in the winter, leading one to wonder why they chose to
live there in the first place. Thankfully for Tara, all wa
not lost.

The glorious Sandias, mountains that had stood watch
over this land since the beginning of time, remained stal
wart. Pink and surreal in the sunset; formidable in the
light of day. Real New Mexicans preferred to live properl'
on the land, respecting it as they blended into their sur
roundings. Here, in Tara's Albuquerque, adobe house
with their flat roofs and long porches, low walls and weath
ered gates were the norm; brush, sage, and cottonwood
the natural landscaping. Wreaths of chiles still hung on
front doors. And five days into the new year, Christma
luminaria still lined roofs and walls, lighting the way o
Mary and Joseph and Jesus.

Tara's home was like these. It had been in the Linley
family for generations, on land they had claimed when a
neighbor was the person a hundred miles to the south
The souls of all those who had gone before still dwelt in
the walls, looked out of the deep-set windows, held tigh
to the heavy beams that crossed her ceiling, and warmed
themselves by the cavernous fireplaces. Each ancestor had
added something more to the original structure: a barn
a small nursery (now her office), a corral, the lean-to by
the river, a guest house. Her home was Tara's reward for
a young life at the mercy of politics, spent in cities so alien
they might have been half a world away. She loved this
house and the tradition and the stability of her life.

She hated change, but her life was changing. Carlos, the
man who had tended the Linley land for as long as she
could remember, was needed elsewhere to deal with family

usiness. He had stood on this porch, hat in hand,
xplaining how it was.

Tara watched him drive away. She pulled the blanket
e had thrown over her shoulders tighter even though
e couldn't see the truck any longer. It had been an
wkward conversation, since Carlos was a man of few words,
ut already she missed him.

She poked her hand out from beneath the blanket and
oked at the note he'd given her. Neatly printed were the
hone number of the place he'd be in Arizona, and the
ame of the boy who would come to take care of her horse
r the duration: Joseph. She hoped he would be as good
s Carlos said. She knew he wouldn't be.

"Tara, hon? Where do you want the gold ornaments?"

Tara closed the door and sloughed off the blanket. She'd
alf forgotten she wasn't alone. Folding the blanket as
e went, Tara entered the living room just as Charlotte
nished packing the gold ornaments from the tree into the
rong box. Charlotte looked up and smiled with prettily
owed, very pink lips.

"Is this the right box?"

"Sure." Tara tossed the blanket onto the couch and
ok over the dismantling of the Christmas tree. "You
ouldn't do that. I don't want you to get messed up
efore—wherever it is you're going."

"The high school. Woodrow's giving a speech. Recep-
on afterward so he can listen to everyone's complaints."
harlotte waved a cigarette, unapologetic for her displeas-
re at the upcoming event. "You don't mind if I smoke,
o you?"

"Woodrow thinks you quit," Tara said. Charlotte arched
ne well-defined eyebrow. "All right. Your secret's safe
ith me." With her hands full of strung chiles, Tara nod-
ed toward the fireplace. "There's a lighter over there."

"Don't think I need one." Charlotte snapped open her
urse. "Oops, wrong." She was across the room in three
ng steps. Tall and slender, she was nonetheless substan-
al. She was a doer, and a perfect political wife for Wood-
ow. Charlotte could sit with her ankles daintily crossed

for hours, or run roughshod over a room full of volunteer until they dropped from licking too many envelopes.

They'd known each other since high school, and Char lotte Weber still intrigued Tara Linley with her single mindedness and generosity. Thankfully, she always man aged to get what she wanted, too.

The cigarette was lit, the first drag taken, and Charlotte was happy.

"Oh that tastes good." She leaned back against the hug fireplace. "You know, I still can't figure out how you man aged when you were a kid. Keeping up with the schedul of a man in public life is difficult even for an adult. Knowin what to say, when to say it, what to do—" Another dra and a thoughtful expulsion of a spirit of smoke. "Bu you followed your father around through three federa appointments and an elected office. That was a big caree for a man on his own with a little girl." The next puff wa more perfunctory. "The gang and I didn't sympathize ver much. We went out cruising while you hung out at th high school watching him give speeches."

"I liked being with him. I didn't need any sympathy. Tara pulled a box toward her with her toe and laid th dried chiles in a nest of tissue paper. The mis-boxed gol ornaments went in after.

"Yes, you did. You're just too proud to admit it," Char lotte said.

"Okay, a little would have been nice." Tara grinned "Happy to know you were right?"

"No. I like guilt," Charlotte sniffed.

"You've never felt guilty in your life." Tara laughed.

"You're right. But it's only because I've never really don anything to feel guilty about." Charlotte put her hand t her neck, tired of rehashing history and uninterested i delving into her psyche. "Do you think these pearls ar too much?"

Tara looked over her shoulder and shook her head "No, they're fine. You look like you could take over th governor's mansion tomorrow. Hand me those scissors will you?"

Charlotte looked around, tossed what was left of he

;arette into the fireplace, and grabbed the scissors off
e mantel. Though she handed them to Tara, her eyes
re locked on the cards neatly displayed on the rough-
wn wooden mantel.

"You got one too, I see," Charlotte said evenly.

"What?"

"Ben's announcement." This time her voice was flat.
ıra's snipping stopped but she remained stooped over
e box. Finally, pulling a piece of tape across the seam,
e sealed it tight.

"I think everyone did," she said. "I saw Charlie in court
e other day and he mentioned getting one. No big deal."

"It might not be a big deal to Charlie," Charlotte said,
ɪnversationally nudging the opening into Tara's private
e wider. "But he's kept in touch with Ben. You haven't."

Tara nodded and lifted the box, neatly stacking it on
e one she had managed to pack before Charlotte arrived
ırty minutes early. It gave her an excuse for not looking
ɪarlotte in the eye. She could kick herself for even both-
ing to display that card.

"He sent flowers when Dad died last year. He was in
ɔs Angeles, I think. Didn't even mention coming back.
ot that there's any reason he should. It's been over twenty
ars." Tara straightened and put her hands on the small
˙her back. She smiled at Charlotte. There was less sparkle
ɪd more strain in her expression. "Look, I've just about
ɪd it for tonight. You can toss those Christmas cards in
ɪe fire. At least the mantel will be cleared. I'll finish
ɪcking up the tree tomorrow."

"You don't want to save Ben's card, just in case?" Char-
ɔtte ignored her given task and fingered the red card
splendent with gold cherubs, one with its hand on the
her's breast. Ben always did have a subtle, but healthy,
ɔido. Fleetingly Charlotte wondered if it was still intact.
someone like him could even manage to—

Tara interrupted her thought. "No. Thank you very
ıuch. And if I hear another word about it, I won't go to
ɔur fund-raiser tomorrow night."

Charlotte quietly put the card back. "In that case, I'm
ıt of here." Charlotte gathered her things, the subject

of Ben Crawford closed. She glanced in the mirror abov
the hearth, gave her St. John suit a tug, and grinned. "I'
really sorry I couldn't stay longer. I hate leaving you alor
tonight of all nights."

"Not the first birthday I've been alone. Besides, Carolin
took me out to lunch and the court reporters sent flowe
to the office. Two judges even remembered. The bouqu
you brought was icing on the cake, and I'm thrilled yo
thought of me, considering how much you have to d
tonight."

"It was nothing," Charlotte said, lifting her chin a tac
Tara leaned in for an air kiss and walked her friend to th
door.

"Tell Woodrow hello for me and wish him luck."

"Certainly will," Charlotte murmured, her spouse voic
fully in force, her face closing, changing into the publi
one that no one could read but every voter loved. Whe
she looked up, her smile was in place and wouldn't droo
until the last reporter had left the high school. Tara ha
long since ceased to be amazed. She'd watched those i
public life morph since she was ten. It was an art she'
never perfected.

" 'Night then." Tara opened the door and shivered.
was a cold, clear January night. The last place she wanted t
be was in the high school auditorium listening to Woodro
Weber wax poetic on various and sundry political agenda

"We could meet you for a late dinner and celebrate,
Charlotte offered.

Tara shook her head, too quickly. "No, thanks. I'll se
you tomorrow. Where is it again? What shall I wear?"

"La Posada Hotel. Right after work. Everyone will be i
a suit and tie. Do me a favor. Wear a dress instead of pant
I'm going to put you in front of the cameras with Woodro
and your legs are fabulous," Charlotte said. Suddenly he
arms were around Tara. "Wish us luck tonight."

"Of course." Tara patted Charlotte lightly, then hel
her away. "I always do, you know that."

"He just wants it so much, Tara," Charlotte said quietl

"I know."

What else could she say? Woodrow was a politician

here was always hurt for the women who loved that sort.
lurt and joy. Rejection and acceptance. It was all the luck
f the draw, the whim of the people. Thank goodness her
ortunes were dependent only on her actions.

Charlotte's public face had slipped. She took a moment
) put it in place.

"All you can do is your best, Charlotte," Tara reminded
er. Charlotte fingered her purse as if the thought made
er nervous.

"I know. I guess I just keep thinking there's more
omehow."

"There isn't. Just keep smiling. That's what the voters
ant."

"Guess you should know. See you tomorrow. Happy
irthday."

With that, Charlotte was gone in a cloud of lavender
erfume. Tara closed the door with a chuckle, picked up
ie mail that the cleaning lady had laid neatly on the hall
ible, and wandered back to the living room.

Bills, an invitation to speak at a women's conference in
`aos, a letter from Franklin, the last in her short list of
ivers, and the dearest. She opened that envelope swearing
he smelled his aftershave as she pulled out the card. Frank-
n was getting married. Good for him. He would make
ome woman a marvelous husband. At one time she
hought she might have walked down the aisle with him.
ut Franklin wanted to live in the bustle of New York, and
`ara clung to her Albuquerque roots, unlike many of her
riends and family. Those she had liked, and some she had
oved, had left. But now Ben was back and that wasn't
omething Tara had counted on in this lifetime. Thank-
ully, Albuquerque had grown. They wouldn't be running
ito one another anytime soon.

Impulsively, Tara stepped up to the mantel and gathered
he Christmas cards into a haphazard stack. They were in
he fire, curling at the edges, before she could think twice.
`he red card with the gold cherubs was the first to go.
Vatching awhile longer, Tara finally turned away. Knowing
;en was close again made her feel lonelier than ever. She

didn't want to question the choices she'd made, not o
this particular birthday, anyway.

Feeling antsy, Tara went to her bedroom, and peele
off her sweater and her too-short-for-court skirt. She pulle
on her jeans, tossed on a flannel shirt, tied back her hai
and grabbed her denim jacket. A night ride was in orde
Shinin' would love it as much as she.

Tara tugged her boots on, groaning with the effort, an
heard a knock on the front door at the same time. He
heels sounding an echo on the tiled floor, Tara flipped o
the lights in the living room and reached for the doorknol
Charlotte must have forgotten something. She pulled o
the huge knob. Impossible to fling, the massive doc
opened slowly but it wasn't Charlotte who waited on th
other side.

"Surprise!"

"Oh, my God," Tara breathed, sagging against the door
her forehead resting on the thick wood. She lifted he
head.

"You didn't think I'd forget, did you, Tara?" The woma
on the doorstep burst into Tara Linley's house, handin
over a bouquet of roses that had half hidden her, pressin
on Tara a magnum of champagne. "God, if you only kne
what it took to get here! You have no idea, I swear. Happy
happy, happy, you old broad, you!"

Tara laughed as Donna Ecold filled every available b
of space with her gifts, her chatter, her laughter, and he
presence.

"I don't care what it took to get here. I'm just gla
you made it." Tara kissed her friend's cheek, holding he
shoulder as if she were afraid she might flit away.

"Of course you are, my love," Donna trilled. "I kne
you'd be bummed. Everyone is bummed when they h
forty. So here I am, to get you through your birthda
crisis."

Donna chattered, but not without noticing that Tar
wasn't listening any longer. The tall woman's face ha
fallen to a look of bewilderment. Donna looked over he
shoulder and giggled. She flung her arm around Tara'
waist, pulled her close, and gave her a little squeeze.

"Okay, so it's a little more than me, myself, and I. Tara
inley, this is Bill Hamilton. Bill, this is my very, very best
iend in all the world. The smartest woman you'll ever
eet. The best attorney on the face of the earth, Tara
inley."

Donna's little head swiveled from one person to the
ther. Her grin could have lit up Albuquerque from one
ecember to the next, but its radiance was lost on Tara.
er eyes were locked with Bill Hamilton's and she had
e strangest feeling that she should shut the door before
e stepped over her threshold.

If you enjoyed the riveting legal suspense

of R. A. Forster's *The Mentor*

then please turn the page for

a sneak peek of R. A. Forster's

Character Witness

on sale at bookstores everywhere

Chapter One

"Got your basic cleaner in forty-gallon drums." Arthur grunted as he grabbed one and rolled it toward the stainless steel cart. "Bad stuff. Bad." He shook his head and gave the drum another twirl, held it against his substantial thigh and looked at the kid. "This is going to clean up any of the gunk you're gonna find, and you're gonna find some real gunk, kid, 'specially over there in that building that looks like a sausage. That's where you're headed, 'kay?"

"Absolutely. No problem. I can handle anything. You want me to do the windows, too?"

Arthur rolled his eyes. This kid was green as green could be. "You see any windows in that building?"

Arthur grunted again and twirled the drum hand over hand. The drum toppled when he let it go and rumbled as it settled down. Arthur glanced over his shoulder and saw the kid's anxious face. This kid was okay. A real go-getter. Arthur liked to help that kind along 'cause he didn't see many of 'em.

"You know this place gives you help on tuition for school if you want to do more than push a broom." Arthur lifted the top and sniffed the green crystals like a gourmet, dumped some into a small, plastic-lidded jar, and attached

it to the side of the kid's metal cart. He opened a smaller
can and sniffed again. He jerked his head. "This one'
strong. You wear gloves when you get to them sinks, okay?'

"Okay. Sure. Whatever you say. I want to do it right.'
The black-haired kid took his place behind the cart. It wa
almost as big as he was. "I know about the tuition. Th
benefits are real good, too. My sister works here. She started
at the bottom, too. Now she's an analyst over in the space
division. Tysco's been real good to her. Me, I'm going to
do better than that. You just wait and see."

Arthur slapped the kid on the back. "I wouldn't doub
I'll be seeing you in a suit one of these days. Just remember
to treat the bottom folk like me good when you get up
there on top."

"You bet. You bet, Arthur. I'm going to be the best, bu
I'll never forget all this."

Arthur gave him one of those old, evil-eye warning look
that was filled with admiration. "You ain't there yet, kid
'Till you're some big manager, you don't forget all wha
you gotta do here."

"No problem. I got it straight. Dust the desks and th
chairs, empty the wastepaper baskets, don't take anything
from the desks or open the drawers. Dust the sills on th
windows dividing the manager's offices from the mair
room. I get a break after two hours. I do the bathroom
next. Then breakfast after the next two hours. Then you're
going to take me over to the cafeteria and we're going to
dress that down before the office workers get here."

"You got it, my man." Arthur put his hand up. The kid
high-fived him and beamed. "See you in four, back here
First breakfast's on me."

They went their separate ways, the kid humming. He
dusted with a flourish and waved at someone vacuuming
way down a hall; but, for the most part, he was alone and
happy to be that way.

Tysco was a wonderful place. While he worked, the kid
checked out the drawings on the walls that showed the
stuff Tysco manufactured. Stuff that helped feed people
stuff that helped educate people. The stuff that helped
kill people he didn't think about. That was in a whole other

ection, and special people cleaned over there. Besides, it
as depressing to think a company this big, a company
hat would pay him to go to school, a company that had
credit union, could do anything that wasn't good and
elpful and excellent. There was the space division, too,
nd that was exciting. Maybe when he'd paid his dues and
earned enough, he'd work in the space division like Verna.
He'd make things that reached up to the stars. That would
uit him. His ma always said he reached for the stars.

Invigorated by the vision of his future, undaunted by
he tasks that lay before him, the kid didn't even stop for
is first break. Someday he'd run the whole place and
omeone would give a speech about how he'd been one
ell of a janitor.

Gently he swiped at a wedding picture on the last desk
n the row and adjusted it just so. More pictures were stuck
o bulletin boards. A big pink bow had been left on a table.
The calendars with funny sayings on them were all turned
o the next day. The kid smiled at these testaments to the
uman face of this big, now dark place. People were happy
nd busy here, and he wanted to be a part of it all.

Stuffing his rag in the back pocket of his bright-orange
umpsuit, the kid whistled and headed across the hall to
he bathrooms. He couldn't remember which container
eld the floor cleaner and which was for the toilets and
inks. Making his first executive decision, he poured the
rystals from the smaller pail into the sink and turned his
ace away just in case the stuff blew up or something. It
ure smelled like it should. When nothing happened, the
id smiled, replaced the canister and pulled on the huge
loves that were meant for larger hands than his.

Ten minutes later he looked back on a gleaming row
f porcelain sentinels.

"Good job." He patted himself on the back, then pushed
pen the stall door of the first john.

One, two, three. Only six more to go. The kid was sure
o one had ever done such a fine job.

Grinning, he whacked open the fourth door, and that
vas when his jaw dropped. He stepped back, embarrassed
eyond belief. There was a guy on the john. A guy in a

suit on the john. Oh Lord, a manager doing his business.
The kid stumbled back until his butt was up against one
of the newly cleaned sinks.

"I'm sorry. It's my first day. I didn't think anybody would
be here. . . ." The kid was sweating; his mind was going a
mile a minute. ". . . I'll get out of here till you're done. I
can't tell you how sorry I am. I really, really am. . . ." He
leaned forward as he started to walk out. But when he
passed that stall, the one where the guy was doing his
business, it dawned on him that it was awful quiet in there.
Not like embarrassed quiet. Not like rude quiet. Quiet like
scary quiet. "Sir? Hey, sir? Are you all right?"

He touched the door. It swung open again. The kid
blinked, then froze. The stall door swung gently back with
a mild little clunk and bounced against the locking mechanism. The kid swallowed. The place was way too hot. He
was sweating bad. He called once more.

"Sir?"

Mechanically, the kid pushed open the door once more.
He didn't bother to push it again.

The man in the suit—the man sitting up so weird on
the toilet—was dead.

"What kind of craziness is this, to try to fix something
that isn't broken? You're not broken, and I'm not going
to let anyone—not anyone in Los Angeles or Washington—try to fix you."

The thunderous applause made Carl Walsh feel like a
god, but no one would ever have known it by his expression.
Humble, a tad surprised, a bit delighted was how he looked.
It was the expression of a man who was just saying what
everyone else knew. He was one of the gang. He was just
hanging out with the rank and file. He was a politician.

Today, the street corner where he planted himself was
the Beverly Wilshire and the folks who'd stopped by for a
chat were the three-hundred members of the court reporters' union. Carl had been briefed on their concerns,
tweaked the speech someone else had written for him,
then convinced this group that he had what it took to fight

ashington now that he'd conquered City Hall. Not that
ashington had a damn thing to do with their problems,
ut it made them feel important to think that.

He called to them through the last spattering of
oplause.

"I know you feel like you're alone and you don't like
eing told you're expendable. I understand that, because
m there every day. I'm responsible for sorting out the
any voices in the city the way you are responsible for
orting out the voices in the courtroom. No machine can
o what I do, and no machine can do what you do!"

This time he let passion come into his voice and was
ewarded with whoops and hollers of ecstasy. He'd pushed
ll the right buttons without breaking a sweat. The courts
ere pushing for electronic recording. If that happened,
e reporters would be out of a job forever. Court reporters
ade a lot of money. The judges didn't. There were more
eporters than judges. Reporters could give more to his
ampaign coffers, and there was more of them to cast a
ote. So, Carl Walsh talked to the court reporters' union,
ot the judges association.

"I'm asking for your support now, at the beginning of
y campaign, not the end. You're not an afterthought.
ou, above all, know how important it is to keep the human
ouch in the business of lawmaking. Make me your senator
om California and I'll keep the humanity in politics.
hank you for having me. Thank you for your support."

The woman at the head table was up and shaking his
and. He was looking her in the eye when he pulled her
lose and turned to face a camera that was suddenly
ointed their way. She was in seventh heaven. He couldn't
emember her name. Only the most important names,
ates, and details were kept in his head; and at this
noment, he was scanning the crowd to confirm that no
ne on the A-list was present. Buoyed by the good words,
he pats on the back, Carl was grinning when he was pulled
orward.

"Mr. Walsh." Another woman was tugging on his arm.
"This is Mr. Pullet. He heads the division."

"Happy to meet you. What a great turnout." Walsh

shook the man's hand heartily. "I can't thank you enough."

Carl led the man away, escaping the dais and his hostess in one swift move. With a few well-chosen words, a guy-to-guy slap on the back, Carl lost Mr. Pullet and fell into step with his two bodyguards. Carl could barely remember their names either, even though his life rested in their hands. They would follow him to the ends of the earth. Right now he just wanted them to walk him to the facilities.

On his way, he gave the high sign to two men who were headed his way and picked up his pace. Life was glorious. The spring in his step was meant to propel him into fast forward; instead, he collided with a man coming out of the rest room. The bodyguards reached for the mayor; the mayor grabbed the man, and everyone righted everyone else.

"Sorry. I wasn't looking where I was going. Stupid of me, really."

"Sure, 'tisn't a problem. No problem at all," the other man assured him, and then they looked at each other.

"Gerry O'Doul!" The mayor laughed; and even he, seasoned politician that he was, couldn't keep the surprise out of his voice. "How are you?"

I thought you were dead.

"Well, well. Look who I've run in to. Mr. Mayor, is it?" Gerry chuckled.

I'm glad you're so predictable.

His gentle voice, the last whisper of an Irish broque that Carl Walsh's father swore—with grudging admiration—was put on for the jury, hadn't changed. It was the only thing about Gerry O'Doul that hadn't. "What's this I hear about your leaving us for Washington? We'll be calling you *senator* then, I suppose."

"I sure hope so." Carl smiled broadly. Gerry, still kicking, took Carl back to a time when he'd proudly watched his father and dreamed of the wondrous things he would do when he grew up. Carl sighed. Never in a million years had he dreamed he would do some of the things he had. The business of the city had had class in Gerry's time. Gerry still had it. Carl knew he did not.

"Wouldn't your father be proud of you! Why I remem-
er when we used to stand against one another in court—
e at the defense table, he the prosecutor. We made fine
emies, we did."

"You think I could ever forget? I was weaned on those
ories. We had many a dinner where the name Gerry
'Doul was taken in vain." Carl chuckled. "My dad used
talk about you often before he died."

Gerry leaned closer to Carl. Memories were such a lovely
nnection, so useful. Gerry was happy to see that he could
ill connect with the handsome, more practically con-
ected Carl Walsh.

"Did he, now? So long ago, 'twas. So many are gone
ow. Things change so quickly, don't they, Carl? One min-
te you're surrounded by great friends and great enemies;
e next, you're alone."

Gerry's eyes misted. Carl Walsh reached out and put his
and on the old man's shoulder. Something flashed. A
hoto op. Carl thought there was something sad about
at. Gerry turned into the flash even though the intent
as to capture Carl doing his thing. It went off again, and
erry didn't miss a beat. He brought back the misties for
n encore. "So he talked about me? That's lovely, sure
is."

"Absolutely."

The crowd around Carl had diminished, but people still
ung on the periphery of his space in an ill-defined circle,
aiting for his ear. There was a ringing. A portable phone
as handed to Carl. He took it, simultaneously nudging
erry along with him to the semi-privacy of the anteroom.
'Scuse me a second." He listened. Gerry waited patiently,
eading the signs of a happy man and noticing that Carl
as trying very hard not to appear too happy. He couldn't
ave chosen a better time to bump into his old friend's
on.

"Good news?" Gerry asked the minute the phone was
olded.

"The best." Carl nodded, no longer beaming. "First
rm, city budget was down by three percent." Strangely,

Carl didn't look Gerry in the eye. How surprisingly mode:
he was.

"If that isn't wonderful! That's what it's all about, mal
ing a difference."

"I'm going all the way no matter what, Gerry." Car
seemed to be talking to himself, but Gerry wasn't quit
ready to be discarded. He put his hand on the younge
man's arm.

"Success is powerful, Carl. Just remember, it doesn'
always bring what you expect," Gerry warned.

"Then again, sometimes it does," Carl bantered bach
He rejuvenated himself with that thought. "Listen, I'v
got to ..." He held his hands toward the men's room.

"Of course. So ungracious of me." Gerry laughed an
took a step back.

"Don't rush off. I've got a half hour or so before m
next appointment; we'll have some coffee."

"No, no, no. I'm running, too, I'll have you know."
Gerry was as proud as punch but kept a tight rein on hi
excitement. "I'm taking on a new associate. O'Doul &
Associates is going to be back in business, Carl."

"That's great. Got the old fire lit again, huh?" Car
shook Gerry's hand heartily. "Well, you just let me knov
what's happening. Maybe I can ride your coattails, ge
some good press standing next to Gerry O'Doul."

"Be happy to oblige, Mr. Mayor. Happy, indeed. I'd b
especially proud if we could be seen shaking hands o
a bit of the city business before you're off to conque
Washington."

"Gerry, you never change. My dad always said once yo
set your sights on something you were dangerously tena
cious. He also said you were so smooth when you saw ai
opening that nobody saw the bite coming."

"Your father was a smart man. I'll ask for only a momen
Mr. Mayor, to try to convince you O'Doul & Associates i
as fit as a fiddle and ready to perform. You've got th
business. Last I read, it was almost thirty-six police officer
alone who were being sued by the citizens of your fiscall
well-run city."

Carl Walsh cocked a wry grin, knowing it was useless to y to deflect Gerry's advances. Sidestepping had never orked with his father either.

"Call my office for an appointment. But I'm not promis- g. Shay, Sylvester & Harrington is still the city's firm of cord. I'd hate to get on Richard's wrong side even for ou, Gerry."

"I wouldn't either." Gerry's voice lost some of its twinkle; is eyes darkened just a shade. He recovered nicely. Besides, I'm a little long in the tooth to cause Richard any ouble. He might even find it amusing that I'm mentioning is at all. Crumbs is what I'm looking for, Carl. If you don't k, you'll never know what you might have had." He raised is hand, the signet ring he'd worn since the day he gradua- d from law school flashing as they parted company. Gerry ot back a last reminder, "Crumbs is all, Carl."

Gerry walked sprightly out of the Beverly Wilshire alone, small, content smile on his face. There was change in e wind. A second chance had come his way, and Carl /alsh had a big 2 emblazoned on his forehead. Poor boy idn't have a clue what was about to hit him.

Behind him, Carl was watching. Gerry O'Doul had a oring in his step that a man half his age would envy. arl allowed himself one small sound that he thought nderscored the surprising pleasure he felt at seeing Gerry nd being reminded of his father. Actually, it sounded ore like a noise to ward off an evil spirit. Carl Walsh felt s if someone had just walked over his grave. The phone ing again. He flipped it open and turned away from Gerry 'Doul's retreating figure.

"Yes?" He listened. "Of course. Of course, I'm thrilled." Ie listened a bit longer and responded as he knew his aller wanted him to. "I can't thank you enough. We're a reat team. Nothing can stop us now. The election is in e bag."

Carl flipped the phone closed, thought of the man on e other end, and wished he were more like Gerry O'Doul.

Then Carl Walsh changed his mind and thanked his ucky stars he wasn't.

* * *

"Your three o'clock is here, Mr. Jacobsen."

"Show him in."

Richard Jacobsen laid his fine hands on the desk, hi
eyes darting over his office. Everything was in order: There
was good news to tell; the future looked bright; the billing
statements were on target, and, of course, the relationship
with this particular client could not be paralleled.

The door opened.

Richard rose to greet the handsome young man with
dark hair and the look of someone on the way up. Richard
had always admired that look. He only wished he had had
it as a young man. He could have gone so much further
so much quicker. But what was a little time? Richard, a
firm believer in fate, knew that it was better this way. The
look of success might have made him stand out sooner
but his history, and those he had fatefully encountered in
the last few years, put him light-years ahead of his more
comely peers. Money, power, prestige. Richard Jacobsen
had all this city had to offer; and soon, he would make
the country his business. She had always wanted this for
him, and he appreciated her sacrifices that had brought
him to this point. Luckily, the young man coming through
the door wanted quite a bit, too. He was willing to do just
about anything to get what he wanted, and that benefited
Richard quite nicely. Unfortunately, neither this man, nor
the woman who gave her life to him, understood what
drove Richard Jacobsen. His lips tipped up just a tad. Even
he, humorless as he was, thought that was quite amusing.
They would be so amazed—or would it be appalled?—to
know what passion drove him.

"So nice to see you. And right on time."

"I'm glad to be here. Have you spoken to our friend?"

"Yes. Everything is on schedule. He's elated."

"Fine. Fine."

The younger man walked straight up to Richard Jacob
sen. They met beside his desk, looking at each other the

ay men will who understand their power over one
10ther. They were both very clear on that.

"I haven't been able to find anything in the office regard-
1g the problem we had this morning. I searched every-
here."

"Not to worry. Everything's been taken care of." The
>unger man didn't look convinced. Richard put his hand
1 his shoulders and said sincerely, "I promise. You
eedn't worry. I needn't worry. There's nothing that can
1ange what's already been done, but you'll never have to
/er think about it again."

"Didn't anyone ever tell you never to say never?" the
>ung man asked peevishly.

"No," Richard answered quietly. In his business he saw
ts of people upset over lots of things. He knew what to
>. The hand on the man's shoulder was surprisingly tight.
ichard slipped it down toward the elbow. He held on a
1oment, then, with the gentlest of pressure, led the man
cross the huge office. "You'll want to freshen up."

"Yes, that would be good," the young man said. He
idn't look well at all. Richard felt terrible that he hadn't
oticed the moment he came in. That had been terribly
1considerate.

"Do you need anything?"

"No, I have it all. Right here." He patted his breast
ocket, and Richard thought it was dangerous to carry
>mething so important so casually.

"All right. I'll wait. I've blocked off the afternoon for
ou."

The young man looked over his shoulder. He smiled
>r the first time. It was shaky, but a smile nonetheless.

"It won't take that long. It never does."

"There's always a first time," Richard answered quietly
s the other man walked toward Richard's private bath-
oom.

It was only after the door had shut that Richard remem-
ered her picture was still there. He wished he'd remem-
ered to put it away.

Richard was, after all, a very, very private person.

* * *

"Dorty & Breyer, how may I help you? Miss Cotter? Yes, I believe she's here. Just a moment, and I'll connect you."

She pushed the hold button and zoomed around the reception desk.

"You didn't fool anyone," Cherie called, but Kathleen barely gave her a glance. By the time Kathleen was in her chair, Cherie was kneeling on her credenza, her arms dangling over the top of the carpeted wall that partitioned their cubicles. She tapped Kathleen's head with a pen. "You can't disguise that voice of yours. No way."

Kathleen brushed at her hair. Cherie tapped again when Kathleen pushed the line that was lighted.

"Kathleen Cotter, may I help you?" Her voice was back to normal. Sweet and girlish in pitch, professional in tone. The caller didn't seem to sense her duplicity. Kathleen listened intently, then hung up without another word. Cherie waved a hand, hoping to catch Kathleen's peripheral vision.

"Earth to Kathleen. Who was it? I hope it was a murderer. We need something to perk this place up. I don't have anything fun to do."

"No, it wasn't a new client. It wasn't anyone. I mean, it was someone. He wanted to know if I was going to be busy Saturday night."

Cherie tapped Kathleen's head again and laughed, but it didn't sound as if she were happy. "You've been holding out on me. I didn't know you'd started dating again."

"I haven't, and what that caller had in mind wouldn't be called dating anyway. He just saw me on the commercial, that's all. Will you stop it!" Kathleen brushed away Cherie's pen and stood up so fast the other woman almost lost her balance. By the time Kathleen was standing in the opening of Cherie's cubicle, the other woman was settled on the credenza, her legs dangling, her arms crossed. "You know you've been getting very strange over the last few months. We're attorneys, Cherie, not children. I really think you should start acting like you take your profession seriously."

"Oh, you mean like pretending you're the secretary then running to your chair and pretending to be a lawyer."

"I am a lawyer." Kathleen raised her chin proudly. "Dorty & Breyer may not be a fancy firm—"

"It's the McDonald's of the law, Kathleen. We're legal bimbos." Cherie grabbed her cigarettes without taking her eyes off Kathleen.

"It's a general law practice and the people who come here need us. They haven't anywhere else to go. You should be proud of that. I know I am."

"Oh, yeah, so proud you're going to leave. You're going to go to Beverly Hills, la-de-da." Cherie lit her cigarette and inhaled deeply, letting her statement slap Kathleen in the face. They'd never been best of friends outside the office, but inside they clung to one another. There was no one else except Jay Dorty, and neither of them would want to cling to him.

"You've been going through my desk." Kathleen's red lips pulled tight. It wasn't anger that flared, but disappointment. She never indulged in the former without the latter, and the former usually crept up on her late at night when there was no one to yell at.

"I wasn't snooping. I was in your desk looking for something and I just happened to see that letter. I mean, wow, what can I say? Beverly Hills and everything. Geez, you start fixing yourself up a little bit here and there, and suddenly you're not good enough for this place. You're even too good for Riverside. You went all the way to the top."

Cherie sniffed. She took another drag, tossed back her head, raised her chin, and exhaled loudly. Kathleen had seen the tough girls in high school act like this. She hated women who acted like they were better than everyone else when everyone else could see they weren't. Funny thing, though, all those everyones were usually intimidated by those girls. That was the funny thing.

Cherie, tired of looking at the cloud of gray smoke above her, swung her head back and let her lids lie low over her eyes. "Are you going? 'Cause if you expect a going-away party, I can't afford it."

It sounded like an accusation, as if Kathleen were contemplating murder.

Kathleen sighed and plopped herself in Cherie's chair, crossed her legs, and considered the other woman. One arm was crooked to hold her cigarette up; the other was crossed over an androgynous chest. Her color-stripped hair was pulled back in a short ponytail. Cherie wouldn't look Kathleen in the eye. She probably thought Kathleen wasn't worth the effort.

"I was going to tell you about it when I decided what to do. Really I was." In truth, Kathleen had thought of sneaking out in the middle of the night just to spare Cherie's feelings. After all, news like this would be like announcing she'd won the lottery just when Cherie showed her the dollar she'd found in the gutter. "I was just waiting for the right time."

"Well, when was the right time going to be? I mean, when were you going to drop this on me? When we had a couple of new clients and this office needed both of us? When my car broke down and I didn't have enough money to repair it and needed a ride in? When my ex called to let me know that he'd found another perfect woman? Get real, Kathleen. This isn't the kind of news I would want to hear, now is it?" Another drag. The chin went higher. "I thought you were my friend."

"I *am* your friend, Cherie." That wasn't exactly true, but Kathleen didn't want to disappoint her. She tried again. "I mean, I'm your friend but that kind of thing goes both ways, you know. I could just as easily ask why you're not happy for me? I think a real friend would be excited for the other one, don't you?"

Kathleen uncrossed her legs and considered her black patent leather pumps, on sale because there wasn't much call for Italian square-toed, high-heeled pumps in Banning, California. Kathleen had bought them just because they were beautiful and different. There was nothing Kathleen loved more than something that looked beautiful, something with color and form, something other than the desert and a sickroom and a mother who could only speak about disappointment and despair. Listening to Cherie, Kathleen

emembered so well the words that had made her long
or a change of scenery. They were words that had changed
hings around until Kathleen felt everything not quite right
vas her fault. Her mother had the knack. Cherie had the
nack. Kathleen had had enough.

"I'm thirty. I've never been out of Banning except to
o shopping at the outlets near Palm Springs and to go
vith my parents for a weekend in Las Vegas when I was
leven. I went to law school just down the road in Riverside.
've never been challenged except to see how patient I
ould be waiting for my time to live. I've tried very hard
o be kind to everyone; in fact, I've been over backward
o be kind to everyone.

"Now, given all that, you can see why I didn't rush to
ou with this incredible news. I'm very patient; I was trying
o be kind so I wouldn't hurt your feelings by leaving you
ere, and I was trying to be cautious because I know I'm
ipe for disappointment. I know what this place is and,
ıntil this moment, I wasn't sure I could leave it behind.
)orty & Breyer is predictable and safe. I could probably
vork here until I retired or died. There's a lot to be said
or that."

Finally, Kathleen paused for breath. That was more than
he'd ever said about herself at one time in all her years.
;he felt better already.

"On the other hand, I could go to Beverly Hills to work
vith an uncle I haven't seen in fifteen years, a man whom
 admired greatly and who disappeared without a word to
ne . . . a man neither of my parents would talk about in
ıll those years. I don't know what I feel about him because
've never been the kind of person to hate. I'm not even
ure I carry a grudge. But I do know what I think about
ıis offer to have me work for him. It's an opportunity no
)ne else is going to give me because I come from Banning
ınd I'm thirty and I didn't have enough guts to grab for
he brass ring before this. And all you've done by trying
o make me feel guilty for wanting to go, and for having
he chance to go, is to make my decision for me. I think
t's the best thing that happened to me, thank you very
nuch. I'm going to leave here and not look back."

"Well, then, I guess that shows what your home counts for," Cherie said. "Guess that shows what it means to live your whole life in a place that you can just leave it in a snap. Guess that shows what your commitments count for, doesn't it? I mean what are you going to do with your caseload?"

Kathleen was already halfway down the hall. "I wouldn't walk out on the firm."

"You think you're going on an adventure?" Cherie called and Kathleen stopped for a moment. "You're not. Just remember I'm the one that said that. They'll chew you up and spit you out, Kathleen Cotter. I don't care how much you think you've learned from those dumb magazines. They'll see right through you. They will. I don't care if you graduated top of your class. It was still a second-rate school. You won't be able to handle anything bigger than a thirty-dollar divorce. They'll know that the minute you open your mouth."

Cherie laughed until Kathleen turned her head. She didn't bother to look at Cherie; she just stood there, her face in profile. Cherie stopped laughing just in time to hear Kathleen's voice, hurt and suddenly hard.

"At least I'll have tried. And another thing, I won't hate you for trying to make me feel bad about it . . . so that puts me two steps ahead right there."

There didn't seem to be anything more to say. Much as Kathleen wanted to apologize, to beg forgiveness for putting herself before others the way her mother had always insisted she do, this time she wasn't going to. This was the beginning of a new life—her life—finally. She was going to take a chance and grab this opportunity, unless, of course, she got there and her uncle came to his senses.

By the time she'd reached the only office with a real door, Kathleen considered the notion that Beverly Hills would roll up its sidewalks the minute she appeared, the way Cherie said. Then again, they might love her. Kathleen threw back her shoulders and put her hand on her hip. She was as good as anyone in her situation could be and she worked hard. There was always that. Holding the good houghts, Kathleen raised her fist and knocked on Jay orty's door.

"Come."

She went in.

Jay was hunched over his desk, a bad imitation of an nitation heirloom that served its purpose beautifully. It as as big and intimidating as the balding man seated ehind it. But now Jay and Breyer Dorty were over. She as Kathleen Cotter, soon to be associated with the firm f O'Doul & Associates. She wouldn't be intimidated by nyone. Still, she faltered a bit when Jay slid his eyes up riefly. He never made eye contact.

"Mr. Dorty?"

"Yes?"

He had been laboring over a letter. He did that a lot, et she never saw a stack of mail waiting for the postman.)nce she had offered to take his correspondence to the ost office. He hadn't spoken to her for a week. That's hen Cherie had become her friend, ushering her out of ie office and explaining what was what. Dorty's name was n the door; they labored for Dorty; it was useless to try) be friends with a man who had invented an imaginary artner. Kathleen had taken her words to heart, yet se- retly longed for some sort of connection, professional-to- rofessional. Now, before she made it, she was going to ever it. Kathleen hated leaving something so important ndone.

"Jay." Kathleen cleared her throat and changed her act. She was headed west, to Beverly Hills, she might as ell start acting like someone who would do that. "Jay, I ave something to tell you. I'm leaving Dorty & Breyer."

She waited. The pen wasn't scratching anymore. Slowly, ay Dorty sat back. His eyes slid from the top of her blond ead to the middle of her knees. Her ankles were hidden y the desk or he would have traveled the whole route. Ie looked downright surprised; and when he looked her n the eye again, he actually looked sad. Kathleen answered im with an equally sympathetic look, then remembered hat she was about.

"I want you to know how much I've enjoyed working

here. Not only did I learn a lot handling all those personal
injury cases and divorces, but I was honored when you
asked me to be your spokesperson on your cable commer
cial." She smiled, closed-mouthed. It made her eyes crinkle
mischievously. When he didn't smile back, she recomposed
herself. "But, Jay, I've got an offer and it's big. I'm going
to work in Beverly Hills."

Jay Dorty put his hands over his eyes and bowed his
head. Kathleen felt horrible. It had been wrong to come
on so strong; her voice softened, but the message was clear.
"I'd like to leave as soon as possible, but I'll stay as long
as you need me. As long as my clients need me."

Jay dropped his hand. His eyes were red rimmed, but
there were no tears. He took a great deep breath through
his great broad nose.

"No problem. Take off whenever. Cherie can pick up
the slack."

He was scribbling again.

Kathleen smiled wanly.

That hurt.

When she left his office, she had no idea that Jay Dorty
was regretting her departure. There was no one, after all,
who left a room the way Kathleen Cotter did.

ABOUT THE AUTHOR

Married to a Superior Court Judge, R. A. Forster lives
Southern California. You can write to her at P.O. Box
81, Palos Verdes Estates California, 90274 or FNNK34A@
odigy.com

<u>BOOK YOUR PLACE ON OUR WEBSITE</u> <u>AND MAKE THE</u> <u>READING CONNECTION!</u>

We've created a customized website just for our very special readers, where you can get the inside scoop on everything that's going on with Zebra, Pinnacle and Kensington books.

When you come online, you'll have the exciting opportunity to:

- View covers of upcoming books
- Read sample chapters
- Learn about our future publishing schedule (listed by publication month *and author*)
- Find out when your favorite authors will be visiting a city near you
- Search for and order backlist books from our online catalog
- Check out author bios and background information
- Send e-mail to your favorite authors
- Meet the Kensington staff online
- Join us in weekly chats with authors, readers and other guests
- Get writing guidelines
- AND MUCH MORE!

Visit our website at
http://www.pinnaclebooks.com